The Shadow Universe II
Running in the Shadows

William G. Davis, Jr.

Published by
William G. Davis, Jr.

Acknowledgments

Special thanks to Pastor E. C. Fulcher, Jr. for his support. To Ursula Crouse, Linda Shoaf, and Alyx Bliesener for feedback on continuity, spelling, and grammar corrections. Finally, to Sergeant 1st class Marc Schenker, his valuable help explains certain unclassified army procedures and jargon specifics.

The cover design is courtesy of www.Pixabay.com

Chapter 1

Akil
Argi City
The 22,277[th] Terrestrial Rotation of the Second Summer

Olan woke in Dolas's guest room. His eyes were open, yet he could not see anything because there was only darkness. He thought a moment and remembered that Dolas's guest room was against the city wall, which meant the room had no windows. Olan sighed, "Lights." Several polished stones on the ceiling gradually illuminated. As the room brightened, he found himself stretched out on a bed with body pillows propped on either side to keep him from rolling over.

Methodically, he took count of all his fingers and toes, moving each one independently, awaiting the slightest hint of pain or discomfort from Dolas's interrogation on the prior Terrestrial revolution; he also moved his arms and legs. Not feeling pain or discomfort, he believed they recovered, so he sat up in bed and visually checked his midsection. In the dim light, he could only find a few minor bruises. *There is nothing to worry about; by mid-Terrestrial Rotation, they will vanish.*

The polished stones stopped increasing at their brightest, triggering Dolas's family holograms to automatically project images around the room. He shook his head. *Not an attractive female in the bunch. What a pity.* He found a fresh set of clothes at the end of the bed; he bathed, dressed, and went to the kitchen to eat. It, too, was dark. "Lights." He retrieved some moss from the cold box, threw a handful on a platter, and set it on the white stone table in the middle of the room. There was a small monitor set on the tabletop.

Using his index finger, he touched the glass, and the Information League came on. His body cried for sustenance to replace the vast amount of energy used for recuperating. He watched the video and inattentively grabbed several handfuls of moss, dropped them on his plate, and devoured it. Dolas walked in, retrieved a plate, got some food for himself, sat in front of Olan, and did not speak. They ate in silence as Dolas studied Olan.

"What is wrong?" Olan finally inquired.

"The warden will discover that you are missing soon and must inform Zorion of your escape. I cannot keep you here because it is not safe for either of us."

"Do not worry. I can hide in other places. Secret places."

"How will we keep in touch if I do not know where you are?"

Olan studied him, "Considering my recent predicament, I think it is time to choose my successor."

Dolas chuckled at the remark, "Zorion already gave me your old position as Chief Administrator of Argi's Intelligence Department. You should have figured that out during your interrogation in prison. Now lie down; I do not think you have fully recovered yet."

Olan grinned, "You may hold my office, but you do not have access to all of my resources."

Dolas looked at him quizzically, "I have the highest level of authority. I oversee everything. What else is there?"

"You are only responsible for the things Zorion gave me. Follow me, and I will show you what I mean."

Olan rose from his chair, shoving the last morsel of food into his mouth. Before opening the door, he changed his appearance to one of his preferred undercover disguises, an elderly Akilian. The impersonation did not surprise Dolas because Olan showed him the value of using it many yellow harvests ago. Dolas followed Olan and changed his likeness to someone older too. Olan led him down the avenue, and a hundred paces farther, stopped, turned to face the wall, and pointed.

"What do you see?"

Dolas looked at Olan, looked at the wall, looked back at Olan, and in a weak raspy voice replied, "Rock, dirt, essentially an undeveloped section of the city."

"Exactly. There are thousands of these small areas around the five cities. They were declared unworkable due to instability or dense rock."

A group of young Akilians, who had not seen more than sixteen Yellow Harvests, approached their vicinity on the avenue. Dolas paused before responding until they left.

"Yes. I remember reading the city map during my training to become an agent. These areas are markers."

Olan's smile grew, "You missed it, just as I did and everyone else who has read the maps."

Dolas looked baffled, "What did I miss?"

Olan pointed at the wall again, "Take a closer look and tell me what you see."

Dolas walked up to the short rail that prevented little ones from trying to climb the rough surface of the undeveloped city wall. Using a portable light, he shined it at each crevice and hole within sight but could not see anything; he faced Olan and shrugged his shoulders. Olan jumped over the rail with little effort and disappeared into one of the fissures.

Dolas heard another group of Argians approaching. Before they arrived, he whispered a warning to Olan, urging him to return, but he had vanished. As they walked past, Dolas leaned against the railing and smiled at them. Having forgotten his disguise, he accidentally pushed his tongue through the gap in his front teeth and blushed because one of the young females looked at him pitifully.

She walked away, saying, "That just breaks my heart."

As they moved down the avenue, he shined his light where Olan stood last and could not see him. Dolas looked right and left to ensure no one saw him, jumped over the rail, and walked to the fissure. It appeared slightly broader than just a tiny crevice, and he discovered enough room in the opening for him to walk through, unencumbered.

Within moments, the darkness engulfed him. The light from the avenue did nothing to illuminate the area. Granted, it hid him, but it also made it impossible for Dolas to see Olan until an unseen hand grabbed him out of the darkness and pulled him farther into the tunnel. It had a firm grip on his shoulder and guided him around a corner to an area with a dim light, where Dolas saw Olan's face.

He had changed back to his original likeness. Dolas, in turn, did the same and turned his attention back to the passageway, which only had enough space for one. Confirming what his eyes told him, he moved his hands over the rough surface left by the machines used to burrow through the hard rock. Over Olan's shoulder, he saw the path split into two directions.

"Where does it lead?" Dolan whispered.

"Everywhere."

Dolas was astonished, "You mean I can go anywhere in the city from here?"

"No, you can go anywhere in the five cities from here."

"Why is this not public knowledge?"

"Follow me, and I will explain along the way," Olan urged, veering toward the left tunnel. "It has been nearly eleven Yellow Harvests since my predecessor showed me this network of hidden corridors. I asked him the same question as you. He told me that Urki, who was Argi's sovereign at the time, built the cities and bribed the lead engineer to construct a network of tunnels behind their walls."

"It must have taken thousands of workers to complete. They must have known what the passages were for."

"Urki told them the tunnels were for an air filtration system and ventilation, but after they built the cities, the engineer told his men that they had abandoned the idea in place of a better one."

"We do not use an air filtration system because the moss converts carbon dioxide to oxygen and cleans the air simultaneously."

Olan smiled, "Precisely. Urki instructed the engineer to condemn the tunnels, calling them a hazard."

"That is when they put up the rails," Dolas noted.

"Yes. The fences keep the young ones from going into the crevices and accidentally finding the tunnels. Since there is only rock and dirt, no one else has a reason to go beyond them."

"Interesting," Dolas paused, contemplating. "You are right. I have never paid any attention to these areas before."

"It has been hiding right in front of you all this time."

"Did any of the workers slip up and tell someone about the project?"

"The laborers were each forced to sign a confidentiality agreement before they could work on the project. To encourage their silence, Urki promised them large bonuses once they finished the job, but the agreement said that if they ever told anyone about what they knew, even their significant others, they would be sent to prison for breaching the government contract and he would retract their bonuses."

"Did anyone ever say anything?"

"Sovereign Cubes and the threat of prison can be a powerful motivator, and to our benefit, they all kept their word. They believed that the government made a mistake and paid them to keep it quiet. As a result, they had no reason to suspect Urki would use the tunnels for anything else."

Dolas craned his head to look back from where they came, "Obviously, you had other uses for them."

"Yes, because I know their true purpose. I have recorded videos and conversations of citizens, business owners, city officials, and even other city sovereigns from the shadows, and they never knew I was there. Their design allows me to be privy to many private discussions."

"We should tell more agents; we could have them take shifts in the tunnels. Imagine the information we would collect!"

"No!" Olan snapped. He stopped and turned to face Dolas, "The rule states that only two can know of these tunnels at one time; even Zorion is not aware of their existence."

"Why have you not told him?" puzzled Dolas.

"Urki gave his Chief Administrator of Argi's Intelligence Department instructions. The tunnels were for his use only, and at the right time, he would choose a successor and reveal all the secrets these tunnels hold."

Dolas peered sightlessly at a wall, drifting off into thought until Olan regained his attention, "Dolas."

"What?"

"I appointed you to be my assistant because I trusted you. Also, I knew I would have to confide in you eventually, so it is now your responsibility to find someone you have confidence in and appoint him to be your assistant. You can only reveal these tunnels to him once I am dead." Olan glared at Dolas, "You must swear to me with an Akilian Oath that you will do this."

He secretly moved his hand toward his sword.

Dolas thought carefully before replying, "I swear. So how often have you used them?"

Olan quietly sighed in relief. If Dolas had not sworn with an Akilian Oath, he would have killed him. That would not be good for him because Dolas was his only ally. Abruptly, Olan spun around and walked forward.

"I only use them for emergencies. If someone catches me leaving one of the exits, it will expose their mystery, and they would become worthless, so I strongly suggest you use them only if necessary."

They walked about four hundred paces until reaching a circular room that was well lit and spacious. They sat to rest.

Olan faced Dolas, "Zorion will find out I have escaped and will call Broll and you into his office to order you both to search for me. You will be busy most of the Terrestrial Rotation, pretending to look for me. Be careful with what you say around Broll because he pretends to be slow of thought. Be even more careful around Zorion. He can read your expressions and interpret your feelings. He will know if you are lying. You must *believe* that you have no idea how I escaped, or else you will give yourself away."

"I understand," Dolas answered, pausing briefly. "What do you plan to do?"

Olan thought momentarily, "There is a hunch I want to follow up on." He looked at the time, "Zorion should be getting up soon. I will observe his level and see if I am right."

"What do you suspect?"

"Someone wants Zorion dead. Whoever it is, tried to use me to do their dirty work."

"But you failed."

"Exactly, which means…."

"He or she will try again."

"Yes, and I want to be there if it happens."

"Do you have any idea who it might be?"

"It is hard to say for sure. It may be one Akilian or several. Sovereigns often make many enemies. One thing is for certain."

"What is that?"

"Whoever is trying to kill him will not commit the act himself."

"Do you think your female companion is behind this?"

Olan paused in thought, "She calls herself Nayrah. During the interrogation, I told you that if she has the power to make me attack Zorion, there is no telling who is under her control. I still do not know if she is working for someone or if she is the one making all the decisions."

Dolas thought until his eyes lit up, "You think she already has a backup in place."

Olan nodded.

"Who could it be?"

"Anyone, or it may be more than one. I must stay close to Zorion and protect him if the assassin strikes."

"I thought a Screener would notice an intruder."

"Remember the first lesson I taught you?"

Dolas nodded, "Nothing is impenetrable."

"Right, which means if someone wants in, they will find an opening. You got into the prison without being detected."

"Correct, which means someone has found a weakness in Zorion's top-level security and is exploiting it. I must warn Broll!"

"No, we have to let the assassin reveal himself, or else we may never know who it is. Once we have the killer, we can interrogate him or her to find out who is behind this."

"You are taking a very significant risk with Zorion's life."

"*We* do not have any other choice."

"What will you do about Nayrah?"

"I will deal with her later. My first duty is to protect Zorion."

"I wish you good hunting."

"Before you leave, take this," Olan handed him a small device. "It is a communicator that uses my encryption so that we can speak to each other without detection. Do not engage in long conversations or use our names. Just use it to set up a time and place for us to meet."

Dolas put the device in his pocket, nodded, and left. Olan pulled the hood of his black cloak over his head and returned to the tunnel. *Now, let us see who is behind all this bloodshed.*

Chapter 2

Akil
Argi City
The 22,277[th] Terrestrial Rotation of the Second Summer

Zorion tossed and turned in his sleep. Even now, unconscious, his mind searched for her. Since he and Thea were no longer together, Zorion hoped she would not interfere with his dreams, but that was not the case. It had been only a few Terrestrial Revolutions since his last dream of her, yet he missed her terribly. Although Zorion kept calling out to her in his dream, there was no answer. He approached the avenue (their usual meeting place), overwhelmed with sorrow, and frantically searched for her. Moments away from giving up, he called out to her one last time.

"Where are you?" His voice echoed down the empty corridor.

There appeared a bright light. Zorion's heart leaped with joy. *Finally*! He held his hand up to block the sparkling illumination before her appearance. As it dimmed, he ran, embraced her tightly, and whispered, "I did not think I would ever see you again."

Several moments later, he released her and stepped back to see her beautiful face. She smiled at him, and it meant everything. Although it was a dream, he did not care. If possible, he would sleep to be with her for the rest of his life. As they gazed into each other's eyes, their lips gently met. The dream felt more real to him than life itself, and just as he was about to speak, breaking the silence, she put her fingers to his lips to silence him and spoke.

"I am coming for you."

"What?" he inquired with wide eyes.

It was the second time he heard her voice. Not only did it excite him to hear her speak, but the news of her arrival made him overjoyed.

"Soon, we will meet," she smiled knowingly.

"Where?"

"You will see. Do not worry. Everything will be fine."

"Please! Tell me where so I do not miss you!"

He started to hear soft music playing, "No! Not yet!"

She faded from his sight and yelled, "Do not worry, my love. We will find each other."

He reached for her, but his arms went through her translucent body, "Do not leave! Please, not yet!" As the dream faded, he yelled, "No!"

He woke, sitting up in bed and reaching out into thin air. His bedroom door flew open, and Broll came rushing in with his sword drawn.

"Where is he?" Broll bellowed.

Two guards entered the room moments later. Embarrassed, Zorion covered his face with his hands.

"I am sorry, my friend. It was just a bad dream."

"We must search each room, Sir. Protocol," one of the guards asserted with a deep throaty voice.

"Do what you must, but hurry," Zorion responded.

Broll stayed behind until they left.

"Did you dream about our sun exploding? I have that one from time to time. It is not very pleasant."

"No, this was something else," Zorion paced, contemplating whether to tell Broll the truth.

He stopped and stressed, "I do not want you to repeat what I am about to tell you to anyone. Understand?"

Broll nodded, with deeply furrowed eyebrows, "As a rule, I would never repeat anything you tell me."

Zorion cringed, thinking he had insulted him, "I am sorry, my friend. I did not mean to imply that you would. It is just that this is a very personal matter."

Zorion motioned for Broll to sit on a small, cushioned lounge, and he sat on his bed across from him. He took a deep breath and told Broll the details of his dreams, including how long ago they started, the incident with Thea, and how she somehow entered his dream.

"She said we would meet soon," Zorion added grimly, giving him the final details of his last vision of her.

"Do you believe she is real?"

"During the dream, she seems very real; it is hard to explain whether she is or not. I have been searching through the photo database for hundreds of Terrestrial Rotations, hoping to find someone who looks like her. Sadly, I have not found anyone who even comes close. Some had certain features, yet none were an exact match."

"If she is real, it sounds like you will meet her soon enough."

"I guess. I still do not know her name or where we will meet. I tried to get her to tell me, but she refused."

"If she did not tell you, it is because you do not need to know. At least, that is how I would look at it. Try not to think about it and go about your usual routine. If the universe wants you to meet, you will see her during the Terrestrial Revolution. Assuming she can get past me," he jested with a sly grin.

Zorion smiled halfheartedly, "Just in case, for the following few Terrestrial Rotations, I want you to promise me you will not kill anyone trying to approach me, especially females. You may subdue, but do *not* kill."

"I promise to do my best not to kill anyone; you know as well as I that it will depend upon the circumstances."

"All I ask is that you be mindful of my request. Now, if you will excuse me, I need to get ready for work."

Broll stood, gave a slight bow, and closed the door behind him. Zorion heard the other guards telling him that the apartment was empty. Later, he heard the front door close.

"Who are you?" he wondered aloud in a whisper.

In his bathroom, he reached down and touched the water in the tub. The temperature was perfect. It was not a surprise; if nothing broke down, the container would automatically fill at a specific temperature before waking. He disrobed and sank into the warm, inviting water. As he pulled the cleaning comb through his hair, he thought about what he had told Broll. The possibility of meeting her ruled his thoughts.

It occurred to him that she would not be in his dreams if she were real. *Is my subconscious playing tricks on me?* Questions flooded his mind, and he became more resolute in finding her. Upon arriving at his office, he brought up the photo database and continued searching for her. *I will at least know your name if I can see your picture.* By the time Shilda called on him, he had looked through more than a few hundred photos, which was a new record for him, yet still had not found one that resembled her.

"Sir, Vul is here to speak with you. He says it is urgent," Shilda announced.

He sensed the worry in her tone and hoped the following photo might be the one, "Can it wait a little longer?"

"He says it concerns Olan," Shilda urged.

I will look for you later, my love. "Very well, send him in."

Vul stood at the door, waiting for Zorion to give his approval to enter his office. Zorion waved him in and noticed that Vul trembled. That was never a good sign. Obviously, he was afraid to tell him about whatever happened. Since he was not forthcoming, Zorion prodded.

"What happened?"

"Olan, Sir. He has…" Vul gulped, terrified to speak, knowing his life would change for the worse.

"Dead?"

"No, Sir. He is not dead."

"Speak, Vul! Tell me what happened!" Zorion yelled, losing his patience.

"He escaped, Sir."

Zorion stood, simultaneously slamming his fists on his desk. The searing look of shock and anger caused Vul's heart to skip a beat.

"How in the universe did he get out?" Zorion yelled.

"Someone impersonated one of the guards. I have brought the checkpoint video where he entered," Vul's hands shook, handing Zorion the data file.

Zorion snatched it from his grip, "How could anyone get past a Screener?"

Just as the words left his mouth, Zorion remembered the new drug that suppressed pheromones. The only way to get it was through the shadow economy. *If a concoction can hide someone's essence, I wonder if a scientist could duplicate it.* The thought sent chills down his spine as he inserted the data file into his Information Terminal. The video appeared, and he watched the event unfold.

"My preliminary investigation shows that the invader came and left at a busy time. Many Akilians waited in the line, so the guards waved him through."

"I want a full investigation, Vul. Also, I want the guards, who allowed him through, removed from their post!"

"I already have, Sir. You will have a full report before by the end of the Work Cycle."

"I better. Now get out of my office!"

"Yes, Sir!" Vul tripped over himself, spinning around to leave.

Before reaching the door, Zorion stopped him, "One more thing, Vul! If this ever happens again, you will take the prisoner's place. Do I make myself clear?" Zorion warned through gritted teeth.

Vul's face went pale, "Clear, Sir."

"Now, get out of my sight before I change my mind!"

Vul opened the door and fled.

"Shilda!" Zorion bellowed.

He did not bother using the intercom, knowing that his voice would carry to her seat.

Shilda ran to the door, "Yes, Sir."

"Tell Broll and Dolas I want to see them now!"

"Right away!" Shilda spun around and ran back to her desk.

Zorion paced. *Incompetent fools*!

Broll arrived and did not wait for Zorion's permission; he entered and stood in front of his desk, waiting for Zorion to tell him what was wrong. However, Dolas did not have that privilege and remained at the door. Zorion paced for several heartbeats until his anger subsided enough for him to talk rather than yell and, having reached that level of calm, waved Dolas in, who took a position beside Broll.

"Olan has escaped."

Zorion's gaze traveled back and forth between them. He wanted to read their reaction; both seemed genuinely surprised at the news.

"I will notify my staff at once. Every level will be on alert," Broll vowed.

"I will have my second in command work with Broll's team and begin searching the city," Dolas added.

Zorion repeated Vul's account of how the intruder got in and out of prison and showed them the checkpoint video where it happened.

"Whoever did it must have been an agent," Dolas offered.

Zorion and Broll looked at him suspiciously.

"I thought it was obvious," Dolas commented, scratching his cheek.

"What do you mean?" puzzled Zorion.

"He denies it, but I believe Olan is working for Elzer, so it only makes sense that Elzer would send an agent to break him out of prison before he confesses," Dolas concluded.

"Olan would never admit to working for Elzer even if it were true," Zorion countered.

"Still, Elzer is the only one who has a motive. Since he has top-level clearance, Olan must have arranged a deal with Elzer if we caught him, Argi's secrets for his freedom. Therefore, I should contact all our undercover agents in Vlor to ensure Olan has not compromised them and to put them on high alert," Dolas stated.

Zorion nodded his agreement, "It is up to them whether to return. I do not want our agents to fall at Elzer's hand."

"I will relay the message," Dolas replied.

"I cannot believe this is happening," Zorion whispered.

There was a deep sadness in his voice, but he pushed the feeling aside.

"I want every checkpoint alerted to what happened. Ensure they understand that if they allow anyone they have not screened, I will remove them from their post and imprison them because we cannot let Olan leave this city. He is too much of a security risk. Tell them there is a bounty of 250,000 Sovereign Cubes, dead or alive!"

"Yes, Sir!" Broll and Dolas responded simultaneously.

"Very well, you can leave, Dolas," Zorion ended curtly.

As Dolas left, Zorion motioned for Broll to close the door. Zorion stepped from behind his desk so he could whisper.

"I want you to keep an eye on Dolas."

"You do not trust him?" Broll questioned.

"I trust my gut."

"What does your gut tell you?"

"He scratched his cheek, suggesting that Olan was working for Elzer."

"You do not think it was an itch."

"No, it was a nervous response. I have been a sovereign for a long time, and I have discovered that when someone lies, a quirk usually accompanies it, like a scratch or flinch."

"I will have two of my best guards watch him," Broll reassured.

"Tell them to be careful. Dolas is almost as good as Olan at his job."

"I will tell them to use extreme caution."

"Very well, dismissed."

"I think it best that I stay by your side from now on. Olan is free and may try to kill you again."

"I understand your concern, but I refuse to live in fear," Zorion insisted.

"It will not be permanent, just until he is apprehended."

"My answer is no. Now leave," Zorion answered flatly and returned his attention to his Information Terminal to begin working.

Broll knew not to push the issue any further because it would only anger him, so reluctantly, he bowed slightly and left. Now alone, Zorion decided to get some fresh air.

"Shilda, I am going out on the terrace. Let Broll know where I am."

Shilda responded as Zorion left, making her voice like an incoherent whisper. Once outside, he grabbed the guard rail and looked out over Argi. It was still early, and only a few elevators and hover vehicles were active because most of the city was asleep. *First, Olan attacks me, and now someone helps him escape. Broll is already trying to increase the number of guards around me. If this keeps up, he will be standing over me during the sleep cycle!*

Chapter 3

Akil
Argi City
The 22,277[th] Terrestrial Rotation of the Second Summer

Olan stood hidden in the darkness and watched Zorion enter his office through his secret door. A little later, Olan walked out of the dark corridor and sneaked around the corner, keeping his back to the wall. The terrace led to an avenue opposite the front of Zorion's office building. There were only a few guards allowed to walk these platforms. Olan could see three, standing about twenty paces away, chatting with each other. One of them was Broll.

Everything was normal, so he returned to the darkness to wait, and about three thousand heartbeats later, Zorion unexpectedly burst out of his office from his private entrance, walked to the guardrail, and stared out over the city. From his vantage point, it was clear something upset him. *He must have just heard of my escape.* Olan grimaced, knowing that a good friend now considered him an enemy.

Olan saw a guard turn the corner and approach Zorion. He recognized Molo right away. It might have been the way Molo walked, or it might have been the look on his face; whatever it was, it made the skin on the back of his neck bumpy, which cried out a warning. Olan watched Molo closely, waiting for any sudden moves for his sword.

Unexpectedly, Molo announced his arrival, "Sir, is everything all right?"

"No."

"Is there anything I can do to help?"

"No, thank you. I want to be alone."

"Sorry to have bothered you, Sir."

Olan narrowed his eyes, watching Molo turn to leave. He stopped, and Olan felt his stomach tighten. Molo scanned the area and spoke softly into a wrist communicator. Olan could not hear the conversation because he was too far away, and the noise of passing hovercars blocked his hushed tones. *Is he speaking with another guard? To an assassin? To an accomplice?*

Molo ended the communication, scanned the area one more time, turned around, and crept back toward Zorion, who did not notice him because the city had his attention. Not only was Zorion looking away from him, but passing vehicles drowned out any noise Molo's boots made.

Olan knew an attack was imminent. Molo approached, and his right hand drifted toward the hilt of his sword. *He is going to kill him!* Olan almost yelled. If he shouted, Zorion would look toward him and not at Molo, which would still give Molo a perfect opportunity to kill him. *It seems like I must do this the hard way.*

Olan unsheathed his sword and appeared from the shadows at his fastest pace. He used his momentum to clear the small fence guarding the secret tunnel and sprinted to Zorion's side. By then, Molo had unsheathed his sword and held it at the ready. *I am not going to make it in time.*

Seeing he had no choice, Olan screamed, "Behind you!"

Zorion turned and saw Olan approaching from his right. Had he not seen movement out of his peripheral vision at that moment, Zorion thought Olan was attempting to kill him again. He turned his head farther and saw Molo standing with his sword raised. Looking him in the eyes, Molo swung, but Zorion ducked, avoiding the death blow that would have certainly removed his head.

Zorion reached for his Gaddar; it was not there because he had given it to Yanamai. The few heartbeats he wasted trying to retrieve it made him vulnerable to another attack. Molo caught his chin with a left-handed hook, spinning him around. Molo stabbed Zorion in the back, under his fifth rib, puncturing the right lung and paralyzing Zorion's breathing; it took less than a heartbeat. Molo pulled his sword out roughly, and Zorion fell to his knees, facing away from Molo. Olan drew near, knowing it would be close.

Molo raised his sword and swung with all his might. Olan leaped in a desperate move to clear a span of several paces and landed feet first on Zorion's right side, knocking him out of the path of Molo's blade. At the same time, he raised his sword defensively and blocked Molo's attack. Seeing that Olan took his target from him, Molo growled and swung widely at him, forcing Olan to defend himself from an awkward sitting position.

It did not take Olan long to block and maneuver himself back to a standing position. Soon, the sound of their swords clashing would attract Broll's attention and the other sentries on duty. Olan trained his whole life for this scenario and usually toyed with his opponent to humiliate him. Sadly, there was not enough time, so he had to end it quickly. The fight lasted less than seventy heartbeats before Broll, and one other guard came sprinting toward him. It had been a thorough disappointment to him all around. Molo's skills as a fighter were hardly up to the level he expected, even for a guard. *Obviously, an imposter.*

Olan had to thrust him through the chest to escape. Molo fell to his knees. The look of surprise on Molo's face had to be his reward for now. Broll and the other guard were getting close, so Olan propped his foot against Molo's chest and pulled his sword from him. Molo fell backward, unconscious. The momentum and direction of Olan pushing off with his foot directed his fall.

"Do not kill him!" Zorion whispered.

He wanted to yell, but his injury prevented him.

"I did not plan to kill him," Olan revealed, reaching down to search Molo's pockets.

Inside, he found a communicator, put it into his cloak's pouch, unrolled a cable from his tool belt, and secured it to the protective terrace rail.

As he climbed up the railing, Zorion challenged in a breathy explosion of words, "Where did you come from?"

"I am always around."

"This does not change anything."

"I did not think it would," Olan replied in a gravelly, deep voice.

Broll tried to grab him but missed.

Before leaving, Olan insisted, "I am not your enemy."

He leaped off the rail and swung down to the level below. Broll lunged over the steel bar to try catching him and missed. If it had not been for the other guard, who grabbed his legs and pulled him back to the terrace, Broll would have fallen to the bottom. Instead, Broll spoke into his communicator to alert the patrol on the next level that Olan was there; he turned and saw Zorion pointing to Molo.

Although his words slurred and lisped, Zorion managed to tell him that Molo tried to kill him, so Broll put restraints on him. The sentries from the level below contacted Broll via his communicator; somehow, Olan disappeared, making Broll very unhappy with them. Zorion looked at the rail that Olan jumped from and thought, *you got away this time, but I <u>will</u> find you.*

Chapter 4

Yanamai sat at her desk, reviewing the information the probe sent back on its earlier mission five Terrestrial Revolutions ago. It found two planets within a solar system in sector twenty-five. One orbited within the 'Life Zone,' which was the proper distance from the sun, giving it the potential to sustain life. Its surface had water and a breathable atmosphere, and a more detailed scan revealed that it was at least four to five times Akil's size. The increased gravity of such a large mass would make it impossible for them to walk on the surface.

In her frustration, she exhaled loudly. They needed a backup world if the occupants of the newly discovered planet turned them away. She examined data on the second planet; it was beyond the 'Life Zone,' and its mass was closer to Akil's size. If the occupants rejected them, they could dig through the icy surface and continue to live underground. It was a practical alternative to her first choice. At least they would have more time because the sun was still young.

Having lived underground her whole life, she had become used to the lifestyle. She hoped to live on the surface of some flourishing planet before death came for her. She completed her report and sent it electronically to Zorion's office. Her timekeeper chimed, alerting her that it was time for lunch. Due to her busy schedule, she resorted to electronic reminders to avoid forgetting to eat. Yanamai approached the food box but heard Tadra's voice over the intercom and stopped.

"Yanamai, the scout has sent a signal to return home."

"I am on my way."

Yanamai initiated the portal. The power coursing through the cables to the eight metal spheres vibrated the room, the portal opened, and the tremors stopped. Standing on the other side of the event horizon, Yanamai saw Kraeth, who stepped onto Akil. Yanamai noticed a system warning light, alerting her that one of the power cables needed replacement. The alarm distracted Yanamai and Tadra, forcing them to take their eyes off the vortex.

"We need to shut down the portal!" Yanamai exclaimed.

Tadra agreed, so Yanamai checked the Interstellar Transport Bay to ensure the scout was clear of the portal and started the shutdown sequence. Looking back, she saw someone run through the event horizon, just a heartbeat before it closed. Instinctively, she hit the intruder alarm.

Chapter 5

Akil
Argi City
The 22,277[th] Terrestrial Rotation of the Second Summer

Assistants rushed Zorion to a private Recovery Station on the top level. He sat on the edge of the bed and, with their help, removed his blood-soaked shirt. Other aides used rehabilitation towels to soak up the vital fluid from his torso. They gave him water and moss to aid his recovery. About a thousand heartbeats later, his lung recovered enough for his breathing to return to normal, but the attack left him shaken. Broll paced nearby, shaking his head in frustration.

"I should *not* have left your side again."

Zorion took a brand-new shirt from one of the helpers, put it on, and faced Broll.

"You cannot be with me every heartbeat of every Terrestrial Revolution."

Broll stopped pacing, "I can, and I will. I will not take no for an answer this time. You can put me in prison if you do not like it."

Zorion smiled halfheartedly. He knew that Broll genuinely cared for his wellbeing, which was why he was the only Akilian under his authority allowed to speak to him so plainly. Still, he did not want to give up any more of his privacy.

"Although I appreciate your enthusiasm, I do not want you close to me all the time."

"Too bad! I will not allow you to keep me from doing my job any longer! Your life is at risk!"

"Fine, you win."

Satisfied, Broll exhaled loudly in victory until seeing Zorion frown, "What is wrong?"

"Why would Olan try to kill me on one Terrestrial Rotation and save me on another? It does not make sense."

"He is a spy. Who can understand their logic?"

"If Olan wanted me dead, why stop Molo's attack? All he had to do was allow the assassination to unfold, I would be dead, and he would have completed his mission."

"Perhaps he is trying to extort more sovereign cubes from Elzer for your death."

"I guess it is possible, but before jumping over the side, he claimed he was not my enemy."

"He is using your friendship against you. Convincing you that he is on your side will cause you to lower your guard, allowing him to strike at you later. I am sure Elzer is paying him a great sum for his services."

"Sovereign cubes will not do him any good. He will always be looking over his shoulder. Surely, he knows I will search for him for the rest of his life."

"Greed can make an Akilian do crazy things."

Zorion nodded absentmindedly, "Perhaps."

"In the meantime, I have an idea that I want you to consider concerning your protection."

"What is it?

Before Broll could tell him, the Interstellar Transport Bay intruder alarm sounded.

"Stay here," Broll cautioned.

"No, I am going. Just stay by my side and keep your hand on your sword."

Zorion shook his head, starting for the door, "Can this Terrestrial Revolution get any worse?"

Broll disapproved of Zorion's decision but had no choice. He had to follow his orders. Aside from tying his hands and feet to a chair, Broll had no other way of restraining him, and since doing something so drastic would land him in prison, he decided against it. They ran to the Interstellar Transport Bay with their hands gripping the hilt of their swords to find out what had happened. Along the way, Broll signaled for more guards to join them.

Chapter 6

Akil
Argi City
The 22,277[th] Terrestrial Rotation of the Second Summer

Julie landed on the other side of the portal and realized they were no longer in the Regime because she and Kraeth arrived in a room with strange and unfamiliar markings on the walls. To make matters worse, she noticed that the architecture differed significantly from anything in the Regime or any other country. *Where am I? Russia?*

Hoping to retrieve her laptop and return home, she grabbed it from under Kraeth's arm and spun around to exit through the event horizon only to discover they had closed it. *Oh, crap.* Kraeth turned, saw Julie, and froze. With nowhere to run, Julie turned around to face Kraeth.

She saw a woman standing behind a large glass window. Surprised by Julie's presence, she triggered an alarm, which blared. Julie covered her ears to block the noise, securing the laptop between her elbow and waist. Shortly after the alarm sounded, Julie saw two huge men run into the room with swords drawn. The sight of their blades made her panic at first, but she remembered something one of her instructors told her: *if you're ever in trouble and can't run away - bluff, bluff, bluff.*

"I guess you thought you could get away with stealing this, huh?" Julie yelled over the alarm.

Kraeth signaled for the woman to shut off the noise allowing Julie to finally uncover her ears and lower the volume of her voice.

"I thought you were asleep," Kraeth replied.

"I woke up. Just in time," Julie reflected, becoming more indignant. "I mean - I take you into my parents' home. I treat your wounds, feed you, let you use our computer so you can communicate, and this is the thanks I get!"

"I can explain."

Julie pointed at the two guards. "Are they the police?"

"They are our equivalent of police, yes."

Julie walked toward the guards and yelled, "I want this man arrested!"

The guards, not understanding her, looked at each other quizzically.

"They do not recognize the English language, Julie," Kraeth explained.

She pointed at Kraeth and looked at the guards, "Arrest - this - man - now!"

"Slow speaking will not help them understand you. Again, they do not speak your language," Kraeth insisted.

Zorion, Broll, and four more armed sentries ran into the room. Julie and Zorion looked at each other at the same time.

"It is you!" Zorion gasped.

Not understanding him, Julie urged Kraeth to translate, but before Kraeth responded to her, he spoke to Zorion in the Akilian language, "How do you know her?"

Julie interrupted, "Hey, I asked you a question!"

"Please, just a moment, Julie," Kraeth insisted.

Crossing her arms, she frowned and waited for them to stop speaking, which was utterly unrecognizable. Zorion realized his error and changed the subject.

"I will ask the questions. Why is she here?"

"She was in bed resting, so I took the opportunity to return. She woke and saw me leaving through the portal with her computer," Kraeth answered, pointing to the laptop in her hand.

Julie saw Kraeth point to her computer, approached Zorion, and yelled, "I want him arrested!"

Broll sprung from Zorion's side and raised his sword until Zorion grabbed his arm and stopped him.

"She is not to be harmed!"

At the same time, Broll raised his sword; Julie brought the computer up to block his attack and stepped back, saying, "Hey! Wait a minute! He's the thief!"

Zorion, not understanding her, looked at her quizzically and faced Kraeth, "Interpret for me."

"She wants me arrested for stealing her computer; she called me a thief."

"Did you take it from her?" inquired Zorion.

"Yes, but…" Kraeth started to say; Zorion interrupted him.

"Then *you are* a thief."

The remark brought laughter from the guards.

Silence!" Zorion yelled and faced Kraeth, "How can you understand what she is saying? You have only been there four Terrestrial Revolutions."

"That will take some time to explain. For now, you must understand that we need that computer. With it, I can upload their language into our mainframe, and using the translation software I have created, we can communicate with the citizens of her world. I have developed a mobile device that will translate conversations. We can use them until we learn to speak their language ourselves."

"What is her name?" questioned Zorion.

"Julie," Kraeth answered Zorion.

"What?" puzzled Julie.

"He asked me your name," Kraeth informed Julie.

Zorion finally allowed himself to look at her again and was careful not to gaze adoringly at her. Since she looked exactly like the female in his dreams, it was tough not to embrace her. The last vision he had of her flashed in his mind. She told him they would meet soon, but he never imagined she would be from another planet. Even more perplexing was that Julie did not recognize him and could not speak Akilian as she did in his dreams.

"Tell her my name and that I am the sovereign of this city," Zorion ordered.

Kraeth did as Zorion commanded.

"Now ask her if we may borrow her computer. Be sure to tell her why we need it and that I promise to return it once you finish," Zorion said calmly.

As Kraeth did as Zorion commanded, Julie noticed that Zorion kept looking at her strangely. It was as if he recognized her and his familiarity made her feel uneasy.

Kraeth finished his translation, and Julie disputed, "You are not making any sense. Every country on Earth has interpreters. You do not need my computer to learn English."

"We are not on Earth, Julie," Kraeth stated flatly.

"What?" she shrieked.

Zorion flinched at the sound of her cry.

"You are on Akil. It is on the other side of the Milky Way," Kraeth remarked.

"That's not possible! The farthest we can go is to the moon," Julie yelled in disbelief.

"It is not possible for you, but we have had the technology for many of your years, so please, allow us to borrow the computer so our sovereigns can communicate with you and your people."

Julie decided it would be best for her safety to give them the computer. Refusing to hand it over could cause them to take it from her forcibly. At least, if she willingly gave it to them, they might treat her better. She gulped, walking toward Zorion, and hoped the others would not try to attack her again. She brought the laptop up in front of her with both hands and held it out for Zorion to take.

"Tell him that he may have it."

Kraeth translated.

She turned to Kraeth, "Now, please send me back home."

"I am afraid we cannot do that," Kraeth commented.

"Why not?" Julie nervously responded.

"It takes our capacitors a full twenty-four hours to recharge, so you must stay until tomorrow."

Kraeth relayed the conversation to Zorion in the Akilian language.

"How long will it take you to create the earpieces?" Zorion queried Kraeth.

"Not long, three, maybe four thousand heartbeats. I have been preparing for my return nearly thirty Terrestrial Rotations."

"Thirty Terrestrial Revolutions? You were only gone for four."

"Yes, as I said, I have much to tell you."

"Before my team debriefs you, escort her to apartment number one in the guest area. Assure her that no harm will come to her," Zorion ordered, paused, turned to Broll, and continued, "Post sentries at the elevators. No one is allowed in or out unless I give specific approval." He started to leave but stopped abruptly and, without turning around, spoke to Kraeth, "Tell her I will visit once you have the language application working."

Kraeth obeyed Zorion's orders and motioned to Julie, "Now, if you just follow me, I will show you to your accommodations."

Kraeth escorted Julie out of the lab and noticed Yanamai alive and well in the control room. *Since Garbi did not kill her, did Yanamai kill Garbi? Either way, the mission failed, but I do not believe it is my fault. I told Domeka that I must be around to ensure success.*

Chapter 7

Akil

Argi City

The 22,277[th] Terrestrial Rotation of the Second Summer

Dolas left his office and noticed someone following him. Initially, he thought of killing him but decided it was better to discover the pursuer's identity before ending his life. Knowing whom you were dealing with in the field was always essential. Gathering information was the cornerstone of his job, enabling him to do his best. He took an inconspicuous image of his hunter and ran it through his office's database while moving along the avenue.

A few hundred heartbeats later, the search results showed he was one of Broll's guards. Knowing Broll would not move without the sovereign's permission alerted him to Zorion's suspicion. However, with Zorion watching him, killing the guard was not a choice, so he must evade him. Keeping that in mind, Dolas entered a crowded elevator at the last moment, making it impossible for the guard to follow him.

As the elevator descended, he changed his likeness, removed his outer jacket, and appeared as someone else. Had the guard done the same, Dolas would not have noticed him. *Never send a sentry to do an agent's job.* He changed his clothes and physical features several times to ensure no one else followed him. Using extra caution made him a thousand heartbeats late for his meeting with Olan. It was unavoidable.

At the corridor entrance, Dolas hid in the shadows, near an area of the undeveloped wall, where he waited for a few hundred heartbeats and then scanned the avenue one last time to ensure he had lost the pursuer. He entered the tunnel and vanished into the darkness, it was the first time he had accessed the secret passage on his own, and it gave him a sense of euphoria to be one of only a few chosen to know of its existence.

Nearing his destination, he saw a bright light coming from an opening that illuminated the hallway. He entered the doorway and saw Olan sitting at a table, working on a timekeeper.

Seeing bloodstains on his clothes, Dolas inquired, "What happened?"

"Molo attacked Zorion, and I intervened."

"Is Zorion dead?"

"No, he only wounded him. Zorion should recover soon."

"What about Molo?"

"I let him live with the intention that Zorion would interrogate him, so you must be ready if he calls for you."

"I do not think he trusts me. One of Broll's guards followed me. That is why I am late."

"If I were Zorion, I would not trust anyone; if you are careful, he will continue to employ you."

"Now that they are following me, you must allow more time before our meetings begin."

"Agreed, there is nothing we can do to change it."

"The attack must have just happened because I have not heard about it yet."

"It happened earlier this work cycle."

"Does Zorion know you saved him?"

"Yes, but he still does not trust me, which means I must find the ones responsible. Even if I do, you can never reinstate me."

"You will be *running in the shadows* for the rest of your life if you do not allow me to clear your name."

"Working as a rogue agent allows me to do my job with anonymity. No one will look for me if I am 'running in the shadows,' as you put it.

"I am sorry. You are the best agent I have ever met."

"It is better this way."

Dolas watched him tinker with the timekeeper and inquired, "What are you working on?"

"I removed Molo's timekeeper before I fled, the one he talked into before attacking Zorion, and I have inserted a tracker to locate his accomplice."

Remembering he had a bag with food and clothes, Dolas set it down and walked over to look closer, "Have you identified the signal yet?"

"Yes. I have programmed it to connect to the other communicator in a random micro-heartbeat pattern. The other communicator responds, and this one will terminate the connection, so the target will not know I connected this device to his."

Olan switched on his portable data device, which displayed a small flashing red dot in the middle of a map of Argi.

"Where is he?" questioned Dolas.

"Level twenty."

"I will go."

"No. If you arrest the accomplice, you must take him into custody. I want to speak to him first. You can have him later. It is a benefit of being a rogue agent."

"You do all the work, and I get the credit. It sounds like a good deal to me," Dolas responded, smiling playfully.

"You will have plenty to do, but your most important task is to ensure you do not let Zorion know you are helping me. If I lose you, it will be much harder to find and capture those who set me up."

Olan retrieved the clothes that Dolas had brought him.

"What do you want me to do?" Dolas queried.

"Redirect the agents on level twenty for a few thousand heartbeats. I will also need Broll's guards' identities and station locations on that level to avoid them."

"I will send it electronically to our secret server once I return. Is there anything else?"

"Yes, be ready in case I need you."

After Dolas left, Olan changed his clothes and checked his locator. *He is still on level twenty. Good, Molo's associate is stationary.* He fastened his sword to his waist, threw a new cloak over his shoulders, changed his appearance, and headed for the elevator.

Chapter 8

Akil

Argi City

The 22,277[th] Terrestrial Rotation of the Second Summer

As his finger moved across the face of his tablet, scrolling to another page of Kraeth's report, Zorion marveled at its length. *At least he was thorough, but an abbreviated version would have been better.* With a yawn, he looked away from the screen and rubbed his eyes. The amount of detail certainly lends credence to Kraeth's claim that he accidentally traveled back in time. This data would have been impossible to accumulate in only four Terrestrial Revolutions. The "accident," Kraeth mentioned, helped their mission, putting it ahead by thirty Terrestrial Rotations. Time was something they dearly needed.

The idea of time travel was not new to him. After Zorion's inauguration, Kex, the Chief Administrator of the Science Division, told him and the other sovereigns, who had just started their rule as well, that the technology to build such a machine existed, but it was known only to them and a couple of scientists on Akil. Researchers from each generation passed the knowledge along to two students they selected. They hoped that someone would find a way to use it without destroying themselves, which is why they vigorously guarded the technology.

Kex and his assistant chose to train Yanamai and Garbi. Now, they must teach two students of their choosing. When the newly instituted sovereigns heard that they could move back in time, they nearly jumped at the opportunity, but Kex had told them that the technology came with a warning: *You cannot cheat time.*

The phrase had many interpretations; Kex believed the timeline was fixed or predestined, and if they tried to save themselves by using a time machine, it would not change their situation. Somehow, their sun would still become a red giant with a river of plasma streaming to the nearby star. Other scientists believed that if an Akilian went back in time, he or she would be the cause of their sun turning into a red giant. Only a few scientists believe they could create an alternate timeline.

As part of the curriculum, Yanamai and Garbi had to draft a thesis on the benefits and dangers of time travel. Yanamai argued that historians did not know enough about antiquity and how their sun changed into a red giant to guarantee they could reverse it or even stop it. All they had were legends of Gau, the deity credited for their sun's destruction, so she was vehemently against it. Garbi argued that they could change the events and create a new timeline, even if they did not know the past. She tried to convince Zorion it was worth the risk.

Zorion did not trust legends; he believed in science. There had to be a logical reason for their sun's abrupt depletion. One theory he held was that a black hole passed by close enough to drain its precious plasma. This event weakened the sun, causing it to expand and burn cooler. If that theory turned out to be correct, going back to the age of antiquity would not save their planet. At the same time, Zorion believed that if they traveled back a few yellow harvests, bringing their portal technology and records of where they had already explored would give them the advantage they needed to survive.

He presented his opinion to Yanamai and Garbi, who argued for many Terrestrial Revolutions; ultimately, it was the sovereigns' decision. Yanamai had convinced the other sovereigns, except Elzer, not to use the technology. Outvoted three to two, Zorion had to stop his pursuit from traveling back in time. Now that Kraeth had breached time, Zorion wondered what changes, if any, came with it. If the timeline changed, it would be impossible to know. It left Zorion wondering if Kraeth's unintentional actions resulted in their dying sun. *Did we cheat time, or did time cheat us?*

Zorion knew for sure that time was running out for them. Akil moved toward its destruction with every heartbeat, making him wonder if he should have secretly built the machine. The power needed to make such a journey required a hundred Terrestrial Revolutions to accumulate and was an unacceptable risk. In Kraeth's report, he met Julie after landing thirty Terrestrial Rotations in the past. He hoped the impact on the timeline was minimal. *Julie*. The name, though alien, sounded familiar.

He fought hard to keep her out of his thoughts; still, her image always crept back into his mind. Their meeting was a complete disaster, and he could not imagine a scenario ending with them being together, yet even against surmountable odds, he could not push aside his ardent desire to speak or be in her presence. There was something about her that drew him.

While waiting for Kraeth's return, he visualized their first encounter again. The look on her face was priceless. He smiled. She stumbled upon a situation unprepared yet managed herself exceptionally well. In comparison, he would not have done the same, landing on an alien planet and finding himself surrounded by armed guards. His instincts would have driven him to fight his way out, which would have ended with his death.

Her strength and confidence made her a desirable candidate for a companion, but he could not imagine she would ever consider him due to their unusual introduction. He paced, fretting over the situation until it occurred to him that he did not know anything about her mating rituals or customs. *Great, another wall standing between us.* Staring at the tablet, he wondered if Kraeth included anything on the subject in his report. Using the search engine, he typed in some keywords, and within moments the item appeared on his screen: <u>Mating Rituals</u>.

Hesitating, his finger hovered over the execute button. *What am I doing? There is no way this will work.* The words she spoke to him in his dream echoed in his mind, "I am coming for you." Seeing her in the Interstellar Transport Bay caused reality and the dream world to collide. Even now, he finds it hard to discern between fiction and non-fiction. She also made it a point to use the term *my love* in his last dream, which is a phrase that has a special meaning in his culture. *I need to know.*

He started the process and spent the following three thousand heartbeats reading everything Kraeth accumulated on the subject, yet he still had not seen all of it. Sadly, he found himself even more confused than at the start. There were many different traditions. For example, in some cultures, the parents decide whom their children marry. He cringed at the thought.

In comparison, other societies disregarded old traditions, and the responsibility fell upon the males to start lasting relationships; again, not everyone held to that custom either. Some forsook any entanglements and remained unattached for most, if not all, of their lives. He sighed at how unpredictable Earthians tended to act. Also, Zorion guessed her to be at least twenty yellow harvests. Since

Akilians joined houses at the eighteenth yellow harvest, he wondered if she was still single and if it was by her choice, making him think she favored remaining unattached. If so, their relationship was over before it began.

The Akilian custom was simple. The burden of starting the relationship fell upon the females. There were no variations to their tradition. Although society had put its trust in their heightened gift, Thea proved to him that they could not rely on everyone to be truthful. *There are no guarantees in this life.* It was a lesson he learned the hard way.

Tired and frustrated, he turned the tablet off and pushed it away. *Why did you not warn me? Why did she not recognize me? Why could she speak Akilian fluently in my dreams but did not understand a word when we met?*

He stared at the ceiling for the longest time, contemplating the situation until the stress got to him, so he walked and found himself standing in his private dressing chamber. In front of his mirror, he saw his reflection wearing his best uniform, complete with all his medals. Based on Kraeth's report, some Earthian males wore the best quality clothing to capture a female's attention. Zorion hoped Julie would notice his effort to present himself in the best attire he had, or the past two thousand heartbeats were for nothing.

He pulled his jacket to straighten it and saw the touch-up comb lying on his dresser. In his report, Kraeth wrote that older Earthian males sometimes dye their hair to appear younger. Prior to reading the article, he did not care about the gray hairs that had rudely infiltrated his dark, black mane, but now he felt embarrassed by them. Before the dye was even dry, Shilda contacted him on his communicator.

"Kraeth is here to see you."

"Send him right in!" he shouted, darting back into his office.

In an unusual move, he opened the door and anxiously invited him inside. Kraeth noticed the unexpected gesture and moved cautiously toward him.

"Do you have the translators?" Zorion excitedly questioned.

"Yes, Sir. I have them right here."

Kraeth removed the devices from their box and handed them to Zorion, who placed one in each ear. Zorion gestured with his chin, and Kraeth spoke in English.

"Do you understand me?" quizzed Kraeth.

There was a slight pause until Zorion nodded. Kraeth handed him a small box.

Zorion frowned, "What is this for?"

"Julie. It translates our language to hers. Also, there are several more like yours that you can distribute to whomever you wish."

"Thank you. You have done an outstanding job!" Zorion trumpeted, patting him on the shoulder.

Kraeth smiled politely, "Thank you, Sir."

"I want the translators mass-produced. Also, make copies of the application that taught you how to speak their language because I want every Akilian to have one of each."

He paused to make sure he thought of everything.

"That will be all for now; I will contact you if I need something else. Dismissed."

Zorion called Broll into his office, "How do I look?"

Broll raised an eyebrow, "You look overdressed. Our visitor is not a dignitary. Why would you go to such lengths to impress her?"

Zorion closed the door and whispered, "It is her."

Broll furrowed his eyebrows, "Her?"

"Julie! She is the one from my dreams," Zorion continued with a loud whisper.

"How is this possible?" puzzled Broll.

"I do not know. It does not make any sense to me either."

"At least now, you know her name."

"Yes. That is one part of the mystery solved."

He opened the door, walked out of his office, and onto the avenue. Broll stayed by his side.

"Have you dyed your hair?" Broll teased, grinning.

Zorion smoothed his hair back with his hand.

"It is part of their custom. Older Earthian males will alter their appearance to look more appealing."

"Why not simply change your form and make yourself look twenty yellow harvests younger?"

"I did consider it, but if she is the one from my dreams, I want to ensure she will recognize me."

"Are you sure she will even notice? She has other pressing issues to concern herself with."

"All I know is that I must get her attention. I cannot let this opportunity slip by."

"I do not mean to sound insensitive, but do you think you have a chance?"

"I left out something from our earlier conversation. Last night she used the phrase *My Love* before she vanished."

He stopped walking and faced Broll.

"It is something Thea has never said to me."

"Never?"

Broll looked surprised. Zorion shook his head and started walking again.

"Now I understand why you separated yourself from her," Broll commented.

"It is one of many reasons."

"From my point of view, I would guess *many* other reasons."

Zorion stopped to face Broll again, "I am frustrated because she did not tell me the circumstances of how we would meet. You saw how it happened. I do not see a way to overcome that disaster."

"She will know if you should be together; it is up to her to tell you, and the brutal way you met will be meaningless."

Zorion shook his head as they moved forward. He explained what little he knew of Earthian mating rituals.

"I see your dilemma. It does hamper things if she does not have the Akilian gift."

During a brief silence, he took the opportunity to think of some advice to offer his friend.

"You have no other choice than to be yourself. You are a good friend and a great sovereign. If this Earthian female is honorable, she will find you attractive even with her disability."

Zorion nodded, "I hope you are right."

"Have you considered if she has already joined houses with someone else?"

"I recently discovered there is a way to find out. Kraeth's report made me aware that their custom is to wear a ring on a finger on their left hand; it will be the first thing I check."

They arrived early at Julie's guest apartment, and the caterers showed up within a couple of hundred heartbeats.

"Wait for my signal to bring the food in," Zorion instructed, just before knocking.

Chapter 9

Akil
Argi City
The 22,277[th] Terrestrial Rotation of the Second Summer

Julie looked at her wristwatch; it had been three hours since Kraeth left. She had just finished exploring the apartment, in which the builders carved every room out of the rock and strategically placed thick stone pillars throughout the area to support the roof. The floors, ceilings, and walls were all polished and smooth, reminding her of marble. Decorators set furniture around the apartment, made of glass and stone with cushion seats and backs. Florescent-like lighting emanated from select stones that hung flush with others from the ceiling. There were three bedrooms and three full bathrooms.

She found warm water cascading from an opening at the top of the wall above the tub. It flowed over magnificent rock formations, creating a miniature waterfall. Every room was accommodating; in some respects, it reminded her of Earth. *Earth. This place is surreal.* She discovered a large, transparent glass plate stationed in what might be the living room. She found out it was like a television from home by accidentally touching the correct place. Unable to understand the language, she turned it off and returned to her pacing.

Frustrated, she decided to step outside. Before leaving, Kraeth told her that the apartment was the first of many that curved around one end of the city limits to the other side. All the dwellings were vacant, reserved for Zorion's guests during special occasions. Kraeth also explained that Zorion dedicated this level to his staff, assistants, cooks, and the like.

Since they would be moving about the level, she had to stay within the guest area's boundaries but had permission to step outside her apartment and wander around. Kraeth said the guards would tell her if she went too far. Feeling claustrophobic, she decided to venture onto the avenue.

When she opened the door, fresh, warm air blew past her into the home. The sentries stood visible at each side of her doorway. She smiled politely and walked toward the rail ahead. Their boots hitting the ground let her know they were close. She estimated they kept a five-foot distance behind her. If there were a safe place to run, she would risk it, but there was nowhere to go.

She looked over the city and saw an elevator junction only a few hundred feet away to her right. She saw each apartment door to her left. They seemed to go on for at least a mile in a semicircle; it ended on the other side, where the avenue straightened. Beneath her, thousands of lights, as far as the eye could see, lit up the city. Although she tried to find the bottom, it was too far.

Traveling on hundreds of various levels, hover vehicles of all shapes and sizes dashed about in every direction. Above, the ceiling looked like a giant projection screen. It first caught her attention on her way to the apartment. On it, she saw a crescent red giant sun looming on the horizon. It had fountains of plasma spewing from its surface into space. The sight of it gave her chills. Turning, she faced the guards and smiled. Although there was no direct sunlight to stir up the air, she could feel a constant warm breeze moving around her. At times, it was strong enough to blow hair into her eyes. She pushed the strands over to the side where they belonged.

"You have a beautiful home."

The guard responded only with a dead-tone stare. She sighed at the silent reply, returned to the apartment, and, unable to burn off her nervous energy, paced for several minutes until plopping down on the couch. *Oh, where is he? Kraeth said the sovereign would visit in a couple of hours.* Kraeth insisted she was not a prisoner, but it had been three hours, and she wondered if it was a lie; she heard a knock at the door and used her jittery energy to answer.

The door flung open, and she came face to face with Zorion. At once, she noticed a few subtle changes in his appearance. His red suit was now blue and decorated with a lot more medals than before. Also, his grey, peppered hair was now solid black. *Why did he dye it?* With a slightly shaky hand, Zorion handed her a small black box. She opened it to find a strange-looking device inside. Zorion motioned for her to put it in her ear, and without thinking, she did. *Oh, crap, what if it was a mind control device? Way to go, Julie; now you will end up someone's slave on a faraway planet that even Alex cannot reach you.* Unexpectedly, the device emitted static until she heard English words.

"Can you understand me?" inquired Zorion.

Julie blinked, pushing the translator farther into her ear, and, having secured it, replied, "Um - yes, I can understand you. How is this possible?"

"Kraeth created it so we could communicate; it is temporary until we learn to speak your language. I realize you already know my name, but I would like to introduce myself."

Stepping forward, he extended his hand to greet her. He did not use the standard Akilian greeting. Instead, he held his hand, palm facing to the left, which, per Kraeth's report, was the customary greeting for Earthians.

"I am Zorion, Argi's sovereign."

Hesitantly, Julie extended her hand and shook his.

"I'm Julie."

Hours of frustrated energy had built up inside her. Now that the pleasantries were over, Julie could no longer contain herself.

"Are you planning to invade my world?"

The words came out so quickly that she did not have time to think them over or consider their ramifications. The straightforward question caught Zorion off guard, who raised his hands defensively.

"I can assure you that is not our goal. We sent Kraeth for the sole purpose of retrieving material we could use to communicate with your government. His accident put him in your care, and he tried to return undetected, but since you followed him here…."

"I'm now your prisoner," Julie interrupted.

"Not at all! I was going to say that since you followed him here, you will be our guest until you return."

"Where I come from, guards are for prisoners, not guests."

"Please, may I come in?" pleaded Zorion.

It was clear that she was anxious and apprehensive. All he wanted to do was make her feel at ease, but not on the avenue.

"Sure," she answered, stepping back to give him room. Before Broll could step inside, she slammed the door in his face and locked it.

Soon Zorion saw him standing, looking through the window. Before he broke it, Zorion held up his hand to stop him.

He faced Julie and spoke softly, "The guards are here for your protection and ours. If you were to leave this level, someone might see you, even with an escort. I have not officially announced that we have found your planet yet, so I do not know how my citizens would react if they discovered alien life in their city. They could try to hurt you out of fear, and we both do not want that to happen."

"I can see your point," she conceded. *Wow, I'm the alien. I always imagined it the other way around.*

By the tone of her response and body language, Zorion believed that he had set her mind at ease, at least a little.

"I brought some food with me. If you do not mind, I would like to let the caterers bring it in."

"Sure, I'm hungry."

He opened the door and motioned for the caterers to bring in the food, hoping the offer would help to relieve her worries. The cooks entered and set out a grand buffet for her. Covered plates of all shapes and sizes filled the kitchen table. Zorion took the opportunity to look at her left hand and was happy to see no ring on her finger.

"I do not know what you like to eat, so I had them make everything," he offered, lifting one of the lids.

Steam rose from the plate. He grabbed a tiny morsel and ate it.

"Kraeth's report indicates that you have a vast assortment of foods in your world. I am afraid we only have a small variety of one type of vegetation. It will satisfy your hunger and nourish you."

He swallowed, put some on a plate, and set it on the table.

"Please, eat."

Julie walked over and sat in the chair. She sniffed the strange-looking entrée, which had almost no fragrance, and nibbled at it. *It doesn't have any flavor at all. I've eaten lettuce with more zest than this stuff.* Nevertheless, she politely smiled and chewed the bland dish, trying not to offend her gracious host.

"What is it?" she asked.

"Green moss, there are others with different tastes."

Julie spat it out of her mouth and yelled, "Moss? What the hell?"

He flinched at her disgust.

"I am sorry. Moss is all my planet can provide for your sustenance."

He removed the lids from the other platters, hoping one would satisfy her palette.

"Perhaps one of these might be to your liking."

Nervously, Zorion uncovered the rest of the dishes, hoping she would at least try one. Seeing how hard he tried to please her, Julie tasted a small cluster from each plate. Sadly, none of them had any flavor worth mentioning. Even the purple moss, which he said was dessert, left her longing for the rice cakes she ate during training. *I sure could go for a cinnamon bun right now.* Somehow, through guilt or pure hunger, she managed to eat enough to fill her stomach and noticed an increase in her energy level.

She wiped her mouth, "How long will I be your guest?"

"If I have correctly calculated how you perceive time, it takes twenty-four hours to recharge the capacitors." Zorion paused, looked at his timekeeper, and continued, "In twenty-one hours, you will be free to return home."

"Will you tell me why you want to talk to my government?"

"Of course. Our sun is close to the end of its life, which means our planet will die too. We have been searching for a habitable planet for a long time. Your world is the first one we have found that can support life. We hope your government will allow some or all our people to stay on Earth until we find another habitable world."

Julie stood and exclaimed, "You mean to tell me I'm on a planet that could die at any moment?"

Again, Zorion held his hands defensively, "Please, do not panic. Our scientists believe we have a few hundred of your days left, if not more, so you are not in danger."

"You only have a few hundred days?"

"It is difficult to be precise with something vast and unpredictable, so it is only a conservative estimate."

He tried to sound as soothing as possible. She felt genuinely sorry for Zorion and his people but could only think of her peril.

"Do you promise to send me home tomorrow?" she coaxed.

"I do."

Julie exhaled loudly and sat.

"I realize it is a lot to take in all at once. Please do not worry. You will be home before anything happens," Zorion assured.

He forced a practiced smile. *All right, Julie, just a few more hours, and you will be back home safe.* A few minutes passed, and she calmed down enough to push her fears aside and consider his peril.

I will be fine, but soon, everyone will die if they cannot get off this planet. She placed herself in his position and understood the tremendous weight that rested on his shoulders. *It must be a terrifying burden.* Overwhelmed with compassion, she began thinking of a way to help him.

"I have an idea. Can you record a video?"

"Yes, we have that capability."

"If you can make a recording describing your situation, I will take it back with me and give it to my brother, so he can give it to his boss, General Saunders, who can hand it to our Supreme Commander. Once he learns of your predicament, I'm sure the Regime would be willing to help you."

"How long do you think it would take to get the video to your Supreme Commander?"

"Considering the circumstances, I'm sure General Saunders would take it to Supreme Commander Porter the moment my brother gives it to him, so by tomorrow, you should be in negotiations."

"This is wonderful news! I will have my assistant type a brief petition, and since he is already fluent in your language, I will have Kraeth make the recording."

The news was bittersweet. Zorion was tremendously grateful that she would speed up their introduction to her Supreme Commander, yet at the same time, he hated the thought of her leaving. *It is hard to accept that I will only have you here for a brief time.* He extended his hand again, per the protocol Kraeth wrote down in his report.

"You have been a tremendous help to us. I will be forever in your debt. Someone will be by tomorrow to escort you to the Interstellar Transport Bay."

Although he did not want to leave her presence, sending a recording to her government was especially important, so he had to begin at once.

Julie called out to him, "Wait! Where are you going?"

"I am sorry; I must prepare this before your departure."

"Will it take you all night?"

"Well, it should only take about three of your hours. Why do you ask?"

"There must be somewhere you can take me without being noticed. It would be a shame to travel such a long distance and only see the inside of an apartment."

"No, I am sorry. It is too risky."

Julie nodded sadly, "Sure, I understand."

Seeing the look of disappointment on her face, Zorion became determined to find something to entertain her. He agreed with her statement. She did come a long way, and it would be a shame not to show her something about his world.

"After I finish preparing the video, most of my staff will be off duty, so there are a few places I could safely take you."

Julie smiled, "That sounds wonderful! I look forward to seeing you later."

Zorion returned her smile and left, closing the door behind him.

"That went well," Broll observed.

Zorion looked at him incredulously, "You cannot be serious."

"There were some rough patches, but you are returning later; it is a start."

"She is still leaving tomorrow!"

"Perhaps she will stay. You never know how things will change."

"I do not want her to stay. She could die with us."

"In that case, you should be happy that she is leaving."

"I do not want her to go either. I want to spend more time with her."

"It seems you have a double mind on this issue."

"I agree. My heart wants her to stay, but my mind knows she must go."

"Let it be her choice and support whatever decision she makes."

"What if I never see her again, Broll?"

"If she is the same person from your dreams, I believe she will never leave your side."

"My heart hopes that you are right."

Chapter 10

Akil
Argi City
The 22,277[th] Terrestrial Rotation of the Second Summer

It was lunchtime, and Olan used the crowded promenade to cover his movements from Broll's search parties, looking for Molo's accomplice. Olan assumed a business owner's attire within the financial district, allowing him to move around invisibly and in plain sight. Looking at the numbing sameness of all the others around him, Olan realized Molo's accomplice had the same idea. Olan pulled the locating device out of his pocket and casually checked his prey's position. *No more than five quick steps in front of me.*

The red dot he used to track him moved toward a food court. The avenues had three sections, with the passenger shuttles using the center lane. Olan decided to move from the inner path to the outer path, allowing him a better view of all pedestrian traffic. Once on the outer road, he checked the locator. His quarry stopped moving. The device showed his target several paces away. Akilians crowded the walkway, and Olan could not determine which one was his quarry. Looking back to the locator, he saw the red dot moving again. With the practiced moves of an agent, he inconspicuously slipped back into the crowd and continued his pursuit.

A couple of thousand heartbeats later, as the crowd on the avenue thinned, someone bumped into him, knocking the personal timekeeper from his hand. He retrieved it and discovered it had inadvertently sent a garbled message to his target's communicator. *If he does not panic, everything will be fine.* Patiently he waited, hoping the transmission did not go through and scanning the avenue to see who would raise their wrist to their ear. Olan frowned because the target raised his arm and spoke into the communicator.

"Shafe, Shafe, is that you? Come in, over."

Olan made a mental note of the guard's name, who posed as Molo. From his vantage point, he could tell that his quarry adopted the nondescript image of a mid-level accountant. Everything about him was mundane: average height, average weight, no distinguishing features. *The kind of disguise I would have chosen.* Having seen his prey, Olan leisurely moved back to the inner lane and hid, hoping not to spook him. He used the shuttle lane as a barrier and followed the other from a distance.

The target crossed the outer lane and got in line for the hover bus. Olan followed him, instinctively looked down at the locator, and noticed that the signal was now behind him. It meant only one thing; his target ditched the communicator. Keeping a weather eye on his quarry, Olan retrieved the device from the trash bin where the other tossed it. However, the agent shoved the Akilians out of the way, tossed the driver onto the avenue, and sped off. *Blast! He has commandeered the vehicle!*

As the bus pulled away, he saw its marking number *452*. Now, he needed another vehicle to chase him. On cue, another bus pulled up, and the driver stepped out to help the other bus driver, who was still lying on the ground. Seizing the opportunity, Olan ran onto the bus, shut the door, and sped away in pursuit. The driver banged his fists on the door, ordering Olan to stop. Olan ignored him. Glancing up at the rear-view mirror, he saw three passengers, two middle-aged socialites, and one young maintenance worker.

"I am an agent with Special Security forces. I am in pursuit of a wanted felon. Do not yell. Hold onto your seats, and it will all be over soon," Olan shouted, pushing the throttle to its maximum.

In the mirror, he saw the passengers grab onto the rider restraints to secure themselves. *I hope this does not get messy.* He frantically weaved through traffic, trying to catch up, and had several near misses. *Where in Abadose is bus number 452? Ah, there it is.* Olan swerved to pass a vehicle ahead of him and heard a loud crunch. In the rear-view mirror, he saw metal confetti flying everywhere as the other driver spun out of control. *That is why you have insurance.*

The vehicle continued to spin into another, and together, they slammed into the sturdy guard rails. He saw metal bending and glass breaking. *It is a good thing I am no longer an agent, or else Zorion would have to pay for it.* The accident distracted Olan, causing him to miss the bus in front of him, which he hit from behind, pushing it into oncoming traffic, where two other vehicles careened into it. The jolt forced him forward, cracking the windshield with his forehead.

Slightly dazed, he blinked and saw the rear of the vehicle drop below its level plane, which was a sign that the magnetic suspension unit had failed. *That is why they make backup systems.* Although the collision slowed him down considerably, it did not deter him. He restarted the engine, pushed the throttle to its top speed, and searched for the other bus speeding past traffic. *I have lost him.* In the distance, he saw his target make a dive, going down several levels. Realizing he had to maneuver the same way to stay in pursuit, his excitement faded. Olan sighed, knowing the situation would not end well.

"Hold on tight," he yelled to his three passengers.

He overrode the system's safety protocol, pushed the steering wheel forward, and plunged the bus in the same direction. As the driver, he expected the fall. Even so, his stomach lurched, and the passengers did as well. He clipped the fender of another bus driving in its correct lane on the way down. The collision sent him into a spin, and his passengers screamed.

"Do not panic! I have everything under control!" Olan shouted, pulling against the steering wheel.

The vehicle's control panel flashed a warning. Olan pulled with all his might against the counter forces that kept them spinning until he regained control, leveled the bus, and pushed the throttle to its top speed again. In the distance, he saw bus number 452. As the vehicle sped toward his target, poles, doors, and citizens flew by in a blur. He continuously pitched the bus up, down, and sideways to avoid hitting anyone else until a small vehicle ahead of him suddenly stopped. *Oh, no, not again.*

Unable to turn out of the way, he hit the hovercar from behind, forcing it into traffic, where another vehicle hit its side. The impact shattered the windshield of Olan's bus, ripping it from its molding. The windshield fell forward and slid off the hood, plummeting thousands of levels to the bottom. Without the windshield, Olan felt the full force of the winds created by the bus's high speed but did not slack on the throttle.

Within a few hundred heartbeats, he again found bus number 452. *Ah, that is why I caught up with him so quickly. His bus is full of passengers.* Just as he was about to ram him, the bus Olan drove started to smoke. *No, not yet!* Stealing energy from other sources, he directed more power to the engines. It kept him close to the other bus, but it was not enough to ram it.

He saw some of the passengers move against the driver in unison. As they struggled, the bus slowed down. *I cannot let them arrest him. I need to continue to track him.* Having gained on the other, he steered the right side into the left rear of bus 452, sending them both into a wild, uncontrollable spin toward a crowded avenue. Those who saw it coming scattered in every direction.

Due to their size, the guardrail was unable to stop both vehicles. As they struck the rail, the buses tumbled top over bottom. Everyone inside was flung around like rag dolls as they bounced off the walls and seats. The buses smashed through a department store's grand display window and slid to a stop amid the wreckage of merchandise and the bodies of those who could not get out of the way.

Having landed upside down, Olan unhooked his safety restraint and fell to the vehicle's roof. Bruised and bleeding, he crawled through the front, where the windshield had been. He scanned the area and saw everyone running toward the accident to help the injured, except one. *Aha!* His target changed his form to a younger, more athletic Akilian. On pure adrenaline, Olan ran after him.

Reaching the upper level of the department store, the other disappeared amid hundreds of clothing racks. Cautiously, Olan walked down the center aisle, feverishly looking for some clue as to his quarry's whereabouts. With everyone observing the wreckage, the store was tranquil. Just in case his target was nearby, he retrieved his sword. To flush out his prey, he methodically walked each secondary aisle. He searched for a few hundred heartbeats until returning to the main corridor empty-handed. *I have lost him.*

Having given up, he sheathed his sword and moved toward the stairway, where he saw his target's reflection in the store's corner mirror. The distorted image showed him well hidden beneath a rack of clothing. He unsheathed his sword again with renewed vigor and walked to his position. As Olan approached, his target shoved the clothing stand he was hiding under into his face.

The metal bar hit Olan's chin, sending a wave of pain through his jaw. Olan pushed the rack aside just in time to block an overhead attack. Olan was ready for his opponent's ferocity but not his skill: Parry, thrust, counterthrust, slash. *He is as good as I am.* Olan tripped over some clothes that fell from the rack. Seeing an opportunity, the other swung his sword across Olan's forehead, leaving a gash that bled profusely. Olan fell, and blood poured down his face and into his eyes.

Before his target could attack again, Olan rolled underneath a clothing rack to hide. He used his sleeve to wipe away the blood from his face. *Damn, there goes another good suit.* His opponent was on him again, whaling away with his sword without rhyme or reason. The brute force of the attack knocked the sword from Olan's hand, making the sound no fighter ever wants to hear, the sound of his weapon clanging on the ground as it slides away.

The other smiled, knowing he had the advantage. As his target raised his sword with both hands, preparing to strike, Olan jumped up and grabbed his wrists before he could swing. His opponent tried to get free until Olan swept his feet from underneath him. They hit the ground simultaneously, and his quarry dropped his sword. The fight changed from blades to wrestling and punching. They rolled around on the floor, kicking, biting, and pummeling each other.

Olan wrapped his legs around the other's waist and squeezed tightly, crushing the air out of his lungs. His opponent struggled to breathe and dug nails into the skin around Olan's eyes. Olan punched him in the throat several times and removed his gouging hands from his face. Finally, Olan secured his target's head, preventing him from moving, and head-butted him unconscious.

Olan rested on the floor, catching his breath, and bleeding. *This is not what I want. I must let him escape to follow him, but how do I track him?* Olan stood, swaying over his target's unconscious body, and removed the communicator from his pocket. *If I conceal this in his clothes, he might find it or change clothes, and I would lose him. However, if he changed his clothes, would he change his shoes?*

He gutted the communicator, removed the tracking chip, knelt, and hid the chip in his quarry's left shoe. *Now for the hard part. I must make him think he has only been out for a few heartbeats.* Getting back on the floor, Olan rewrapped himself around his opponent and rolled around as if they were still fighting, waiting for him to wake up. Moments later, his target regained consciousness and cracked Olan several times on the side of the head with a rack bar.

Since he was still tired from being unconscious, the blows barely made an impact; even so, Olan reacted as if hit with the force of a stone hammer. Using a practiced move, he rolled away and feigned unconsciousness. It was a considerable risk, but Olan trusted his instincts. The other got up and, seeing that Olan was not moving, turned, and ran away. Olan smiled, knowing his plan worked. His target fled, so he stood, grabbed some clothes off the rack, and limped to an emergency exit to hide until his wounds stopped bleeding.

A few thousand heartbeats later, he changed and returned to the avenue where a crew cleaned up the accident. The Information League set up cameras near the buses. Olan was not worried about his cover because he was still in an unrecognizable disguise. The accident destroyed the front of the department store. Glass, debris, and blood were scattered about everywhere.

The accident left many wounded on the avenue with loved ones or onlookers nearby, helping them get comfortable until they could take them to a Recovery Station. A crane hoisted the buses evenly off the avenue. Olan cringed at the sight of several motionless bodies lying underneath. Even though the crane operator did his best to lift the bus safely, preventing further injury, Olan thought it was too late for them.

As the bus rose in the air, it appeared as if one of the injured was trying to get up; a closer look revealed his hand stuck in the frame. Someone nearby yelled for the crane operator to stop and ran under to unhook his hand. As towing vehicles hauled the buses away, Olan started to leave but stopped after seeing a young socialite running toward one of the bodies trapped underneath the bus. Seeing the injured up close, she screamed a blood-curling shriek that could only mean one thing. He felt a knot form in his stomach.

Even though the crushing wounds would have healed over an extended period, he noticed that shards of metal from the bus severed his head, making it impossible to recover. The weight of several more deaths now lay on his shoulders, and sometimes it was unbearable. Whenever things like this happened, he tried to console himself by believing it was for the greater good; it never seemed to help. For many Terrestrial Revolutions to come, he would question himself, hoping to prevent the loss of life in the future, and with one last look at the horrific scene, he turned and disappeared into the crowd.

Chapter 11

With her new translator secured in her ear, Julie decided to turn on the transparent glass monitor in her room. Her finger glided across the smooth surface, searching for the spot that turned it on earlier. *Ah, there it is.* The monitor came to life, and she stepped back to take in the image. A TV show came on calling itself *Argi Information League*. As they played live footage of a bus accident, recorded by a pedestrian, she watched, enthralled by the event. *Man, that doesn't look good.*

The reporter went on to say that there were many injured and several fatalities. The accident appeared catastrophic. The fact that only several people died amazed her. She watched the *Argi Information League* for a while and looked at her watch. Since Zorion would not arrive for at least another hour, she decided to explore the area to the side of the apartment.

Stepping outside, she saw one of the guards patrolling the section. He disappeared around the corner, so she turned her attention to the beautiful courtyard with a fountain that abutted a part of the undeveloped wall. Its construction had many details; it took several minutes to view the whole sight. The fountain's round base had a two-foot barrier that held water in the pool, which doubled as a seat. Water flowed from several bowls held by statues of women with long hair.

The sculptor arranged each woman with a different pose so that one woman's hair flowed into the bowl of the one beneath. The container poured the water onto her head, running down her hair to the basin below. The design formed an intricate weave for the water to flow, creating a pleasant melodic sound. Looking at its peak, she estimated it was at least twenty feet high. Enticed by the sound of soothing water, she walked over, sat, and dragged a few fingers through the pool.

The water was warm and inviting, so she took off her shoes, pulled her pant legs up, and let her feet dangle in the tranquil water. She rested on the stone seat, keeping one foot and one hand in the water, staring at more artwork on the ceiling. Before too long, her eyes became heavy, and she drifted off to sleep. Somewhere between reality and the dream world, she smelled something familiar. *Is someone making pastries?*

The cinnamon aroma brought her out of her stupor. She sat and looked around, expecting to see her brother walking toward her, holding a bag of cinnamon rolls from the market bakery, until she remembered following Kraeth through the portal. She realized it was not a dream and decided to put on her shoes and sniff the air, trying to find the source of the pleasant smell.

She walked around in circles for several minutes and found herself near an area of the undeveloped wall. At first, she hesitated to climb the small railing, but her newfound ravenous hunger drove her forward. She traversed the rail, searched the area for clues, and felt a warm breeze blowing toward her, rich with the smell of cinnamon.

Julie followed the gust to a small opening in the wall. Inside, she noticed that a fraction of the fissure partition completely blocked the courtyard's view, which explained why it was hard to find. Turning, she saw a faint light illuminating a narrow tunnel. The aroma was getting stronger, and her stomach started to growl from the teasing, enticing smell. Without another thought, she traversed the passageway, going deep into the rock.

Although the channel was narrow and not too high, she had no problems moving through it. Up ahead, she saw the tunnel open into a larger area. Carefully, she walked to the opening of a sizable circular room. Standing in the doorway, she looked for a chef. The room was empty except for thick swirling black and white moss covering the walls.

The tunnel continued farther to the opposite side of the room. Before moving forward, Julie decided to explore the space. Cautiously, she stepped inside to examine her discovery. With every breath, the smell of cinnamon grew stronger. Now, more than ever, she decided to find its source. Twirling, she saw that the room was dome-shaped, and the only space that did not have moss was at the top center, where a stone light shone.

Black and white moss hung in clusters like grapes from the ceiling and walls. She grabbed a handful and brought it to her nose. The smell of cinnamon was overwhelming and powerful; it made her dizzy. Hesitantly, she tasted a small morsel. As she ate the tiny leaves of the plant, they melted in her mouth like the sweet, creamy icing of a cinnamon bun. One small bite led to another and another.

A few minutes later, she had eaten several clusters of the plant. She used her trousers to wipe her hands and moved forward to explore the rest of the tunnel. Two steps later, she stopped and grabbed her belly from the pain. *Oh, no, I've poisoned myself.* Before she could call for help, the pain made her double over and fall. Her breathing became increasingly difficult, and her throat closed shut.

She screamed for help, but it only came out as a whisper. She tried to claw her way back to the apartment until her body convulsed. As she shook, foam spewed from her mouth. Now her breathing almost ceased, and her hands and feet went numb as she lay on the floor. The sensation traveled up her legs and arms into her torso. Finally, she closed her eyes and died.

Chapter 12

Otsoa heard a knock and went to answer it. On the other side, Durnah's parents waited impatiently. It was not hard to figure out that they both cried over the grim news he gave them.

"Where is my daughter?" Gloz, her dad, asked.

"She is lying in bed. I will show you the way," Otsoa remarked solemnly.

"Tell me what happened?"

"It was something she ate. We received a tray of red moss as a gift."

"Red moss? That is rare," Gloz admitted.

"I know, which is why she prepared it for the mid-day meal. I returned home and found her lying on the floor, with some still in her mouth. She must have tasted a few leaves while preparing it," Otsoa recalled.

"Who gave it to you?"

"I do not know. The delivery service said someone sent it anonymously."

"My poor Durnah."

"I found her too weak to walk, so I carried her to bed. Within a few thousand heartbeats, she progressively got worse; her skin, which did not have blemishes, became pale and blotted, and she developed a fever and began sweating. I keep bringing her pitchers of water, but it is not enough. Her body sweats more than she can drink. In time, I saw blood mixed with her sweat; I called you because I do not know how much longer she will live."

His last words caused Jornah, Durnah's mother, to exclaim loudly and cry harder. Otsoa briefly paused, so her parents could compose themselves. They entered Durnah's room, where they stood opposite her bed. Gloz gently took her hand. Feeling a touch on her skin, Durnah struggled to open her eyes.

Seeing Gloz, she smiled weakly and, with a raspy voice, whispered, "Thank you for coming."

"Do not worry, dear. You will be fine. Just rest," Jornah quivered, doing her best to comfort Durnah.

Hearing Jornah's voice, Durnah struggled to turn her head.

"I have the sickness, and we all know there is no cure."

Durnah's voice was just above a whisper. Otsoa did not love Durnah and wanted her out of his life, allowing him to pursue Yanamai. Still, he did not want to see her suffer this way. It seemed as if her illness came at the will of the universe. Sadly, no one survived the sickness.

"Is there anything I can do to make you more comfortable?" inquired Gloz.

Again, Durnah smiled weakly and whispered, "Just having you here is enough."

She closed her eyes and drifted off to sleep. As they waited for her to take her last breath, Otsoa heard a knock at the door, excused himself, and left to answer it. He found Nayrah with her head down and her cloak covering her face.

"Why are you here?" he wondered.

"I hear Durnah is ill, so I have come to offer my services."

"She has the sickness. There is nothing anyone can do."

"Show me to her room."

"Her parents are with her."

"I know."

Otsoa sighed because arguing with her was pointless.

"Very well, follow me."

Nayrah entered Durnah's room.

Gloz and Jornah looked at her angrily, "Who is this?"

"This is Nayrah," Otsoa answered.

"Why is she here?" Gloz challenged.

"I have come to help your daughter recover," Nayrah explained.

"No one can help her. She has the sickness."

Nayrah removed a vial from her cloak with a knowing grin and walked to Durnah's side, moving Jornah out of the way. She gently placed her right hand under Durnah's neck, woke her, lifted her head, and put the vial to her lips.

"What are you giving her?" inquired Gloz.

Nayrah ignored him and spoke to Durnah, "Drink, child."

Durnah took a few sips, and Gloz saw her complexion return.

"How do you feel?" queried Gloz with amazement.

"Much better," Durnah sighed with relief, and her voice returned to her.

"How is this possible?" Gloz questioned.

"She has not completely recovered yet," Nayrah warned.

"What do you mean?" puzzled Gloz.

"I have only given her a sip. If she does not drink the rest of the cure, the sickness will return, and nothing will save her."

"Let her drink the rest of the potion!" Otsoa exclaimed.

Nayrah faced Otsoa and yelled, "Silence!"

She turned her gaze to Gloz, "I will let Durnah drink the rest for a price."

Gloz's face turned red from rage. He tried to snatch the vial from Nayrah's grip. She moved out of his reach and released a wall of energy toward him, forcing him to fall onto the dresser behind him. Gloz slid to the floor, stunned. Jornah ran to his side to help him until he regained his composure.

"What is your price?"

Nayrah handed him an electronic contract. Gloz and Jornah read it.

This is outrageous!" Gloz exclaimed.

"It is a small price to pay for Durnah's life. Is it not?"

Jornah gently touched Gloz's arm, who faced her.

"Sign it, Gloz. I do not want to lose Durnah," Jornah insisted.

Having no choice, Gloz signed the contract. Nayrah reviewed the agreement and gave the vial to Durnah, who drank it greedily.

"Durnah will recover unless you fail to live up to your end of the contract or tell anyone what happened here; the next time Durnah gets sick, her mother will join her, and I promise, you will not stop it," Nayrah threatened.

"You will have your Sovereign Cubes, you *putok*! I hope you choke on them!" Gloz spat. Turning to Otsoa, he groused, "You are both despicable Akilians!"

"I had nothing to do with this!" Otsoa objected.

"Get out of here and leave us alone!" Gloz yelled.

Nayrah smiled, but Otsoa frowned, knowing she did it to him again. Now, he knew the real reason she wanted him to choose

Durnah. It was all about Sovereign Cubes. Outside Durnah's room, Otsoa confronted Nayrah.

"You poisoned the red moss, knowing she would eat it."

"Since you failed your mission in Zorion's office, I have no choice. I need Sovereign Cubes."

"Are you blaming me?"

"Do not test me, Otsoa. I *will* strike at you!"

"I could have eaten it too!"

"I would have given you the antidote, and you would be fine."

"If you needed currency, I could have given it to you. You did not need to do this."

Nayrah chuckled, "Where would you get the Sovereign Cubes?"

"I have ten thousand in my account."

"That is a drop in a fountain. I need much more."

"Once I become Argi's sovereign, I will have millions. You should have waited."

"I need them now. Besides, it is not easy to steal from Argi's coffer because auditors from three departments examine every account to ensure the sovereigns spend the Cubes properly. Now that Gloz and I are partners, I am entitled to half of his company's profits."

"What are you planning to do with it?"

"That is none of your business."

"Now that you have what you wanted from our union, I see no reason for us to stay together."

"Do not even think about leaving her!"

"Why?"

"Because I know you want to be free to pursue Yanamai. I have told you what would happen if you did."

Otsoa sighed in defeat, "Fine."

Before leaving, she noticed that he was beginning to fill out his clothes. The shirt he wore was snug on his arms and shoulders. *Excellent, the potion is starting to work.*

She nodded toward him and advised, "You should get a new uniform. That one looks small."

Otsoa frowned, "I do not understand. I just had it made to fit me earlier this Terrestrial Revolution." He fussed with the material, "Is it shrinking too?"

Nayrah smiled, "Perhaps, you should consider some stretchable material for a few Terrestrial Rotations."

Nayrah left, so Otsoa shut the door and stood outside Durnah's bedroom because of guilt. He peered through the slight opening in the doorway to look inside. Seeing her smiling and laughing with her parents made him feel better. His thoughts turned to how Nayrah used him, and anger filled his heart. Again, he would be the one to take the blame for her dirty work. It would not surprise him if Gloz believed that he was the one pocketing the Sovereign Cubes from Nayrah's latest deception. *I need to get her out of my life!* He sighed, left the hallway, and rested in a guest room.

Chapter 13

Akil
Argi City
The 22,277[th] Terrestrial Rotation of the Second Summer

Julie convulsed, gasping for air. It felt like a defibrillator shocked her back to life. Awake and alert, she collapsed back to the floor, breathing heavily, and tried to remember what had happened. As her breathing returned to normal, she noticed the swelling in her throat had receded. Her arms and legs tingled as the feeling started to return.

A few minutes later, she rolled her body onto her left side. Pushing off the floor with her right hand, she sat awkwardly and forced herself to stand. She felt dizzy until the fog of unconsciousness left. Looking at the white and black moss hanging from the ceiling, she realized that it must have been toxic, or her body had an allergic reaction to it.

She checked her extremities, ensuring there were no broken bones or lesions. Satisfied that her physical being was unharmed, she performed a quick mental check. *I don't feel sick anymore, and all the feeling is back in my limbs; I guess I'm all right.* Looking at her watch, she discovered it was past time for her tour with Zorion.

She moved through the tunnel toward the apartment and felt her body recover. At the cave opening, she was well enough to run. Passing the fountain, she heard someone banging on her front door. She entered the side entrance, hoping Zorion did not see her and ran to the bathroom to clean up. As the sink filled with warm water, she looked in the mirror and almost screamed. Dry saliva with a gray, sticky residue covered her face, so she used the warm water from the sink to remove all of it.

Bang, bang, bang. "Julie! Is there something wrong?" Zorion yelled through the door.

"Just a minute!" she yelled, knowing by the tone of his voice that he was becoming impatient.

She could not fix her hair correctly because she chased Kraeth through the portal and forgot her purse. Had he not stolen her laptop, this entire scenario would not have happened. She did her best to make herself presentable and looked at her reflection one more time before leaving. The water removed the gray mess and all her makeup. *I would kill for my purse right now.*

She rushed to the door and felt the same nervousness and excitement before a date. Zorion did not say it was a romantic engagement, yet it felt like it for some reason. Just as Zorion was about to bang on the door again, she opened it. The first thing Julie noticed was the smell of spearmint. It was her favorite snowball flavor.

Worried that the moss in the cave was trying to lure her back to eat more, she ignored the pleasant smell and focused on Zorion, who could not hide his frustration. She saw his bodyguard just a few feet behind him, smiling and shaking his head. Hoping to turn an awkward situation around, she smiled pleasantly and spoke as if nothing was wrong.

"I would have answered sooner, but I don't have my purse with me."

Being in her presence pushed away any irritation he had waiting for her. Still, her comment confused him.

"Why would not having a purse keep you from answering the door?"

"It has all my makeup and hairbrushes, so it took longer to get ready than usual. Without my things, you're seeing me at my worst."

"I think you look beautiful," Zorion proclaimed.

The words came out before he had a chance to filter them. Embarrassed by his accidental boldness, his face turned red.

"That's very kind of you," she responded with a warm smile and walked toward the elevators. She took a few steps and turned around, "Where are you taking me?"

Both Zorion and Broll looked at each other with astonishment. Neither could understand how she could act as if nothing were wrong, especially after breaking many etiquette rules.

As they stared at each other in disbelief, Broll smiled and whispered, "You wanted to get to know her."

"I am beginning to wonder if it was a good idea."

"Well, are you coming?" coaxed Julie.

Zorion moved to join her with a practiced smile; Broll stayed a few paces behind to watch over them.

"I thought we would visit the tower. I have dismissed all my staff so that only guards will be on duty. This way, no one will question your presence."

"The tower?"

"Yes, it is on the surface. I had hoped that once you see how dire our situation is, it will put your fear of us attempting to invade your world to rest."

"Ok, lead the way."

She exited the elevator and saw things that impressed her.

"This is the Argi House," Zorion said.

"It's beautiful."

As they walked the semi-circle steps, he continued, "Stonemasons carved the steps and pillars out of the existing rock and polished them, so they would reflect the light above, which is why they appear to glow. Also, they hand-carved all the streams on either side of the steps and placed the stones to make it look natural."

"Where does the water from the fountains go?"

"It goes to the level beneath where it feeds many fountains until it lands in a large pool at the bottom, where a machine pumps it back up to the top where we are now. As it flows all over the city, it goes through thousands of natural filters, making it clean and fresh on each level. Also, the stonemasons built several waterfalls around the city to keep the air moist," Zorion remarked.

"Wow. That's amazing."

He held his hand for her to take, "In case you trip."

The closer she came to him, the stronger the spearmint scent became. She wondered if he was wearing cologne. Not willing to ask such a personal question, she smiled and took his hand. Though he felt strong, his skin was soft. It was a sign that he had never seen an exhausting day of physical labor during his whole life. Taking a note from Earth's history, she considered whether the life of a sovereign spoiled him. *Is this all an act? Are you cruel to your people? Would you be cruel to me?* She landed on the porch's top step and reached out with her hand touching one of several tall, white pillars supporting the ceiling. It was smooth.

"The builders made the floor out of Amber Illuminati," Zorion noted.

"I have never seen anything like it before."

"Illuminati are unique stones that can absorb electricity. They accumulate power until the stones begin to glow."

"There must be wires everywhere underneath the floor."

"No. Wires are unnecessary because we send the electricity directly to the receptors from the main unit over there," he pointed.

Broll sent two of his guards ahead to open the large glass doors of the Argi House. As they moved toward it, Julie's eyes followed the thick metal frames to the top. Their height matched that of the pillars. Once inside, she saw a circular lobby with a white dome ceiling. Stonemasons set soft bright, White Illuminati Stones in the dome ceiling, lighting up the area thoroughly. Zorion continued to point out all the structural features, including the polished, dark green stones on the floor, to the light tan walls, where many digital pictures hung.

"And we have the Argi House fountain set in the center of the room," Zorion ended his narrative.

"Who is he?" puzzled Julie, pointing to one of the pictures on the wall.

"Ah, that is Urki. He was Argi's sovereign during the last phase of our move underground. Many Akilians revere him."

"Are you related to him?"

"He is a distant ancestor."

"We consider most sovereigns on my world a king."

"Yes. I read Kraeth's report and certain historical accounts of kings from your world. I want you to know that just like the kings on Earth, some Akilian sovereigns are good, and some are not."

"Are you good?" she quizzed with a raised eyebrow.

"That depends on whom you ask. The latest survey shows that my approval rating has increased. Anyone in my position will always have enemies. I have worked hard to ensure that my citizens survive this tragedy. If we live, I hope they remember me in a positive light."

"They should if you are responsible for saving them."

"Having said that, we have one sovereign that I hope you never meet."

"That bad, huh?"

"Yes. Elzer has caused us a great deal of trouble and even set us back considerably for his gain."

"He definitely sounds bad."

"He is an embarrassment," he paused to open the door for her. "This is my office."

"Very nice," she commented, entering.

He showed her the room and led her into the tower's elevator. Once inside, he signaled Broll to stay behind, who reluctantly obeyed. As the elevator climbed, Zorion helped Julie put on the thermal jumpsuit, helmet, and safety goggles needed to protect against the sun's radiation. At the top, the doors opened, and they stepped onto the viewing deck. Seeing the sun, she spoke through her helmet's communicator.

"How?"

"There are many theories and legends as to what happened. One is that a massive star passed by, pulling plasma from it. You would call it a black hole. It drained most of our sun's energy, causing it to morph into a red giant. That brought about a sudden steep increase in our global temperatures. Our tropical zones became deserts, and our temperate zones became tropical.

"The planet's ice sheets and permafrost regions melted, giving off carbon dioxide and methane, resulting in a runaway heating spiral that destroyed the planet's agriculture. Our plants could not adapt fast enough. The only plant that survived was the moss you are so fond of," Zorion joked.

Julie did not laugh, having missed his attempt at humor.

"Next came the ultimate irony," he cleared his throat and continued, "As the temperatures rose, increasing the amount of water vapor in the air, the clouds began to block the radiation from the sun, allowing the heat to radiate off the planet. The temperatures fell. We had snow instead of rain and ice instead of running water until we reached what you see here, a planet encrusted in ice from pole to pole like a giant snowball. About sixty Earthian years ago, the river of fire appeared; it flows to a nearby star. We always knew we had limited time once the plasma stream emerged."

"The clock began moving faster," she interrupted.

"Exactly."

"At least your ancestors did something about it. They moved everyone underground."

"Not everyone," Zorion clarified.

"No?"

"We lost eighty percent of our world's population. We could not build cities big enough for everyone. Natural selection took care of a few."

"Natural selection?"

"Our agriculture failed, forcing us to look for another food source. We began eating the moss; some could not process the plant as a nutrient and starved to death with full stomachs. For the rest, there was a lottery."

"How horrible," Julie replied, looking out over the snow and the tops of the towers that showed the frozen city. "You mean?"

Zorion nodded, "The cities are still accessible from certain locations; we do not encourage the public to go there, only archeologists or people with in-depth research programs. They found it too unsettling, hundreds of thousands of Akilians frozen in time, waiting for a proper burial."

"You've seen it?"

"Once," his voice was sorrowful, "I still have nightmares."

They returned to the elevator, and Zorion helped her remove the goggles as they descended. He lifted her helmet and saw tears in her eyes.

"Is something wrong? Are you injured?"

"No, I'm fine. It's just that I'm afraid for your people."

"Your empathy moves me, but I did not bring you here to upset you."

"Don't worry about it. I can be emotional sometimes."

Once he removed the remaining protective gear, the smell of spearmint returned. Not knowing its origin, she decided it would be an excellent idea to determine what Zorion knew about the black and white moss.

"I can't remember. Did you, by chance, bring me any black and white moss to eat earlier today?"

Zorion furrowed his eyebrows, "I have never seen black and white moss before, but there is a legend surrounding it. Why? Did you find some in your food?"

"No."

"Where did you hear about it?"

"I was watching a TV show earlier that mentioned it," she lied.

"Ah, yes, you must have tuned into our history network. Well, I can tell you many superstitions about black and white moss. The most prominent revolves around an old myth concerning Saiphs and Skeans."

"What are those?"

"They should have mentioned it during the broadcast."

"I must have changed the channel."

"Ah, I see. Saiphs were emissaries or soldiers (depending on who tells the story) for the High Lord, and the Skeans were the same for the Night Lord. The myth says that those who eat the black and white moss will die. Only those chosen by one of the deities will resurrect and return to defend the Lord who raised them." He smiled. "Those are only fables. If you see any black and white moss, I suggest you stay far from it. Legend says it imitates the scent of the victim's favorite food to entice him or her to eat it. It is very poisonous, so if you find any, you must contact me so that we can eradicate it. I do not want you dying on me."

Julie laughed nervously. *Too late.* "I promise."

Zorion was unhappy with how the tour was progressing. He replayed the conversation in his mind. There were some things he wished they had not discussed, and to make matters worse, she cried. He needed to turn things around fast, or she would never want to see him again. Earlier, he sanctioned a gift for her, and as they returned to his office, Zorion left to contact the vendor. The merchant had finished making the gift, so Zorion instructed him to remain on Julie's level until they arrived. Zorion returned to his office and escorted Julie to a walkway that overlooked the city.

"How do you keep the ceiling from crashing down?" she asked, looking upward. "I don't see pillars anywhere."

"We use a force field to support it." He pointed to specific places along the wall. "You can see the capacitors evenly spaced all the way around," Zorion explained.

"What if you lose power?"

"There is a backup system; if that fails, the ceiling will collapse."

She shook her head.

"Your lives are dangling by a thread. How do you sleep at night?"

"I have grown up knowing that my world could die at any moment. It is unsettling, so I try to focus on my work."

"I don't think I will sleep tonight, knowing that your sun can explode any moment."

"Please, try not to worry. I am sure nothing will happen before you return home tomorrow. Our scientists estimate we have until the upcoming yellow harvest, at the very earliest."

Julie paused to think of everything that happened and had difficulty pushing Zorion from her mind. There was something about him that she could not shake. Just being with him was a delight, yet she worried about developing feelings for him, which would not be suitable for either of them, so she faked a yawn to end their evening.

"I'm tired. I should get back to the apartment and try to sleep."

Zorion hid his disappointment with a polite smile, "Are you sure I cannot tempt you with our fashion stores? I had hoped that you might find something to your liking. You could take it with you tomorrow. Consider it a souvenir of your visit with us."

"That's kind of you, but I've already taken up much of your time. I don't want to upset your wife."

Subconsciously, she knew why she said it. It was a verbal probe to find out if he was single. *Why do I care?*

"I am no longer bound to Thea," Zorion explained.

"Are you divorced?" she asked, suppressing her excitement.

"In a manner of speaking, yes."

"How long were you together?"

It was another probe to find out more details about his personality.

"More than twenty yellow harvests. It equals to about twenty Earthian years."

He seems loyal. Still, I need more information to know for sure.

"Why did you break up?" *Julie, what are you doing?*

"I realized she did not love me anymore, so I carefully reviewed my life with her and discovered that she never cared for me. She only wanted me for my Sovereign Cubes."

"What are Sovereign Cubes?"

"It is our currency."

Awe, that's so sad. "It sounds like you're better off without her."

"It was like waking from a bad dream."

"I imagine you've been dating since your breakup."

At this point, Julie could not help herself. She wanted to know as many details about him as possible.

"No," he responded bashfully, "I am much too busy. Besides, there is - never mind."

"What? Tell me."

She could not believe how badly she wanted to know his secret.

"Perhaps another time."

Damn. Well, continue with the other line of questioning. "Do you have any children?"

"Yes, two boys and a girl, but…."

"But what?"

"They are not who they should be."

"What do you mean?"

"They are not fit to be the heirs of a sovereign. I blame myself. Somewhere I failed in their upbringing. Since they are not ready to take my seat in the Argi House, I plan to give the seat to my cousin."

"Do they know?"

"Not yet."

"Do you think they would try to do something to stop you?"

"I believe my oldest is capable of anything, but enough about them. I wanted you to enjoy your visit, not for me to burden you with my problems."

"I don't mind. Besides, I was the one asking the questions. Remember?"

Zorion smiled, "Are you sure you would not like to see some of our shops?"

Although her desire to spend more time with him was strong, she was close to making herself look foolish by asking too many personal questions. *No, it's best if we call it a night.*

"Maybe another time. I should return to the apartment."

"Of course, I will walk you back."

"How did you get the sun to display on the ceiling?" she queried.

"Our top engineer's daughter wanted to see the sun, which gave him an idea. Since we cannot go to the surface, he devised a way to project the image within the force field. We are currently entering the winter season, so the sun will remain on the horizon as it is for sixty Earthian years."

"That's strange. It means your world rolls on its side."

"Yes."

"We have a planet in our solar system like it. We call it Uranus."

"Interesting."

"Your world is both beautiful and terrifying."

"Yes, it is a shame it is at its end."

She faced him as they approached the door to her apartment; due to his height, she had to tilt her head back to meet his gaze.

"I had hoped to stay with you longer. There are so many things I want to learn about your world. Nevertheless, I am grateful for the time we had this evening. Before we say goodbye, I have a gift for you," Zorion offered.

"A gift?"

He waved to the vendor, who had been waiting nearby. The merchant approached and removed a few layers of cloth, exposing something shiny. Zorion took it from him, the merchant left, and Zorion presented his gift to Julie.

"Wow! It's beautiful!" she exclaimed.

"The sword was my sovereign's. I instructed the merchant to put an inscription on the handle in both languages."

She accepted it and read the engraving aloud, "Hope."

"It is what you have brought us," he smiled, but his grin faded, seeing tears in her eyes. *Oh, no. I insulted her.* "If you do not like it, I can give you something else, perhaps something of your choosing."

"No, I love it. It's a wonderful gift."

"Why are you crying?"

"I told you. I'm an emotional person. Sometimes I cry when I'm happy."

She is very mysterious.

"Thank you. I will treasure it forever," Julie sniffled.

"I will see you early tomorrow before you return home."

Standing on her toes, she reached up and kissed his cheek to thank him for the present and the kind words. Her tongue touched her upper lip as her heels returned to the floor.

She tasted spearmint, "Are you wearing cologne?"

"No, why?"

"I just thought I smelled some."

Baffled by the experience, she turned to go inside but stopped. There was a question that needed answering, still nagging at her, so she spun around to face him without thinking.

"Have you ever seen me before?"

Her question caught him off guard. "I…uh…I…what do you mean?"

"In the Interstellar Transportation Station, you looked as if you knew me and said something. Not knowing your language, I instructed Kraeth to interpret as we walked to the apartment."

"What did he tell you?"

"He told me you said *it is you*. Now that kind of reaction means that you've seen me somewhere before."

"It is tough to explain."

"Do I look like someone you know?"

"Julie, some things are better off left unsaid; I will only say that you look familiar."

"Please, tell me the truth, and don't hide anything from me."

Zorion felt as if someone had placed a boulder on his chest, "You will think I am crazy."

"After everything that's happened to me in the past few hours, it can't be that bad."

Zorion wanted to tell her, yet he knew how it would sound. *She will never come near me again.* Reluctantly, he confessed, "For nearly an Earthian year, I have dreamed of someone who looks exactly like you."

"That's not a big deal. I'm sure it's just a coincidence. You must have met someone here that looks like me. She's the one in your dreams."

"It is unlikely. I meet the same Argians regularly, so I have not seen her in person."

"Maybe you saw her on your television network."

"I have been checking Argi's photo database every Terrestrial Revolution since I first dreamt of her, yet I have not found anyone who even comes close."

"How can you dream of someone you've never seen before?"

"I do not know how or why. All I know is that the dreams were vivid and real; I thought you would recognize me because she knew me in my first dream of her."

"Wow! That *is* a little out there. Are you certain this woman looks like me?"

"I am. She looks like you in every way."

"What did you two do in your dreams?"

"We - talked."

He could feel his cheeks turning red from embarrassment.

"What did you talk about?"

He stuttered for a few moments, giving him time to figure out what to say until resigning to tell her the whole truth, and hated every moment of it. He had never felt so embarrassed in his life.

"And, as we kissed, I woke up."

He faced the floor, unable to look at her. Never had he shared something this intimate with anyone. It made him feel vulnerable and miserable. They remained silent until he felt it was time for him to leave.

"I know how this sounds, so you do not need to worry; you will never see me again. I promise."

He started to leave, but Julie grabbed his arm, "Wait."

As she stared into his eyes, it was as if her mind peeked inside him. She felt waves of different emotions and realized they were coming from him. She sensed his feelings of love, desire, and embarrassment. Never had she experienced anything like it before. It felt like they had a connection. His powerful feelings for her only seemed to fuel her attraction to him.

They stared into each other's eyes for a very long time, and Julie tried to understand her fascination with him until she could no longer help herself. *Oh, I don't believe I'm going to do this.* She put her hands firmly behind his neck, pulled him toward her, and their lips met in a passionate kiss.

At first, Zorion thought he was dreaming again and swore to destroy the alarm with his bare hands if it went off during this kiss.

As she pulled him toward her, he glided his hands to the back of her waist and embraced her. He trembled because her sudden affection surprised him, and he did not want it to end. They pulled away. Julie looked at him, breathless and a little shocked at her impulsiveness.

"I'm very sorry," she sighed.

"Please, do not apologize."

She stumbled, walking to her door, and caught herself; her face turned red.

"I should go inside before I do something really embarrassing."

She closed the door behind her and leaned against it. Her mouth tasted like spearmint, and she realized the sweet aroma came from Zorion, not the black and white moss. She licked her lips, tasting the remnants of their kiss, and breathed in deeply, enjoying the robust and delightful odor until it finally dissipated several minutes later. *What are you doing, Julie? You can't get involved with him; you are leaving tomorrow!*

Along the way to the kitchen table, she carefully examined his gift. It looked much like a Katana. She knew the design well because her brother, Alex, collected them. The finely polished blade reflected the light from the ceiling toward her eyes. Removing a hair strand from her sleeve, she let it fall on the blade's edge and watched it split into two pieces under its weight.

A close inspection of the handle revealed several stones she believed were jewels embedded in a golden finish. *It must be worth a fortune.* Exhausted from her encounter with him, she gently laid the sword down on the table, collapsed onto the soft cushions, and as she drifted off to sleep, her thoughts focused on the tunnel and how she nearly lost her life. Just before falling into the dream world, she tasted spearmint. Zorion's face was the last thing she saw.

*****

Zorion faced Broll, who wore a smile from one side to the other, "You have made a good impression."

"Yes, I am grateful, except she is still leaving tomorrow," Zorion frowned.

"You will meet her again on her planet."

"Maybe, assuming negotiations go well."

He turned toward the apartment door for one last glimpse, wanting to take her in his arms again, but doubt made him think that in the end, she would leave him, just like his dreams.

Chapter 14

Akil
Argi City
The 22,277[th] Terrestrial Rotation of the Second Summer

The elevator stopped on the lowest level, and the doors opened. Nayrah stepped out and took a deep breath, filling her lungs with the damp, chilly air. As a cold draft enveloped her, she felt renewed. She walked the avenue that led to her apartment and noticed the mist was thicker today, making it even darker if that was possible. Lights that hung only a few paces away barely lit her path. *Why is it getting so dark down here?*

She stopped about thirty paces from her door, feeling a ripple from the darkness beyond the avenue. It called to her, so she abruptly turned around, stepped off the street, and moved out onto the moss until the night consumed her. The fog was so thick that it blocked out all the light from the city above and the lamps nearby. In the quiet, a nearby fountain was the only sound she heard.

She felt at peace until sensing another ripple, so she closed her eyes to search. Drawing on the power that surrounded her, she saw the future. As before, multiple scenarios appeared before her mind's eye. *Damn Saiph!* She struggled for several hundred heartbeats until deciding to study each one carefully before the vision vanished.

Gecheana would reprimand her for wasting time. *"If the future is in motion, you cannot rely on anything it shows you,"* she would say. Even though the visions were hard to keep, she pressed on, centering her attention on each specific sequence of events. *Show me!* She strained as sweat poured down her face. The frigid air could not keep her cool anymore. One scheme followed another, presenting itself in her thoughts.

In time, exhaustion made her stop. She sat on the fresh moss and replayed them; each scenario continued to have a different outcome. *Gecheana was right. It is a waste of time.* Just as she was about to leave, something from one of the visions stood out in her mind. *Why would I want to watch myself sleep?*

Seeing the event unfold, she saw a familiar face enter her bedroom. Nayrah found herself within her vision, lying in bed. Her eyes opened to see Jadell standing over her, holding a sword at the ready. Before saying a word, Jadell brought the blade down through her neck. Nayrah gasped and woke from her trance.

She paced, focusing on the vision. All the Skeans on Akil understood that only Gecheana could approve of one Skean killing another. *Gecheana plans to kill me! Is this how you repay me for many Yellow Harvests of servitude?* Rage filled her mind, bringing her more in tune with her powers, followed up with another nudge.

"What do you want me to do?" she asked with an angry whisper.

Her patience was running thin, yet she managed to open her mind, allowing the unseen puppet master to guide her thoughts until an idea came to her. Although she could not see a definite future, the present was clear. *Jadell.* The name came to her mind like a whisper. All the Skeans on Akil could sense the Saiph coming, but none of them knew how or where he or she would arrive.

When the Saiph did appear, she imagined that pinpointing his or her exact location would be impossible unless they were within four or five paces of each other. Notwithstanding, if the Saiph cloaked its power, it would be impossible to discover it even at a close distance. Finding someone with the same power uncloaked was just as hard. She always felt the presence of her sisters and Gecheana. Still, trying to find them was not easy. Usually, she could figure out their general location if they were within fifteen paces of her position yet could only pick them out of a crowd by standing within three to five paces from them. The reason was that their power flowed everywhere, blending them with the shadows.

The nudge she felt urged her to find Jadell, so she closed her eyes, focused on her, and searched the city unsuccessfully. It would be impossible to find if Jadell had cloaked her powers. Again, she opened her mind, trying to discover Jadell's whereabouts, and within a few short moments, Nayrah saw her moving about in her kitchen. *That is why it took so long to find her. She is in my home.*

As if she were an ancient bug on the wall, Nayrah watched Jadell remove vials from her cabinet and add an unknown concoction, which momentarily changed its color and returned to its original. *She is sabotaging my potions! I will kill her!* Nayrah unsheathed her sword and started for her apartment but stopped before reaching the avenue. *If I kill her now, it will force me into hiding while the others pursue me. However, if I act like I do not know what she has done, I have time to prepare.*

She heard the door to her apartment creak open and close as Jadell's soft footsteps faded, disappearing down the avenue. Nayrah entered her apartment and went through all her potions. With all her bottles sitting on the table, she evaluated them to see which Jadell altered, and discovered they were all ineffective. She put them back in their proper place and closed the cabinet door to keep her discovery a secret. Seeing her life was in danger, she decided to buy another apartment and restock her new cabinets with fresh, untampered chemicals. *It is a good thing I extorted that money from Durnah's parents.*

Now Nayrah had a new cause. *I will destroy Gecheana and everything she has worked for, including my wretched Skean sisters.* With the new realization that Jadell had been secretly working to kill her, Nayrah believed that Jadell must have also manipulated Otsoa somehow. Armed with this new revelation, she sat in front of her Information Terminal and brought up all the surveillance videos of Otsoa she had accumulated over time. It was her job to keep a close eye on him, and she could not think of a better way to use the city's Civilian Monitoring Network.

She reviewed the old data to match the time stamp with another video and found her answer; she remembered the Terrestrial Revolution very well. Otsoa insisted he had been with Yanamai, except Nayrah knew the opposite to be true, so she severely punished him for lying; now, the video showed that he might have been correct. On the left side of her monitor, Otsoa stood alone on the avenue. On the right side of her screen, she saw Yanamai at lunch with her friends. It was the video she used to support the fact that Otsoa lied.

She brought up another recording angle, showing Otsoa's location, and discovered that he *was* with someone. After studying the image intently, she could not see the other's face because he or she cleverly stayed out of the camera's eye. Sometime later, Otsoa left. Nayrah could tell by his movements that he kissed the other before leaving. Later, a hooded figure left the shadows, so she froze the image to study it carefully.

Although the other kept his or her face covered, she noticed a small light reflection below the neckline. Her fingers glided over the command board to magnify it. Seeing it made her ill. The item was a necklace she gave Jadell on her fourteenth Yellow Harvest. *You little putok!* Jadell had made the mistake of wearing it a few Terrestrial Rotations before realizing that the camera could catch its image. It explained why she stopped putting it on. Nayrah thought she did not like it but now understood.

Nayrah did not investigate the matter thoroughly, missing Jadell's miscalculation, and her distrust of Otsoa cost them both. In her defense, she never imagined Jadell going to such lengths to destroy her. It all made sense now. By posing as Yanamai, Jadell did not have to manipulate him with her powers or potions, which is why Nayrah could not detect her involvement. It was the perfect deception. Nayrah would have admired it had Jadell not maliciously directed it toward her. Now she knew that Otsoa's memories were accurate, except that it was not Yanamai; it was Jadell.

Remembering the beatings Otsoa received by her hand for pursuing Yanamai made her notice something odd. *Is this guilt I am feeling?* Her right index finger wiped away a tear that somehow escaped her lower eyelid. *Get control of yourself, Nayrah!* She could trace every failure to Jadell; even so, Gecheana would blame her. "*You let a subordinate trick you. You deserve your fate,*" she could hear her say. *That is all right, Gecheana; you and Jadell deserve your destiny too.*

With renewed determination, she left her old apartment without looking back. While walking down the avenue toward the elevator, she sensed anxiety. Reaching out with her mind, she discovered it was coming from the darkness surrounding her. "What is wrong?" she whispered. As the words left her mouth, she felt the Night Lord's power, unlike before. It was so overwhelming that she collapsed against a nearby wall and exhaled loudly. Now she understood why the darkness was so thick on her level. The Saiph had arrived, and the night was gathering its strength for the inevitable battle between them.

Chapter 15

Earth
The United States - Texas - Houston - George Bush Park
May 14, 2452

As Sarah made breakfast, a vehicle pulled up the driveway. Its lights shined through the front door onto the kitchen cabinets. Not expecting visitors, she ran to the closet and retrieved a 16-gauge shotgun. With the weapon in her hand, she went to her front door, turned on the porch lights, and looked outside. The driver parked the vehicle just outside the light's range, and the morning sky was not enough to illuminate it. As she pushed the screen door handle to open, something made it stick. *Damn it. I need to have Larkin fix that the moment he gets home.* She jiggled it a few times until it opened, stepped outside, turned off the safety with her right index finger, and cocked the gun.

"Identify yourself, or I will start shooting!"

"That's my girl."

"Dad, you scared the crap out of me!"

"Sorry, I wasn't tryin' to startle ya. I just came over to make sure you two were all right."

"You could have radioed me for that, so what's the real reason you're here?"

"Let's talk inside."

"Where's Lieutenant Colonel Jones?"

"I told him to meet me at HQ. The matter is personal."

Sarah shut the door behind them and put the gun back in the closet, "It's Larkin, isn't it?"

"Is Sable still asleep?"

"Yeah, I was going to wake her in half an hour."

General Bailey hesitated.

"What is it, dad?"

Her voice was nervous and agitated.

"Murphy and Nelson are back from the mission." He paused, swallowed hard, and continued, "Nelson's dead."

"What? Where's Larkin?"

"He's been captured."

It was every wife's nightmare, and she cried bitterly at hearing the news.

"I told you not to send him!" she snapped, brushing some of the tears from her cheek.

"We need intel, Sarah; he was the logical choice."

"Do not give me that crap! Larkin told me his brother ambushed his men a few days ago, and you decide to send him right into his lap!"

"Mommy!" Sable called from her bedroom.

"Now, see what you've done!"

General Bailey started to follow her.

"No, I will bring her down," Sarah insisted, stomping her feet.

She opened Sable's bedroom door, turned on the light, and saw that Sable had been crying.

"Oh, what's wrong, sweetheart?"

"There is someone outside. They're going to hurt us!"

Not this again. "Come to me." Sarah extended her arms, and Sable jumped into them. "Oomph. Wow, you're getting big."

With Sable in her arms, she walked to the window, and they looked outside. The morning sky was getting brighter, and long shadows made it hard to see. Even though the front porch light lit up a third of the front yard, Sarah could barely see anything beyond it.

"You see, there's nobody here."

She heard a scuffle downstairs, walked into the hallway, and yelled, "Dad! What's going on?"

There was no response. Sarah felt a cold chill run down her spine.

"Pop, Pop!" Sable yelled.

"Shh, Sable."

Sarah shut the door to Sable's room, locked it, set Sable down, and started pushing furniture in front of it. Sarah heard heavy footsteps climbing the stairs, ran to the window, and opened it.

She called for Sable with a whisper, "Come here and climb down the lattice, Sable!"

Too frightened to move, Sable shook her head, so Sarah picked her up, causing Sable to cry.

"Quiet, sweetheart. They'll hear us."

She continued to cry in a lower, whimpering tone until someone started kicking the bedroom door, causing them to gasp. Sable screamed. Instinctively, Sarah shoved her through the window to protect her. Remembering how Larkin showed her how to climb down the lattice, Sable grabbed at the opening beside the shutter and held on tightly. She secured her feet and extended her hand to help her mother out the window. It was too late because the intruder crashed through the door; the furniture kept him from opening it far enough to enter.

Sarah whispered, "Get to the ground like daddy showed you and run to our meeting place in the woods."

Sable cried, "No, mommy, not without you."

"Young lady, you get down there right now, or I will tell daddy you disobeyed me."

The thought of Larkin being angry with her made her eyes widen in fear, so she climbed down. Sarah shut the window and turned to face the intruder. The furniture was heavy, forcing him to take a running start to move it. Each crash into the door was like a clock tick for Sarah, and several pushes later, the intruder forced the furniture out of the way and walked inside, but he was not alone.

"Where's the girl?" one of the men questioned.

Sarah pretended that Sable was in the bathroom, hoping to give her daughter more time to run.

"Do not come out, sweetheart, no matter what you hear!"

One of the men went to the bathroom door and kicked it. It took him several attempts to open it. He found it empty.

He faced Sarah, "Where is she?"

Sarah laughed mockingly, "I didn't lock the door, you idiot! All you had to do was turn the handle!"

The remark made him angry, so he slapped Sarah with the back of his hand. The force of the blow caused her cheek to go numb. In response, she spat at him and discovered that his knuckle had cut her lip open. He raised his hand to strike again but stopped because something or someone was beating against the house outside. He ran to the window, looked down, and saw Sable at the bottom of the lattice.

He turned to his partner and yelled, "Hector, she's outside! Get her!"

"Sable, run!" Sarah shouted.

Hector left to pursue Sable, so the other removed a knife from his belt and smiled. Sarah raised her lip in disgust because he had several teeth missing from his mouth, and the few clinging to his gums were yellow and rotting.

"Ever heard of a toothbrush?"

The other chuckled, "Just so you know, I *am* gonna kill ya right after we have some fun."

As the invader approached, she backed up to a dresser and stopped. With his left hand, he grabbed her hair and brought the knife to her throat with his right. Sarah faced her captor with as much courage as she could muster and frantically searched the dresser behind her for something to use as a weapon. He leaned in to kiss her, and Sarah found a glass knick-knack just in time. She grabbed his wrist that held the knife and hit him just above his left eye with the other hand shattering the glass and creating fragments that cut his skin.

Reflexively, he grabbed his forehead and screamed, allowing her to flee. She pushed him out of the way and ran out of the bedroom. Initially, she had a good lead until stumbling at the bottom of the stairs, which caused her to fall. Fear and adrenaline enabled her to get up and move forward. The delay cost her dearly. She ran to the front door and heard the other's footsteps as he came running down the stairs.

Trembling, she grabbed the doorknob, opened it, and reached for the screen door handle. Again, it jammed, and as the sound of his footsteps came closer, she frantically tried to open it. With his right hand, he lunged to grab her. The handle finally moved, opening the screen door. Sarah screamed and ran outside; the delay had taken away her slight lead. She reached the front lawn and started to sprint; he caught her and pushed her down.

Falling forward, she landed hard, and her face skidded across grass and dirt. Once her body finally stopped moving, she spat a mouthful of turf. Before she could think about standing, he grabbed her by the collar, yanked her up, took a handful of her hair with his left hand, pulled back hard, exposing her neck, put his knife to her throat, and growled, "I was gonna kill ya quickly, but now that you've pissed me off, I'm gonna kill ya *real* slow, right after I have my fun!"

Sarah screamed for Larkin as the intruder dragged her back to the house.

*****

After her mother tossed her onto the lattice, Sable climbed down. The structure supported her weight, and she remembered her dad securing it, so it was safe for her to climb. However, the journey down was not without problems because Sarah planted wisterias to hide the lattice, and they kept getting in her way.

"Take your time and ensure your hands grip the wood before ya make your next move," she remembered her dad saying. She reached the bottom, looked up, and saw a man staring down at her from her bedroom window.

"Sable, run!" she heard her mother scream.

She turned and ran into the woods as fast as her tiny frame could. She was in her bare feet, which slowed her down. During practice, she wore shoes. Without them, her tender feet made her wince whenever she stepped on a branch or stone. Fear kept her moving forward. As it began to dawn, she saw the markings on the trees her daddy made for her. Remembering his words, she followed them to the lean-to and hid.

Although she had a good head start, Hector saw her entering the woods and followed her until she turned into a bend and disappeared from his sight. Hector looked around where she vanished, trying to find her hiding place.

Hoping to flush her out, he began calling her. "Piglet. Where are you?"

His voice was mockingly sweet.

"Don't be afraid, piglet. I'm a friend of your daddy's."

He searched for her, retrieved his gun, and raised it in front of him, ready to fire, on the chance she decided to make a run for it.

81

Chapter 16

Julie had an unusual dream. She saw a hooded figure, wearing a black cloak, standing on a pyramid's summit with his arms stretched toward the sun. Julie saw the sun's color change from yellow to red, and an explosion created a shock wave that hit the planet, causing a quake. Somehow, she could sense that the eruption pushed the world beyond its standard orbit as the sun's surface expanded, losing most of its mass.

Unexpectedly, she felt pain in her chest. For some reason, she knew it was the sun suffering and not her. Telepathically, it cried out to her because it was dying. She knew the cloaked humanoid was trying to destroy it and felt an overwhelming urge to respond; before taking her first step, she heard the roar of a crowd below. Looking down at the pyramid's base, she saw hordes of people fighting.

From within their midst, someone wearing a white cloak leaped onto the pyramid and rapidly climbed the steps to the top where the other stood. The challenger arrived, and the other turned from the sun and unsheathed his sword, which had a crimson red glow. The challenger also drew his sword; his blade emitted natural white light. The two fighters circled each other at the top of the pyramid. Their swords met with a loud clap of thunder. The sound boomed, and she felt the vibration go through her body.

As she watched the dream unfold, they fought each other ferociously, with moves so perfect it looked as if they rehearsed the fight beforehand, making every strike a potential death blow. The defender pierced the challenger through his belly, and he fell to his knees, beaten. The defender raised his crimson blade and swung downward toward the white-cloaked humanoid's neck. The challenger somehow vanished and reappeared behind the black-cloaked being and swung his sword, removing the head of the one that tried to destroy the sun.

The defender fell from the pyramid, and the challenger followed in a freefall toward the ground. Before he landed, Julie woke, gasping for air. She felt her heart pounding, calmed herself, and heard a distant voice call her name. *Julie.* She sat in bed, desperately trying to remember why her bedroom looked different. At first, she thought it was her parents' farm. *Oh, yeah, Akil.*

Julie, a distant voice, called again.

"Lights."

She stepped out of bed and looked for the voice's owner.

Julie.

The sound came from outside the apartment's side door, where she discovered the fountain. Cautiously, she stepped onto the avenue and looked around, but no one was there, not even her guards.

Julie.

This time she knew the sound was coming from inside the tunnel.

Julie.

She walked into the corridor where she had eaten the black and white moss the previous day and sniffed the air to ensure the hallucinogenic moss was not luring her back again. She did not smell anything and re-entered the room full of black and white moss. It is here she had collapsed, or as Zorion suggested, died, and there were still signs of her recent visit. The uneaten moss and residue of saliva, where her mouth foamed just before falling, were everywhere.

"Who's there?" Julie asked nervously.

She heard rumbling and saw two halves of a round stone, embedded in the floor at the center of the room, open upward like a door, and a large vase rose from underneath. The vessel was full of small diamond-like stones, and she felt a slight breeze moving through the room; it quickly became a rushing wind. Soon the gale lifted the diamond-like fragments out of the vase and swirled them everywhere. She covered her face to keep them from landing in her eyes, yet none ever touched her skin. Once the tempest stopped, she opened her eyes and saw what appeared to be a man standing before her, except it was not a man.

They stared at each other for a few moments until he said, "Please, follow me."

Without another word, he turned and walked into the tunnel on the other side of the room. Julie hesitated until her curiosity won out, driving her to catch up with him, "I can tell that you're not human or Akilian, so what are you?"

"I am a computer-generated image of our great sovereign, Urki."

"Urki, Urki, oh, you mean the one who built the Argi house?"

"Yes."

With her right hand, she reached out and touched him. He was solid.

"How did you materialize?"

"My stone fragments, which you would call diamonds, rest in the vase, and my electronic brain is in a secret location. Your arrival triggered sensors that activated the assembling of my avatar. The wind lifted the diamond fragments out of the vase. The diamonds automatically connect with their counterpart, allowing my brain to communicate with you through it."

As he finished answering her question, they reached a large cavern. Urki walked to the center, and Julie followed him, looking around. The room had dim lighting like the tunnels; besides that, there was nothing to see except bare walls.

"How do you know my name?"

"I am linked with Akil's main computer. I have access to everything Kraeth brought back with him. I know who you are and where you are from."

Before asking another question, she heard a loud thud behind her. Turning, she saw a massive stone blocking her exit. She ran over and tried to push it back up into the ceiling, but it was too heavy.

Angered, she faced Urki, "Why did you trap me down here?"

"Because you must face the trial, and you cannot leave until you do."

"What trial? I did not break any of your laws that I know of."

"It is not that kind of trial. Deep below the surface, there are three different metals. One of the metals is the same color as silver from your world; it is neutral. The other two metals are red and white. Using your mind, you must retrieve the silver metal and one of the other two from the ground."

Julie laughed. "Are you insane? I can't do that?"

"You survived eating the black and white moss, so you have the power."

"Sorry, friend. There must be something wrong with your software because no one has that ability where I come from."

"I suggest you try, or we will never leave this room."

Returning to the rock that blocked her path, she unsuccessfully tried to push it back up into the ceiling.

A few minutes later, she gave up, faced Urki, and yelled, "You better let me out of here! Zorion will…."

He interrupted her, "Zorion will never discover you down here. This cave has stayed hidden for many of your years. No one knows of its existence."

Defiantly, she searched the room for another exit.

"There is no other way out of here. All you need to do is complete the trial, and you may leave," Urki replied.

"You're asking me to pull rocks out of the ground without a shovel. I can't do that!"

"You did not have the ability before you arrived, but you have it now." He pointed to the ground. "Please, have a seat and try."

Having no choice, she huffed, sat down near the center of the room, crossed her legs, and whispered, "This is ridiculous."

"Close your eyes and focus on the silver rock," Urki instructed.

"Which one of the other color metals do I bring up?

"Whichever calls to you."

She rolled her eyes and quipped, "Whatever."

She closed her eyes and concentrated, picturing a silver rock. She did not feel or sense anything until something tugged at her moments before giving up. It was like holding a rod with a fish biting at the bait, and at the same time, it was unlike anything she had experienced before. Somehow, she could see a jagged silver rock surrounded by white metal, about a hundred feet underground. That metal had a link to her mind.

Surprised at the new sensation, she turned to Urki with a raised eyebrow and exclaimed, "I can see and feel it!"

"I told you. Now you must pull the two metals you sense to the surface."

"Uh…ok. I will do my best."

With a new sense of enthusiasm, she closed her eyes and willed the metals to the surface. The closer they came to her, the more butterflies she felt in her stomach. Even in her wildest dreams, she never imagined having the ability to sense metal in the ground, let alone bring it up to the surface via telekinesis. It took several minutes for the minerals to make their way to the surface. By the time they arrived, sweat had drenched her clothes. Although dirt and clay covered the metals, she could see silver and white metal fragments mixed within them. Excited by her unique achievement, she looked to him for approval and saw him standing over her with a raised sword. She reflexively raised her hands to defend herself, expecting him to strike.

Nothing happened, so she looked at him quizzically, "What the hell are you doing?"

He lowered his sword, "As part of the ritual, I had to be ready. Had you drawn the silver and red metal, I would have ended your life."

"What? Why would you do that?"

He extended his diamond hand to help her stand and explained, "Because those who draw the red metal are Skeans."

"Skeans? You mean like the ones Zorion talked about earlier?"

"Yes. Since the beginning of time, there has been a war between light and darkness. Each one fights for dominance in this universe."

"Zorion told me that Skeans fight for the Night Lord. Is that true?"

"Yes."

"I dreamt last night that someone tried to destroy a sun. There was a battle at the base of a pyramid. I saw two figures fighting at the top. They both died."

"You just described Gau's last battle when he tried to destroy our sun."

"Gau?"

"History is vague about his life; we know that he was a powerful Skean who lived thousands of Earthian years ago. Using his abilities, he took control of the government and forced rituals of blood and battle that our society still performs today. Legend says he went mad and enslaved our ancestors, forcing them to supply materials to build a pyramid. It still stands at the equator of our planet, beneath the snow and ice. No one knew why he built it until Gau's last battle when they discovered he planned to destroy the sun with it."

"It means a black hole did not come near your sun and deplete its plasma."

"Correct. That is a theory created by those who do not wish to believe the truth. If Lehoi had not stopped him, Gau would have destroyed our sun, plunging Akil into everlasting darkness. Before she killed him, he had already weakened our sun, making it a red giant. Over the following years, our planet underwent changes that killed most of the life on Akil."

"Zorion showed me the surface. It's horrifying. Who is Lehoi?"

"She was a Saiph."

"Zorion told me a Saiph fights for the High Lord."

"Yes. That is correct."

"Are you saying I'm a Saiph?"

"Not yet. I must train you first."

"No way, I'm going home in a few hours."

"You must stay and help us! The High Lord has chosen you!"

"Hey, I didn't ask for this High Lord to pick me! Besides, you don't need my help. I will return home soon with a video of Zorion asking Supreme Commander Porter for assistance. In no time, your people will move to our planet until you can find another one. Isn't that enough?"

"No, Julie. Skeans on Akil will destroy your star, as Gau did ours. Their purpose is to usher in the Shadow Universe."

"Are you telling me these Skeans will try to destroy our sun too?"

"Yes."

"You're not making any sense! If they destroy our sun, they will kill themselves!"

"Bringing the Shadow Universe here is their goal. They will not stop until it is here. They will land on your world and destroy it like they did Akil if you return home, but if you stay, you have a chance to stop them before they can damage any other star."

"I'm sorry. I can't do what you're asking of me. I have a class to teach. I have a life. You must look for someone else."

"There *is* no one else. You are our only hope."

"There must be a mistake. I'm not a fighter. I'm a gymnastics teacher. The two do not go hand in hand."

"Urki constructed me as a failsafe in case the Skeans destroyed the Saiphs. The last known Akilian Saiph died sixty Yellow Harvests ago. A former Saiph named Gecheana forsook the light and killed them. Since that time, many infants have died of unknown causes. I believe Gecheana is murdering them to prevent Saiphs from returning. The fact that you are from another planet is not a coincidence. The High Lord has sent you to us for this reason, Julie. If you leave, billions of Akilians will die, and billions of Earthians will too."

"I don't want to discuss this anymore. I want to leave."

"How can you leave knowing billions will die without your help?"

"Now, Urki!"

He frowned, "You may leave any time you wish."

"I can't leave. The stone is still blocking the way out."

"You have access to the High Lord's power, so simply command the stone to rise as you did for the trial."

"That stone is much bigger than the one I pulled from the ground."

"Do not allow your eyes to deceive you. There is no difference between them for a Saiph."

"I'm not a Saiph, remember?"

"Then stay here and die."

Frustrated, she turned toward the stone, closed her eyes, and instinctively held her hand toward it. Within moments, she felt its mass; it did not deter her because she saw a slot above it with two stone latches, which would hold it in place, assuming she could raise it high enough. She took a deep breath and envisioned the stone moving upward. Moments later, she heard the stone door grinding against the rock wall as the boulder moved upward. Once it was in position, she pushed the latches into place and released her grip. The stone did not fall, and Urki urged her once more as she started to leave.

"The High Lord has given you a great gift, which means you cannot run from the responsibility that goes with it. If you leave, you will regret that decision for the rest of your life."

Without responding, she ran, just in case he changed his mind. At the fountain, she sprinted to her apartment, locked the door behind her, and tried to forget what had just happened, but his last words kept replaying in her mind.

Chapter 17

Special Agent Reed and one hundred fifty TBI agents swarmed the Sanya Electronix building early in the morning. Reed insisted on arming his agents with automatic weapons in case they met resistance. The agents secured the lobby, so Special Agent Reed entered, pulled out his identification badge, and walked to the receptionist on duty.

"Where is Kathryn Wright's office?" Reed demanded.

"She's on the top floor," the receptionist nervously replied.

"All right, now stand beside that agent," Reed pointed. "Give him your information and sit tight. No one leaves until I have what I'm looking for."

He turned to his assistant, "I want two agents on every floor, and no one leaves until I say."

His assistant nodded and carried out his orders. A team of five agents, specially trained for combat, went with him. As he entered the elevator, they followed him inside. At the top, his team exited first, ensuring the area was secure, and gave the all-clear, so he headed straight for Kathryn Wright's office with purpose. Filled with righteous indignation, Reed resolved to remove every brick to find answers, yet strongly suspected it would not go that far.

Kathryn's receptionist saw him and his team approaching and picked up the phone to alert her boss.

Reed yelled from down the hall and pointed his finger at her, "Put it down and raise your hands!"

She dropped the phone and put her hands in the air.

"Restrain her," Reed ordered.

Reed and the rest of his team burst into Kathryn Wright's office, meeting with a client. They both jumped at the sight of Reed and his men.

"What's the meaning of this?" Kathryn demanded.

Reed pulled out his tablet, having the Supreme Commander's Warrant, handed it to her, and advised, "You and your company are under investigation."

Kathryn, baffled by the news, wondered, "Why?"

Reed motioned for one of his agents to take her guest outside.

Moments later, Reed continued, "I have evidence linking your company to the Comptroller's death."

"The Comptroller is dead?"

"Yes. I know your company had something to do with it."

"How?"

"My records show Sanya Electronix deposited a little more than half a million Regime Talons in his account a few months back. Since that amount far exceeds his pay as Comptroller, it was obviously a bribe. I want to know what you paid him to do."

"I did not *pay* him anything. I was unaware that my company paid half a million Regime Talons to anyone."

"You are the one in charge here, aren't you?"

"Yes, of course."

"You are the one responsible."

"May I bring up this year's financial records on my computer?"

"Wait," Reed turned away from her and spoke into his communicator. "Evan, did you gain access yet?"

"Yes, Sir. I just finished downloading their database."

Reed turned back to face Kathryn, "My technical team has a copy of everything on your server, so you don't need to show me your financial records. I have them."

Reed manipulated his tablet until the company's account appeared on his display, showing the date the money transfer took place, causing him to frown, "It's not here."

"That's what I tried to tell you. If I saw such a considerable sum of money leave this company, I assure you I would have stopped it."

Reed spoke into his communicator again, "Evan, I need the names of everyone in the financial department sent to my tablet."

"Yes, Sir."

Moments later, Reed's tablet beeped, and he opened the file.

"What floor are they on?"

"The twentieth," Kathryn answered.

"Let's go."

On her way, Kathryn noticed her secretary in restraints and inquired, "Is that necessary?"

"Yes, until I have what I came for."

"I will return as soon as possible," Kathryn said to her client, following Reed down the hall.

His team gave the all-clear, so Kathryn and Reed stepped out.

"Lead the way," Reed gestured.

Kathryn showed Reed and his men to the financial department.

"This is director Jim Price," Kathryn introduced.

Surprised, Jim stood apprehensively.

"They're here investigating the…" she started to say; Reed interrupted.

"A few months ago, someone in this room transferred half a million Regime Talons into an outside account. I want to know who did it and how."

Jim swallowed hard and looked to Kathryn for help; she offered none, "I swear I have no idea what happened."

"Someone moves half a million Regime Talons, and no one at the top notices!" Reed yelled.

"Let me look at our financial history," Jim remarked.

Nervously, he accessed the information on his terminal and analyzed the data. Patience was not one of Reed's virtues, mostly because he wanted answers now.

Several minutes later, Jim's eyes widened, "I don't know who did it, but I can show you what he did."

"What? What did he do?"

"We complete hundreds of daily transfers, sometimes thousands, so we receive an electron bill and receipt for every transaction. An auditor will review and approve the bill so our system can transfer the funds into the proper account for reimbursement. I have discovered that the biller's account number sporadically changed to one specific account number. If the supplier did not receive their funds promptly, they sent another bill. Since the computer could not find a record showing payment, it approved the second request; the supplier did not file a complaint, making the transfer invisible."

"Why didn't the system catch it?" Kathryn queried, with a severe look of concern on her face.

"It did. Someone overrode the error message and pushed it through."

"Why didn't our auditors catch it?" Kathryn demanded.

"It shows up as an error as if the Regime Talons never came out of our account."

"How is this possible?" quizzed Kathryn.

"I have seen this before. A hacker gained access to your server and loaded a virus that allowed him to manipulate the software," Reed explained.

"If I were to contact the bank right now…." Kathryn started to say.

"It would show that you are half a million Regime Talons shy of what you think you have," Reed finished for her and faced Jim, "Who overrode the error message?"

Jim typed into the computer for a few seconds, "I don't know. Whoever did this erased their tracks."

"Is everyone in the office today?" inquired Reed.

"Yes, but…" Jim paused.

"What is it?" queried Reed.

"I had an employee quit around the same time the virus transferred the last charge."

"What's his name?"

"Kenny Barnes."

Reed told his communicator, "Evan, I want everything you can get on a Kenny Barnes. He quit here a few months ago, just after the company's account paid the Comptroller."

"I'm on it," Evan reassured.

He turned to Kathryn, "My men have the names and addresses of every employee. My team will tell them not to leave the city under any circumstance and don't discuss this raid with anyone, including family members. That includes you, Kathryn."

"I have an out-of-state meeting I need to attend," Kathryn protested.

"Invite them here, use a video conference, or don't have the meeting. In any case, *you* cannot leave the city."

Reed motioned for his team to leave with him.

Evan approached him as he entered the lobby, "I have sent a full dossier on Kenny Barnes to your tablet."

Reed brought the information up and carefully reviewed the material, "I see a sum of twenty thousand Regime Talons, above the half-million, went into his account."

"The transactions show that he sent the money to himself in negligible amounts; the same date the half-million Regime Talons disappeared into the offshore account."

"We need to pay him a visit right now," Reed said to his assistant.

"Yes, Sir. I'll gather the men."

"Oh…send someone up to release Kathryn's secretary. I left her bound in her chair."

Chapter 18

Yanamai woke early before her alarm sounded and sat on the edge of her bed. Her conversation with Zorion a few Terrestrial Revolutions ago still troubled her. Someone she did not know wanted to kill her. They had deduced that Otsoa had given her the wrong sector to search. Also, Zorion checked his Information Terminal and discovered that Tadra, Yanamai's now-former replacement, has an anonymous benefactor.

Over the past few work cycles, Yanamai studied Tadra yet did not see her act differently. There was a good chance she did not know of the assassination attempt. Additionally, she checked her computer and did not find any attempt to search within another sector. Yanamai stayed guarded around her, careful not to say anything about the incident.

It angered her that someone drugged her and Garbi, so she sprang out of bed in her sleep clothes, walked to her Information Terminal, and connected to the Civilian Monitoring Network. She reviewed the images without finding anything new. Whoever attacked her had removed all recordings of her journey, but she had an idea.

Recently, Zorion ordered the transportation companies to install cameras in their vehicles. Since the Information League did not report it, most Akilians were unaware. She used her authority to access the hover bus video storage. Sadly, she did not remember the bus number, so it took time to find it.

Her eyes widened, seeing Kraeth sitting beside her, whispering something into her ear. Moments later, Kraeth moved to another seat as Yanamai mumbled with red puffy eyes. At the bus stop, she watched herself leave and did not remember any of it. Now armed with proof, she copied the images to her data device, dressed, and within a few hundred heartbeats, she was in Zorion's outer office, waiting to see him.

"Zorion will see you now," Shilda gestured.

Inside, she showed him the recording.

"This *is* troubling," Zorion commented.

"Can you arrest him?" Yanamai asked.

"Kraeth is Gwah's heir, a sovereign's heir; this video is not enough proof to accuse him."

"I understand," Yanamai lamented.

"Even more frustrating is that he oversees deciphering the Earthians' language. If I begin an investigation, it will halt that process and delay our ability to speak with them."

"You cannot do it because you must make a video in their language, so we have a chance of convincing them to help us."

"I am sorry, Yanamai. What he did to you and Garbi is unforgivable. I would send an agent to kill him if we did not depend on him for survival."

"You would do that?"

"Without hesitating."

"What do I do now?"

Zorion stood and walked to her. Yanamai rose to greet him.

He embraced her with a firm hug, "You will continue with your work, knowing that on one Terrestrial Rotation, he will pay for his crime. I promise you."

"I thought you could not accuse him."

"I cannot do anything until we find a new home, and I swear to you, an agent will visit him."

"Please do not kill him. I could not live with that either."

"Do not worry; if harming him displeases you, I will send him to a remote prison, where he will spend the rest of his life behind bars," he lied. *You do not try to kill someone I care about and live.*

"I can accept that outcome," Yanamai replied.

"After Julie returns home, take the rest of the work cycle off and try to relax. Understood?"

Yanamai nodded.

"Good, now go to the Interstellar Transport Bay. I will be with you shortly."

As Yanamai left, Zorion called Shilda to his office.

"Yes, Sir."

"Shut the door behind you."

Shilda did as he ordered.

Instead of calling her to his desk, he walked to where she stood, leaned in, and whispered into her ear, "I want new surveillance equipment installed on the top two levels. I want the images loaded to a separate server and give me exclusive access to it. Hire one contractor and instruct him to work during the sleep cycle. Make him and his employees sign a confidentiality agreement. I do not want anyone to know about this."

Shilda nodded.

"I will start immediately."

Later, he was finally free to think about Julie without interruption. A wave of sadness hit him at the thought of her leaving. He lay awake during the last sleep cycle, trying to think of something to say or do to convince her to stay; nothing came to mind. Now, he had to prepare himself to say goodbye to her forever.

Chapter 19

Earth
The Regime - Washington, D.C. - Capitol Building
May 14, 2452

Supreme Commander Porter returned from the vault, sat, and opened the file before his daily briefing. The only instructions were for financial matters; it was silent concerning Jared. Frustrated with the Founder, Porter pushed the record aside, wondering why he did not shed any light on Jared's situation. It was a few minutes past 9 AM Regime time, and in Frankfurt, where the Tech Revolutionaries held Jared, it was a few minutes past 3:00 PM.

It was getting late, and Brandy Miller, Mrs. Bradshaw's temporary replacement, opened the door, "Secretary of Defense, Neil Long, is here to see you."

"Send him right in," Porter stood, they shook hands, sat, and he continued, "I hope you have good news for me, Neil."

Neil placed a hologram tablet on his desk and showed him a detailed image of the mountain, highlighting specific areas.

"We've analyzed Jared's recent movements. Based on the bacteria Michael injected into his body, Jared moved up a corridor and stopped here," he pointed to the highlighted areas. "He was in this area briefly, left, and returned. We believe they're holding him there. We also determined that his descent was much quicker than when he ascended the corridor."

"Isn't it normal to descend at a faster pace?" Porter asked.

"His descent rate indicates that he was running."

"Why would he run back down to where they were holding him?"

"We're uncertain; we think he may have returned to help other prisoners, or his exit is blocked."

"It means he either went back to free someone, or he's trying to avoid their sentries."

"Yes, Sir. That's our best guess."

"Either way, he's still trapped, and assuming he's running around without an escort, they'll want to kill him."

"I agree, which is why I want to send an extraction team. We can get to Jared with a portal if they can destroy the generator."

"Do you know where they keep the generator?"

"We're not one hundred percent certain. The disruption field is making it hard to pinpoint its location."

"Have a team ready but give Jared just a little more time. I'm sure he'll figure out a way to destroy the generator; if he doesn't do it within a half-hour, send the team, and don't forget to prepare for his arrival. You know how he tends to return from an assignment."

"I have already added it to my list."

"Now go bring our boy home."

Chapter 20

Waking from a good night's sleep, Chu Lian rolled over onto her left side and faced Michael. The rays of morning sunlight, peeking through the blinds, softly illuminated Michael's features. She expected him to wake from her stirring; he did not, so she took advantage of the opportunity and watched him. The slow, steady sound of his breathing gave her comfort.

Using her index finger, she gently stroked his cheek, causing him to squint and brush her hand away, not knowing it was her. She moved her hand farther up and twirled a few strands of his hair around the same finger; still, he did not respond. She smiled and playfully touched other areas of his face and neck, nearly waking him. He rolled over onto his side, leaving his back to face her. She thought about her feelings for him and realized something very frightening. *I love him.*

She stopped touching him. Years of training smacked her mind like the back of her instructor's hand. *What am I doing?* Somehow, Michael got through her best emotional defenses that she and her instructor meticulously put into place to protect her from this exact scenario. *"Remember the mission. Always remember the mission,"* she could hear her instructor say.

Precaution always protected her behind enemy lines when she was most vulnerable. Fear and paranoia dominated her thoughts. She stared at the back of his head, wondering if he was a Regime spy cleverly planted to catch her. *No one is this perfect.* With her emotions spiraling into a freefall, she jumped out of bed, making enough commotion to wake him this time. As he groggily opened his eyes, she left the bedroom. Moments later, she heard his footsteps. He found her in the living room, pacing.

"What are you doing up so early on a Saturday?"

Using moves rehearsed a thousand times, she grabbed his nightshirt and pushed him against the wall, pinning him.

"Who are you?"

"What?"

"Stop playing games, Michael. If that *is* your name."

"Of course, it's my name. What the hell is wrong with you?"

Wu Luli studied him and discovered that he was telling the truth. Confusion replaced anger conflicting her thoughts. She struggled against her loyalty between General Ming-tun Fu and Michael until realizing she had him pinned against the wall. She let him go.

"What's wrong? What happened?" he demanded.

She took a moment to assess her situation and realized she had made a critical error by falling in love with the target. *I should have gone through with my original plan. I should have killed him the night I invited him over for dinner. The night he first told me he loved me.*

"We can't see each other anymore," she answered indifferently, hoping to put some distance between them.

"What? Why?"

"It was a mistake! *You* were a mistake! The past eight months have been a mistake! Get your things and leave now!"

"But…"

"Go before I call security!"

She saw his eyes well up as he collected his clothes and dressed. *Oh, you are good at playing the victim, but your tears will not move me.*

"Why are you doing this?" he challenged.

Ignoring him, she opened the door and yelled, "Leave!"

As he stared quizzically into her eyes, she felt a lump in her throat. There were still two powerful voices fighting for control. One shouted to kill him, the other to embrace him.

"I'm sorry for whatever I did to make you hate me," he lamented.

He closed the door and left with his head down. For what seemed like hours, she paced, analyzing her situation, and struggled to decide if Michael was a brilliant spy who tricked her into falling in love with him or if her emotions had tricked her. She had dealt with men richer, better looking, and more charming than him during her career. None of them came close to tempting her with the emotional entanglements of a relationship. Yet it left her with a nagging question. Why, of all people in the world, did this nobody capture her heart?

She reached a breaking point and collapsed onto the couch in tears, struggling to push away her feelings for him. Eventually, the emotional storm ended, and she realized her mistake. Michael had been honest; she was the one lying. Now she faced a fork in her life's journey. If Wu Luli went left, it meant staying loyal to her employer. If she went right, it meant changing her allegiance to Michael. She chose the latter and swore to be on Michael's side forever, no matter what. She ran to his apartment and knocked; no one answered. Putting her ear to the door, she listened for any sign that he was there. It was quiet until she heard footsteps.

"Michael, it's me. I know you're in there. Please, open the door," Wu Luli continued to use her cover as Chu Lian.

"Go away, Lian. You've made it clear how you feel. There is no need to review the highlights."

"It's *not* how I feel. I had a moment of uncertainty. I wasn't thinking. I did not mean what I said."

"It sounded to me like you did. Now go away."

She paced outside his door, angry with herself for allowing this to happen. She had to speak with him and tell him her identity. She wanted to tell him she was a spy and planned to defect. Most importantly, he had to know that she *did* love him, yet it was not the kind of conversation to have in the hallway.

She found the keycard to his apartment in her pocket and unlocked the door; Michael had hooked the chain, which prevented her from entering. Adamant, she stepped back and kicked the door. Although the first attempt failed, it loosened the chain from the wall. By the fifth try, the door flew open, and she stepped inside.

"What the hell are you doing?" Michael yelled.

She closed the door and paused, seeing wet cheeks and red eyes. She had hurt him badly, and it made her angry with herself. Knowing she caused him so much pain only made her more resolute in telling him what she came to say.

"Look, I'm sorry about the door. I will pay to have it fixed, but I need to speak with you."

He turned away; she grabbed his arm and stopped him. With his arms folded, he refused to move, so she walked in front of him.

"You must be bipolar. I have never seen anyone go from one extreme emotion to another in such a brief time."

"I acted the way I did because as I watched you sleep, I realized something."

"What? That you hated me!"

"No, Michael," she shook her head adamantly, "I realized I love you. I have for some time now. I didn't know it until this morning."

"You have a bizarre way of showing it."

"I acted irrationally, but there's a good reason."

She paused, trying to collect her thoughts. Before revealing that she was a spy, it came to mind that telling him would put his life in danger and her dad's. Once her employer discovered that she defected, he would certainly end his life and try to kill Michael. It was clear she had to take care of a few things before letting him know the truth, so she thought of a lie instead.

"Well, I'm waiting," Michael challenged.

"I was scared."

"Huh?"

"I've been on my own most of my life, and I have never trusted anyone until now. You made me feel vulnerable, and it scared me."

"We all take a risk with relationships; that doesn't excuse the way you acted toward me this morning."

"I know it doesn't, yet that's why I acted the way I did. Please, forgive me?"

There was a long silence between them until he conceded, "I forgive you. Just don't do it again because I can't take that kind of emotional abuse."

"I won't. I know now that I don't want to live a day without you in my life, and I will do whatever it takes to keep us together."

"I hope so because I don't want to be without you either."

She smiled and whispered into his ear, "I will love you forever."

She kissed him.

*****

Back to Oz! Back to Oz! The strange words echoed in her ears. She did not know what to make of them until waking from her sleep, which made her realize it was a dream of a past argument with

Michael. Jared's voice brought her back to reality, making the memory slip away like a vapor. With her eyes still closed, she assessed her surroundings.

Jared kept repeating the phrase that woke her, which meant he had difficulty contacting the Regime. She remembered hearing a motor as the guards dragged her into the cave. Since Jared could not contact the Regime, the Tech Revolutionaries must be jamming all signals within their area. Clearly, he would need her help, so she opened her eyes.

"Hey, are you all right?" queried Jared.

She nodded, tried to sit up, and regretted it.

"Ow."

"You've got a nasty bump on your forehead."

"One of the guards did that. I didn't give him the answer he wanted."

"Can you stand?"

"I think so."

She stood, with help from Jared to balance her. Later, she managed to stand on her own.

"Ok, I've got this. Thanks. By the way, how did you get out of your cell?"

"I got free in the interrogation room. I can't contact the Regime. We must get out of here on our own, most likely through the front door."

"There are too many of them. We won't make it out alive," Wu Luli warned.

"We don't have any other choice. The Tech Revolutionaries are using a disruptor, which is blocking communications and quite possibly our ability to open a portal here," Jared responded.

"How would the Regime even know where to open one?"

"They just do," he moved forward.

"Wait! I heard something on my way in that sounded like it could be a generator."

"Are you sure?"

"I think they would want to keep it hidden from the Regime's satellites. It would be vulnerable to an airstrike if they left it outside."

"It would have to be big to create the power needed to block a portal."

"Combustible engines need lots of fuel," Wu Luli noted.

"You would have made a good Regime agent," Jared joked.

"Thanks. Maybe you can put in a good word for me after we return."

"Let's hope we can get back. Follow me."

They raced through the tunnel and stopped at an intersection. The sound of excited voices to their right caught their attention.

"They must have found Diederich," Jared concluded.

"What did you do to him?"

"I let him know how I felt about being tortured."

"I guess he didn't take it very well."

"No, he didn't. He's dead, which means the Tech Revolutionaries will want revenge, which means we don't have much time."

He pointed to the tunnel on their right, where they heard the voices, "I'm fairly sure that's the entrance. I counted two hundred twenty-three steps until we made a left, which must have been here at this intersection. Also, I counted fifty-two more steps to the cell, so the interrogation room is straight ahead."

"That means the generator must be down the right corridor," Wu Luli surmised.

They paused to listen.

"Yeah, I can hear it too; it's very faint. The guards must have been talking the last time I was here, which is why I didn't hear it," Jared surmised.

"What are you going to do?"

"Stay here a moment. I'm going to the interrogation room to see what I can find."

"Hurry back!"

He found the interrogation room door open and Diederich lying against the wall. The dead guards were there, too, meaning whoever found them must have run to get reinforcements. Soon, a swarm of Tech Revolutionaries would flood the tunnels at any moment, so he grabbed all their weapons and ammunition and returned to where Chu Lian waited for him.

"Can I have one?" she inquired, nodding toward one of the handguns.

"Do you know how to use one of these?"

"Yes. I've fired one before."

"All right, here ya go."

"What do we do now?"

"I need to disable the generator; the moment it shuts down, the Tech Revolutionaries will go there to find out what happened."

"You distract them, and I will shut down the generator," Wu Luli offered.

"Are you sure you can do it?" Jared wondered.

"My life depends on it. Don't worry. I'll disable it somehow."

"The moment you take it down, return to this intersection. There is enough space for the portal to open without causing a collapse."

"I'll see you in a few minutes."

As Jared disappeared down the tunnel, she ran to her right and stopped, hearing voices. She peeked around the corner with her back pressed against the wall and saw two sentries standing near the entrance. Between them, she saw an exhaust tube running out of the room and farther down the tunnel, which meant another exit. The loud noise from the motor would mask the sound of her gun firing. Having memorized their positions, she stepped out from the corridor, aimed, and fired two quick shots to the head, dropping them.

Years ago, she had mistakenly shot her targets in the chest; one had a bulletproof vest under his shirt. He recovered, surprised her with an attack, and almost killed her. She swore never to take any chances and began shooting her quarry in the head. She waited about a minute to ensure no one heard the gunfire and entered the room to find three large fuel tanks about fifteen feet from the generator. A closer examination revealed that each container had hoses hooked to the fuel valve at the bottom front. Now all she needed were some tools.

She searched the nearby cabinets and found a toolbox and a gas can. Considering what was available, she developed a plan. After evaluating the weight of the can, she determined it was half full and put a hole in the generator's fuel tank at the bottom using a hammer and screwdriver. As gasoline poured out onto the rocky floor of the room, it began to puddle, so she grabbed the can, set it down over the small pool of gas, removed the lid, ran to the other large tanks, and opened their nozzles, releasing their fuel onto the ground.

The room quickly flooded with combustible fuel. With everything in place, Wu Luli only needed a match. Since most assignments did not give her many options for accessories, she had to choose them carefully, so before leaving on her mission, she requested one thing from General Ming-tun Fu, a match. She moved her fingers up to the base of her neck and unclipped one single wooden stick. Yes, she could have chosen a small, sharp metal rod to subdue one or two guards by surprise, but it would not help against the considerable number she expected to face here. Instead, she chose a match because most outposts had fuel.

Wu Luli wrapped the match in plastic to prevent moisture damage; the stick broke during her interrogation. She removed the cover and looked for a rough surface to use before the fumes could overtake her. Scanning the room, she found a rusty bar on the generator. Pressing firmly against the tip, she dragged it across the rough surface (once, twice, and three times); still, nothing happened. *Damn it! Come on!* Holding her breath, she pulled it across the surface again, and it finally lit. Carefully, she set it down beside the metal can, near the puddle of gas, and set it on fire.

She waited for the generator tank to empty, which caused the motor to shut off, and ran from the room, hoping to find Jared before the blast. She expected two separate explosions. The first would be the gas can, which would spray gas and fire all over the room, preventing anyone from fixing the generator anytime soon. The second would be the three fuel tanks. That eruption would be massive, and she did not want to be in the cave when it happened. Arriving at the intersection, she heard and felt the gas explode. Jared had not returned yet. Now that the jamming signal was down, they could contact the Regime and leave if he made it back alive. *Come on, Jared; it's up to you now!*

*****

Jared reached the end of the tunnel and found the entrance to the cave. Near the door was a stockpile of guns and ammunition. Beyond that, he saw about twenty-armed Tech Revolutionaries. *This confrontation is going to be messy.* The thought of starting his subcutaneous body armor caused his stomach to growl, reminding him to eat. The interrogation weakened him, leaving him two more uses before replacing the chemical, and he hoped his body would have enough energy to finish the mission.

Besides his body armor, Jared had only one added advantage, surprise. He took a headcount and realized their numbers were increasing. There were at least fifteen more than before, and several arriving every few seconds. *Well, it's now or never.* He released the chemical into his bloodstream, walked outside, pointed at them with a gun in each hand, and nervously laughed.

"Surprise!"

Everyone froze until one man started for his gun; Jared shot him before he could reach it.

"Fire!" their leader yelled.

In unison, they all brought their weapons to bear on Jared. *Oh, man, this is going to sting.* Both sides fired their guns. Bullets ricocheted off Jared's skin, hitting the wall and some of the Tech Revolutionaries as they bounced around aimlessly. Every time a slug hit him, it stung, yet it did not penetrate his skin. He carefully aimed before firing, trying not to waste ammunition, hoping to get the most out of his supply.

There was an explosion, and everyone stopped firing. *She did it! The disruptive field is down!* He took down several guards, but they still outnumbered him. Even during their momentary cease-fire, more Tech Revolutionaries arrived. *It's time to go.* He shot a few more rounds, turned, and returned to the tunnel, trying to contact the Regime.

"Home Base, this is Jared. Do you copy?"

"This is Home Base, Jared. You didn't give the secret code. Are you ready to return home?"

"Not yet; wait for my signal."

"Roger that; waiting for your signal."

Gunfire rang out behind him as he negotiated turns through the rocky corridor. He slammed into the wall repeatedly, trying to keep his speed up through the winding tunnel. Not having enough energy to support it and run simultaneously, his body armor dissipated, leaving him vulnerable and even more exhausted. The passageways were extensive and twisted, slowing his journey back to the intersection. A couple of minutes later, he arrived, winded and tired.

"I heard the explosion," Jared panted loudly.

"There will be another one soon, a bigger one. We don't have much time," Wu Luli warned.

Gunfire rang out from where Jared came.

"Run back toward the cells. We can't stay here. Keep in front of me!" Jared yelled.

She nodded and ran down the tunnel with Jared behind her.

"Home Base, this is Jared. Back to Oz! Back to Oz!"

Summoning the last of his strength, he started his body armor one more time and ran, even though his legs felt like lead. It was good that he used the ability again because bullets ricocheted off his back, and he grunted from their sting.

Having moved far ahead of him without realizing it, Wu Luli turned to see why he had stopped running, "What's wrong?"

"I can't go any farther."

She ran back to help him.

"No, keep going, Lian!"

"I'm not leaving here without you!"

She placed her shoulder under his arm and did her best to support him, and they moved forward. She occasionally fired her weapon at the Tech Revolutionaries to prevent them from getting too close.

"Where will they open the portal?"

"They must open it somewhere in front of us, and since we're moving and descending inside a winding tunnel, it may take them a little longer to figure exactly where to open it."

"They better open it soon, or there'll be no one here to rescue."

"Just make sure you hold your breath as you go through."

"Why?"

"You'll see."

Chapter 21

Akil

Argi City

The 22,278[th] Terrestrial Rotation of the Second Summer

Olan entered a store that rented Information Terminals in his usual traveling disguise. Reaching into his pocket, he removed Sovereign Cubes and paid the clerk for a private room. Olan closed the door behind him, sat, and typed in the password the cashier gave him. The terminal came to life within moments, and he entered his credentials. Although Dolas removed his access to the central database, Olan still had many of his former subordinates' identifications and passwords.

Olan decided against using Dolas's because if someone discovered his entry, they might suspect Dolas was helping him, so he used a lower-rank's identity. Also, the information he was looking for only needed low-level clearance. The database came online, and he entered the city 'Vlor' and the name 'Shafe.'

A list of thousands of Vlorians showed on the screen. *Hmm, I need to narrow this down. Let me see. If I were to infiltrate Elzer's guards, who would I use? Well, I would use my best agent, except this agent failed, which is rare and can only mean one thing. He did not use an agent. But why?* He thought for a few hundred heartbeats until it came to him. *Ah, he was in a hurry, and an agent would need time to familiarize himself with a guard's routine; if Elzer gave my counterpart the assignment at the last moment, he had to go with the best choice, one of Elzer's guards.*

Olan chuckled to himself. *I wonder how many Sovereign Cubes he had to promise the dupe to get him to commit.* He opened the dossiers of every member of Elzer's security team. There were several named Shafe. *Figures, it is a popular name in Vlor.* He read each one carefully and found the guard best suited for the job. His background was typical of a patsy because he had no family. *I would have picked him too.*

Olan copied his name and position, downloaded the information to his new portable data device, and entered his counterpart's name into the Information Terminal. Later, he planned to give the information to Dolas. Igon's dossier appeared on the screen, with an image of him in the top left corner; the picture did not match his quarry, which meant he had changed his appearance. Since this was not a standard mission, it made sense that Igon put himself out in the field because if Zorion had told *him* to assassinate another sovereign, he would have personally overseen the operation himself from beginning to end.

Now, more than ever, he was sure Igon was here but had to capture him to prove it, so he downloaded Igon's profile, shut down the Information Terminal, and went to the avenue. He walked the promenade, felt his wrist communicator vibrate, and checked his locator device. The assassin was on the move. Olan inconspicuously headed for an area of the undeveloped wall, checked to ensure the avenue was clear, and disappeared into the shadows.

Chapter 22

Earth
The United States - Texas - Houston - George Bush Park
May 14, 2452

Larkin had been running for about five hours because the vehicle he stole at the auditorium ran out of gas some miles back, forcing him to finish his journey on foot. The concrete and chains weighed him down, slowing his pace for most of his journey. Sweat flowed from every pore of his body as he climbed another hill in his arduous trek.

As the sun crested the horizon, he looked for something familiar to get his bearing; the terrain seemed the same. His last meal was just before his fight with Marco, and his hike home took its toll on his body. He was hungry, tired, and desperate to reach his family in time. . He climbed another hill and saw his house in the faint morning light, about a mile away.

Stopping to catch his breath, he saw a vehicle parked in front. He felt relief, hoping it was General Bailey until the shadows unexpectedly urged him forward. *Oh, no. There's something wrong.* Knowing there was not enough time, he tried to teleport, and nothing happened again. *Damn it! I need this ability back now!* He tried repeatedly, but his ability to teleport did not resurface.

It puzzled him because the aloe should be out of his system by now. *They are in danger.* The thought came to him like a whisper. Seeing he had no choice, his mind moved closer to the deep within him. Power surged through his body. He liked it a lot and hated himself for it. He willed himself forward again and teleported his body, landing several feet ahead. Looking down, he saw that his bloody wrists and ankles were finally free of the chains. Power flowed freely through his mind and body. He felt an urgency coming from the direction of his home. *Sable!* He sensed her fear. In her mind, she was calling for him. *Don't worry, Darlin'. I'm comin'!*

The energy rejuvenated his strength, so he ran toward his home and used his ability to teleport vast distances. Each time, he landed closer to home. Within seconds, he arrived on his front lawn and saw a man dragging Sarah toward his house. Rage owned his mind and fueled his power to the point that the ground shook beneath him.

The miniature earthquake caused the man holding Sarah to stumble. He regained his step, looked back, and saw Larkin. Chills of fear ran down his spine, so he pressed the knife firmly against Sarah's throat, hoping it would be enough to save him.

"Don't come any closer, Larkin, or I'll cut her! I swear I'll do it!"

Larkin did not hear the other man's words because his only thought was Sarah and the blood on her face.

"Sarah, are you hurt?"

"Yes."

"I said back off, or I will cut her!" the intruder yelled.

As if to make his point, he pressed the knife harder against Sarah's throat, drawing blood. Instinctively, Larkin focused on the knife hand and, with his mind, pulled back on it. As the intruder struggled against the unseen force, he frowned because it was winning. Once the blade lifted from her skin, Sarah moved her right hand to his wrist, pushed away, elbowed her captor in the stomach, and ran. Now that Sarah was out of harm's way, Larkin swiftly moved toward him.

Seeing Larkin approaching, the intruder pulled his gun. Larkin grabbed his wrist before he could bring the weapon up to bear. Using his other hand, the attacker tried to cut Larkin with the knife; Larkin also grabbed that wrist. The would-be killer struggled against Larkin's strength and reflexively squeezed the trigger, forcing the gun to fire a shot into the ground.

Using his brute strength, Larkin broke the other's wrist, which held the gun. He screamed from the pain and dropped the weapon. Larkin moved the intruder's knife hand to his own throat. Finally, the moment arrived. Larkin wanted to savor it and pressed the blade into the man's skin.

"Hurry, Larkin. Sable is in danger!"

Without a second thought, Larkin used the attacker's hand to push the blade through his trachea. As the knife cut through flesh and cartilage, he gurgled and tried to fight against Larkin's unreasoning power, and as the blade passed through his vertebrae, he went limp.

Larkin tossed him aside like a rag doll and faced Sarah, "Where is she?"

"In the woods. The lean-to."

*****

Hector noticed that the woods became eerily silent. The crickets, birds, and other insects that filled the air with their song, stopped. It was as if all the animals and insects sensed a super predator nearby. Goosebumps rose on his arms, and he felt a cold chill. Adrenaline coursed through his veins as he scanned the area nervously. He had no idea what was out there. In the quiet, he called out to the little girl again.

"Piglet, where are you?"

She did not respond, so he indiscriminately fired his weapon a few times. One of the bullets must have struck close to her position because he heard her scream. The sound of leaves rustling got his attention, and he saw her appear out of her hiding place only a few yards away. As she ran away screaming, he took careful aim and fired again. The bullet ricocheted off a tree that she had just ducked behind. He was angry at himself for missing; it did not matter because he now knew her position and would kill her soon.

He walked in a semicircle around her location behind the tree. Now that she was stationary, he had a better chance of hitting his target after getting her in sight again. She came into his view as he walked around. He remained concealed behind a nearby tree and smiled, watching her vain attempt at finding him. As she craned her head around the tree, searching for him, he raised his weapon and aimed.

He had her in his crosshair, but something grabbed him and threw him in the air. He landed several yards away, looked over, and saw her running. A tall figure caught his attention, so he looked up and saw Larkin glaring at him.

"It's nothing personal, Larkin. I'm just following orders," Hector remarked.

Without replying, Larkin moved toward him. Hector raised his weapon and fired; Larkin disappeared into thin air before the bullet left the chamber. Hector searched, unable to find him, so he panicked and aimlessly fired a few shots, turning around in a circle, hoping to wound him by chance or flush him out of hiding. As the echo of his last shot faded, the deafening silence returned. The continued eerie feeling only helped to make him even more nervous.

He felt a thick, unyielding hand grab his wrist that held the gun. Before he could resist, Larkin snapped it in half like a twig. Hector screamed from the pain, held his injured wrist with the other hand, and knew there would be no mercy. Larkin effortlessly spun him around to face him.

Hector never feared anyone in his life until he stared into Larkin's solid black eyes for the first time and realized Larkin was some magical thing. The longer they glared at each other, the more it felt like he was gazing into the great abyss. Its darkness called out to him. Terrified of what was to come, Hector tried to pry open Larkin's fist to free himself, but it was no use. Larkin drew back his other hand, preparing to strike Hector, who closed his eyes, not wanting to see it coming. A moment later, he felt Larkin's fist land in the center of his chest.

Hector fought many times during his life, yet no one had ever hit him this hard. The blow forced the air out of his lungs, breaking most of his ribs. Pain raced through his body, making it impossible to breathe normally. Feeling a tickle in his trachea, he coughed uncontrollably, and blood trickled out of his mouth, letting him know the end was near. He stared defiantly at the two black voids on Larkin's face with wide eyes and mockingly laughed.

"Is that all you got?"

Larkin drew back his fist again. This time, Hector's broken ribs could not withstand the impact. The punch pushed his sternum into his heart, stopping it. As Hector's life drained from his body, he felt the great abyss pulling him in, it swallowed all the light around him, and he died.

"Larkin! Larkin!" Sarah yelled.

As if tossing aside garbage, Larkin threw Hector into the brush, his anger dissipated, and his eyes returned to normal before Sarah reached him.

"Where's Sable?" she questioned.

"I don't know. She ran that way. I think," he pointed toward the west.

They heard Sable scream and ran toward her. By the time they arrived, Sable had stopped yelling because she had tried to cross the creek and ventured into a deeper area. She floated face down, and the current carried her downstream. They both ran to help her, but Larkin, the faster swimmer, advanced where the water got deep.

He reached her first, rolled her over, brought her head out of the water, and supported her, swimming back to shore. He set her down on the sand and checked her vitals. She was not breathing, and her heart had stopped. Larkin began CPR, and Sarah, knowing what was happening, began to cry.

"Come on, sweetheart. Don't you leave me!" Sarah's voice trembled.

Precious seconds passed like hours, and a minute later, Sarah cried even more hysterically because they could not revive her.

"She's dead! She's dead!" Sarah kept shouting, weeping.

Larkin did not give up, nor did he allow Sarah's cries to distract him; he focused on only one thing, saving Sable. He blew another breath into her lungs and heard a voice whisper, "Shock her." Reflexively, he put his hands on her chest and felt power flow into his arms, through his hands into Sable. Sable arched her back as her muscles contracted from the jolt. Still, nothing happened. Larkin shocked her again, and again, and again.

Sable coughed up water. Larkin rolled her onto her side to help clear her lungs. She got rid of most of the water, gasped, and inhaled a deep breath of air. The coughing continued for a few more minutes until her breathing returned to normal. Still crying and shaking from the ordeal, Sarah stroked her hair and tried to comfort her; she seemed stable enough to move, so Larkin picked her up and held her in his arms. Sarah walked behind him on their way home, watching her child closely. Exhausted, Sable rested her chin on Larkin's shoulder and her right cheek against his ear. Sarah realized that she did not know what had happened to her dad.

"Larkin, you need to hurry home and find dad! I haven't seen him since he arrived this morning!"

He handed Sable to her mother and ran to the house. Sarah held Sable and followed.

Larkin stepped inside and called for him, "General Bailey! General Bailey!"

There was no answer. Larkin saw signs of a struggle because every room had tables and chairs turned over, and broken knick-knacks were lying everywhere; in the dining room, he saw him lying on the floor face down. There was a gash on the back of his head, where one of the intruders hit him. Also, there was a trail of blood that led from the wound to the floor. He rolled him over and took his pulse; it was weak. Larkin gently smacked the General's cheek to wake him; the General did not respond, so he ran to the radio and called for help.

"HQ, come in, over."

Sarah entered and inquired, "Where is he?"

"On the floor in the dining room."

Sarah ran to help him.

"HQ here. Who's this?"

"This is Sergeant 1st class Larkin Burke, platoon sergeant for 3rd platoon Charlie Company. General Bailey is at my home, and he's unconscious. I need you to send help now!"

There was silence for about fifteen seconds until the operator returned and announced, "Sergeant Burke, an emergency team will be there shortly. Stay away from the front lawn. They'll be using Emergency Portal Transport."

"Roger that."

Larkin returned to the dining room, where Sarah held an ice pack on the General's head.

"Dad, come on, dad, wake up!"

Sarah felt helpless.

"I can't get him to wake up!" she yelled to Larkin.

"They're sending a team now," Larkin advised.

General Bailey stirred, "Ouch! That hurts!" He reached for the wound on his head and found an ice pack instead.

Sarah sighed in relief, "Sorry, dad. You took a serious blow to the head."

"They're here," Larkin yelled from the door.

"Good, I want Sable to go too."

Larkin looked at Sarah, "You need medical attention too."

"They need to help my dad and Sable first."

The medics brought a stretcher with them, and after they were sure it was safe to move General Bailey, they placed him on it and wheeled him through the portal. Larkin, Sarah, and Sable followed. Larkin stepped through the event horizon, where an entire team of doctors waited for them. Once the paramedics wheeled General Bailey in, they started working on him.

Sarah pulled one of the nurses aside and told her what had happened to Sable. The nurse called for another gurney and put Sable in the treatment room beside General Bailey. As they stood outside, waiting for the doctors to finish their diagnosis and treatment, Sarah took her first close look at Larkin.

"Your wrists are bleeding!"

"My ankles too."

Sarah disappeared for a moment and returned with a nurse.

"They can take care of me at HQ. Right now, I'm more concerned about Sable, you, and your dad."

"Absolutely not. You need medical attention, and if you don't let her help you, I'll do it myself."

"I'll let her fix my wounds if you let her look at you too," Larkin responded defiantly.

Sarah sighed, "Fine."

The nurse called for help and directed them to the room beside Sable. Sarah needed stitches, and Larkin needed an antibiotic ointment with bandages.

Later, Sarah faintly smiled, "What a pair we make, huh? You with your wrists and ankles and me with my cheek and lip."

"I'm glad I got there in time. I was worried about you and Sable."

A doctor approached them.

"How are they?" Sarah questioned.

"We're going to keep Sable overnight to ensure there is no brain damage. Do you know how long she was unconscious?"

"No, we're uncertain. I think it was at least a couple of minutes," Sarah guessed.

"We'll do some further tests, but so far, everything looks good."

Sarah sighed in relief, "And my dad?"

"General Bailey needed stitches for the cut on his head, and he has a severe hematoma, so we're going to keep him overnight as well."

“Thank you, doctor.”

“You two can sleep in the bed alongside Sable. You both look like you could use some rest.”

“Where’s the cafeteria?” queried Larkin. “I haven’t eaten in a while.”

“I’ll have something sent up.”

“Thanks, doc.”

Sarah and Larkin walked into Sable’s room, and Sarah faced Larkin, “What happened?”

He explained everything that took place within the past twenty-four hours, “I wish I would have left the moment I had the dream.”

“It was a dream. You couldn’t have known.”

“The strange thing is it didn’t happen as I dreamed, yet there were some similarities.”

“Maybe, it’s because you waited, and that changed the outcome.”

“Yeah, I guess.” He looked down at Sable. “She’s been dreaming of this day for quite a long time. It must have been what scared her.”

“Yeah, maybe she can sleep now. I could use a good night’s rest myself.” She laid her head on Larkin’s arm and held it tightly. “I’m so glad you’re safe.”

Chapter 23

Akil
Argi City
The 22,278th Terrestrial Rotation of the Second Summer

Nayrah decided to create an alter ego named Reenah after seeing Jadell kill her in a vision. This new character in her repertoire was a single, beautiful, prim, and proper socialite. It was necessary to develop such an alias to hide from Gecheana, her Skean sisters, and Jadell. To celebrate Reenah's birth (as it were), Nayrah shopped for a complete wardrobe proper for her status.

It was not a coincidence that both Nayrah and Reenah loved to shop. *We have so much in common.* For Reenah to be convincing, Nayrah had to buy a stylish home on level ten, where all the elites lived. Her new home and wardrobe's cost took a large chunk of the Sovereign Cubes she extorted from Durnah's parents. Since Nayrah discovered that Gecheana planned to kill her, she ensured that every Sovereign Cube ended up in Reenah's account.

It would not take long at the rate of her spending until she would need more funds to support Reenah's lifestyle because the tenth level had a high cost of living. Hiding from Gecheana would not be easy. Nayrah knew she hated level ten with a passion, so it only made sense to live there. *"Skeans only dwell in darkness. It is where our powers are strongest,"* she could hear her say.

Another reason Gecheana hated the level was that many Argians occupied the walkways. The hardest part for Nayrah was traveling along the avenue and hearing all the friendly greetings. Smiling was something she did not like doing; in fact, it was painful. She settled into her new surroundings and prepared to restock her potions. This time, she would leave nothing to chance. Only she would buy every ingredient, using one of her many alter egos, and bring them to Reenah's new home, returning her confidence in her potions.

The thought of making a toxin, especially for Jadell, brought a smile to her face. *I will have my revenge one way or another.* As Nayrah fantasized about beating Jadell, she felt joy at seeing the look of defeat on her face; her smile unwittingly caught the attention of a young business owner on the avenue. Thinking she flirted with him, he introduced himself with his palm forward. She almost dismissed him but remembered her financial dilemma and returned his greeting.

As he approached, his pheromones reminded her of Olan; lately, everything reminded her of Olan. Nevertheless, she gave this newcomer the benefit of the doubt and studied him carefully. Within a few heartbeats, she decided that he would do, for now. Her timekeeper chimed, letting her know it was the middle of the Terrestrial Revolution. *I do have enough time for a brief distraction. I hope his other talents are equal to his bank account.*

"My name is Kren; I know everyone in this section of level ten. You must be new to our area."

"I just arrived. You may call me, Reenah."

Believing that Reenah was single, Kren lingered to see if she was interested in him. Since the offer to join houses was not forthcoming, he thought their association was over and started to leave until she made him a surprising offer.

"Would you like to accompany me to my home? I just purchased it during the earlier part of the Terrestrial Rotation."

Confused, Kren paused, not knowing how to react, "This is highly irregular."

"What is so irregular about two consenting Argians walking to an apartment?"

A few heartbeats later, he started to waver, so she looked directly into his eyes and, using the Night Lord's power, pushed away his inhibitions.

"I see no reason I cannot escort you home. It is, after all, a dangerous city," he answered, blinking.

"Lend me your arm."

Her unorthodox offer made him both hesitant and curious, and without his inhibitions, curiosity won. He absentmindedly extended his arm and noticed a strange feeling wash over him. It was as if something else had control of him. Although it made him doubt his decision to go with her, somehow, those questions disappeared like vapor. Reenah took hold of his arm and walked back to her apartment.

"What kind of business do you own?"

"I own a chain of furniture stores. Certainly, you have heard of Kren's Comfort Furniture."

"Ah…yes. I thought your name sounded familiar. I own several sofas made by your company."

"I am honored."

"You seem very young to own a business."

"I purchased it from my parents. They intend to move on to other things."

"How long will it take to pay them off?"

"I am making small payments, so it will take several yellow harvests before I own it outright; I can assure you that I make a good living with it."

"I am sure you do," she whispered, grinning.

Upon arriving, she opened the door and invited him inside. Again, he hesitated, but with a little push from the shadows, his new doubts vanished, and he stepped inside. He first saw one of his couches in the main entrance room.

"I recognize this model. It is very expens…. I mean, it is well made."

She smiled at his comment, "Please, have a seat. I will return shortly."

Left alone, Kren surveyed the foyer. Several pieces of furniture made by his company set about the room. Knowing they were high-end pieces, he was sure Reenah came from a wealthy family. He caressed the soft cushions with an open hand and felt a sense of pride. It had been a family practice to use a one thousand thread count of the first-rate woven yellow moss for the material.

As his hand moved toward the seat's leg, he saw polished *Moret,* a rare rock made up of recrystallized carbonate minerals, covering the floor. *Expensive, very expensive.* The green in the Moret complemented the walls. Most apartments had uncovered walls, except for a modest coating of paint. However, tan fiber from the extinct *Baobatin* plant covered the enclosure of Reenah's apartment. *Phew, I could have bought two homes for what she paid for those upgrades.*

She returned to the foyer, and as he stood out of respect, her appearance surprised him. She twirled to let him admire the sheer, white garment clinging to her light brown, elegant figure; he stood speechless. The dress was so snug that it appeared as if someone had painted its design onto her skin, which stopped just below her buttocks. As she spun, her wavy, long, black hair flowed through the air with a slight arc until she stopped to face him with a smile. Her red, painted lips made her teeth appear white as the snow on Akil's surface.

He stared into her deep brown eyes and felt himself losing control. They had a lure he had never felt before. She extended her hand, and without thinking, he took it; as their bodies drew close, she embraced him with a kiss.

A few moments later, he pulled back and inquired, "What about protocol? We must publicly join houses before consummating our relationship."

"Why should we endure a boring ceremony when we can have our pleasure now?"

"Because of tradition?"

He tried to say it with conviction, except his words seemed lame even to him.

She replied with pouted lips, "Well, all right, if you do not want to enjoy our time together, you can leave; just know that if I meet someone else before the ceremony, and he is better than you, I could change my mind."

"Perhaps you are right; we do not need to wait for a ceremony. It is only a formality."

"I was hoping you would agree."

Having fallen under her spell, he took her in his arms and kissed her with great enthusiasm, and as things heated up between them, he pushed her against the wall and pressed his body firmly against hers, kissing her lips, face, and neck. She took control, spun him around, and did the same, and her actions surprised him. It took strength to move someone of his size, and with her petite frame, he could not understand how she managed it.

They paused to stare into each other's eyes, and he wondered if she was playing games with him; the thought soon passed, replaced with his desire for her. He believed it was his turn to spin her around, but his aim missed, pushing her back into the small table near the wall.

"Ouch! You stupid *putok*!" she exclaimed, rubbing her back to ease the pain.

"I am deeply sorry, my love. Are you all right? I did not see the table there."

Realizing her mistake, she closed her eyes and let the anger drain away. *Elites do not show their rage as the commoners do. You must be careful, Nayrah, or you will make him suspicious.*

A few moments later, her smile returned, "It is all right. It was an accident."

Trying to salvage the rest of their encounter, she gently took his hand, guided him to the bedroom, shut the door behind her, and hinted, "Now, where were we?"

Chapter 24

Earth
The Regime - Washington, D.C. - Fort McNair
May 14, 2452

General Green paced in the facility's observation room. Engineers designed the building to receive agents back from dangerous missions. On the other side of the thick, viewing glass from where he stood, soldiers filled an empty pool with special foam made to cushion against severe impact. Thick, blast-resistant steel walls and ceilings would withstand most explosions. If an unwanted guest arrived, he ensured a strike team was ready to go into action. It had only been a few minutes since Jared made contact. He requested that the General wait before opening the portal. That made him nervous. Since Jared did not have time to elaborate, no one at the facility would know what to expect.

"Where is he now, Michael?" General Green demanded, with tension in his voice.

"The tracking device shows that Jared is still deep within the mountain. He's descending back to his prison cell."

General Green faced his portal technician, "You must be ready. The moment he gives us the secret code, I want a vortex opened in front of him."

"Yes, Sir, but if he's moving, it'll take more time. I must guess where he will be, not where he is."

"How about opening up a larger event horizon?"

"I planned to do that, Sir, but there's a cave-in risk."

General Green groaned, "Do whatever you think is right. Jared will do his part."

He turned back to face the foam pool, and his communication officer yelled, "General! Jared just gave us the code!"

"Lower the blast doors!" General Green yelled.

Thick, steel walls came down over the viewing glass. Once everyone was safely behind the protective barrier, General Green faced the portal tech and looked back at the monitor, showing the portal's status.

"What's taking so long?"

"I'm trying to calculate the best position to open it. It isn't easy. He's moving through a winding tunnel."

Precious seconds passed, and General Green was about to yell at the technician until hearing the portal machine activate. When the event horizon became visible, he saw a strange sight on the other side. The portal's diameter was about thirty feet, and most of it opened within solid rock. Since the portal tech had to guess, it put the tunnel at the bottom right of the vortex's opening.

"It looks like you only got half the tunnel!" General Green yelled.

"There's enough room for him to get through," the technician replied.

"Zoom in on the tunnel!"

The monitor showed two blurry images running awkwardly toward the event horizon. It was just as they thought. Jared was rescuing a prisoner.

"Hurry!" General Green yelled, knowing they could not hear him.

Everyone in the observation room anxiously awaited their arrival. They were five feet from the portal's opening, and it seemed like they would make it until something exploded behind them. The force of the blast pushed them through the portal at an accelerated rate. The explosion tossed their bodies through the air like rag dolls. They flew through the event horizon and headed straight into the foam, which swallowed them up, making a protective encasement. Behind them, large tongues of fire shot through, scorching the upper layer of foam.

"Shut it down! Now!" General Green yelled.

The technician disengaged the portal, and the fire disappeared. The rescue team rushed in, searched for a few seconds, found them, and pulled them out of the pool. Fearing for his brother's life, Michael ran downstairs and onto the patio surrounding the foam-filled pool. General Green briskly followed and saw Jared lying on the pavement with an oxygen mask on him. With his focus solely on his brother, Michael did not notice his companion lying nearby.

"Are you all right?" inquired Michael.

Jared removed the mask, "I'm fine."

He smiled.

"Why are you so happy?"

"Have you seen her yet?"

"Who?"

Jared nodded his head toward Chu Lian. Michael's eyes widened with surprise, and he ran to her side.

"Chu Lian! Are you all right?"

"Sorry, Sir. She's unconscious," one of the medics advised.

Michael faced Jared and mouthed the word, how?

"I think she should tell you."

Michael faced the medic and insisted, "I'm coming with her."

The medic looked to General Green, who nodded his approval, "It's all right; he can go."

The paramedics took Chu Lian through the Emergency Portal Transport to the hospital; the stretcher bucked, waking her. She opened her eyes, and everything seemed blurry. Her cot shook again, causing her head to roll over to her left side. At first, she thought it was a paramedic until he spoke.

"Don't worry, Chu Lian. You're going to be fine."

"Michael, is that you?" she whispered in a raspy voice.

Before he could reply, she fell unconscious again. Michael nervously waited outside while the doctors examined Jared and Chu Lian. An hour later, they wheeled them out of the examination room.

"How is she?" queried Michael.

"She's resting with a mild concussion. We'll keep her for 12 hours to ensure she is well."

"What about Jared?"

"He'll be fine. A few bruises, nothing serious."

Michael sighed loudly, "Thank you, doctor. Can I see them?"

"Sure, they're taking Jared to room 115. Chu Lian will be in room 116."

Michael left in a hurry to catch up with them and stopped at Jared's room first. Jared was sitting in bed, hastily eating his fourth plate of food.

"That is a nasty side effect," Michael admitted.

Jared stopped chewing, "It's only a problem if I can't find food."

"I've recently created some new time-released power bars for you. Have you had a chance to try them?"

Jared gulped down another bite, "Yeah, you went heavy on the power and light on taste."

Michael smiled, "Sorry, I'll have to work on that. How are you feeling?"

"I'm fine." Jared paused and looked at Michael. "Go and be there when she wakes up."

"All right, I will. And Jared, thanks for everything."

"It wasn't just me. She helped a lot."

Michael shook his brother's hand, stepped into the adjacent room, and found her resting peaceably. He saw a small bump on her forehead, just over her left eyebrow. There were also scratches on her arms and face. They might have died if the foam had not protected them from the flames. As he held her hand, waiting for her to wake up, memories of their time together came rushing back. He thought of the day they met, their first kiss, the day she broke up and made up with him, and the most painful of all, the day she left the Regime.

*****

"I don't understand why they're transferring you."

"The Chinese ambassador requested me specifically, and I'm still under the Regime contract, which means I must go," she zipped her suitcase closed.

"I've already applied for a visitor's pass to China. It'll be three months before it's approved, and we'll have a whole week together!"

"Except when you return, you'll have to restart the process, so it'll be another three months before we can see each other again."

"I don't mind waiting. You're worth it."

"I don't want to go. If I had a choice, I would stay with you; remember, the decision isn't mine to make," she answered solemnly.

"Can't you get the ambassador to cut through the red tape so I can see you on the weekends?"

"I already tried. There's nothing he can do." She paused before continuing. "I think you should start seeing other women after I leave."

"Don't say that! It means you're giving up!"

"I don't want to give up, but I have ten years left on my contract. The ambassador has said he plans to keep me there until I fulfill it."

"I don't care. We can video chat, and I can speak to General Saunders. I'm sure he could negotiate reoccurring admission so we can see each other every weekend."

She tried to smile, but her true feelings of remorse prevented her, "It doesn't seem likely. The Chinese government has a strict policy concerning Regime visitors."

"We can meet somewhere neutral like France, Germany, or Spain."

"You know I won't be able to do that. The ambassador will want me around in case he needs me, so going out of the country will be impossible."

"I don't care. We can make this work."

"Michael, stop thinking with your heart and start using your head. You know that long-distance relationships never last."

"You're not even going to try? You said you would love me forever. Obviously, you didn't mean it."

"Just because I want what's best for you doesn't mean I don't love you. I meant what I said. I *will* always love you, and if you think it's easy for me to tell you to see other women, you don't know me. I don't want you to waste the best years of your life waiting for my contract to expire. No matter how much it hurts, I want you to find someone who will make you happy."

"*You* don't know me. I would wait twice that long for you."

His eyes welled with tears as the emotions of that day returned. She pulled him close and, with tear-filled eyes, stared into his. Their farewell made him anxious. Although he tried to find a way, no scenario would keep them together. He wanted to be her hero but failed as usual.

"I want you to remember that you are the best thing that ever happened to me," she wept.

Even though her words made him feel loved, he could not bring himself to let her go without a fight. He tried to convince her to run away with him; nothing he said changed her mind. He stood on the International Transportation Station platform feeling emotionally exhausted and made one last attempt to keep their relationship intact.

"Promise me that you won't give up on us," he begged.

This time Chu Lian did not answer. Instead, she kissed him one last time, turned, and walked through the event horizon to China and out of his life forever, or so he had thought. It had been a little more than a year since he last saw her. He struggled with an emotional rollercoaster of abandonment, bitterness, fury, hate, regret, and even suspicion during that time, yet he never stopped loving her. He wondered if her return was temporary or permanent.

*****

"Hello?" a distant voice brought Michael out of his thoughts. Turning, he saw Nurse Hayes entering the room.

"I'm sorry. I was thinking about something," Michael noted.

"Not a problem; you can continue to think. I'm just here to check her vitals," she articulated.

"Has she regained consciousness during your visit?" Nurse Hayes asked.

"No, she's been sleeping. Is that normal?"

"Knowing what she's been through, yes. She's exhausted and has a mild concussion too. I will wake her every three hours to check on her."

Gently, she smacked the top of Chu Lian's hand and called her name, "Chu Lian. Chu Lian. Wake up, honey. Come on, dear."

A few moments later, Chu Lian opened her eyes, "Huh, where am I?"

"You are in a Regime hospital. How do you feel?"

"I have a headache."

"Here, take these. They should help with that."

The nurse held her head up while Chu Lian took the small paper cup holding pills, swallowed them, and drank the water.

"Can you tell me your name?"

Chu Lian looked at her quizzically.

"I need to ensure you know who you are, sweetie."

"I'm Wu Luli."

The nurse looked at Chu Lian's chart and, seeing a different name, faced Michael, "A friend, perhaps?"

"I have never heard that name before," Michael responded.

129

Hearing his voice, Chu Lian turned her head toward him, "Michael!"

She brought her other hand to set it on his, and he held hers.

Michael smiled, happy that she was excited to see him, "You need to rest."

"At least she recognizes you. I'll come back in a few hours and see how she's doing," the nurse remarked and left.

"I've missed you so much. You have no idea what I had to do to get back here."

Michael frowned, "I've sent messages every day; you never returned them. I was sure you moved on."

She shook her head, "No, I didn't. The government has been watching my communications, so responding would have put us both in danger. Believe me; there's so much I need to tell you."

"Rest for now. You can tell me when you're feeling better. You've suffered a minor concussion. You should refrain from making any decisions."

Chu Lian smiled, "I will tell you tomorrow."

"Don't worry. I'll be right here."

Knowing he was by her side, she fell into a deep sleep.

Chapter 25

Akil
Argi City
The 22,278[th] Terrestrial Rotation of the Second Summer

Pacing in the living room, Julie replayed her meeting with Urki. His warning about leaving Akil prevented her from having any peace. *Would I regret this decision for the rest of my life?* The situation was too much for her to absorb. She had read fantasy novels about telekinesis but doing these incredible things in the real world was unthinkable. The more she thought about it, the more it seemed like a hallucination.

To prove that it was her imagination, she reached out with her mind and tried to lift the kitchen table. As it rose in the air, she began to question her sanity. *How am I doing this, or am I doing this?* She set the table back down and commanded the three pillows on the couch to float. As they levitated, she exhaled nervously and made them move in a circle around her.

There was a knock on the door. The noise distracted her, causing the pillows to fall. With a thought, she made them fly across the room, back onto the sofa, and into their respective places. The sweet smell of spearmint assaulted her senses when she opened the door. She took a deep breath of the pleasant fragrance.

"Zorion, what are you doing here?"

"I hope I am not disturbing you."

"No, please, come in."

He faced Broll, signaling him to stay outside, and stepped into Julie's apartment. Zorion bit back a smile, hearing Broll mumble about making his job harder.

"I was hoping you would not mind reviewing the video we plan to send to your Supreme Commander. Your opinion would be most valuable."

"Sure, show me."

He retrieved a small, rectangular object inside his jacket and handed it to her. It looked about ten inches long, six inches wide, and about one-eighth inch thick.

"Press the play icon. I hope it resembles what your applications use back on Earth."

"Yes, it's close enough."

Gently, she pressed the play icon; a picture of Earth appeared on the screen, and the view zoomed out to show the solar system, showing the whole Milky Way Galaxy. The image moved toward the left and stopped in orbit around Akil, and as its dying sun loomed behind it, she heard Kraeth's voice narrating.

"Earth: a planet full of life and possibilities, existing in the Milky Way Galaxy. Its inhabitants believe they are alone in the universe. However, another planet supports life on the other side of the Galaxy. We call it Akil. Unlike Earth, Akil is nearing the end of its life because its sun has grown cold."

The image focused on the plasma stream as Kraeth continued, "Every day, a nearby star drains valuable plasma from our sun."

Again, the depiction changed into an aerial view of the underground city, and the camera lens zoomed in for a close-up of a busy avenue.

"Beneath the ground, billions of citizens go about their lives, hoping our scientists will one day discover a suitable planet."

The view of the avenue faded to black, and Zorion's image appeared with him sitting behind his desk.

"Hello, Supreme Commander Porter. My name is Zorion. I am Argi's sovereign, one of five cities beneath Akil's surface. I oversee the scientists who daily search for a new planet we may call home. For thousands of Earthian years, Akilians have been looking for a world capable of supporting life. We have been unsuccessful until now. That planet, of course, is Earth. A few days ago, we discovered your world by accident.

"During that time, we sent one scout to your country, hoping he could somehow learn your language. He was successful. Now, I can speak to you in your native tongue. I appeal to your good nature and ask that you allow my people to temporarily live somewhere on Earth until we can find an uninhabited planet of our own. I would not ask this of you unless it was necessary. We are desperate. The fate of billions rests in your hands. I hope you will be gracious.

"We have advanced technology we are willing to offer in exchange for your hospitality. We are prepared to accept any terms you see fit for us. Along with the tablet you have, there is a cylinder. When you are ready to speak with us, press the blue button. It will send us a signal, and we will open the portal several feet from the cylinder's position. I will leave it up to you whether negotiations occur here or on your planet. We can only open a portal once every twenty-four hours because of the vast distance between our worlds. Therefore, the earliest we can respond is 9 AM, your time tomorrow. I hope to hear from you soon, and thank you in advance."

His image faded, and she faced him, nodding, "That looked and sounded good to me. How did you learn English so fast?"

"I had Kraeth help me memorize the brief statement. He confirmed that I pronounced the words properly. Do you think Supreme Commander Porter will believe me?"

"There is only one way to know for sure."

"Right," he answered, opening her front door. "It is time we send you home."

Before leaving, she ran to the kitchen to retrieve the sword he had given her, held it in her left hand, and hurried outside.

"Will we meet again soon?" queried Julie.

Shrugging, he explained, "I have no idea; it's up to your Supreme Commander. Even if he agrees, this will not be a quick process. It will take time to move billions of Akilians to Earth."

"Oh, I had not thought of that. If he says yes, you will be busy for some time."

"It will be a daunting task. Even if we start evacuating tomorrow, I do not know if we have enough time to save everyone. Our sun is depleting at a rapid pace."

They reached the Interstellar Transport Bay, and Zorion signaled Broll to stay outside. Ignoring his grumblings, Zorion led her to the waiting area adjoining the Transport Bay, where they were alone, so he felt safe to stare into her eyes. He tried to smile, but his disappointment surfaced.

"Don't look so sad," she tried to lighten the mood. "The moment you land on Earth, find me. I will be waiting for you."

"I will do just that; before you go, I want you to know that I am happy to have met you, even though it was brief."

The door to the Transport Bay opened, and Yanamai remarked, "We are ready to send her home."

"I guess this is it," Zorion lamented.

Like Zorion, Julie felt terrible about leaving because they might never see each other again, so she leaned in and kissed him. Yanamai looked away, feeling uncomfortable.

She cleared her throat and interrupted, "Shall I start the process, Sir?"

Zorion loved Yanamai like a daughter yet sometimes wished she was not so diligent about her duties.

"Yes, you may begin," he replied, pulling away from Julie.

Zorion held her hand as they walked into the Transport Bay, "Once the portal is open, you can go through. Stand here until the process is complete, so you can safely return to your parent's farm."

Yanamai started the procedure to open the portal. Julie licked her lips and could still taste spearmint. The floor began to vibrate as power surged into the capacitors. An image of Urki flashed in her mind, and the conversation they had earlier began to replay. *The High Lord has given you a great gift; you cannot run from the responsibility that goes with it.*

Running was what she wanted to do, what she had to do because staying on a dying planet terrified her. At the same time, she could not ignore her feelings for Zorion. The thought of leaving him to die bothered her. Based on their last conversation, they did not have enough time to get everyone to Earth, which meant he would die here trying to save his people. Yanamai's hand moved to a large blue button on her console. Time was running out. *What are you doing, Julie?*

"Wait! I want to stay!" Julie yelled.

The request surprised everyone in the room, including her.

"Yanamai, stop!" Zorion yelled.

"Sir, I cannot just shut it off. The power must go somewhere. We must open a portal, or it will burn up the capacitor and explode."

"How much time do we have?"

"About a hundred forty heartbeats, give or take."

He faced Julie, "I would like nothing more than for you to stay, but we must get the video to your Supreme Commander."

"I have an idea. Does this thing record?" she queried, holding up the tablet he gave her.

"Yes."

"Good. Now, is it possible for Yanamai to change the location of where the portal opens?"

He faced Yanamai, "Can you do it?"

"It depends. Where do you want to open it?" Yanamai responded.

"At my brother's home. He lives just outside the Fort McNair base."

Yanamai brought up a map created during her preliminary search of Earth.

"Can you pinpoint the location?"

Julie saw an aerial view of the Regime and frowned. There were no lines to divide the states, which did not make it easy. She pointed to the general area with her finger, and Yanamai magnified it. Again, she directed her to another region. They repeated the process until they found Alex's home.

"There, can you open the portal in his backyard?" Julie asked.

"Yes, if the capacitor does not explode," Yanamai advised.

Yanamai and Tadra nimbly moved their fingers over the control panel, calculating the unexpected change for the portal landing. Yanamai computed most of the figures in her head. Meanwhile, Zorion showed Julie how to use the tablet's record function until alarms sounded, grabbing Zorion's and Julie's attention.

"How much time?" Zorion yelled over the alarm.

Yanamai tapped an icon, shutting down the siren, "Not much. I am going as fast as I can. If we are off by even a fraction, we could kill someone or open the portal in the planet's core."

The room shook violently as the power built inside the capacitor.

"Just use the original coordinate; I do not want to risk destroying our only way off this planet!" Zorion yelled over the rumbling noise.

"I can do this! We are almost there!" Yanamai yelled a reply.

Other alarms sounded, alerting her that the capacitor was in danger of exploding. Yanamai selected another icon to shut down all current warnings and any future ones and continued to recalculate their new destination. Just as she finished her calculations, Tadra gave her confirmation and the blue light, declaring everything was a go, so Yanamai raised her hand and slammed the execute button.

Due to the delay, an increased amount of energy moved through the portal machine. The moment the event horizon appeared, it came with a loud clap of thunder, shaking the city to its lowest level. Yanamai wiped the sweat off her brow.

"Please, do not do this again."

Feeling guilty for having caused so much trouble, Julie apologized to everyone in the room.

Before leaving, she faced Zorion, "Leave the portal open. I will be right back."

Zorion watched her step through the event horizon with a sense of excitement, knowing that she would return. Julie landed in Alex's backyard and noticed the smell of fresh-cut grass. She wondered why the aroma was so intense, mainly because Alex had not mowed his lawn in a couple of days. She pushed aside the distraction, retrieved his key underneath a potted plant, and unlocked his back door.

She set the tablet on the table, recorded a message, and set it to repeat, so he would hear it upon arriving home. Satisfied, he would find it; she looked at the time. It was a few minutes before 9 AM. Every day, just like clockwork, Alex stopped by his home for lunch and to feed his pets. *Ok, he should be here in about three hours. Alex will walk in, hear my voice, and come to the kitchen to find me. He'll see the tablet, listen to my message, and contact General Saunders, who'll contact Supreme Commander Porter. If things go right, they should have it on his desk no later than 1 PM today.*

Before leaving, she took the liberty of contacting her employer. She felt obligated to let him know that she would not return for an undetermined amount of time. Also, she left a video message for her parents, who would return home in a couple of days. Knowing that the androids would take care of the farm until they returned, she was not apprehensive about abandoning her promise to farm-sit, so she closed the door, locked it, and placed the key back into its hiding place.

She saw the vortex was still open in Alex's backyard. On the other side, Zorion anxiously awaited her return. Goosebumps moved down her arm. *I hope you're making the right decision, Julie.* On Earth's side, she inhaled deeply one more time and committed the smell of fresh-cut grass to memory. She stepped through the event horizon and landed on the alien world, Akil.

Chapter 26

Special Agent Reed sat behind his desk, reviewing Barnes' dossier. It was not surprising to learn that he was thirty years old and single. His dad passed, but his mother was still alive. The only other family member was a brother who lived with his mother in the Atlanta area. Barnes' last known address is a one-bedroom apartment in Avalon Gardens, found within Georgia's Inner Circle. That could only mean one thing; he was a natural-born Regime citizen.

He graduated high school at fifteen, typical for Regime students, and took several college courses in computer science. Reed saw a virus that Barnes used against Sanya Electronix a few years ago. Although he would not admit it to his peers, the skill it took to create one of these applications was admirable. He just did not like how the designers used it. These viruses were super complex, leaving him with only one conclusion. Someone trained in computer science must have developed it.

Even without a criminal background, he still fit the profile, which placed him at the top of his suspect list. Reed reviewed Barnes's financial records, revealing that he owed thousands of Regime Talons. Most went to casinos, making it clear that Barnes had a gambling problem. Being in debt, having a background in computer science, and access to corporate funds made Barnes a desirable target for any enemy company. Before reading another page, his video com beeped. Agent Ross's face showed up on his monitor.

"What do you have for me?" Reed asked.

"I arrived at Barnes's apartment and found a body lying on the floor, so I called the local Police Department. Forensics and the medical examiner are here too."

"I'll be there in a minute."

Reed disconnected, stood, and headed for the TBI Interstate Transportation Station, where he swiped his identification card, entered, and handed the technician his destination data stick. The technician downloaded the information and moved his hands across the control panel with speed and precision. Within seconds, a portal opened. On the other side, a secure room waited for him. The protocol demanded that every building have a Safe Emergency Transport Room (SETR). Reed thanked the technician for his help and walked through the event horizon.

Chapter 27

Earth
The Regime - Georgia - Atlanta - Avalon Gardens Apartment Complex
May 14, 2452

Stepping out of the SETR, Special Agent Reed headed straight for the elevator. Moments later, one arrived, and he selected the sixth floor. He entered Barnes's apartment and saw the body lying on the floor, just as Agent Ross had described.

"Ah, that did not take long," Ross commented, noticing his boss had entered the room.

"Have you identified the body?"

"Not yet; I wanted to wait for you."

Kneeling, Reed took a closer look at the victim lying face down in a pool of blood. He could tell it was a man wearing black trousers, a white shirt, and a sports coat.

"Ok, roll him over," Reed instructed the medical examiner.

Special Agent Reed saw the deceased's face and frowned, "It's not Barnes."

Agent Ross walked over, checked his pockets, and removed a badge.

"He's a Detective with the Atlanta PD, Immigration District," Ross explained.

"Check his fingerprint to confirm his ID."

Agent Ross received confirmation in only fifteen seconds, "Yep, Detective Frank Mitchell."

He checked his holster and gun.

"He didn't fire it," Agent Ross added.

"How long has he been dead?" Agent Reed inquired, looking at the medical examiner.

"Based on his current body temperature, I would say he died last night between 11 PM and 1 AM."

"That means Barnes has about a fourteen-hour head start, so he could be anywhere in the world by now," Agent Ross speculated. "Check all transportation records in the area. If he used his transport card, we would know which direction he went," Special Agent Reed instructed Agent Ross.

He looked at the dead detective and whispered, "Now, what was an Immigration Detective doing in the Inner Circle?"

"I'll check the transportation records and explore what cases the detective was working on," Agent Ross suggested.

"Excellent idea; maybe Barnes participated in other crimes that led the detective here," Special Agent Reed remarked, turning toward the Forensic Officer, "What do you think happened here?"

"First, it's important to note that no one has ransacked the room. Someone shattered a vase near the detective's body, and at the same time, a full glass of water sits on the coffee table. Other than normal living clutter, everything else is in its place."

"Where was the vase originally?" queried Special Agent Reed.

"In his bedroom, there's a picture of two people sitting on the couch. I can only guess it's Barnes and his mother. The picture shows that the vase was sitting on the coffee table unless he moved it after he took the photo."

"Which means Barnes must have thrown it at the detective," Special Agent Reed deduced.

He looked at the medical examiner and quizzed, "Does he have a head wound?"

The medical examiner checked, "There appears to be a small bump on his forehead. It must have happened moments before he died because I don't see any bruising. I also pulled a slug out of the wall above the sofa. It is a .38 caliber. The angle of entry supports the detective shot from the floor. There's also blood spatter on the coffee table and surrounding area," the Forensic Officer added.

"So, the detective is interviewing Barnes. He asked questions that made Barnes think he suspected him of a crime. Barnes throws the vase before the detective can arrest him, hitting him in the head and knocking him down. The detective is lying on his side, unable to reach his sidearm, so he grabs his ankle gun. He shoots Barnes, hitting him somewhere in his upper body, causing a through and through. The bullet doesn't stop him; Barnes reaches him, and they struggle. During the fight, the detective tries to get on his feet; Barnes overpowers him because he's suffering the effects of the head injury.

Barnes wrestles the gun from him, shoots him, and the detective falls face forward, dead," Reed concluded.

"Sounds about right to me," Agent Ross concurred.

"I still need to verify the blood spatter, but so far, the evidence supports your theory. Also, it would help if we could find the murder weapon," the Forensics officer suggested.

Special Agent Reed faced Agent Ross, "Put out an all-points bulletin. Consider Barnes armed and dangerous, and make sure you notify all Regime hospitals; he might decide to get medical help."

Agent Ross left to talk to the local PD as Special Agent Reed inspected the small apartment rooms.

"What's wrong?" puzzled Agent Ross.

"I don't see any evidence that Barnes was about to flee. He had the money and could have left for any warm, sunny destination, so why hang around here in this small, dingy apartment?"

"What if he had one more score he wanted to collect before leaving, and the detective stopped him?"

"We'll know more once you find out what cases he worked on."

Special Agent Reed started to leave, stopped at the door, and turned around, "Did he leave behind a computer?"

Agent Ross looked at his inventory, "We haven't found one."

"Did he leave anything behind to indicate where he might have gone?"

"No, nothing. The place is clean."

"His dossier indicated he has a mother and brother in Atlanta. I want you to interview them personally. Leave officers stationed outside their homes until we find Barnes."

Nodding, Agent Ross entered the orders into his datapad.

"One more thing," Special Agent Reed stated, "I want our TBI agents conducting the interviews with the tenants, just in case."

"Understood," Agent Ross acknowledged.

"I'll be in my office. Contact me the moment you have something."

Chapter 28

Akil
Argi City
The 22,278[th] Terrestrial Rotation of the Second Summer

Olan stepped out onto the avenue, only a few levels up from the bottom of the city. His tracking device showed that the spy he tagged was down here. Over time, these abandoned levels became the home of Akil's poor. The city donated power, food, and water. Still, their passageways were always dim due to the lack of funds. There were never enough sovereign cubes to keep these levels fully functional. Zorion had to divert much of the city's capital to keep the other levels running smoothly because of the crisis. That way, the government could continue to function and support the Science Departments.

He walked the dingy corridor and passed many families standing in line for their daily ration of food and water. It was a pitiful sight. He dressed the part of an unemployed maintenance worker and designed everything (clothes, unkempt hair, and unshaven face) to allow him free access anywhere on the level without suspicion.

Olan casually looked at his timekeeper and saw that Igon (or so he believed) was nearby. Walking by a fountain, he saw someone lurking in the shadows. *That must be him.* Having found his mark, he moved on until finding a place to enter the secret tunnels. Satisfied that no one was looking, he disappeared into the passageway and returned to where Igon hid. Near the opening, he heard voices, moved to the fissure, and listened carefully to what they were saying.

"What do you want me to do?"

"You must dispose of him. Someone on Zorion's team captured my agent."

"Do not worry. I will ensure no one will find him."

"Thank you, my friend. I will reward your loyalty."

Before they dispersed, Olan noticed that the agent in charge did not look like Igon, but that did not deter him. After separating, Olan did not follow the one he thought was Igon but pursued the other agent instead. It was clear that Igon ordered a murder, and Olan felt that the real Molo was his victim. It made sense. Now that his mission had failed, he had to remove all witnesses, including Shafe.

If it were his operation, he would kill Shafe while impersonating Molo, ensuring he received the blame for the assault on Zorion's life, which would sever any link to Elzer. Olan could not allow that to happen, so he spun around, ran through the hidden tunnels, and stepped out at the nearest opening. Once on the avenue, the other agent was about fifty paces ahead.

Olan tailed him for a time and concluded that his target was a professional. The other regularly took an interest in his surroundings and found many creative ways of looking behind to ensure no one followed him. Knowing for sure the spy had experience, Olan focused on details most would ignore: how he walked, how he swung his arms, how often he turned to look behind him within seventy heartbeats. All these subtle *tells* would help him find the enemy agent if he changed his appearance and clothes.

The accomplice reached the elevator, and Olan stepped into a food line, pretending to wait for a meal. The collaborator scanned the area until satisfied no one had followed him and stepped onto the elevator. Olan did not enter the cab with him because the enemy agent was alone.

The doors closed, and Olan raced to summon a car and watched the numbers go up on the other elevator. It stopped at the four hundredth level. His car arrived, he jumped on and selected the same stop. As it climbed upwards, he hoped the other agent got off and did not decide to continue upward as an evasive tactic. Along the way, he shed his ragged clothes. Underneath was another layer of modest attire for just such an emergency. Olan was alone, allowing him to change his physical appearance too. Before the elevator stopped, he combed his air differently to ensure the accomplice would not recognize him.

The doors opened, and he merged into the crowd. *Now, where are you?* It was lunchtime, and the boulevard was busy; soon, the crowd would thin. There were only two choices for him: go left or right. He decided to turn right. He walked briskly and scanned everyone on the avenue, paying attention to how they moved. A few hundred heartbeats later, he decided to step onto a balcony to get a better view. It was frustrating not knowing if the other agent was on this level. There were so many variables in play that he had little hope of finding him.

Trying to keep his cover, he asked a nearby Argian for directions. She pointed toward the east end of the avenue, and he used the opportunity to survey the crowd. Just as she finished speaking, he spotted the enemy agent standing in the doorway of a restaurant. He thanked her for the help and returned to the boulevard to resume his pursuit. On his way, he saw the collaborator step onto the avenue and pause briefly. Again, he was ensuring no one had followed him. The enemy agent turned in his direction, unwittingly allowing Olan to see his face. He had changed his clothes yet kept his physical appearance the same.

Reaching the thoroughfare, Olan hesitated. The agent could have made a simple mistake or done it on purpose, ensuring Olan would follow him into a trap; it was a chance he had to take. The accomplice moved down the avenue, and Olan followed him despite the risk. During the chase, Olan repeatedly stopped, pretending to window shop. At least it was enough to fool his target. A few moments later, the collaborator finally reached his destination. The sign above said *Zuine Cleaners*.

Olan put the pieces together and smiled to himself. *That is how they moved Molo's body. They used a laundry basket.* He set up a position across the street and used special magnifying lenses to watch the enemy agent inside, who sat at the service counter and ate his lunch. Although it did seem like the other agent was not in much of a hurry to carry out his orders, Olan was unsure if he was baiting him to enter, so instead of rushing in, he decided to wait a little longer.

Customers entered and left for a few hundred heartbeats to pick up or leave their clothes. Later, the business slowed down, and the accomplice locked up and changed the sign over the front door from 'open' to 'closed.' Moments later, he disappeared into the back. Taking his cue, Olan walked to the door, picked the lock, opened it just enough to get his hand inside, and disarmed the customer chime that would surely give him away.

He disconnected the bell, opened the door farther, walked in, quietly closed it behind him, and locked it. Olan surveyed the room and saw the light illuminating from a door in the back. He crept to it, heard a voice, and put his ear against the door to listen.

"If you hold still, I promise to make this as painless as possible. If you struggle, it will only make it worse."

The words sounded familiar to him. It was a phrase used whenever he had to end a life. Armed only with his dagger, Olan kicked the door open. The loud and unexpected intrusion got the enemy agent's attention, who already had his sword drawn and held it over Molo's neck.

Before he could swing, Olan threw his dagger at him. It plunged into his wrist, causing him to drop the sword. The collaborator reached down to recover his blade, but Olan leaped at him, landing a solid kick to his ribs.

The enemy agent fell backward with a grunt and onto the floor with the wind knocked out of him. As he landed, the dagger in his wrist dislodged and slid underneath a cabinet out of sight. Olan heard bones breaking, which gave him the advantage. The other agent recovered enough to stand. They wrestled, punched, dodged, and kicked each other until the accomplice unexpectedly sent Olan into the wall headfirst.

The collaborator ran to retrieve his sword, and with it firmly back in his hands, he held it high above his head and approached Olan with one purpose. He swung down, trying to cut Olan from the collar bone to his groin. Olan recovered just in time. Grabbing the enemy agent's wrist with both hands, he turned and twisted until wrestling the sword out of his grasp. With a hard thrust, Olan drove the blade into his opponent's belly.

The other fell to his knees and, with both hands, held onto the blade lodged in his stomach. Using his foot to push the enemy agent away, Olan pulled the sword from his stomach and pierced his heart to immobilize him. With his counterpart subdued, Olan untied Molo, and they tied the spy to the chair where Molo once sat.

"I owe you my life," Molo stated.

"Yes, you do."

"Tell me your name so that I may honor you."

"You do not need to know my name because *I* did not save you."

Not knowing how to respond, Molo looked at him quizzically.

"Just watch him. I must contact someone," Olan added. Before leaving, he turned around and continued, "Be sure he does not escape during my absence."

Olan left to find the business's communication station, contacted Dolas and told him to help. A few thousand heartbeats later, he arrived at the store, and seeing the prisoner's condition made it evident that Olan had already started interrogating him.

"What did he tell you?" Dolas asked.

"Not much," Olan paused and glanced at his prisoner, who slumped forward with blood dripping from his mouth, turning, he faced Dolas, "I did get him to tell me his name and admit that he is from Vlor City."

"Is he?" Dolas started to ask.

Olan shook his head, "Not here."

He faced Molo, "Watch him."

Olan shut the door behind him and whispered, "He is not Igon."

"If he is not your counterpart, who is he?"

"His name is Qual. He is one of Igon's agents stationed in Argi."

"How did you find him?"

"I overheard a conversation he had with the Akilian, I believe, is Igon. Igon gave him orders to dispose of someone. I figured it had to be Molo, so I followed him, and now you have something to give Zorion, which will hopefully remove any suspicions he has of you."

"You should be taking credit for this, not me; I want Zorion to reinstate you."

"No, I can never return to my former position. Besides, you will need this victory to gain Zorion's favor and, hopefully, Broll's," Olan explained.

"Agreed. I am tired of dodging Broll's guards every time we meet."

Olan rubbed his chin, thinking, "Before you tell Zorion about Qual, take him to a safe house."

"Why?"

"I do not want Igon to discover that we captured him; I will take on Qual's likeness for a stretch."

"What about Molo?"

"He owes me his life, so I will have him guard Qual until we are ready to bring him in."

"What do you plan to do?"

"I believe Qual oversees a team located in Argi. I will take them all down."

"Why not interrogate him a little longer? I am sure he will give us the information we need."

"I want you to finish his interrogation while I search his apartment."

"I see. We work it from both ends."

"Correct."

"Do you think he would keep their names in his apartment?"

"I assembled similar teams in other cities, and they do not know each other. That way, if authorities catch one, it does not compromise the whole group. He has been here at least several yellow harvests, by the looks of things. Assuming Igon works as we do, they would not contact each other unless prompted by their superior. I think this is the first time Igon contacted him, which means he should have their names and activation codes listed somewhere in his home. That way, he would not forget them.”

"It makes sense, but what if he does not have them written down? What if he memorized them, and I cannot get the information out of him in time?”

"If we cannot find anything by the following Terrestrial Revolution, bring him and Molo in with you and make it official. After that, I will resume my pursuit of Igon. Using my wrist communicator, I should be able to track and bring him in.”

"All right, I will hide them until I hear from you. If Qual gives up any information, I will contact you.”

With sincere appreciation, Olan put his hand on Dolas's shoulder, "Be safe, my friend.”

They returned to the room, where Molo and Qual waited.

Olan faced Molo, "Before you return home, I want you to go with Dolas and do what he says.”

"Does this mean I cannot go home this Terrestrial Rotation?” Molo inquired.

"Not just yet. It is essential to delay your reappearance.”

With a frown, Molo nodded.

"Very good,” Olan pointed to Dolas and spoke to Molo, "Just one more thing, if anyone asks, including Zorion, he is the one who saved you, not me. Is that understood?”

"If that is what you want,” Molo replied.

"It is. Now get this *putok* out of here.”

Chapter 29

Earth
The Regime - Washington, D.C. - Fort McNair - Mars Outreach Facility
May 14, 2452

Having spent the past few days repairing the "cone" to his portal machine, Alex was in his lab going through the final inspection in preparation for another attempt to reach Mars. During his last experiment, the eight cumbersome, superconducting cables he used to send the high voltage needed to run the machine melted. Engineers used heavy equipment to unhook the old wires and attach new ones, taking a toll on his budget for the year. As they removed the last burned-out cable, Alex entered the details into his tablet, making General Saunders aware of their progress. Just as he finished putting in the last words, Vincent walked in.

"Are you ready?"

"This is a waste of time, Vincent. I've said it before; it's not likely we'll find anything because it's been three days. Even if we did find a trace, the signal would be weak, so I can't give you an exact location."

"I only need you to point me in the right direction; besides, Supreme Commander Porter told me to contact you," Vincent responded.

Alex sighed, "Just one more time."

"One more time. If we don't find it today, I'll give Supreme Commander Porter my final report, telling him I failed to locate Dragon."

"Fine, I'll meet you at the International Transportation Station; before we leave, I need to go home and pack my gear and feed my pets."

"Ok, meet you there in an hour."

Alex notified his team that he had to leave early and headed home. Once inside, he heard a familiar voice.

"Julie. Is that you?"

He went from room to room and ended up in the kitchen, where he found a strange-looking tablet on the table with her voice speaking out of it. He moved in front of the display and saw a recording of his sister standing in his kitchen. It reached the end of the message, and it cued itself back to the beginning.

"Alex, you're not going to believe this; I have been on another planet for the past twenty-four hours!" she exclaimed. "I know it sounds crazy, but it's true! I'm going back, which is why I can't be here to tell you myself. Don't worry; we'll meet again soon, I'm sure." Her demeanor changed into a severe frown. "Their sun is dying, and they need our help. I trust you'll give this tablet and the cylinder lying on the table to General Saunders when the message finishes. Please hurry!"

She continued, giving him directions on accessing Zorion's plea to Supreme Commander Porter. It ended and started to replay again. He followed her instructions, played the other message, and ran to see General Saunders.

Chapter 30

Akil
Argi City
The 22,278[th] Terrestrial Rotation of the Second Summer

Julie returned from Earth, and Zorion assigned sentries to protect and escort her to *her* apartment. Although she asked him to join her, Zorion regretfully declined because of work; he did ask to join her for supper, which Julie gladly accepted. Soon, the guards left her alone at the kitchen table, wondering if it was the right decision.

To prevent feelings of anxiety about staying from troubling her, she remembered that Earth was only twenty-four hours away. That thought settled her nerves, freeing her mind to think of other things. She looked at the side door, thought of Urki, and decided to see him again. As her hand reached the side door latch, someone knocked at the front door; she found a young woman, about her age, fidgeting with an earpiece.

"Hello," the woman said. "Can you understand me?"

"Yes, I understand. My earpiece is working fine," Julie confirmed.

The woman held her hand out palm forward. Julie did not respond correctly, so she took Julie's hand and moved it to touch her palm in the same manner.

"That is how Akilians greet one another."

"Oh, I didn't know."

"That is why I am here. My name is Tionah. May I come in?"

"Oh, yes, of course." Julie closed the door behind her. "What can I do for you?"

"I am here to help you," Tionah explained.

Julie looked at her quizzically, "What do you mean?"

"I am your domestic."

"Domestic?"

"I believe Earthians refer to my position as a personal assistant. I am here to ensure you get anything you need or want."

"Oh, I don't need a domestic. I can take care of myself."

"On Earth, you could, but here, you are a stranger, so Zorion told me that for now, he must keep you restricted to this floor, which means if you need or want something, I must get it for you."

Julie thought a moment and asked, "Can you tell me when someone will bring my meals?"

"We will bring your meals at the time you tell me."

"What time do you…scratch that…what time does Zorion usually eat Supper?"

Tionah's fingers danced over what Julie thought resembled a tablet back on Earth, except that it was transparent glass with images.

Tionah found the information and faced Julie, "Zorion usually eats his supper about 8 PM your time on Earth, assuming my conversion table is correct."

"All right, please have food for both of us delivered here at that time. He plans to join me."

Tionah entered the information into her tablet.

"Would you like lunch and snack?"

"I guess 12 PM and 4 PM."

"Very well. What else can I get you?" queried Tionah.

Julie thought a moment. "Nothing."

Tionah looked at her quizzically.

"What's wrong?" Julie questioned.

"Nothing!" Tionah responded, surprised.

"Yeah, I'm just going to sit around and wait for Zorion."

"Since you plan to have supper with the sovereign of our city, may I suggest that you order a formal gown?"

Julie looked in the mirror. She had cleaned her jeans and T-shirt after returning from the cave. Still, she would need better clothes for entertaining a dignitary.

"I think you're right. I want to look nice for him."

"Excellent. I have taken the liberty of copying some pictures Kraeth brought back with him from Earth."

Tionah's fingers gracefully moved over the glass, and in just a few moments, the large viewing screen in her living room came to life with pictures of models wearing different outfits.

"Just tell me if you see something you like," Tionah smiled.

Julie watched Tionah scroll through a few images and inquired, "These are all beautiful, but they are from Earth, so how can you get them?"

"Our tailors can create any of these garments from the pictures."

"What do you think Zorion would like?"

"I think you should choose what you feel most comfortable wearing. I am sure Zorion will like it if *you* are wearing it."

Julie blushed, wondering, "It is that obvious?"

Tionah only smiled and did not answer. "How about this one?" Tionah quizzed, changing the subject.

Turning to the monitor, Julie saw a woman wearing a beige evening gown. The dress's top fit snugly against the model's figure and was see-through, except for the areas covering the breasts. The pleated material began at the lower part of the model's hips and almost touched the floor. Also, there was a slit on the right leg from her upper thigh to her feet.

"It looks good on her, except she's tall. I'm unsure how it will look on me," Julie frowned.

"That will not be a problem."

Tionah removed something from within her bag resembling a laser pen that scanned Julie from head to foot all the way around.

"I have just sent your holographic measurements and a picture of the dress to our best tailor. You should have it in a few hours."

"Wow! Thank you!"

"Do not thank me; you paid for it."

Julie looked at her quizzically, "How? I don't have any money."

"Yes, you do. Zorion opened a bank account in your name. You have enough Sovereign Cubes to buy anything you want or need. All you have to do is let me know."

"Sovereign Cubes?"

"It is our currency."

"I didn't realize he did that for me."

Tionah smiled, "He favors you."

Again, Julie blushed.

Tionah added, "If you like how the dress fits, perhaps you would let me have the tailor create a full wardrobe. If you plan to stay, you will need a change of clothes."

Julie rubbed her chin in thought, "You're right," she paused to look at the side door. "I will also need workout clothes; only make a couple of sets because I do not know how long I will be here."

Tionah frowned, "I thought your stay was permanent?"

"I'm taking it one day at a time."

"I am sure that once you get used to our hospitality, you will never want to leave."

Again, Julie unconsciously looked at the side door.

"I hope you're right," she stated absentmindedly.

"Is there something wrong?" queried Tionah.

Julie faced Tionah and smiled politely, "No, everything is just peachy."

"Peachy? I am sorry. My translator indicated you said everything is like fruit from your homeworld."

"I'm sorry. I meant everything is fine."

"Ah, I see. If you ever need someone to talk to, please feel free to let me know."

"I'm a private person."

"I'm your domestic. You can tell me anything, and I will never divulge it to anyone."

"Even Zorion?"

"Yes, even Zorion. I have taken the oath of a domestic. If I break my vow, the law demands my execution."

"What? That's barbaric!"

"I have read about some cultures in your world that are more primitive. For example, some governments on your planet oppress and kill their citizens for pleasure or to keep control. I realize our way of life may seem strange to you, but I can assure you that your world seems just as alien to me. There are many reasons someone in my position takes the pledge, and the most important one is 'trust' because a domestic will see and hear private and intimate moments in an employer's home. Think what would happen if I revealed personal details of Zorion's life to our Information League."

"I see your point. By the way, did you say that I'm your employer?"

"Yes, you are. Your Sovereign Cubes pay for my services, not Zorion's. It is one of the reasons why he set up the account in your name. This way, you have complete privacy and a friend to talk to."

"Friend, huh, may I ask you a personal question?"

"You may ask me anything."

"Did someone force you to become a domestic?"

"No, I chose to become one."

"Why?"

"First, the number of Sovereign Cubes I receive gives me a good living. When you see my bill, you will understand," she smiled playfully. "Also, I am good at it because I am organized. I can get things done, and I want a job with variety."

"How did you get assigned to me?"

"I used to be in Thea's service. She used to be Zorion's wife, as you Earthians say."

Julie nodded knowingly, "He told me he had three children and was separated."

"Good, you are already aware of his social status."

Again, Julie blushed.

"His separation finalized a few days ago," Tionah added.

"Is that when Thea fired you?"

"Thea did not dismiss me; Zorion did. I understood because she had three domestics."

"Three?"

"Yes, and she kept all of us very busy."

"She sounds spoiled."

Tionah smiled, "During my search for a new employer, I interviewed several different families before Zorion contacted me. Since I already had a level five clearance, he said I would be perfect for the job."

"I'm surprised you accepted."

"I must admit, knowing you were from another planet, I was expecting something with twenty appendages and eight eyes."

Julie snickered, "I hope I'm not a disappointment."

"No, I was relieved to find out that you look Akilian. That reminds me, we have many pictures of clothes to review. I will need the information to put together your wardrobe. Do you mind if we start?"

"Of course not. Put them on the screen."

Julie spent an hour going through a video catalog with her. Afterward, Tionah left to ensure the tailor did not have any questions. Before Julie could leave to see Urki, her lunch arrived, and the caterers left her alone to eat her bland meal of assorted mosses.

Chapter 31

Earth
The Regime - Washington, D.C. - Capitol Building
May 14, 2452

Supreme Commander Porter sat at his desk, mulling over the day's vault file. It only had five words written: "You will make new friends." Sometimes it felt like he was opening fortune cookies instead of daily briefings; since the Founder wrote it on red paper, it was a pivotal day in the Regime's history. Therefore, he had to follow the instruction; to the letter. The only problem was that Porter did not know who these new friends could be. At times like this, he wished the vault did not exist because it only made his job harder. Jay sipped his coffee, contemplating the short statement until Brandy Miller paged him on his intercom.

"General Saunders and Alex Sutton are here to see you. They say it's urgent."

Supreme Commander Porter groaned, "Very well, send them in."

They stopped in front of his desk, and he noticed they both looked excited about something.

"You need to see this, Sir," General Saunders handed him the tablet.

Porter watched both videos, looked at Alex, and asked, "Are you sure this is authentic?"

"I have no reason to doubt that's Julie in the first video."

"Do you think she is playing a trick on you?"

"I don't think it's a trick. If it is, she would not involve you or the General; of that, I'm sure."

Supreme Commander Porter sat in contemplation for a spell. *Now I know where my new friends originate.*

"Sir, you know what this means, don't you?" Alex quizzed.

Supreme Commander Porter frowned, "What?"

"If these aliens can open a portal beyond their solar system, they will advance our vortex technology by hundreds of years! I never thought I would live to see the day we would make it to another solar system!"

"Yes, there are endless possibilities with that kind of technology, except there are always risks, Alex. You heard what he's asking for."

"Yeah, so…they need a place to stay for a brief time. What's wrong with that?"

"How about a passive invasion for starters? Even if they do plan to leave, where do we put them? We're talking about billions of beings. You can't just transport them over without a support system. They would all starve and die in a matter of days."

"What about the Sahara Desert?" General Saunders interrupted.

"It's certainly big enough, but we only have a few buildings finished, not nearly enough for what they need."

"Wait, did he say the Sahara Desert?" puzzled Alex.

"What the General is referring to is a purchase the Regime made a few years ago. I bought the Sahara Desert from the countries that once occupied it. It was briefly in the news because there was not much of a story. I bought the land to create a vast solar farm. We are manufacturing high-producing solar panels to stretch out over the desert and a few nuclear power plants. I agreed to give free transport to the countries who agreed to give up the land they weren't using, so we both got what we wanted."

"Wow! That would create a great deal of energy!" Alex exclaimed.

"You use a lot to open those portals to Mars, Mr. Sutton; I had to figure out a way to fill the demand."

"I think it would be worth the trade for them to stay here. That technology is worth every grain of sand," General Saunders added.

Supreme Commander Porter glanced at the manila folder containing the vault's red paper. *You will make new friends*, a voice whispered in his mind.

"I'm inclined to agree. I will send a representative tomorrow at the appointed time with a contract."

He faced General Saunders, "If everything goes well, perhaps you will be the head of our new science division."

"Really? What would we call it?" General Saunders questioned.

"Deep Space Exploration and Acquisitions."

"Sounds like I'm up for a promotion," General Saunders mused.

"Don't get too far ahead of yourself, General. First, we must see if our new alien friends will honor their word and agree to all my terms."

Chapter 32

Akil
Argi City
The 22,278[th] Terrestrial Rotation of the Second Summer

Posing as Qual, Olan reopened the cleaning store, finished the rest of his work cycle, locked up, and changed the sign over the front door from 'open' to 'closed,' allowing him to search Qual's home freely. Starting in his bedroom, he rummaged through the whole apartment, hoping to find something that would give him answers.

Having found nothing, he searched in the business area and explored for more than an eighth of a Terrestrial Revolution; there was no sign of a list. Frustrated, he kicked over a garbage container and sat at the Information Terminal. He scanned through the files for a couple of thousand heartbeats and found nothing, so he decided to review his suppliers. He saw several, but nothing was out of the ordinary, just the usual data associated with outside contractors: contact information, past and future delivery schedules, and Sovereign Cubes paid and owed. *Think Olan! If you oversaw this operation, where would you keep the names and activation codes of the team?*

Left without ideas, he opened a list of all his customers over several yellow harvests, sorted through them several times, and again came up empty. He felt frustrated yet admired that the business appeared legitimate on every level. No identifying symbols or numbers were associated with any of his suppliers or customers, and after performing a background check on all their businesses, they appeared legitimate. Stumped, he stared at the Information Terminal for several hundred heartbeats, trying to imagine how Qual did it. The business communicator beeped, bringing him out of his brooding; an older male appeared on the monitor.

"How can I help you?" Olan asked.

Olan tried to listen, but the puzzle took all his concentration, and the communication ended without him realizing it. Still focused on his mission, Olan absentmindedly turned off his transmitter and stared hopelessly at the Information Terminal until his wrist communicator vibrated. It was a written message from Dolas. *No need to meet; we just spoke.*

At first, his message confused Olan until realizing what Dolas did, so Olan reopened the business communicator and replayed the conversation with the old business owner. This time, he listened carefully to what he had to say, transcribed the message into the Information Terminal, and deciphered it. It read, "Supplier identification number."

Olan brought up the suppliers again and looked at their identification numbers. *Could it be that simple*? As the head of Argi Intelligence, Olan had several undercover teams placed in different areas over the other four cities. Each unit had a few ways of contacting each other but did not communicate regularly. This setup was completely different. If what Dolas told him was correct, Qual often met with his team members because they were his suppliers. *That must have taken many heartbeats and planning to create.*

He hated to admit it; Igon's system was much better than his. Qual could contact his team at any time, and even if the authorities were watching him, they would not know the other agents' identities. All he needed now was proof. *There is only one way I can find out.* One by one, Olan sent an electronic message to each supplier. The subject line read: *Zuine Cleaners.* In the body of his text, he entered the supplier's identification number, which would activate the agent. He also included a list of supplies and a note telling them to meet to negotiate new pricing.

Olan waited for the first supplier to arrive, sitting at a table outside a popular restaurant. The supplier sat opposite him as the server set a cup of brewed moss on the table, took the supplier's order, and left.

"What is the mission?" the supplier inquired.

"An undercover agent has been captured. We must kill him before he divulges his identity," Olan replied, pretending to be Qual.

"Where is he being held?"

"The prison interrogation center."

"Hmm, that will be difficult. I have heard the warden has increased the number of guards in front and more inside, so we will need everyone on the team for this one."

"I agree. I will contact the others by the end of the Terrestrial Rotation. Before it begins, I will get the guards' names and street addresses scheduled to replace the night shift. We will meet on the prison level at the fountain nearest the elevator. Make sure you are heavily armed. I do not want any mistakes."

"I will be ready."

"See you later."

Olan repeated these steps, informed each spy of the urgent mission to kill the captured agent, and returned to Qual's shop because he had to meet with Dolas and plan an ambush.

Chapter 33

Earth
Switzerland - Zermatt
May 14, 2452

Having received a message from Alex that he would be late, Vincent decided to go on ahead and scan the mountainside until his arrival; finding the Transportation Station that helped Dragon escape would not be easy. Since the avalanche fell down the mountainside, the snow completely covered the terrain, making it too dangerous to hover over. Still, Vincent had to take the risk, or else Dragon's trail would disappear.

Using his binoculars, he tried to find a familiar landmark to get his bearings and saw the couloirs that caused the avalanche to shoot him forward during his descent. Now, he had found the general area where Dragon had disappeared. Jumping on his hovering snowmobile, he drove over the mountain base to the aisles between the large boulders and turned on his beacon so that the Regime would know his exact location.

Looking at his watch, it was about 8:30 PM Switzerland time, which meant 2:30 PM Regime eastern time. *What the hell is keeping him? We're about to run out of daylight.* He decided to set up camp. Later, he heard his beacon beep, and a portal opened nearby. On the other side, Alex drove through the event horizon on his hovering snowmobile and parked beside his tent.

"Sorry I'm late; something important came up. I had to see Supreme Commander Porter."

Although Vincent prepared to thrash him verbally, there was no point after hearing his reason for being tardy.

"You are here now. I've been studying the mountainside, and I found the area where we came down."

He pointed to the gorge Dragon took between the large rocks on the mountainside.

"That's about where he vanished."

"All right, let's give it a try."

Behind his snowmobile, Alex attached a small trailer to carry his equipment. Vincent jumped on his vehicle, and they moved closer to where Dragon disappeared. Vincent motioned for Alex to stop near the location and pointed to the spot.

"Somewhere around here," he yelled over the engines.

Looking around at the devastation the avalanche caused, Alex shook his head, "It's a wonder you didn't slam into one of those trees on your way down."

"It was close. Too close."

Alex turned off his snowmobile, removed a scanner from the trailer, and started surveying the area. Vincent walked with him.

"I meant to ask, what does that device do?"

"Portals leave behind a power signature." With a raised eyebrow, he looked at Vincent. "They usually don't last more than twenty-four hours, which is why this will be difficult." Looking back at his meter, he continued, "If it was opened by a Transportation Station somewhere outside the Regime, we could still detect a signature no more than three days later because they use much more energy than a Portable Vortex Transmitter."

Glancing over his shoulder, Vincent looked at the readings as Alex pointed to the categories and explained each.

"There are three sections here: red, yellow, and green; we should be close enough to set up the tracer if it hits yellow."

"How does the tracer work?"

"It shoots a laser beam into the remnant of the event horizon, where the portal opened. If enough energy is still lingering in the air, the beam will shoot to the other side, and our satellites will find the exit. Over time, the energy will spread out and vanish, causing the beam to exit far from the original point or not at all. Since it's been more than twenty-four hours, there may not be enough energy left to allow the beam to go through."

"Just do your best and get me close to the station that opened it; I will work with the government to find any building using the power needed to run one of those machines."

"They must be generating the power themselves, or else they would burn out the power grid every time they opened a portal," Alex's scanner started making noise.

"Did you get something?" Vincent asked excitedly.

"Yeah, it's picking up a signal, but it's weak."

As they followed the instrument's beeps, they walked another hundred feet, and Alex stopped. "Here's where we should start the trace because the meter is dead center in the yellow."

Vincent nodded.

"That means we're as close as we're going to get to it."

"All right, I'll help you unpack your vehicle so you can get started."

Chapter 34

Akil

Argi City

The 22,278[th] Terrestrial Rotation of the Second Summer

Julie ate and turned on the viewing monitor to look for something to occupy her mind until Zorion arrived. She flipped through the different channels but could only find news, historical shows, and informational broadcasts. The reporters read the daily news as her gaze moved to the side door leading to the tunnel. It took her an hour to gather the courage to open it; she walked back into the corridor to meet Urki. The room was as she left it. The large vase was still sitting out, and the evidence of her encounter with the black and white moss was still on the floor. She peeked into the vessel and saw that it was empty.

"I see you have returned."

With a gasp, she jumped at his voice and yelled, "Damn it, Urki! You scared the crap out of me! Don't you know you shouldn't sneak up on someone like that?"

"It was not my intention to frighten you."

"Next time, make some noise, so I can hear you coming."

"Last we spoke, you were adamant about returning home."

"I know. I'm still not sure how long I'll stay."

"If you are not committed to the cause, I will not train you."

"Why is it all or nothing with you?"

"It must be that way. A Saiph must commit herself completely because lives depend on it."

For a long time, Julie stayed silent, contemplating her response, "Fine, I won't leave."

"You must understand that you are now bound to me until you finish your training. If you turn from the path you are about to embark, you will walk out of the light, and the darkness will swallow you."

Gulping, she responded, "I understand."

"Now, let us begin."

"Wait, we still have one problem."

"What is that?"

"I'm expecting Zorion for supper in a few hours. Perhaps we should start my training tomorrow."

"We must start now. You have already wasted precious time running from your responsibilities. Now follow me."

"You know, you're very bossy," she complained, following him.

Without responding, he briskly walked back to the chamber, where she somehow pulled the metals from underneath the ground.

"Your first task is to build your weapon."

"I don't know the first thing about building weapons."

"That is why you must allow me to train you."

"I don't have any tools."

"Your weapon cannot be formed with hands or hammers. Instead, you must use your power to form the sword."

"Great. Now, exactly how do I make this weapon?"

Near where he stood, a hologram appeared before her, displaying a three-dimensional schematic of a sword.

"You have everything you need right here. As you can see, the blade has five layers."

As he talked, the hologram of a single blade separated into five thin, distinct layers.

"Each layer is thinner than one strand of hair. The blade will be in three sections, allowing it to contract into the handle, making it easier to carry and conceal. Creating each layer, which has three sections, is your first task. To begin, you will make the first, third, and fifth layers from the white alloy you pulled from the ground; and the second and fourth layers from the silver alloy. The silver metal conducts electricity, which is why they have a small prong connector at their end in the schematic."

He paused to point at the couplings on the hologram and continued, "The white metal will not conduct electricity, which is why it is placed on the outside and between the silver layers. Do you understand so far?"

She nodded, "How do I turn those lumps of rock into thin blades?"

"You must focus all your power on the metal because it must be heated until it melts."

"Are you saying I can melt metal with my mind?"

"Saiphs and Skeans make their weapons this way. The metal you removed from the ground is very dense. No furnace is known to any Akilian that is hot enough to melt it."

"How hot do I have to get it?"

"Ten thousand degrees Fahrenheit."

She laughed, "You must be kidding. That's like the surface of the sun hot."

"No metal listed in my database is equal to it."

"Something that dense must weigh a ton."

"On the contrary, it is very light."

She sighed, "Where do I begin?"

"Please, have a seat where you are."

Julie sat and crossed her legs.

"Now, focus on the white alloy," Urki instructed.

With her eyes fixed on the white, clumpy metal, she focused all her attention on it.

"Use your power to lift it in the air and keep it suspended before you."

Using her powers, she made the rock float.

"Now think heat."

The instruction was so simple that she almost laughed but did as Urki told her.

Several minutes later, she inquired, "Is it working?"

"No, not yet. It takes time. You must concentrate on the alloy's atoms and make them vibrate. That motion will cause friction, which will create the intense heat we need."

She looked at the metal floating before her until it magnified. It was as if someone had slipped a microscope in front of her eyes. She could see the tiniest details of the white metal, yet it was not enough. *They're so small, how can I see them?* She pushed herself until straining and somehow saw the metal on an atomic level. Now that they were in her view, she willed them to vibrate. The heat began to build, and the metal started to glow.

"You are doing it, Julie! Now make them move even faster!"

As before, every time she used the High Lord's power, it made her sweat, and the heat generated became so extreme that all lesser metals melted away until only the white and silver alloy remained.

Once the metals turned to liquid, Urki instructed her to separate the white from the silver and drop the silver metal so it could cool.

"Excellent. Now take a part of the white metal and let it flow into the shape of the blade you see in the schematic."

Using her mind, she willed the metal to take on its new shape, and the molten alloy streamed into the form of a thin blade.

"Now, in one swift motion, pin each side of the blade, but you must pinch its full length simultaneously. It will make the edges razor-sharp."

In her mind's eye, she could see the border of the blade, and with a thought, she willed the edges to squeeze together.

"Now divide the blade into three even sections and levitate it until it cools."

She did as Urki instructed and stopped moving the atoms; the metal hardened and cooled quickly. It was ready, so she gently allowed it to fall into her hands.

"Be careful; the edges are very sharp," he warned.

She inspected the three sections of the blade and saw the white metal glisten in the cave's dull lighting, "There is no flaw in it, amazing."

"You have taken your first major step toward becoming a Saiph."

"I wish you would not say things like that."

"You need to be reminded of what I expect of you. Now, repeat the process four more times."

Before beginning, she looked at her watch, "Zorion will be at my apartment soon. I need to get back, or else he'll think I'm missing."

Regretfully, Urki said, "I agree; you must be there when Zorion arrives, or else he will become suspicious of your absence."

"Where do you want me to put the blades?"

"Give them to me; I will guard them."

Julie carefully handed the three sections to Urki.

"I expect to see you back soon."

"I will get up early. How does 4 AM sound?"

"Acceptable," he acknowledged and disappeared from her sight.

"I wish I could be invisible sometimes," she whispered.

She returned to her apartment and heard a knock at her front door.

"Man, I can't get a break around here."

Tionah stood on the avenue, patiently waiting with the dress she picked out earlier.

"Come in."

"I hope you like it. I think our tailor has done a wonderful job. I cannot wait to see you wear…" she stopped talking, seeing Julie's clothes soaked with sweat and dirt, "You are filthy!"

"Oh, yeah. I was working out."

"Zorion will be here soon. You must get ready. I will draw your bath."

"That's not necessary. I can do it."

"It is part of my duties. Now get undressed."

Reluctantly, Julie accepted Tionah's help, removed her clothes, and stepped into the tub. Warm, soothing water surrounded her body.

"Oh, that feels good."

Before leaving the bathroom, Tionah explained the importance of their small cleaning cloths. Their purpose was to absorb any dirt or sweat the water left behind. Also, she showed her how to use the cleaning comb; it was different and even strange yet functional. Once the cleansing process was over, Julie tried on the dress, and it fit perfectly; only the shoes were snug.

"I will have them fixed right away."

"There's no time; Zorion should be here soon. I can tolerate it for one night."

"I do apologize."

"There is no need to apologize. It happens."

"Thank you for understanding. Now, it is time to style your hair. I hired a professional. She is waiting for us in your living room."

The beautician had brought a chair, which swiveled in every direction, making it easier to fashion Julie's hair. Having finished, the stylist brought a large mirror for Julie to see the result. She had braided and fastened most of Julie's hair securely to her head, brushed other sections, and straightened some to flow down her neck. Also, she wove small, handmade, flower-like pedals within the braided segments. Although Julie liked the style, it seemed radical, making her feel insecure.

"Are you sure he'll like it?" she asked Tionah.

"Yes. I am very sure. Many socialites have requested this exact style. It is what Earthians would consider the *in* thing."

"All right, if you say so."

"The caterers are here. They will keep everything warm and fresh until he arrives. Do not concern yourself with putting food on your plate; they will oversee everything. Also, it is customary for me to answer the door, so you should sit on the couch until I call for you."

"Yikes! I can't even answer my door," she whispered, walking over to the sofa.

She fidgeted with her dress and shoes, expecting him to arrive any moment; the later it got, the more uncomfortable she became.

"What is taking him so long?"

"He is the Argi's Sovereign, Julie; sometimes, his work delays private affairs."

About fifteen minutes later, Zorion knocked on the door. Sitting nervously on the couch, Julie waited for Tionah to summon her and noticed the smell of spearmint drifting into the room. With a deep breath, Julie took in the sweet, pleasing aroma. Moments later, she heard Tionah call for her. Trying to be poised and graceful, Julie walked to the foyer to greet her guest. When she saw his smiling face, all insecurities about her appearance faded.

"You are beautiful," he flattered, with a fascination that reminded her of her first date.

Unwittingly, Julie blushed, lowered her eyes to look away, and stopped, seeing something in his hand.

"Are those for me?"

"Yes. I almost forgot. I brought these for you. I hope they will remind you of home. I believe they are called roses."

"Yes. They're lovely. Thank you."

Zorion handed them to her, and she set them in the center of the table where they were about to eat. She faced them and noticed an odd look on their faces.

"Is there something wrong?"

"You cannot eat them. The flowers are not real," Zorion warned.

Julie snorted softly, trying to suppress her amusement, "I have no intention of eating them. We customarily place them on a table to see and admire them. It's a gesture of gratitude."

"Then, I am pleased to see them there."

They stared at each other until Tionah pulled their chairs out for them.

"Please, have a seat."

They sat, and the caterers set their plates in front of them, already full of various moss spread about in a decorative pattern. She stared at her plate and wondered how the chef could make something so unpalatable look appetizing. They often glanced at each other during the meal, making the dinner an exciting adventure.

Zorion held his hand out, "I was wondering if you would like to accompany me to one of our museums. It would give me immense pleasure to show you what our planet was like before our sun grew cold."

"That sounds wonderful."

As they walked out together, she put her hand in his, and he led her to his vehicle. A feeling of happiness came over him, holding her hand. He did not want to let go. Eventually, he did so that she could get inside the hovercar. After he sat, his driver drove off to their destination.

"I want to thank you for Tionah; she's been accommodating. I don't know what I would do without her."

"I am glad you approve. Tionah tells me she is very fond of you already."

"She also tells me you created a bank account for me?"

"Yes. You should have enough funds to purchase anything you need."

"I'm very grateful, but won't that upset your people if they find out you gave me government Sovereign Cubes?"

"They came from me," he answered.

He saw her frown and realized there was something wrong.

"Have I offended you?"

"No, of course not. It's just that since I left home, I've taken care of myself."

"I in no way meant to imply that you cannot manage yourself; considering your circumstances, I only wanted you to be comfortable."

Now worried that his gesture had upset her, he looked away and frowned. She reached over and touched his hand, so he turned to face her.

"You *have* made me feel welcome. It's just a little awkward for me. I don't know how I'm going to repay you."

Zorion looked surprised, "If I gave you everything I own, it could not possibly compensate for what you have done for my people and me. You will never owe me anything. It is I who will always be in your debt."

"I didn't do anything."

"You delivered the video to your Supreme Commander."

"We don't know for sure if he got your message."

"You said your brother would deliver it to his General, who will take it to your Supreme Commander. It is a sound plan."

"What happens if he doesn't respond?"

"I believe he will."

"How can you be so sure?"

"Because I am beginning to believe in miracles."

"What makes you say that?"

"You make me believe that anything is possible. I never thought I would find you, but I did, and when you were going to leave, I never thought I would see you again, yet you returned. You took my message back to Earth, and I know the Supreme Commander will receive it and contact us because of you."

"You think I'm that woman from your dreams?"

"I do. Even if you are not, my life will never be the same again, and I am grateful for it," he gazed affectionately into her eyes.

She blushed yet did not turn away.

"Stop it; you're embarrassing me," she whispered.

They moved closer, and just as they were about to kiss, the vehicle came to a stop, interrupting their moment.

"We are here, Sir," the driver remarked.

They softly laughed as guards opened the vehicle door. Zorion stepped out first and held out his hand for her to take. As they walked into the museum holding hands, he felt like a young Akilian again. Inside, a tour guide fidgeted with an earpiece as they approached.

"Greetings, my name is Tamer. I will be your guide for the evening."

Julie looked at Zorion with a raised eyebrow, "A private tour? Nice touch."

"Being Sovereign does have its privileges," he remarked with a smile.

As Tamer led them through several dioramas, each displaying exotic plant and animal life as it was, she did her best to explain how they lived before their sun went cold. As Julie walked by some animal displays, their enormous size amazed her. In many respects, they resemble the depictions of dinosaurs from Earth's Jurassic period. Later, they came upon an exhibit that reminded Julie of her dream the night before. Speechless, she stopped and pointed at it.

"Ah, that is Gau's pyramid," Tamer responded excitedly.

"It looks like the ones from Earth."

"Do you have a pyramid on your planet?" Zorion wondered.

"There are hundreds; this looks more like the Great Pyramid in Egypt."

"Interesting. Do you think your people worshipped Gau?"

"No. I had never heard of him until I met you. Still, there must be a reason both of our worlds have them."

"Once we move to your planet, maybe we can research this phenomenon together."

She nodded distractedly, "Sure, I would like that."

"Tamer, send any information we have on Gau's pyramid to Julie's Information Terminal."

"As you wish, Sir."

They moved to another exhibit, and Zorion knelt before the displayed animals. The artists tried to make it look like a baby of a furrier species that had roamed the forests.

"I used to spend hours in this exhibit. Our ancestors lived with these little ones. They were pets at one time."

"They look like a distant cousin to the dogs on our planet."

"Really? Tell me, what are they like?"

"They're playful and loyal. They have enough intelligence to obey commands. They also have exceptional hearing and an acute sense of smell."

"I like this animal already."

"Once we get to Earth, I will help you choose one. There are many different breeds."

"Thank you; I would be most grateful."

The museum had thousands of exhibits, which would take days to see. A couple of hours later, Julie started feeling tired and asked Zorion if they could return another time.

"Certainly, I will take you home."

During their ride, she reached over, took his hand, and rested her head on his arm, "I had a wonderful time."

"I did too."

Zorion looked down at his hand, the one intertwined with her fingers. Just the touch of her skin excited him. To have her head resting on his arm made him imagine the impossible. As the vehicle drew closer to her home, he felt sad, wishing the Terrestrial Revolution would never end. They arrived at her apartment, so he walked her to the door and stopped before entering.

"I think we should end the evening here," she tried to be firm.

"I understand; you need your rest."

Yes, there's that, and I don't trust myself to be alone with you for too long, either. For the longest time, they silently stared at each other. It was hard for her to leave him. The smell of spearmint was abundant in the air, and she felt mesmerized, gazing into his fierce blue eyes. They moved close to each other and kissed until she pulled away, or else the urge to invite him inside would win.

"Will I see you tomorrow?" she hoped.

"Yes. I would like that very much."

"What time should I expect you?"

"Tomorrow will be a momentous day. I will host Yetta's coming-of-age ceremony.

"Yetta?"

"She is my daughter. I was hoping you would be there by my side. I believe Tionah said it would begin at 6 PM, Earth time."

"Won't other Akilians be there?"

"Yes. Many of the city's elites will attend."

“I thought you wanted to keep my presence here a secret.”

“I have changed my mind. I decided to make an official announcement at the end of the ceremony and tell everyone that we had contacted another world. I want to introduce you and tell everyone what you have done for us.”

“Don’t you think it’s premature? I mean, we haven’t heard from Supreme Commander Porter yet. If you get their hopes up and something goes wrong, won’t they be angry with you and me?”

“Since you have sent our message to your Supreme Commander, I was obliged to notify the other Sovereigns of Akil. Now that they know, one of them will undoubtedly leak the news of your presence to the Information League. None of them can keep a secret. They also requested to meet you, so I had hoped to introduce you in a private room before the ceremony. We will walk onto the dais, and I will introduce you to the citizens of Akil.”

“All right, if you’re sure about it.”

“Excellent! I am pleased that you agree!”

“I better get my rest. I have a big day tomorrow.”

“I look forward to seeing you again,” Zorion replied.

She kissed him on the cheek, stepped inside her apartment, and closed the door. Zorion walked away, singing an old Akilian battle song from his youth. He patted Broll on the shoulder with a smile that reached from one ear to the other.

“I do not have to ask how it went,” Broll smiled.

“She is wonderful, Broll!”

“Will you be seeing her again?”

“Yes, on the following Terrestrial Rotation!”

“It sounds like everything is going well.”

“I hope so, my friend. I hope so.”

Chapter 35

Earth
The Regime - Washington, D.C. - Mercy Hospital
May 15, 2452

Chu Lian woke and felt much better than yesterday. She still had a slight headache from where the guard struck her during the interrogation. She sat and saw Michael sitting in the chair beside her bed. Just having him nearby brought a smile to her face. *Even after everything that's happened, he stayed with me all night.*

At that moment, she knew, beyond any doubt, that he would be loyal to her, assuming he could forgive her for lying to him. Today was the beginning of a new life for her. She planned to do whatever it took to be by his side. She slipped out of bed and put on her clothes without a sound. Ready to face the day, she gently woke Michael with soft kisses on his cheek.

"What are you doing?" he asked.

"I'm waking you with kisses, the way I used to. Don't you remember?"

"Why are you out of bed? You still need rest."

"I've had enough rest. Come on, let's go back to your place."

"You can't leave. You must check out of the hospital and register with Regime security."

"They know where I'll be. Besides, I'm going to make an appointment with General Saunders today. I'll tell him something that will change everything."

"What do you mean?"

"I mean that I'm back to stay. Now come on!" she pulled his arm and forced him out of the chair.

On their way, he inquired, "How can you stay here? You're still working for the Chinese ambassador to the Regime."

"Not anymore. As of this morning, I'm looking for a new employer."

"You told me your contract was for ten years. I remember it clearly because that was your reason for breaking up."

"I've figured a way to get out of the contract, and the only reason I broke up was to spare you the pain of a long-distance relationship."

"We still could have met every three months; I would have preferred it over what you did."

"Let's not argue about a moot point. I'm here now, so let's focus on the future."

"It's not a moot point to me! I haven't heard from you in a year!"

She sighed, "There were circumstances beyond my control that made it dangerous for us to continue our relationship."

"That doesn't make any sense. There wasn't any danger here in the Regime."

"You'll understand everything once I speak to General Saunders."

Aggravated by her evasive answers, he huffed, "Whatever."

"Don't say that."

"What?"

"*Whatever*," she huffed, mocking his tone. "My decision to leave the Regime protected us."

"How?"

"Just be patient. You'll know everything soon enough."

They arrived at his apartment, just outside of Fort McNair, stepped inside, and he slammed the door shut. Ignoring his tantrum, she took a moment to reacquaint herself with his home because, during her absence, she only thought of returning to him. She closed her eyes, breathed deeply, and thought of better times.

"I missed this place," she exhaled loudly.

"Why are we here? You made it clear that you planned to see other people."

"I did no such thing."

"You told me to start dating other women, and you wouldn't have said that unless you planned on dating other men."

"I told you to date other women because, at the time, there didn't seem to be any way for me to get back here without putting us in danger. I didn't want you living the rest of your life hoping for something that would not happen."

"I can't do this again. I feel like a yoyo. One moment I'm happy that you're here, and the next, I'm frustrated because you're still keeping secrets from me."

Again, she sighed, "As I said, you'll know everything when I speak to General Saunders."

As she spoke, he repeated the exact words, knowing the routine. For a time, they stared at each other defiantly in silence.

"Well, did you?" she questioned.

"Did I what?"

"Is there someone else in your life?"

"A few days ago, I went on a blind date that Alex set up."

"Do you plan on seeing her again?"

He laughed mockingly, "No. Just like every relationship I've been in, I got hurt."

Using his index finger, he pointed to the skin around his eye that was still lightly bruised. She was relieved until realizing that someone had physically hurt him, making her angry.

"Did she hit you? Is that how you got the black eye?"

"No, it was an old boyfriend from her past."

I will have to look him up later.

"What about you?" he queried suspiciously.

Although rightly deserved, she knew he would be skeptical and angry at her. As she expected, he vented a year's worth of frustration toward her. She patiently waited for him to let his guard down. His interest in her social life allowed her to let him know how much she cared for him.

"There have only been two men in my life I have loved, my dad and you."

Her confession seemed to break through some anger built up inside him.

"I don't believe you," he commented, lowering his head.

His response hurt, but he was pouting, which meant he was wavering. It was clear that he wanted her to persuade him to give in. Taking her cue, she moved closer to him.

"I know this has been hard on you, but it's been just as hard on me. You *know* I didn't want to go. I said it a thousand times, and I meant it. I've missed you every day we've been apart. Sometimes I stared out over the ocean, wondering if you found someone else yet hoping you didn't. I wanted you to be happy, so I prayed that someone would notice you and take my place while I worked diligently to find a way back. Now that I have, I swear to you, no one else has been in my life since we last saw each other."

His eyes wandered to her beautiful, brown, almond-shaped eyes, and he questioned if he could ever feel safe with her again. Having left him once, she could leave him again. The threat of her leaving would always linger. *What would be the reason next time? If I do something that angers her, would she run away again? Sometime in the future, would she stop caring for me and leave me with no hope of seeing her again?* These doubts haunted him.

"You're telling me what I want to hear," he disputed.

Vehemently, she shook her head, "I'm telling you the truth."

She carefully placed her hands on his chest, moved them upward to his collar, and pulled him closer, thinking he might resist her, yet hoped he would not turn away.

Since he did not leave, she moved her lips to his ear and whispered, "I still love you with all my heart. That hasn't changed. It never will."

She moved her lips from his ear to his mouth and breathed softly against his skin, sending chills down his spine. Their lips met, and they embraced until she gently pushed away; with a flirtatious grin, she nodded toward the bedroom.

"I don't think it's a good idea," he frowned.

Although it was sudden, she knew his weaknesses. As with any couple, there were arguments in their past. All it took was for her to wear him down until he agreed, and to accomplish it, she kissed him repeatedly.

In between kisses, she said, "Michael," kiss, "in case you have not noticed," kiss, kiss, "I'm trying to seduce you."

With each kiss, he could feel his resolve weakening, so he tried to look at the situation logically and replayed his adopted philosophy to get over her. *Remember, your mind is more powerful than your body. You are not in love. It is only a chemical reaction.* He repeated the saying, trying to mentally will the chemicals away. It became clear that the concept did not take hold. With every kiss, he grew weaker. Once she started nibbling his earlobe, his urges took control.

Firmly, he grabbed her hair at the base of her neck and gently pulled her toward him. Their lips met, giving him butterflies in his stomach. The love he tried to suppress surfaced at once, and his feelings for her were more significant than before. He worked to quell his desire for a year, but it was always there, hoping for her return. It had been a year since he tasted her lips, smelled her hair, and felt the warmth of her body. Finally, he had her in his arms again and did not want to let her go. He whisked her off her feet and carried her into the bedroom, where they raced to remove their clothes.

Chapter 36

Akil

Argi City

The 22,279th Terrestrial Rotation of the Second Summer

The alarm resonated, and Julie rolled over, struggling to wake from a sound sleep. "Off!" she yelled. Before getting up, exhaustion prevented her from moving. She buried her face under a pillow and slept. The backup system kicked in, detecting that she had not left her bed, and produced an even louder alert. "Damn it. I said off!"

The night before, Tionah explained their alarms. Once set, it would sound an increasingly louder alert until she got up. Julie was not an early riser and would not have gotten up without the persistent warning. The fourth alarm chimed, several decibels louder than the first, and Julie finally gave in. "Lights!" she growled. Standing in front of the mirror, she waited for the White Illuminati Stones to brighten enough to see her reflection. As usual, her hair was in complete disarray, and there was a clear trail of drool on her cheek.

She freshened up, slipped on the workout clothes Tionah brought her, combed her hair into a ponytail, carefully sneaked out the side door, ran to meet Urki, and entered the room.

"You are late," Urki remarked,

"Get over it," she snapped.

"Every minute you delay is a minute lost."

"I'm not a morning person, so you better tread lightly."

"Please, have a seat. You must complete your sword."

"So that you know, Zorion invited me to a ceremony tonight."

"This is unexpected. We have little time as it is."

"I'm here. Let's get started."

She sat, closed her eyes, and continued to create the other four layers of the blade and separated them into three sections. The process took a few hours. She stopped only to eat breakfast and returned to finish her work.

"Now that you have the five layers and three sections finished, you must form a handle out of the silver and white metal," he advised.

"Why, Silver? I thought it was conductive."

"It is. You will need a conductor, so the power can go from the transfer gem to your blade and back again."

"I thought the power source would be inside the handle."

"No, *you* are the power source."

"Me?"

"You must finish the handle to find a suitable Power Transfer gem. Once you have completed its construction and learned how to manage it, I will show you how to ignite it."

He revealed several different schematics of hilts, giving her a choice. She selected one and started heating the white and silver metals, leaving two half pieces ready for the Power Transfer Gem. Waving his hand, he motioned for her to follow him. He led her into a room with a hidden entrance. She could see tiny dots of light covering the wall, reflecting off his diamond body.

"They look like White Sapphires."

"These Sapphires, as you call them, can transfer power from the High Lord to the sword's blade. Saiphs call them Power Transfer Gems. Select one."

"Does it matter which one I choose?"

"You will know because the light will draw you toward it."

To vent her frustration with Urki's teaching techniques, she exhaled loudly and walked toward the wall. As she approached, the stones glowed brighter and brighter. It was like each one was competing for her attention. Several seconds later, she found one with a peculiar pull. Intending to grab the Sapphire with her hand, she reached out, but before her fingers made contact, something inside her invisibly lurched forward and grabbed it. The stone leaped out of the wall and into her hand. As it rested in her palm, it glowed even more brilliantly than before until it illuminated the whole room.

"Are they alive?" she asked.

"No, they are merely gems that respond to the High Lord's power within you."

"Neat."

"Indeed. Now we must return and complete the final phase."

She sat, and he continued his instructions, "There are three sections to the blade. Each section has five layers. You must reheat each section separately, melting the five blades simultaneously. At the same time, you must hold the blades firmly together to make them one, so the blades must not move from their position, or you must start the process all over. After finishing each section, you will reheat the ends and insert them into the other sections, making one blade."

Great, that's all I need is to start over. Julie closed her eyes again and reached out with her mind. The five layers of the first section lifted out of his hand and floated before her. Carefully, she set them one on top of the other so that each surface lined up evenly on all sides and heated them. The blades merged, so she worked on the following section until completing all three.

Combining the three sections was the most difficult because Julie had to ensure that the white and silver parts lined up perfectly, allowing the power to flow through the blade uninterrupted. Once she finished, it stopped glowing. Urki snatched it out of the air. He evaluated it to ensure the three sections moved freely, allowing the blade to extend and contract, and nodded his approval.

"Excellent. You have made a perfect blade."

"Phew. I was not looking forward to doing that again."

"Now, place the gem in the cradle within the hilt. Simultaneously, insert the blade at the top of the handle. Once you have set everything in place, you will perform the last step, which is to heat the remaining portions until they bind together."

With her mind, she took the sword out of his hands, levitated it, set the gem inside the cradle, inserted the blade at the top of the handle, set the pieces together, heated the metals as before, and allowed them to cool. Again, he snatched the sword out of the air and slashed as if mimicking a fight, swinging the blade back and forth. She could hear a whooshing sound as he spun, swung, and thrust the sword in every direction as it sliced through the air; he stopped and turned to face her.

"Excellent. You have built a well-balanced weapon."

He pressed the button on the hilt with his thumb, causing the blade to retract, and handed it to her. Thinking it would extend by hitting the same button, she pushed down on it; nothing happened.

"What's wrong? Why won't it extend?" puzzled Julie.

"The blade extends by air pressure, so you must '*will*' air into the small inlet on the handle. Once you have extended the blade, press the button on the hilt to secure it. To retract the blade, simply press the button again. The air will release, and the blade will disappear into the handle as before."

Frowning, she focused on forcing air into the small opening and tried several times before succeeding. Since it took her many attempts, Urki had her repeat the steps until she did it reflexively. He had her swinging the sword, performing a pretend fight; the sword slipped out of her hand and bounced across the rocky floor. He materialized in front of her as she ran to pick it up, blocking her path.

Julie frowned, "I'm sorry. I hope I didn't break or scratch it."

"The metals will never break or scratch; you obviously have much to learn."

"What do you expect? I have never held a sword before in my life!"

Peaking over his shoulder to look at the sword, she questioned, "Are you going to let me get it?"

"You must become accustomed to using your powers because if you drop your sword during a fight and run to retrieve it, the Skean will kill you before reaching it.

"What am I supposed to do?"

"Use your power to call the handle toward you before your opponent's sword cuts you down."

He stepped aside. She extended her arm, and the sword leaped from the ground, flying awkwardly at her. It spun end over end as it approached her, forcing her to move aside to avoid it.

"No! No! No! You must control the sword the entire time it is in the air, or else your enemy will snatch it from you! Even worse, you will cut your head off!"

Biting back a retort, she focused on the sword where it rested and tried again. It flew toward her and wobbled a little less this time; it still was not stable enough for her to grab out of the air. Nevertheless, she managed to catch it several times by mid-day when her watch chimed.

"Tionah will be arriving soon with my lunch."

"It is inconvenient, but we have made some progress. I will show you how to ignite it during your next class."

Pressing the button, she contracted the blade and extended her hand, expecting him to take it from her.

He held his hands up, "No. You must keep it with you at all times."

"Not only do I not know how to use it yet; I also don't have anywhere to put it."

"If a Skean finds you, it is the only weapon that could save your life. Regarding where to put it, I remember reading that the women of your world carry purses."

"Yes, I left mine back home."

"Akilian women carry something similar. Tell Tionah to have one made for you, large enough to fit the handle inside. No one will notice."

"I will tell her." She turned to leave but stopped, "Should I tell Zorion about this Saiph business?"

"It would be best that he never finds out."

"This isn't something I can keep hidden from him forever. He will find out somehow."

"You must keep our work here secret from everyone until you have completed your training because if anyone finds out, even Zorion, it will jeopardize your life. Remember, we do not know who the Skeans are or who is working for them."

"I can't believe Zorion is working for them."

"Even so, he may unwittingly know someone who is, and you would be in danger if he says or does something to reveal your identity. The fact is you are already in danger of being discovered."

"How?"

"Skeans and Saiphs can sense each other's presence. The closer you get to one another, the more powerful the sensation becomes. I am positive they sensed you when you woke from eating the black and white moss. I believe that they are looking for you now. So far, your isolation has prevented them from discovering you."

She swallowed hard, "Are you saying, if I get close to one, he or she will know I'm training to be a Saiph?"

"No. He or she will not know that you are in training, only that you have the High Lord's power on your side; if a Skean finds out that you are a novice, he or she will not hesitate to strike you down, even in a public setting. Therefore, it is important to keep your presence here a secret."

"Zorion plans to introduce me to all of Akil tonight."

Urki frowned, "One moment, please. I am accessing Zorion's files." A few seconds later, he continued, "Protocol dictates that he must introduce you to the other Sovereigns. Even if you convince him not to introduce you to everyone on Akil, I am certain one of the other rulers will leak the news. It would only put Zorion on the spot for not telling everyone you are here."

"What do I do?"

"We have no choice. Once Zorion makes the announcement, the Skeans will undoubtedly suspect that you are the Saiph they have been sensing, so during your next training session, I will teach you how to cloak your powers. It may be enough to fool them, at least briefly."

"Why didn't you show me how to do that first?"

"Because I did not realize he would introduce you so soon. Also, it needs a great deal of concentration. Since you are a novice, you will not be able to maintain the shroud for long."

"What do I do if I have to fight? Everyone will see me wielding this sword. They'll know I'm a Saiph."

"I will access your account and order a special uniform for you. It will hide your identity from any Akilian."

"Be sure to rush it because I won't have much time before the ceremony."

"You will receive it before the celebration. Now go, and hurry back so we may continue your training."

Chapter 37

Earth
The United States - Texas - Houston - George Bush Park
May 15, 2452

Jared heard the whisper of the portal closing behind him as he walked to Tim Martin's apartment and knocked. It was early, just a few minutes before 5 AM. Tim answered the door, still half asleep.

Seeing Jared, he frowned, "Where have you been?"

"I had to take care of something, but I'm back now. I have a plan to speed up Texas' secession from the U.S."

"You're too late. The governor is holding a special session today. I've heard a rumor that she plans to strike it down."

Jared glowered, "She is supposed to wait five days!"

"What else did you talk about during your last visit?"

"The details don't matter. What's important is that she's already breaking her word. We need to get there before they vote on it."

"It's a six-hour ride to Austin. We won't get there until 11 AM, assuming the gangs don't attack us along the way."

"You better get ready. If we're late, Texas will see blood before it's free from President Martinez's grip."

Tim changed clothes in only a few minutes and wore army fatigues upon returning, making Jared raise an eyebrow.

"Where is your suit?"

"I want to be ready just in case someone attacks us. I don't want to traverse the suburbs in a suit and tie. I'll be a target for sure."

"We better get going."

Inside their SUV, they left with haste, followed by the protective convoy assigned to them. The ride was bumpier than their last trip to Austin because Jared insisted they go beyond the comfortable driving speed. The vehicle's tires bounced violently in protest as they drove over large potholes on the abandoned roads; the faster pace did get them there sooner than expected, even though bandits attacked them during their journey, which caused another delay. Jared and the others in the convoy thwarted any attempts of high jacking the vehicles.

As the SUV slowed down in front of the State Capitol Building, Jared jumped out before it could come to a complete stop. He sprinted to the front door, where the Capital Guards scanned his body for weapons. Jared kept looking at his watch until they let him through and ran to the House of Representatives Chamber, where a guard told him the governor was speaking. He quietly stepped inside and saw Sonya standing behind the podium. Her speech made it clear that she opposed the Secession bill. Jared saw her eyes move across the assembly and stopped to look at him. A few minutes later, she called for a brief recess, and Jared approached her, visibly upset.

"What are you doing?" he asked.

"I told you I would call a special session on the Secession bill."

"You gave me five days!"

"I didn't lie. Today's session was merely for debate. I scheduled the actual vote for tomorrow; I can move it up to today, assuming you have some good news for me."

"I have what you demanded," he handed her a small tablet. "Supreme Commander Porter digitally signed it."

Sonya shuffled through the electronic pages on the small screen. Inside, she found Supreme Commander Porter's signature and seal, guaranteeing her Regime citizenship, a home in the Inner Circle, and a bank account number having the sum of one million Regime Talons. Also, it detailed the compensation package for each state's house and senate legislatures; it all depended upon the immediate vote to secede from the U.S.

She reviewed the documents, smiled, and hugged him tightly, "Thank you. You have no idea what this means to me."

Surprised by her uncharacteristic reaction, he frowned as she embraced him. *Why is her forwardness replaced with gratitude and her confidence with relief?* He only knew her briefly, and it never occurred to him that she might have a softer side.

Without thinking, he replied, "You're welcome; just don't forget that I'm doing this for Texans."

She smiled warmly, "I know, and I realize this will be a big sacrifice for you. Honestly, I didn't think you would go through with it, but I promise to make it worthwhile."

Chills ran down his spine as he remembered the words she whispered in his ear the last time they met.

"Right now, all I care about is getting this vote through. After that, we have plenty of time to sort out our relationship."

"Speaking of which, I was hoping you would be willing to do one more thing for me," she smiled hopefully.

"It depends on what it is."

"I would like a formal marriage proposal, like a normal couple."

"There is nothing normal about us. Getting married was your idea!"

"I simply want to make this a memorable moment, just in case things work out for us."

There was silence between them for a stretch, and it seemed clear that he was not interested, so she frowned, "It's all right. I understand. Although I had hoped for more, our relationship can be a business arrangement if that's what you want."

"I don't have a ring and don't know what to say. What can I say? I don't know you!" he responded frustratedly.

Sonya carefully slid her hand into her purse, retrieved a small diamond ring, and held it out for him to take.

"This was my grandmother's; she gave it to me when I married my first husband. After he died, I stopped wearing it because his memory was too painful. If you put it on my finger, we can create new memories. It's not part of the deal, so if you refuse, I will understand, and it will not affect my decision. The choice is yours to make."

He stared at the ring and tempered his expression to hide confusion. Having known her briefly, he could not tell if she was manipulating him again or being honest for the first time. During their earlier meeting, it was clear to him that she had a way of getting inside his mind. Somehow, she knew what to say to get him to do her will.

For example, the offer she made was one he obviously could not refuse, mainly because so many lives were at stake. He had given in to her demands, and it appeared as if she had handed control of the relationship over to him; it made him feel uncomfortable. *The choice is mine to make, but where is the trap?* It did occur to him that she was letting him feel a false sense of control, and at the right moment, she would present him with a situation where he had to fulfill her will again. The cost of that decision would be unknown until it happened.

The path seemed simple enough. He could pursue an intimate relationship with her or leave it as all business.

Part of him was yelling, *run!* Another part wanted to give her a chance because he had never met anyone who could best him the way she did. He chose to pursue her against his better judgment (the part telling him to run). He took a moment to think of something to say, got down on one knee, looked up at her, and, seeing tears welling up in her eyes, took her hand.

"From the day we first met, you got my attention. You are bold, unconventional, beautiful, confident, and intelligent. I have never met anyone like you before. Sometimes I think you know me better than I know myself, and I believe you'll be a good match for me. So, Sonya Gonzales, would you do me the greatest honor and be my wife?"

"Yes, Jared. I will marry you!" she sniffled and laughed joyfully.

With the ring between his thumb and index finger, he slipped it onto her hand and stood. She surprised him with a kiss that lasted a long time.

He pulled away, "What do we do now?"

"Why don't you wait for me in my office? The session will resume soon, and I will convince them to vote yes for the Secession Bill, making it effective at once."

"How long will this take?"

"Just a few hours. The House will approve it, and I'll do the same with the Senate. You'll be back home by dinner."

"Ok, I'll see you in a few hours."

Her eyes did not leave him until he disappeared through the door; before continuing her work, she heard another door closing, which caught her attention, and her happiness faded seeing the familiar face.

"Alonso, what are you doing here?" she questioned grimly.

"The President sent me. He's heard about what you're planning to do," he warned, approaching her.

"What is that?"

Standing in front of her, he held out a phone, "Treason. Call him now."

Taking the phone out of his hand, she contacted President Martinez.

"Sonya, my darling daughter. Please tell me the rumors aren't true."

"I don't know what you're talking about."

"The Secession Bill, the one you're debating right now."

"You must have heard that I've been speaking against it."

"Publicly, yet I've heard some little birdies singing a different song."

"What do you want?"

"When I heard you betrayed me, I planned to have Alonso remove you from office, leaving your lieutenant governor in charge; Alonso had a better idea."

She looked warily at Alonso and inquired, "I see. What idea does he have in mind for me?"

"Based on the songs my little birdies have sung, I hear that you'll be living in the Inner Circle, with a Regime agent no less. Very bold, my dear; even I'm impressed."

"Texas is collapsing. Even if I continue to fight against the bill, the Regime will own it in time."

"This situation has given me a rare opportunity. With you behind enemy lines, I'll have an invaluable spy."

"I will not spy for you."

Alonso removed a gun from his holster and pointed it at her head. Sonya did not flinch.

"Right about now, I imagine Alonso is showing you the consequences of that decision."

"Go ahead, kill me. I don't care anymore. I *will* be free of you one way or another."

With a chuckle, President Martinez responded, "You're brave; I'll give you that. Fine, since you don't care about your life, perhaps you care for someone else's."

"Who would that be? You've made sure I have no one."

"I could send Alonso to visit Jared."

"I barely know him."

"Good, you won't miss him."

There was a brief pause; Alonso touched his ear, where his communicator fastened, nodded, turned, and started to leave.

"Wait!"

Alonso stopped.

"Maybe we can make a different arrangement," Sonya offered.

"What do you suggest?"

"What if I give you a one-time deal? I'll do whatever you want, only if you promise to leave Jared and me alone, forever."

"Hmm, it seems very light, considering all I've done for you."

"Do you agree or not?"

"Yes, I'll agree to that arrangement."

She sighed in relief, "What do you want me to do?"

"Alonso cleverly found a leak within the Regime; the source demands physical Regime Talons for the information we want, so all I'll need you to do is deliver the money."

"I can't bring it with me. They'll check my bags, see the money and confiscate it."

"Naturally, you'll have to retrieve it once you're there."

"I'll be living with a Regime agent. He'll be watching my every move."

"You'll have to be clever as well. Alonso will give you the instructions. I expect to hear from you tomorrow. If not, Jared moves to the top of Alonso's list. His blood will be on your hands."

Abruptly, she disconnected the phone and held out her hand.

"Give me the instructions," she stated flatly.

"You should thank me," he handed her the list. "The President is very angry with you. He wanted to lock you up and throw away the key."

Ignoring him, she studied the list, "I will need a few things."

"Just tell me what you need, and you will have them."

Chapter 38

Akil
Argi City
The 22,279[th] Terrestrial Rotation of the Second Summer

Posing as Qual, Olan stood by the fountain near the elevator on the prison level, waiting for Qual's agents to arrive. The work cycle started early for him, and he already met with Dolas to ensure his agents were in place, and one by one, the Vlorian agents appeared from the shadows until all ten finally arrived. Earlier, Olan gave each one an address. Their mission was to gain access to that home, restrain the guard and his family, take his uniform, assume his identity, and meet by the fountain nearest the detention center.

At his assigned home, Olan changed his likeness to match Zorion. It would be a surprise to throw off even the most cautious household. The door opened, and Olan looked down to see a petite female, still wearing her sleeping clothes, looking up at him.

With a pleasant smile, he asked, "May I speak to your parents, little one?"

Since it was her first time answering the door, she smiled and ran to get her parents, leaving the door ajar. Although it was tempting, Olan resisted the impulse to barge in because the guard would react defensively, which was the opposite of what he wanted, so instead, Olan patiently waited until the guard approached the door. As he hoped, his impersonation of Zorion surprised him.

"Hello!" Olan exclaimed. "I hope I have the right home. Are you Shoth?"

He nodded nervously.

"Ah! Excellent! May I come in?"

Stepping aside, Shoth cleared a path for whom he thought was Zorion to come inside. Olan closed the door behind him and noticed that Shoth had not yet changed into his guard uniform.

"Zorion! It is an honor to see you, but why are you here? Have I done something wrong?" Shoth queried.

Olan laughed and answered, "No…not at all! I am here with good news."

He paused to take a quick scan of his home.

"Is there somewhere we can speak privately?"

"Yes, right this way," Shoth gestured and walked to a room adjacent to where they stood.

With his senses at full alert, Olan waited for the opportunity, which came quickly. For just a moment, Shoth had his back to him; before he could turn around, Olan snapped his neck, and Shoth fell to the floor. He removed restraints from his utility belt, bound Shoth to a chair, and put a gag around his mouth. Satisfied that Shoth was secure, Olan opened the door and called for his partner to hurry into the room.

Thinking something was wrong, she ran inside, where Olan subdued her within moments. Now that he was in control, Olan changed his likeness to Qual to ensure the child would not think Zorion did it. Olan told her it was a game, so the incident did not traumatize her; she gladly played along. Olan safely secured the whole family in less than a few hundred heartbeats. He instructed Dolas to free all the guards and their families once the mission ended. Olan changed into Shoth's uniform, morphed into his likeness, walked outside to meet the others near the fountain, and they approached the prison in a single file.

Chapter 39

Earth
Spain - Madrid
May 15, 2452

It took Alex half the night to find where Dragon landed on the other side of the portal. Alex insisted that it was impossible to give Vincent an exact location due to a weak signal, saying that it could even be in the wrong country. Since it was the only lead, Vincent followed it. Before leaving the Regime, he contacted Diego, a Police Detective in Madrid and a good friend. They met a few years ago when Vincent pursued a serial killer who fled the Regime.

In cooperation, Vincent let Diego know about the pursuit and followed the killer to Spain. They worked together for several weeks until they finally apprehended him. During that time, they became friends and agreed to keep in touch. Over the past two years, Vincent visited Diego several times and invited his family to the Regime for a few visits.

It had been a couple of months since they saw each other, and he was glad to be back in Madrid to visit with him again, even though it was work-related. Vincent had told Diego that an assassin might be using Spain as a hiding place, so Diego was very eager for Vincent to arrive and urged him to hurry. Vincent stepped through the event horizon, handed his passport and visa to the check-in clerk, and walked to the security station, where they scanned his body. His implant set off an alarm.

Security approached him, so he handed them medical records saved to his tablet. The documents explained in detail why metal wires ran through his upper body. As the sentry read the report, his eyes glazed over, trying to make sense of the medical jargon. The guard set aside the tablet and asked Vincent several security questions until satisfied that Vincent was not a threat and stamped his passport to let him through.

The protocol demanded that travelers send their luggage through a separate portal to protect them against someone who may have packed an explosive. A department scanned his suitcase; he picked it up at the baggage collection point and walked through customs. The process took about thirty minutes; he did not mind the long wait because it was much quicker than flying. He knew some countries still did not have a Regime contract to use their portal technology.   Without it, they had to use outdated means of transportation. Vincent finally made it through customs and hailed a cab outside the International Transportation Station.

"Museo del Prado por favor," he remarked, closing the door.

The cab sped off, and he thought back to when Diego's wife gave birth to their first child, Sabina. *Has it been a year already?* Going from job to job made time move fast for him. Realizing that her birthday had passed, he had the cab stop at a store to pick up a present. He returned to the cab, set the gift on the seat, and smiled, remembering the night she was born. Diego was euphoric, and they celebrated at a small bar in the neighborhood. They planned to have a couple of drinks and return home, except two bottles led to three, and three led to more than Vincent can remember. One thing he did not forget, though, was how different an intoxicated Diego acted.

Usually, he did not smile because the job often showed him Madrid's seedier side. He was a completely different person off duty. At some point during the evening, his arm ended up on Vincent's shoulder, and he told him, in a drunken slur, how much he admired and respected him. Also, he considered him a good friend. Alcohol, Vincent noted, seemed to have a way of tearing down emotional barriers for some. He remembered making Diego promise to call on him if he was ever in trouble. It was his way of letting Diego know he considered him a friend, too, without saying it.

Later that night, they staggered back to Diego's home. Vincent could not keep him quiet. The joy of having a daughter, combined with several drinks, put him in such a good mood that Diego could not stop himself from singing; the noise woke his daughter, who started crying. That did not make his wife happy at all. His grin widened at the memory of her whispering an argument with Diego, who was too drunk to understand.

The cab stopped before the museum; the cabby stepped out and retrieved Vincent's suitcase from the trunk. Vincent paid him, picked up his briefcase, and entered the museum, where he handed the attendant his Madrid Tourist Card. Once inside, Vincent walked straight to room 16b, where the painting 'Jacob's Dream' by José de

Ribera hung. He admired the picture because it was about a thousand years old, and the museum did an excellent job preserving it.

The history of the portrait was well known, even though the dark colors and rugged landscape made the painting remarkably dull. The man depicted was Jacob, clothed with the drab and modest apparel associated with his nomadic status. Initially, Vincent thought it was merely an odd picture of a shepherd sleeping near a tree; learning its history and whom it was made the image come alive.

The artist painted the sky above Jacob's head with great delicacy. Ribera subtly painted wispy, imaginary angels descending on an imaginary ladder. Vincent gazed at the portrait, finding it easy to imagine himself in the depicted space and Jacob's company. He raised his hand into the view and stared at his digits, imagining the complicated wires that ran through his upper body. *We've come a long way since then, or have we gone backward?*

"It has been a long time, my friend," Diego cheerfully walked up behind him.

The voice brought him out of his thoughts, and he turned to see Diego smiling at him. Vincent grinned and extended his hand, but Diego embraced him in place of a handshake. They patted each other on the back to keep their reunion as manly as possible, happy to be in each other's company again.

"It's good to see you, Diego. How's Isabella doing?" Vincent wondered.

"Good, she looks forward to seeing you."

"And Sabina?"

"She's taken her first steps."

"Man, they grow up so fast. Oh, here's a belated birthday gift for her," he retrieved the package from a nearby bench.

"Thank you. I'm sure Isabella will appreciate it." His smile faded, "Let's go to the cafeteria. I want to know what we're dealing with."

Diego was always careful; it was his business to be cautious, so he insisted on discussing their cases in a crowded room, like the cafeteria. It proved one of the best ways to hide their conversations from listening devices. Having used a sonic ear before, Diego knew would-be spies would have a tough time discerning their discussion from everyone else's chatter, so they walked into the lunchroom and took a seat.

Diego scanned for any would-be operatives as Vincent opened a pocket in his suitcase and handed him a sketch.

"This isn't much to go on."

"It's all I have, so I would appreciate any help finding him," Vincent urged.

"How long do you think he's been here?"

"I lost him about four days ago. Assuming Dragon did come here and is still here, he will be staying at a safe house somewhere in Madrid. I would if I were Dragon."

"It would be like…how do you put it? Finding a pin in a stack of leaves."

"I think you mean finding a needle in a haystack."

"The outcome is the same. It's nearly impossible."

"I have a team reviewing the Regime transport video. Since this guy has access to a personal portal device, he must have already landed somewhere in Madrid and used the local Transportation Station to his destination. That's why I was hoping you could obtain any or all the surveillance videos in Madrid, including the airport, train stations, taxi cabs, and checkpoints."

Diego sighed, "You don't want much, do you?"

"Start with taxi cabs. He'll use one until reaching his safe house, where he'll keep a vehicle."

"Sounds like a good place to begin."

"Diego, please try to keep it as quiet as possible. Don't let anyone know what we're doing. If Dragon discovers it, you'll be his next target."

"That won't be a problem. There are many criminals I can say I'm trying to find, so I'll just pick one."

"Good. The last thing I want is to put you in danger. Isabella would put a hit out on me herself."

Diego laughed, "You're right. She would. Speaking of which, she's expecting us."

Vincent stood and felt a twinge of pain in his left shoulder where Dragon shot him. It was a reminder of just how dangerous it is to pursue the man. Instinctively, he grabbed his shoulder with his right hand and massaged it, trying to ease the discomfort. Diego noticed it right away.

"Are you injured?"

Vincent nodded, "Yeah, a gift from Dragon; it's only a flesh wound."

"You need to toughen up."

Vincent laughed as they walked to Diego's car, "Yeah, maybe I do."

On their way to Diego's home, he asked, "How is your social life?"

Vincent looked at him quizzically, "Huh?"

"Are you dating anyone special?"

"I'm sorry, Diego. I prefer women."

"Don't be an idiot! I'm not asking for me."

"Then, who?" Vincent smiled wryly.

"A couple of days ago, Isabella met a new tenant in our development. They've been inseparable. As I was about to leave, Isabella told me she invited her to dinner."

"Let me guess; she's on a matchmaking bender again."

"I'm afraid so."

"We don't have time for this, Diego. We must retrieve the video."

"It's too late to get it tonight; we must wait until morning, which means your schedule is open."

"I don't have a girlfriend or a wife for a reason, which you should understand being in the same business."

"Remember, Isabella believes that you are a business owner who travels the world, not a Regime agent, so she doesn't know how dangerous your job is."

"Is there any way you can get her to cancel dinner?"

Diego laughed, "Are you kidding? You know how she gets after putting her mind to something."

"Have you done a background check on this tenant?"

"Yes. I've done a background check on all my neighbors. She moved here from Seville to work for Terra Networks. I didn't find anything suspicious in her past, just the normal stuff like a few speeding tickets. By the way, her name is Sofia."

"Isn't there anything you can do to stop this? I'm chasing a dangerous man. I don't need this distraction."

"Relax. It's just dinner. Make small talk, and you don't have to see her again once she leaves. In the morning, we'll continue the search," he paused to look at Vincent, who was contemplating the idea. "Consider it a goodwill gesture, like what I'm doing for you by obtaining the videos."

"Wow, you've resorted to blackmail. Fine, I'll make small talk and keep my distance.

"That's all I ask."

Diego pulled up to his house; they got out and headed for his door.

On their way, Vincent questioned, "What does she look like?"

"Why do you care? You're keeping your distance."

"I want to know what to expect. I don't like surprises."

"I have no idea. I haven't seen her yet; Isabella says she's a nice girl."

"Oh man, I know what that means."

"What?"

"It means she's probably homely."

Shaking his head, Diego opened his front door, and they stepped inside. Vincent smelled tantalizing Spanish food cooking, and his stomach growled, reminding him it had been some time since he ate. *Easy boy, I'll feed you soon enough.*

"Diego, is that you?" A woman's voice yelled from the kitchen in her native tongue.

"Yes, my love. I'm home."

Isabella walked in, wiping her hands on her apron, greeted her husband with a kiss, hugged Vincent, and stepped back, smiling, "It's been far too long, Vincent! I'm very pleased you're here."

"It's good to see you too, Isabella, and may I say, you look as beautiful as ever."

Blushing, she gently slapped his arm, "Stop. I know you don't mean it."

"Yes, I do. Diego is very blessed to have someone as lovely as you."

Sensing something was off, she furrowed her eyebrows, studying him, "He told you, didn't he?"

"Told me what?"

"Diego!" she yelled, walking into the kitchen.

Vincent could hear them arguing from the small foyer, where he waited.

"Why did you tell him?" she snapped.

"I had no choice, Isabella! Vincent doesn't like surprises. It would have made him uncomfortable."

They continued to argue about why Diego could not keep a secret, which solidified Vincent's opinion on marriage. Knowing how quickly she figured out what Diego told him, he smiled. *She would give the MR a run for its money.* Hearing someone knock at the door, he spun around and opened it. In the hallway, a beautiful young woman with long, dark hair and brown eyes stared back at him. Vincent knew she was trouble. There was silence as they sized each other up until she spoke in her native tongue.

"You must be Vincent."

As a prerequisite to his job, Vincent had to be fluent in at least eight different languages, and Spanish was one of them, so he spoke in her native tongue, "Yes. Yes, I am. It's a pleasure to meet you, Sofia."

He extended his hand to shake; she smiled and returned his greeting, "You know who I am?"

"Yes. Diego told me about you on the way over."

"Isabella has told me about you as well."

"Good things, I hope."

"Mostly," she responded playfully until Isabella's voice caught her attention, "Have I come at a bad time?"

"No, she's just lecturing Diego on how to keep a secret. She wanted your arrival to be a surprise."

"She thought you would not come if you knew of the setup."

"Honestly, when I heard what she was planning, I considered staying at a hotel, but Diego talked me out of it, and I'm glad he changed my mind."

"That's very nice of you to say."

He realized they were holding their conversation in the hallway.

"Please, come inside." He shut the door and yelled to Isabella, "Sofia is here!"

She stopped arguing with Diego, and they came to greet her. She smiled as if nothing had happened, yet anyone with functioning ears knew they had been arguing.

"Ah, Sofia. I'm so glad you made it! I see you've already met Vincent."

"Yes. We introduced ourselves."

"Isn't he handsome!" Isabella stated enthusiastically in English.

Sofia smiled, looked at him, and spoke in English, "Yes. He's just as you described."

Her remark made Vincent blush. He smiled politely, hoping no one noticed.

"Please, have a seat. Diego and I will finish getting dinner ready."

They sat, and Sofia smiled, "Isabella tells me you are from the Regime."

"Yes, that's true."

"You speak Spanish very well for someone who was not born here."

"Thank you. I learned several languages at an early age. My instructors ensured me it would assist in getting a high-paying job."

"Is that why you do so much traveling? Sorry, Isabella told me what you do for a living."

"That's all right. Yes, my company compensates me for traveling; I also enjoy meeting new people in diverse cultures."

"Who do you work for?"

"Ultimate Construction. We supply all kinds of tools and equipment that companies need to construct high-rise buildings in cities worldwide."

"It sounds interesting."

"It's not as exciting as I thought it would be."

"You get to see the world. I'm sure you tour the cities after work."

"Sometimes, but I'm too tired most of the time; I often go straight to bed, and in the morning, I'm off to another meeting."

She frowned, "It doesn't sound like it leaves you very much personal time."

"What do you do?" Vincent quizzed, trying to change the subject.

"I work for Terra Networks. It is the biggest networking company in all of Spain. They hired me to monitor the system to keep out hackers, which is getting harder yearly."

"I understand they're becoming more aggressive."

"Yes. In fact, just this morning, a server from China hacked into two of our databases. We had to shut them down before they could download any of our files and infect other servers. Later, I ran a diagnostic and upgraded the security system to prevent them from using the same attack again."

"It sounds like you know what you're doing."

"If that hacker had downloaded even one file, I would have lost my job. It was close."

"The important thing is that you stopped it in time."

Unexpectedly, Diego popped his head around the corner, interrupting them, "Come into the kitchen. It's time to eat."

Chapter 40

Akil
Argi City
The 22,279[th] Terrestrial Rotation of the Second Summer

Hiding her training from Tionah was exhausting, especially since she showed up every three hours with food or questions. Rushing back and forth was an aggravating imposition. Just as Julie plopped onto the soft, inviting couch to rest, there was a knock at the door. With a frustrated groan, she walked over and let her in. As usual, Tionah was cheerful. It was becoming clear that she loved her job. *A little too much.* Since her help was invaluable, Julie had to keep her employed. The caterers set out food on the table as Tionah brought in another dress for her to try on, along with an assortment of intriguing items.

"What are those?"

"They are potential gifts for Yetta. I picked out several different items for you to choose from."

"Are you sure she'll like one of these?"

"Yes. Yetta made a gift list several days ago, and I have ensured that no one else purchased them yet."

She walked over to a table and set them out. Two dresses looked extraordinary in their style and color, a crystal vase, several paintings, and 'his and her' timepieces.

"There are many choices. You say she likes these?" Julie asked.

"Yes. Any of them will make a fine gift."

"Give her this dress and the timepieces."

"I can assure you that giving her more than one gift is unnecessary."

"I want to give her something personal, which is why I selected the dress; I also want to get something for both. Will I make anyone angry by doing this?"

"No, it is just unusual."

"I want to make a good first impression. She is Zorion's daughter, and I want her to like me."

"I am sure she will, without the extra gift; even so, I will have them wrapped and presented for you."

"Thank you."

Julie finally had a private moment and ate her food. The training made her very hungry, so it did not matter anymore that she was eating moss. Her enthusiasm caught Tionah's attention, who sat beside her and watched in amazement.

"For someone who claims she does not like moss, you seem to enjoy it."

"I can't stand it. It's just that my workouts are making me hungry," she mumbled between bites.

"When you finish, I need you to try on the dress I chose for you. Since you will be on the dais, you should wear something Akilian."

"I agree. I want to blend in as much as possible," she acknowledged and swallowed the last of her meal. "I'll try on the dress now. I'll let you know," she ran to her bedroom. She was back in a couple of minutes. "It fits fine. You can go now."

"Before I go, we should talk about the ceremony."

"I would like to, but..." she faked a yawn. "I should take a nap. I want to be fresh for the ceremony. You understand. Don't you?"

Tionah smiled politely, "Certainly, I will return at 6 PM with your dinner and hairdresser. You must be ready by 7 PM."

Julie rushed to the door, "Sounds good. I will see you then."

Tionah's instructor taught her never to question an employer's eccentricities. Still, her employer's behavior confused her. Julie shut the door behind her and waited a minute before checking to see if Tionah had left her level; seeing that the walkway was empty, she ran out the side door to meet Urki one last time before the ceremony.

"Tionah thinks there's something wrong with me. I rushed her out just now, and the disappointment on her face was heart-wrenching. I can't keep doing this to her. She will find out where I'm going and what we're doing here."

"Tionah will not overstep her boundaries, nor will she be offended by your actions. It is her job to work around your schedule. Just be polite and firm."

"It makes me feel bad that I can't sit down and talk with her. She's only trying to help me understand the Akilian culture."

"I am trying to save your life and the lives of every Akilian on the planet. Which is more important?"

"All right, you made your point. Now show me how to cloak my powers."

Chapter 41

Earth
The Regime - Washington, D.C. - Fort McNair
May 14, 2452

Chu Lian dressed and met Michael in the living room. Their intimate encounters put her in a pleasant mood. It only convinced her even more that she had made the right decision to return home. However, for her happiness to continue, certain things must occur today. First, she must reveal her identity to General Saunders and Michael. Secondly, she must negotiate for the Regime's help to get her dad from the grips of her old employer. The first of the two would not be the easiest. Once Michael learned that she was a spy, their relationship would take a severe blow; her sincere hope was that he would forgive her one day soon.

"Are you ready?" she inquired, feeling nervous.

"Yeah. What are you doing?"

"I want a picture of us, so I set your camera up on the tripod. Come stand alongside me."

Knowing it might be a long time before he would talk to her again, she made sure to take an assortment of photos. Some were kissing, playing, smiling, and several other poses, which she downloaded to her server for safekeeping.

"Now we have a memento of the day we reunited."

"What time is your appointment with General Saunders?"

"You're right. We need to go. We only have a few minutes."

They walked to General Saunders' office holding hands. Sometimes, she would steal a kiss from him if they were alone. Having been away from her for so long, he was very receptive to the attention. It was strange to have felt sad and lonely without her for an entire year. Now with her back in his life again, it seemed as if no time had passed, so he decided that after meeting with General Saunders, he would take her away with him to some tropical paradise to celebrate. He could not think of a better way to spend his vacation days than with her.

Thinking of her lying on a sandy beach, wearing a bikini, made him hasten his pace to finish the meeting. At General Saunders' office, his secretary sent them right in. Sitting behind his desk, General Saunders spoke into a microphone; he waved them in with his free hand. Closing the door behind him, Michael and Chu Lian sat and waited for the General to finish his memo. He put the microphone down a few minutes later and gave them his full attention.

"I hear you have something urgent to tell me," he looked directly at Chu Lian.

"Yes," she paused, knowing there would be no turning back.

The thought gave her butterflies for the first time in her life. One last time, before things changed between them, she turned to Michael and mouthed the words, *I love you.* She had to fight tears, knowing he may never want to hear those words from her again. He replied with a warm smile, so she committed that moment to memory, faced General Saunders, and took a deep breath.

"My name isn't Chu Lian. It's Wu Luli. I'm a spy."

Frowning, General Saunders looked at Michael, who went pale. Michael laughed nervously.

"You're joking, right?"

"No, I'm sorry. It's the truth."

Unable to look him in the eyes, she faced General Saunders, "I have lots of information which I'm willing to trade for three things."

"What do you want?" General Saunders asked cautiously.

"First, I want amnesty for all my crimes against the Regime. Second, I want the Regime to grant me citizenship to live and work in the Inner Circle. Finally, I want your immediate help in getting my dad out of prison. I want this in writing and signed by Supreme Commander Porter."

"Outsiders are not permitted to live in the Inner Circle; you know that."

"I'm sure Supreme Commander Porter can make it happen. The information I have is worth it. Trust me."

General Saunders rubbed his chin in thought.

"Who do you work for?"

"General Ming-tun Fu."

Returning to Michael, he questioned, "How long have you known?"

He deflected defensively with his hands, "I just found out."

Having known Michael for many years, General Saunders knew whether he was lying, and it was not one of those times. The pale complexion and several nervous twitches indicated that the young man had no idea what she did. Having excluded Michael as a conspirator, he returned his attention to Wu Luli.

"Tell me exactly what crimes you have committed against the Regime?"

"Not until I get my amnesty."

"I'll be right back," the General said and left.

Michael stood, letting go of her hand, "What the hell are you saying? You're not a spy! You're an analyst!"

"That was my cover, Michael; General Ming-tun Fu trained me to fit in and become whomever I needed to be."

As he paced, his mind raced, analyzing every moment of their relationship. Unable to hide his pain, his face showed the agony he felt. She had mentally prepared herself for this moment. Still, it was more challenging than expected.

"You can ask me anything. I promise to tell you the truth," she hoped to calm him.

"Truth!" he blurted out with a mocking laugh. "Liars don't recognize the truth because they don't know what it is!"

"You have every right to be angry, but please understand that there are reasons for what I did. Please try to recognize that I'm here now, coming forward, because I want to make things right for us. That is why I'm betraying my employer and my country."

Years of experience helped keep her voice calm, even though a storm raged inside. No matter her emotions, she had to keep control over them because there was too much at stake. Her dad's life, her freedom, and her relationship with Michael were all at the mercy of every word she would say in the following few minutes. Losing control would not help either of them.

"How can you make things right?" he shouted angrily.

Before their conversation went any further, General Saunders returned. It did not take a genius to notice that they were in the middle of an argument; the General had more pressing matters to deal with, so it had to wait until their business was complete.

"Relax, Michael. I know the news is hard to take, but we must listen to what she has to say," General Saunders commented with a forced, comforting tone.

"I've heard enough," Michael turned to leave.

"Not yet, Michael. I have something I need you to do first," General Saunders advised.

Although every cell in his body wanted to run, he stopped to hear what General Saunders had to say.

"Did you get what I requested?" Wu Luli hoped.

"Yes, with a few stipulations. If you disagree, the sentries outside will escort you directly to the penal colony on the moon," he warned, handing her his tablet with the agreement inside.

She read it and nodded, agreeing to everything in it, "I accept your terms."

She signed it, and General Saunders picked up the phone, contacted Captain Yates, and faced Wu Luli, "Security will escort you to Interrogation Room One, where Captain Yates will debrief you."

He faced Michael, "She is to receive a dose of those bacteria you developed. Go to your lab and bring them to the interrogation room now."

"You're going to inject her with the bacteria?" queried Michael.

"No, you are. She just agreed to it. Also, you're to assist in copying her memories."

"Let me send Lisa in my place. She's more than capable of working with the MR machine."

"I'm sorry. Supreme Commander Porter insisted on you."

General Saunders gave them their orders, and they walked toward the door. Michael left first, let the door close behind him, and walked to his lab, disappearing from her sight. Guards handcuffed Wu Luli and escorted her to Interrogation Room One. Upon arrival, the sentries locked her inside, still handcuffed. The air was cold, like a hospital's surgical room.

She first noticed the oversized, cushioned chair fastened to the east wall floor. Hanging just above was a helmet-size dome with hundreds of wires and sensors. She felt a cold chill go down her spine, knowing it was the machine Michael had invented. They had discussed it before, and the process did not seem intimidating, but facing it alone in a cold room was frightening.

She focused on the mirror found on the north wall to distract her mind, wondering if the interrogator was watching her now, hoping to see her reaction to the Mind Reader. She stared at her reflection for a stretch and decided to sit on one of the six chairs surrounding a medium-sized rectangular table in the center of the room. Above, lights illuminated the entire area, almost bright enough to make her squint.

Her thoughts returned to Michael and how he took the shocking news. She wondered how long he would hate her for lying to him. The more her mind lingered on that thought, the sadder she felt until the door swung open, and a man wearing a military uniform stepped inside with his eyes fastened on a tablet. His fingers danced about the clear surface, pressing icons and scanning through information.

His digits stopped moving, and he looked at the guards, "You can remove her handcuffs and wait outside the door."

The guards freed her and left.

He extended his hand, "My name is Captain Yates."

"Wu Luli," she stated, returning his greeting.

"Please, have a seat," he pointed to the MR chair with an open hand.

Fear grabbed her, and she hesitated.

"Don't be afraid. We're not going to hurt you."

She walked over and sat; the cushions were soft and heated, making her feel relaxed. Her training reminded her that interrogators sometimes used pleasure during interviews. She had to fight her body's desire to unwind in the soothing chair, forcing herself to stay on high alert just in case something went wrong. Captain Yates secured her wrists and ankles one at a time using large leather Velcro straps. Restraints always made her feel uneasy, and this time was no exception.

Michael arrived, causing her anxiety to subside, and she smiled at him; he did not return the pleasantry. Instead, he methodically worked to prepare her for the reading. He checked her straps to ensure they were secure, put an IV into her wrist, connected electrodes, a blood pressure cuff, and a heart monitor, which showed an elevated heart rate, along with her blood pressure. She knew it was typical for someone who was feeling high-stress levels.

He brought down the massive dome. As it came to rest on her head, she felt a soft foam band resting on her scalp. She knew it protected her skin from the harsh metal of the dome; its bottom edges blocked her vision, preventing her from seeing Michael or Captain Yates.

"Don't worry, it won't hurt, even though it looks intimidating. Just do your best to relax," comforted Captain Yates, who forced a pleasant smile.

She appreciated the soothing words, but it made her sad that they did not come from Michael instead. She practiced her calming technique as Michael injected the serum needed to map her brain so the machine could read it correctly.

"You're going to see colors of all shapes and sizes as your brain absorbs the serum," Captain Yates warned.

As the words left his mouth, colors of all shapes and sizes danced before her eyes. In the distance, she could hear someone typing keys on a console. The band around her head tightened, and she felt several probes press firmly against her scalp. As the machine revved up, it made a whining sound that did little to comfort her. Once it reached running speed, the whining morphed into a low hum; with the press of a button, Michael activated the machine's recording mechanism.

The monitor lit up, so Michael and Captain Yates sat, waiting for the process to run its course as the images on the monitor flashed instantly from one memory to another. The machine read and downloaded the memories so fast that it was almost impossible to see any single image on the monitor. '*Almost*' being the operative word. To Michael's embarrassment, her recent memories of him started to display.

Captain Yates nervously cleared his throat and politely turned away as some of the memories became intimate. As fast as those images appeared, new ones replaced them, and as the machine went further back into her long-term memory, pictures of other men appeared in a similar circumstance. It was not information Michael had asked her, nor did he want to know. Seeing their faces in an intimate setting opposite his girlfriend forever engraved them into his memory.

As the machine continued, it captured her training under General Ming-tun Fu. The device stored all the memories so technicians could analyze them later. It reached her childhood, so Michael shut the machine off, and it wound down until stopping. Michael lifted the dome from her head, and Captain Yates removed her restraints.

"Lean your head forward," Michael said flatly.

With her neck exposed, he gently moved her hair out of the way, swabbed her skin with an alcohol wipe, and injected the bacteria near her vertebrae. Being angry with her, he quickly pushed the fluid into her muscle, making it painful.

"Ow! That burns!" she protested.

Michael faced Captain Yates, "I'll check her signal with the main computer and return to supervise your team while they review the data we retrieved."

"I'm glad you're going to help us. Since you invented it, I'm sure it will save us a great deal of time."

"Thank you for the compliment, but if Supreme Commander Porter had not ordered me to help you, I wouldn't be here."

"I'm still glad to have you helping."

With a nod, Michael turned to leave; Wu Luli stopped him, "Michael, before you review my memories, I would like to have the opportunity to speak with you privately."

"We have nothing more to say to each other."

"I do. Please, I'm begging you. Give me a few minutes of your time before you begin."

"I'll find you before I start."

"Thank you," she replied, but he ignored her.

"For what it's worth, I admire what you're doing," Captain Yates remarked, hoping to cheer her.

"Thanks, but you're not the one I want to impress."

"Just give him time. I'm sure he'll understand what you're giving up and what you've been through."

"How could you possibly know what I have been through?"

"I've done some spying myself in my younger days, so I know what it takes, and I know the price we pay to get the job done."

"Except that General Ming-tun Fu forced me to become one."

"My dad encouraged me to enter the field. I know it's not the same, but it's close enough."

Looking at the closed door, she thought of Michael, "I should have never fallen in love with him."

"No matter how much training we have, we don't get to choose whom we love."

Chapter 42

Akil
Argi City
The 22,279[th] Terrestrial Rotation of the Second Summer

Olan walked toward the detention center disguised as a correctional officer using Qual's Vlorian agents for his mission. Over the past few Terrestrial Revolutions, he had changed his likeness so often that it almost confused him looking in the mirror. At the jail, he saw six prison sentries and one screener protecting the detention center entrance. *Good, no surprises.* Qual's agents were already in line, pretending to be security as ordered.

Eight of the ten agents were ahead of him, waiting for the screener to clear them. The other two casually walked over to the two sentries already on duty at the west end of the half-cone entrance. They used a surprise attack, giving them injuries to keep them down for a few thousand heartbeats. The other four prison sentries saw it, so two chased them, leaving two behind to guard the main entrance.

The screener saw the attack and moved toward her booth to call for help. Olan removed a dagger from his sleeve and stabbed her in the sternum before reaching it. She fell without a sound, but the two sentries at the half-cone entrance saw what he did and ran toward him. On their way, they unwittingly ordered sentries, Qual's agents, to seize him.

Those agents grabbed Olan by the arms and pretended to restrain him until the two sentries arrived. Like the other correctional officers, they fell, unconscious from their injuries. With the Vlorian agents' help, Olan bound and hid the six correctional officers' bodies and the screener inside the booth.

"Take your places; I will go inside and complete our mission," Olan commanded, walking into the entrance.

He changed his identity midway through the corridor from the guard to his undercover character, Qual, and contacted Dolas for the closing chapter of his plan, "You are clear to apprehend them."

He returned to the front of the entrance and saw Dolas with more than a hundred Argian agents, who apprehended every Vlorian spy. Since Olan looked like Qual, the Vlorian agents sneered at him for his betrayal.

"*Putok*!" one of them spat as an agent took him away for interrogation.

As Olan watched them leave, Dolas walked to his side, "Your plan worked. We have apprehended the Vlorian cell."

"We still need to catch Igon," Olan noted, looking at his tracking device and frowning.

"What is wrong?" Dolas questioned.

"Igon must have found the tracer I put in his shoe. I have lost his signal."

"How do we find him now?"

"Qual."

"He will never tell us where he is."

"No, but if we put a tracer on him and let him escape."

Dolas smiled, "He will contact Igon for us, and all we must do is follow him!"

"Exactly. Do you still have some of that green moss rope?"

"Do you mean the stuff that tightens around the wrists and unravels a few thousand heartbeats later?"

"Yes. I will interrogate him until he becomes unconscious and put a tracking device behind his earlobe. It should go unnoticed long enough for us to follow him back to Igon. This way, we can still track him if he changes clothes."

"How does he escape?"

"I will put the green moss rope around his wrists. Molo and I will leave him alone. Like any captive, he will try to get free of his bonds. Before this Terrestrial Rotation ends, the rope should break with several repeated attempts to tear it."

"You had Molo watching him closely. Will he think something is wrong?"

"I will be monitoring him from the adjoining room. After waking, he will hear us talking and think Molo only stepped out for a moment. He will want to get out in a hurry. I will wear my locator. You and I will follow him a few moments after he leaves."

"What if he decides to execute a surprise attack and try to take us down?"

Olan shook his head, "No, he is tired, hungry, and is in no shape to take on two agents and a guard, so I am sure he will choose to run. I would."

"I will get the rope and meet you there once I finish. I still need to process Elzer's network of spies you uncovered."

"I will see you soon."

Chapter 43

Earth
The Regime - Africa - Sahara Desert - Fort Levan
May 14, 2452

As the suitcase lid closed, Matthew Reynolds smiled. Recently, Supreme Commander Porter gave him a new position, Ambassador to Akil. It took some convincing because Matthew thought it was all some elaborate hoax his friends played on him, and, somehow, they convinced Supreme Commander Porter to take part. However, watching the message sent from the dying world convinced him.

Although his mission excited him, it was still a *dying* world. At first, he was unsure whether it was a bright idea to go or not. It was a significant risk on his part, yet after careful consideration, he decided to make the trek to this strange new planet for posterity's sake. As he stepped outside his room, military escorts waited for him. They walked to the newly named Interstellar Transportation Station, where Supreme Commander Porter waited for him to arrive.

Stepping into the room, he noticed a crew of photographers and camerapeople recording the event. He knew Porter would not release the video to the public until he or one of his successors declassified the mission. If something were to go wrong, his sacrifice might not be known for generations. He imagined that artists would make a full-body sculpture of his likeness one day and place it in a museum in the Regime. A video would play behind it, explaining the mission and his bravery, knowing that Akil's sun could destroy it and end his life. It made him feel heroic. As he imagined his legacy, a familiar voice brought him back to reality.

"Do you have everything you need, ambassador?" Supreme Commander Porter inquired.

"Yes, Sir. All the terms and conditions are right here on the tablet," he looked at the departure zone and gulped.

"What's the matter?" Supreme Commander Porter wondered.

"Sorry, just last-minute jitters. It's not every day we meet an alien culture."

"I hope one day it will be commonplace. We're taking our first step into an infinite universe."

"I'm honored you asked me to be a part of it."

"You don't have to thank me. I gave you the job because you have the necessary skills to succeed."

"Before I go, is it necessary to have armed guards visible? I can see a powerful military presence here, which may cause them some apprehension."

"We don't know for sure who or what we're facing. I tend to lean toward caution. If this is a ploy to start a surprise invasion, there are enough explosives in this room to destroy this whole facility. At the very least, the blast would force itself to their side and slow them down."

Matthew felt his hands shaking at the thought of that many explosives blowing him to pieces, "I certainly hope you don't need to use them, especially since I will be right in the middle of it."

"Don't worry, ambassador. It's only a last resort," Supreme Commander Porter assured.

"Ready?"

"Yes. I guess as much as I will ever be."

Supreme Commander Porter raised his right hand, which held the cylinder the aliens sent him. Pointing it at the Interstellar Transportation Station's northern wall, he pressed the button and waited in a nearby protective booth. About thirty seconds later, a portal opened. Supreme Commander Porter saw the man from the video standing on the other side from his vantage point, waiting to receive his guest. *At least it was not an invasion.*

Matthew moved toward the event horizon. Before stepping across, he turned and saluted Supreme Commander Porter, who returned the salutation. The ambassador stepped through the portal, and it closed. Supreme Commander Porter rolled his eyes and smiled at the ambassador's theatrical display, but his smile faded thinking about the dangers still ahead. *Safe journey, Matthew. Safe journey.*

Chapter 44

Akil
Argi City
The 22,279[th] Terrestrial Rotation of the Second Summer

Zorion worked at his desk until hearing his interoffice communicator beep, "Yes, Shilda."

"We have received our signal from Earth."

It was the call he had been waiting for his whole life. He jumped from his chair and ran to the Interstellar Transport Bay. As usual, Broll and his team were close behind. Just outside, he paused to compose himself. Zorion straightened his jacket, entered, and headed straight to the Transport Bay, where Yanamai waited for him with excitement and anticipation.

"Are you ready, Sir?" she asked.

"Yes. Open the portal."

The moment her finger touched the control panel, the vortex opened in the adjacent room, and Zorion saw their guest standing on the other side through the transparent glass partition. He took a deep breath and walked into the adjacent room, where he saw a figure standing behind a translucent barrier. They stared at each other for a moment until their guest saluted the other and walked toward him; Zorion greeted his visitor with a formal Earthian-style handshake, opened a box with a translator, and motioned to place the device into his ear.

"Can you understand me?" Zorion quizzed.

"Yes, I can. It's remarkable!"

"My name is Zorion. I am the sovereign of Argi City. Welcome to Akil," he bowed slightly.

"I am Matthew Reynolds, Regime ambassador assigned to your world. It is a pleasure to meet you."

Zorion was nervous but kept his composure. His mind flooded with mixed emotions of fear, excitement, and joy, "I am also pleased to meet you." Turning slightly, he extended his hand toward the door, "Please, come with me, so we can talk privately."

As Ambassador Reynolds walked out of the Interstellar Transport Bay and onto the avenue, the underground city's sheer size amazed him.

"I can't imagine how your people did this."

"We would be more than happy to show you."

"In time, in time."

Along the way to Zorion's office, he gave the ambassador a quick tour of the city building, keeping his comments brief because he was desperate to get the negotiations underway.

"My office is right over there. If you would join me, we can discuss our future." Once inside, Zorion offered, "Would you like something to eat or drink?"

"No, thank you. I had something before I left."

"Very well. Shall we begin?"

"If you don't mind, I want to see your sun first."

"By all means, you're welcome to see anything you like."

Although it disappointed him that the ambassador delayed their discussion, he understood his curiosity. If he were in his position, Zorion would also want to ensure their crisis was real, so he summoned the elevator to the surface, led the ambassador through the top of the tower, and gave him the complete history of his world. They returned to his office, and Zorion noticed the dreadful look on the ambassador's face.

"I must say that I have never seen anything like it before. How do you deal with constant impending doom?"

"We simply had no choice until today."

The ambassador sat, retrieved his tablet from the suitcase, and began searching for the contract.

"I am confident we can come to an agreement that will give your people hope. Now, before we begin, I need to know your credentials. How high up in Akil's government are you?"

"As I said before, I am Argi's sovereign. Argi is one of five cities on Akil, and each has a sovereign."

"Is there anyone above the five sovereigns?"

"No. We vote on decisions that affect us all."

"Does that mean the five sovereigns must vote on this proposal?"

"Yes, the moment we finish here, I will call an emergency meeting. By tomorrow morning, you will have your answer. To be clear, I believe we will all vote to accept your offer."

"You should hear the terms first."

"Please, begin."

"We've received your plea for help. An impressive video, I might add."

"Thank you."

"Now, I have been authorized by our Supreme Commander to make you an offer."

"Does that mean you will permit us to come to Earth?"

"Yes, only if you're willing to agree to all our terms listed here in the contract."

Excitedly, Zorion stood, reached over, and shook the ambassador's hand, "Thank you so much. You do not know what this means to me, to us!"

"You haven't heard any of the terms!"

Regaining his composure, Zorion sat, "Forgive me. Of course, I will listen to them, but you know as well as I that we are at your mercy."

"The Regime does not conquer to achieve its goals. Instead, we buy what we want or need. We only seek what is ours, we help only those who ask for it, and we will defend ourselves with extreme prejudice. We still have enemies, so you should consider everything I tell you before accepting."

"I understand; please continue."

"Very well," the ambassador paused to clear his throat and began reading the contract.

"Akil's citizens, including their leaders, shall not associate or communicate with anyone outside their community without the Supreme Commander's or his representative's written permission. Violation of said act would be considered treason and punishable by death." He paused to look at Zorion for any sign of hesitation. "Any questions?"

"I have no problem abiding by this stipulation. May I ask why we are not allowed to talk to anyone outside our community?"

"Yes, the reason is simple. Your migration to our planet is top-secret. Only high-level personnel will know of your presence.

Alerting the public of your existence would only incite war and protests, which would only serve to delay or even halt your migration to our world.”

“Ah, I can see your Supreme Commander is very wise,” Zorion conceded, smiling to mask his fear of the Regime holding his people in prison camps.

He only hoped the Akilians could endure whatever harsh circumstance lay ahead until they moved them.

“Thank you, that’s kind of you to say,” the ambassador remarked and continued, “Akil’s citizens, including their leaders, shall share all technology solely with the Regime and its appointees,” Reynolds paused.

“The rest of this agreement is redundant; it refers to the first agreement because you would have to communicate with someone outside your community to share the technology with someone other than the Regime, which the Supreme Commander would naturally consider treason. Is this acceptable with you?”

“We anticipated this request. Our instruments detected that your scientists were trying to go off-world with your portal technology. We are more than happy to share this information with you.”

“Excellent! I know our Supreme Commander was especially interested in your power generation and portal technology.”

“We hope the Supreme Commander will use it to relocate us.”

“Don’t worry. The contract includes provisions to move your people the moment our scientists can find a habitable planet. Also, Supreme Commander Porter plans to build several portal machines to speed up finding a new world, so I will set the section aside so you can review it later.”

“That is wonderful news!” Zorion exclaimed.

“There are other stipulations that you can have your legal team review later. Since you seem willing to abide by the two main and most important conditions, which I believe the other sovereigns should also agree to, I will tell you about our immediate plan for getting your people off Akil. About twenty years ago, the Regime’s former Supreme Commander purchased a large chunk of real estate.”

Zorion’s ears perked up.

"We call it *the Sahara Desert*. The Sahara, which encompasses approximately three million square miles, was purchased from the surrounding countries," he paused to look at Zorion. "Does that measurement translate?"

Zorion nodded, "Yes. It truly is large."

"Yes, it is. It's twice the size of the American Regime territory. The surrounding countries signed an agreement and voluntarily moved their borders back, surrendering the land to the Regime. The Regime's technology allowed us to begin terraforming the desert, which is a wasteland, for several years now."

"How much progress have you made?"

"Not as much as you will need. We only allotted a small part of our resources to develop it because the Regime classified the project as a long-term investment, so we only have about sixty square miles converted into a suitable living environment. Currently, there are a hundred buildings on the developed land, most of which are for business," he paused to look at his tablet, "there are only a few apartment complexes that can support a total of ten thousand people."

"Only ten thousand?"

"Don't worry. We have another plan that will increase that number greatly."

"Please, tell me."

"There are four basic requirements humanoids need to survive in large numbers: water, food, shelter, and sewage. We can move roughly a hundred thousand people in thirty days if we build community centers that can offer water, food, and sewage within walking distance of temporary shelters such as tents."

"Tents?"

The ambassador brought up an image on his tablet.

"They're mobile and fairly easy to put together."

"There are nearly three hundred billion people on my planet, which means our sun will die before we can make enough tents for everyone, let alone move them to your planet."

"Since we have no idea how much time you have left, I'm afraid it will always be possible. We estimate that the more your people come over, the more community centers we could build, which would nearly double the number of people we could bring over each month. It would also help if your citizens could make tents and provide building materials too.”

“We will do anything you need of us; how long would it take to move everyone?”

“We estimate just a little more than two years if we don’t have any serious problems or delays.”

Zorion sighed, “We have a large population, and you were not expecting us, so I understand.”

“If you first send over essential personnel such as contractors, engineers, scientists, and laborers, I’m sure that together we could save most of your population before your sun self-destructs.”

“What if, while building community centers, we used our machinery to create homes underground? They can carve out quite a large space in a brief time.”

“Interesting idea. It could save us a great deal of time. For one, we would not need as many tents, but we would still need to build community centers. I will bring it to Supreme Commander Porter’s attention.”

Zorion nodded, “At least it would allow us to double our efforts.”

“I agree. It is an excellent idea. Depending on how fast your machines work, it could shorten our estimate by six months.”

“Is there anything else I should know?”

“Just that you will oversee policing your citizens. The Regime has no desire to interfere with your society’s universal laws, especially since we’re unaware of them.”

Considering the meeting to be over, the ambassador stood and handed him the tablet with the contract.

“Here, all the details are there for your review. Please speak to the other sovereigns and let me know your decision; if everyone agrees, sign the contract, and we can get started.”

Having stood simultaneously, Zorion extended his hand to shake it.

“I am grateful for your help. You will have my answer shortly, I am sure. In the meantime, I have assigned a guard for your protection and an aide to help you. His name is Ander. If you need or want anything, please let him know.”

“I appreciate it.”

"Before you go, I was wondering if you would like to attend my daughter's coming-of-age ceremony; I could take the opportunity to introduce you to the citizens of Akil."

"Will everyone be there?"

"No, the auditorium only seats a hundred thousand; it will be broadcast on a network like yours so that everyone on Akil will see you."

The ambassador smiled to himself. *An audience of three hundred billion. Splendid.*

"Absolutely, I would be more than happy."

"Excellent! I will have one of my assistants prepare you for the event." Again, Zorion shook his hand, "Until then."

The ambassador left, and Zorion downloaded the file into his Information Terminal, where Kraeth installed translation software. Within moments it flashed on his screen in the Akilian language, so he sent it to the other sovereigns for their review. He read the lengthy document thoroughly until satisfied that the agreement helped his people. He turned off his Information Terminal as Shilda came to the door to summon him.

"The other sovereigns are waiting for you."

"Good, let us hope this part goes smoothly."

The doors closed behind him, the meeting room went dark, and four holograms of his colleagues appeared in their designated places before him. He stepped onto the pedestal, bringing his image into their view.

"Greetings, my friends. As I am sure you have read, all we must do is give them our technology, and they will help us relocate."

"I have read about the desert. It does not seem very hospitable," Elzer complained.

"Is the surface of Akil any better?" Gwah asked.

"The price is too high. We should not surrender our knowledge to these Earthians," Elzer countered.

"What good is our technology if we are dead?" Gwah disputed.

"If we give them our knowledge, we will be vulnerable," Elzer responded.

"We are already vulnerable, Elzer. The slow destruction of our sun has seen to that," Ruvve added.

"What if they plan to imprison us?" speculated Elzer.

"You have no evidence that they will do that," Quok countered.

"I would rather die than become a slave!" Elzer spat.

"If you do not change your opinion, you *will* die, Elzer," Zorion chided.

"We vastly outnumber them, so if they were to enslave us, we could easily stop them," Gwah added.

"Not if they only take a few of us and leave the rest to perish with our sun," Elzer hypothesized.

"Enough!" Zorion yelled. "I have read the agreement. Yes, we will be strangers in a strange land, but we are strong enough to survive whatever comes our way. I, for one, do not fear these aliens. On the contrary, they have accepted us openly in exchange for our technology. They have given us a chance to survive; I say we take it!"

"I do not give my trust so easily," Elzer remarked.

"I suggest you have your advisors review the contract and consider our options carefully; we should reconvene in a few thousand heartbeats to vote. Remember, the longer we delay, the more Akilians could die. Time is against us," Zorion warned.

Their images faded, and he stood silent, thinking of Elzer's paranoid comments. Yes, there were risks, yet even with them, it was insane to reject the only offer they had for survival. Why Elzer was against it was beyond his comprehension. He turned to leave and mumbled to himself along the way. *Elzer, you fool, do not mess this up!*

Chapter 45

Michael left, and Captain Yates took Wu Luli to a different facility area. As they entered the room, she could tell that the engineer dedicated it to military operations. Analysts occupied workstations that covered every square inch of the room. Also, a large monitor showing live satellite footage hung on the wall directly in front of her.

"I thought you were going to debrief me?" she asked.

"Later, part of the agreement Supreme Commander Porter made with you requires immediate action. All we need to know is where General Ming-Tun Fu is holding your dad."

"Po Toi Island."

Captain Yates nodded to one of the analysts, who heard their conversation. The island appeared on the screen; the compound's image was only visible through the satellite's night vision lens since it was night.

"Magnify," Captain Yates ordered.

As the satellite lens zoomed in on the target, the image filled the screen, becoming more explicit until Wu Luli saw small dots of light surrounding the grounds near the fence.

"Initiate 3D scanner," Captain Yates ordered.

Moments later, red lines appeared on the monitor, depicting detailed schematics of the building. The computer completed the facility's graphic layout.

He faced Wu Luli and questioned, "Is this where General Ming-tun Fu is based?"

"Yes," she paused, walked to the monitor, and pointed, "This is the wing where General Ming-tun Fu keeps my dad; he's not the only one. Up and down this corridor are other rooms. I counted a total of a hundred, including his; I believe that's where he's holding the parents of the other operatives."

"And his office?"

She pointed to a different spot on the monitor, "Right here. He has many guards watching it. There is a bulletproof shield just before the security station. You can't get through it unless they let you in."

"Not to worry, we have ways of getting through that defense."

"When do we go in?" Wu Luli inquired.

"Follow me."

Leaving the Data Gathering and Analysis Room, Captain Yates, and his sentries escorted Wu Luli down the hall to a door where he punched in a code. Moments later, a laser scanned his hand, and the door opened.

"You know, I never liked the idea of hand scanners," Wu Luli commented.

"Why not?"

"I can't tell you how often I had to remove a target's hand to gain entrance to their safes or vaults."

With a raised eyebrow, he paused before opening the door, "Noted. I will speak with our technicians about considering alternatives."

Once inside, she saw that the room was three times larger than the other, with many more people. Monitors covered every inch of the wall with varied information on display. Although everyone seemed busy, the room was quiet. The door closed behind her, and an older man waved them over to a well-lit table, displaying a hologram of the targeted building above it.

Captain Yates saluted, "General Green, this is Wu Luli."

Having read her dossier, he knew her reason for being there. General Green kept his opinions to himself. It is why no one knew he preferred putting a bullet between her eyes after scanning her brain rather than rewarding her for cooperating, but that was not Supreme Commander Porter's order. Knowing that they would work together going forward, he thought it best to be cordial. Pushing aside his feelings, he forced a polite smile and extended his hand.

"It's a pleasure to meet you."

She returned the greeting, and he pointed to the hologram.

"The computer completed a full scan of the building. This table shows a three-dimensional view of every room. Heat scans show at least one hundred guards surrounding the perimeter; we're getting strange readings from within the facility."

"What do you mean?" Wu Luli asked.

General Green pointed to the room where they believed General Ming-Tun Fu kept her dad.

"This marker clearly shows that there is someone in the room where we think General Ming-Tun Fu imprisoned your dad, but throughout the rest of the building, the heat signatures are weak."

"What does that mean?"

"It could be any of a hundred possibilities, so we're preparing for all scenarios. Now, I want you to show us where General Ming-Tun Fu stationed every guard inside."

Wu Luli gave them all the details, showing them every post, and reconfirmed where General Ming-Tun Fu kept her dad with his quarter's location. The hologram made it easy for her to give specifics. Using its capability to enlarge itself, she pointed to every blind spot and post within a small margin of error until a technician approached General Green with some bad news.

"This is the second facility we've encountered using a portal disruptor."

"General Ming-tun Fu had the device installed a few months ago; I don't know where he bought it. How will you destroy it?" she wondered.

He faced the Satellite Technician and asked, "Have you found the power source yet?"

"Yes, Sir. There is heat originating from this area," he showed the location on the monitor. "I'm focusing the lasers on it now."

Everyone watched the monitor as the Satellite Technician engaged the laser. Five thin beams of concentrated light made a circle as they burrowed through the roof and into the basement, creating a large hole about a foot in diameter. Telescopic lenses allowed the Satellite Technician to see inside.

"General, I believe there is machinery in the basement."

"Good, determine the best spot to hit it and check to see if the shield goes down."

"Yes, Sir."

The Satellite Technician analyzed the machinery and found the transmitter antenna, so he focused on taking it out using the lasers that silently cut through the thick metal bar that transmitted the interference. The technician watched it fall to the ground within the confines of the basement and faced General Green.

"Sir, we've severed the antenna."

"Is it down?"

"Yes, Sir. I have just confirmed that the disruptor has been disabled."

"Ok, now all I need is a rifle with a scope, suppresser, and plenty of ammunition," Wu Luli suggested.

General Green shook his head, "We have not cleared the building yet."

"I don't need it cleared! Now give me a weapon so I can get my dad!"

"Young lady, in case you haven't noticed, I'm in charge here, so unless you'd like to spend the rest of this mission in a cell, I suggest you calm down!"

Realizing her mistake, she took a deep breath to soothe her nerves. Being so close to freeing her dad made her emotional.

She quietly exhaled and smiled, "I apologize, General. As you can tell, this is especially important to me."

Being a man of few words, General Green did not reply. Instead, he gave her a look of warning and pressed the communication button.

"1st Sergeant Nick Gordon, is your team ready?"

"Yes, Sir. We've reviewed the intel the War Room sent us. We'll have the outer area cleared in a few moments."

Several monitors on the wall showed video from cameras that the soldiers wore. She determined which screen displayed 1st Sergeant Nick Gordon's view and focused on it.

"It looks like you have a full company of soldiers," Wu Luli watched in amazement.

"We have more, just in case there are any surprises."

"I had no idea you would go to such lengths."

"Perhaps you forget what General Ming-tun Fu did. He's authorized an infiltration onto Regime soil. That's considered an invasion; we haven't attacked China only because we need to know if he acted on his own accord or if your President authorized it."

"If our president authorized it?"

"Let's take one step at a time."

"Sir. I have a request from 1st Sergeant Nick Gordon to open the invasion portal," the technician remarked.

"Do it."

The technician engaged a macro that simultaneously opened sixty portals ten feet above General Ming-tun Fu's roof.

"1st Sergeant Nick Gordon, you're clear to engage."

Having gone radio silent until they were in position, Nick used hand signals, and his team propelled ten feet from their current location, from inside the Regime Assault Barracks, onto the targeted building roof. As the two teams quietly landed, they took their positions, and Nick signaled them to pick a target. Each soldier peered through their rifle scopes and selected a nearby sentry standing outside the facility.

They were not hard to find because the fence lights gave away their location. Now that his men were in position, Nick turned on his communicator and twenty seconds later whispered, "Three, two, one: fire." In one quick sweep, the Regime soldiers quietly dropped every sentry patrolling the lawn outside the facility.

Nick confirmed no survivors and radioed back, "Base, the grounds are clear."

"Get ready for the second assault," General Green ordered, facing Captain Yates, "Get her to the Barracks and put a vest on her."

Trained by the best, Wu Luli knew the military protocol and was ready to go in less than a minute.

"Don't take this the wrong way, but I'm surprised you're allowing me to go."

"It was part of the agreement Supreme Commander Porter signed. Besides, we recorded all your memories, in case something happened to you. Also, if you decide to flee, we have a tracer in your neck," Captain Yates explained.

"I see your point." *Great, I have just become expendable.*

Captain Yates nodded, hearing his orders through the communicator, "Ok, Wu Luli, you're clear to go. Stay with Nick; he'll ensure you get in and out without injury."

Chapter 46

Akil

Argi City

The 22,279[th] Terrestrial Rotation of the Second Summer

Earlier, Yetta ordered Thea to switch identities during her coming-of-age ceremony. Yetta arrived at Thea's apartment, which Zorion bought on the one-hundredth level; Thea was not there. An assistant let her inside, so Yetta went to her bedroom, laid her ceremonial gown on the bed, and admired herself in the mirror. Thea quietly moved behind her. Seeing her reflection made Yetta jump, having not sensed Thea's arrival.

Yetta spun around, ready to fight, only to find Thea holding her gown, the one she would have worn to the ceremony. Even though Thea's surprise entrance made Yetta anxious, Yetta pretended that it did not affect her and spoke in a calm voice.

"You are late. Where were you?"

"I was taking care of a few things. Besides, my timekeeper says I am on time," Thea deflected, handing over her garment.

Snatching it from her hands, Yetta removed the protective cover and changed. At the same time, Thea put on Yetta's ceremonial gown. After dressing, they faced each other and transformed their likeness to match the other. Now the mother looked like her daughter, and the daughter looked like her mother.

"I do not have any wrinkles," Thea frowned.

"You should get a different mirror," Yetta remarked spitefully.

"Fine, if we get caught, do not blame me."

Rolling her eyes, Yetta removed the wrinkles from her face.

"Now you look like me," Thea smiled pleasantly.

Yetta studied her for a moment and nodded her approval of Thea's impersonation of her.

"It is like looking at a three-dimensional hologram. No one will be the wiser."

"You should be glad we are the same size, or you would have to participate in your celebration," Thea noted.

"I am sure I could find someone," Yetta answered.

"Are you sure you want to go through with this? It is *your* special celebration. There will not be another one like it," Thea pointed out.

"I am willing to make the sacrifice. You will fulfill my obligation to Noka, and I will be with Taen as myself. By sunset, I will have found someone to replace you in my stead. At the beginning of the following Terrestrial Revolution, you will stop impersonating me, return to your original identity and continue your duties," Yetta explained.

"Why not take Noka and have Taen on the side? Neither will ever find out."

"The thought of coupling with Noka is repulsive to me. I would kill him before allowing him to touch any part of my body."

"That would certainly be bad for him."

"Are you ready?" Yetta asked.

"Not yet. We need a drop of the pheromone potion. We will be around many Akilians, and our powers will not fool all of them."

They took a drop of the bitter water and curled their lip upward from the taste. Having completed their outward illusion, they left Thea's apartment, each wearing the other's clothes and portraying the other's physical appearance. It took some time to adjust to their new identities. They had practiced responding to the other's name and morphed into the other's personality, completing the deception. At the arena, they entered the preparation room and sat in front of a mirror.

Gecheana's order for Yetta to join houses with Noka forced her into this situation. She could not accept the idea of Noka pawing at her because it made her ill. Still, seeing Thea's reflection staring back at her gave Yetta the creeps. After the stylist fixed her hair, she looked over and saw that Thea had disappeared. Pushing aside her first reaction, which was panic, Yetta searched for her. She did not wait long because Thea spoke with Taen, who thought he was talking with Yetta.

Anger replaced her anxiety as Yetta tried to listen to their conversation; it was impossible to hear from her position. Thea kissed him on the cheek and walked toward her seat, but Yetta stopped her.

"What is he doing here? I told him not to come," Yetta demanded.

"Even though you refused to select him, he wanted to participate. I thought it rather sweet," Thea smiled, remembering.

"I do not want him here because I do not want to see the look on his face when you choose Noka, so you must tell him to leave!"

"I tried, but he refused. I could injure him if you would like."

Grabbing Thea with both hands, Yetta pushed her back against a dresser and growled through gritted teeth, "I will end your life if you hurt him!"

"Calm down, daughter. It was only a suggestion. Besides, you are wrinkling your ceremonial dress. Do you want me to look messy while I am out in the arena impersonating you?"

Yetta released her with a push.

"Perhaps *you* should speak to him. You are the one pretending to be me. A stern warning from Yetta's mother might make him leave," Thea suggested with a raised eyebrow.

Yetta thought for a moment.

"Perhaps you are right; I will insist he go home."

She abruptly approached Taen, who greeted her with his palm forward. Yetta's love for him quenched her anger over his presence at her ceremony. Still, he had to leave.

"Why are you here?" Yetta demanded, pretending to be Thea.

"I am exercising my right to participate in Yetta's celebration," Taen disputed defiantly.

"You know she will not accept you, so why would you enter it?" Yetta quizzed, impersonating Thea.

"I know it may sound ridiculous, but I love her, and she loves me. Yes, that is right, your daughter loves a moss farmer. I will never give up on her, no matter how angry you become. Even Zorion will not keep me from her."

"You are at the opposite end of the social ladder. Your love will not sway her decision. She will not go against Zorion's wishes. He is too powerful and has threatened to have you killed if Yetta chooses you," she lied.

"I am not afraid of Zorion, nor am I afraid to die for Yetta. I came here to show her that she has a choice. We can still be together," Taen asserted.

"If you two joined houses, both of you would have to leave the city and start over."

"I would welcome it if she were by my side."

Since Taen thought it was Thea, it only made Yetta love him more for his bravery and loyalty. Yetta had a life full of treachery and deceit under Gecheana's tutelage, and he was the only one she believed genuinely cared for her. Having such a willingness to sacrifice everything for her was the most romantic gesture she could ever imagine. Seeing that there was no way of keeping him out of the ceremony, even she gave in to his will.

"Very well, but do not get your hopes up."

She returned to her mirror, where an assistant ran to her and said that Zorion was approaching the dais. Before leaving, Yetta looked at her mother again; satisfied that the resemblance was perfect, she left to join Zorion on stage.

Chapter 47

Earth
Scotland - Edinburgh
May 14, 2452

Colin rolled over in bed and extended his arm to pull her close but only found a pillow. His eyes groggily searched the room until he saw her standing on the balcony. Colin dragged himself out of bed, feeling ill due to the champagne they consumed last night. He walked to the French glass doorway and stopped to view the city with her at the forefront.

He reserved their penthouse suite to celebrate their first anniversary, and it gave them a god's eye view of Edinburgh. Leaning against the rail, Dawn stared out over the awaking city. Behind her silhouette, golden sunlight reflected off the edge of wispy clouds floating on the horizon. It was early; she could never sleep for long.

Seeing her hair, he smiled, musing that she reminded him of a chameleon. She often changed the color and had done so once again. This time she switched it from a deep brown to a two-tone brown and blonde combination. With a lover's enthusiasm, he gazed at her body through her sheer silk robe swaying in the gentle cool breeze, leaving nothing to the imagination. Even in the dim morning light, he could see goosebumps on her skin, yet the chill did not bother her.

He moved toward her, put his arms around her waist and his chin on her right shoulder. Her skin felt cold, so he knew she had been there for some time. They stood together in silence; he gazed out over the city with her. It grew exponentially over the past few years due to a large company that rose from a small business into a conglomerate, bringing jobs and wealth to the area.

As the CEO of Shire Inc., one of the leading drug companies in Europe, his business had been in a race with the corporate giant to find a common cold vaccine. Their research pushed them ahead of the competition by decades until finally, they found it. He would soon announce their success to the world, which would push their stock prices to their highest levels. Once the news of their discovery hit the media, he planned to retire because his current schedule afforded him little personal time.

Recently, he tried to convince her to work as his assistant to be with her daily. Sadly, she turned down his offer, saying she wanted to make it on her own steam. He admired her for it but hated knowing she was wasting her time as a secretary for a small business instead of collaborating with him. Obstacles were a challenge, and he always overcame them, which is why he put a plan into motion that would change things for them. By now, his body heat warmed her; her silence told him she was deep in thought.

"Good morning, love," he whispered affectionately.

"Good morning," she replied, raising her right hand, gently touching his cheek without turning around. "It's beautiful, isn't it?"

"What?"

"The sunrise."

"I think you're more beautiful than any sunrise."

"How sweet," Dawn responded.

"I don't suppose you could take the rest of the day off?" Colin asked.

"No, it's getting late. I need to get ready for work," Dawn turned to face him.

He stared into her blue eyes and longed to gaze at them forever, making him more determined to go through with his plan. They enjoyed a long kiss and returned to the room. Before she could get ready, he retrieved a small black box hidden in a dresser drawer. Holding it tightly in his hand, he gently took her arm.

"In a few days, I will announce something special on behalf of my company. We've developed something grand, and it will have a big payoff for me, which means that in a few months, I can retire."

"How wonderful. I'm so happy for you."

"This means I'll finally have more time to spend with you."

"Even better," she remarked, smiling.

He moved his hand to take hers and simultaneously got down on one knee, "Last night is a blur because I drank too much champagne. Now that I've recovered, I want to ask you something," he paused to take a deep breath, "Dawn, you would make me the happiest man in the entire world if you would marry me."

A warm smile grew on her face, "Yes. I will marry you."

He slid his grandmother's ring onto her finger, stood, and held her tight, "This is wonderful, Dawn! You won't regret it! I'll spend the rest of my life trying to make you happy. I promise."

Gently pulling away, she walked to the table and grabbed the opened bottle of Champaign, still sitting in the chiller, "How about a toast to celebrate?"

"Sounds wonderful! Just not too much this time. I want to remember this moment."

As she poured their drinks, he stared back at the sunrise. It was shaping up to be the best day of his life, "I wish my parents were still alive. I know my mother would have adored you."

She returned, handed him a glass of champagne, and questioned, "Were you close with them?"

"Yes. They were supportive. She gave me her ring before dying. It's the one I put on your finger. It's been in my family for more than a hundred years."

She lifted her glass, "To family."

He tapped her glass with his, "To 'family' and us."

They sipped their drinks until their glasses emptied; he set his down on the table, kissed her again, and queried, "When should we set the date?"

"There's no need to rush."

"June is only a month away. I could hire someone to help you plan everything. Think of it, Dawn, a June wedding in London!"

"It sounds wonderful, but..."

"What?"

He felt a sharp pain, causing him to clench his fist and grab his chest. Agony replaced joy because he realized it was another cardiovascular event. He staggered backward and fell onto the bed, struggling to breathe.

"Dawn, call for help! There's something wrong! I'm having a heart attack!"

She did not move.

At first, he wondered if she thought it was a prank; desperate, he reached out to her, "I'm not playing! It's for real!"

She did not reply, so he looked at her quizzically; her only response was a cold stare. He realized she would not help him and tried to reach the phone. Paralysis set in, preventing him from moving. Gradually, his breathing slowed, and he felt cold. As life gently drained from his body, everything steadily grew darker. Before leaving this world, the last thing he saw was his fiancé tossing her engagement ring onto his paralyzed body, and then there was nothing.

Dawn stared at the corpse, detached from any emotional sentiment, retrieved a prepaid cell phone from her purse, and dialed the only number saved in its memory. During the past few years, her job often demanded the other's services. To secure a prompt response, she gave him a retainer. Earlier negotiations set up a system beneficial to both parties. She would deposit his payment in a Post Office Box so that neither would ever have to meet, keeping their identities anonymous.

"Yeah," a croaky voice answered.

"I have made another mess," Dawn said indifferently.

"Where are you?"

"Penthouse suite at the Royal Mile."

"It's best if you leave now. I will be there in thirty minutes."

Without another word, she disconnected the line and tossed the phone onto the bed. Tomorrow, no one would find a trace of her presence in the room, and she would receive another prepaid phone with a number to contact him if she needed his services again. Now that time was of the essence, she dressed and left for work. She did not even bother to glance at Colin's body on her way out.

Chapter 48

Akil
Argi City
The 22,279th Terrestrial Rotation of the Second Summer

Tionah knocked on Julie's door several times with no answer and began pacing along the avenue. The problem with her new employer was her tardiness for their appointments. Considering her relationship with Zorion, Tionah could not understand why Julie was so careless about protocol. Remembering their last conversation, Julie had planned to rest, and since she obviously could not hear her knocking, Tionah decided to try the side door, hoping it was closer to her bedroom. She banged on the door for a few hundred heartbeats; Julie did not answer. Frustrated, Tionah rested at the fountain nearby.

She usually enjoyed the soothing sound of falling water, but the situation removed its relaxing effects. If Julie continued to be late, it would get her in trouble with Zorion. She saw it happen with Thea, and just as Tionah was about to get up to knock again, something appeared in her peripheral vision catching her attention. Tionah turned and saw Julie walking behind the protective railing in front of an undeveloped wall area. Curiously, she watched as Julie tiptoed toward the side door.

As she reached for the knob, Tionah spoke up, "May I ask where you were?"

Startled, Julie jumped and screamed simultaneously; knowing Tionah had caught her, she turned to face her, "I'm sorry, it's personal."

"I do not understand. You told me you planned to lie down."

"I couldn't sleep, so I went exploring."

"Those areas are fenced because loose rocks could fall on you."

Turning to open the door, Julie acknowledged, "Understood, I won't go back there again."

Tionah followed her, "I must warn you that if you continue to be late for Zorion, he will, at some point, become angry with you."

"I'll try harder to be on time. Now, let's get ready for the celebration."

Julie changed and stepped into the living room, where Tionah sat waiting. Upon seeing her, Tionah smiled with pride at her work, "You look like a princess."

"Do you think so?"

Still feeling insecure, Julie looked in the mirror. Everything about her appearance was utterly alien from what she used to wear; the hairdresser wove extensions into her hair, wrapped them in and around a tear-shaped form with holes spread evenly throughout. The tear-shaped fashion disappeared behind layers of real and fake hair, and, at the top, she formed small ball-like ends that hung from hair strands. Even stranger was her dress, which felt like a wrap rather than a fitted garment.

"Yes. I do. I know Zorion will be pleased with your appearance," Tionah's smile widened.

"That's all that matters to me."

"It is time to go. Zorion will be waiting with the other sovereigns. His itinerary says that the ambassador will be there too."

Julie exhaled nervously, "I hope I don't mess this up."

"You will be fine. Just remember to hold your palm forward as you greet the sovereigns."

"I will."

"Now, we must go. Your hover vehicle is waiting outside."

"I hope you didn't buy one."

"I can return it if you are not happy with it."

"No. I'm just saying it was unnecessary to spend all those Sovereign Cubes. We could have taken a taxi."

"Your circumstances require private transportation. Setting aside that you are an alien, we must always guard you because you are also Zorion's friend and, in a sense, a dignitary."

"I don't know what I would do without you," Julie replied and leaned in to hug her.

"You would be like a lost child," Tionah smiled, returning her hug. "Be careful not to show Zorion any public affection. Akilians consider it inappropriate."

"I will make a mental note."

They sat in the back seat, and Tionah told the driver where to go.

Along the way, Julie asked, "What happens at one of these celebrations?"

"She is Zorion's daughter and an aristocrat, so her ceremony will be more elaborate than any other; there will be music and dancing, much like your marching bands back on Earth. Yetta will take her seat at the end of the auditorium; her suitors will come in from the opposite end of the arena in a single file, marching in a complex and difficult rhythm around the stadium. Once the procession is complete, Yetta will stand, walk by each one, sit and announce the name of the one she selected."

"That doesn't sound very romantic."

"It is our tradition. Most couples find romance later in the relationship."

"Do you have someone?"

"Yes. His name is Edur."

"How did you meet?"

"We met at my coming-of-age celebration. It was by chance because not everyone finds someone so quickly."

"You did."

"It was a surprise."

"How so?"

"Normally, invitations are sent out to eligible Akilians within the social class before the celebration."

"Does that mean Edur has a job like you?"

"No, he works in an office. My work is a little more physically demanding."

"How did he end up at your celebration?"

"A carrier accidentally sent one of my invitations to him," she smiled, thinking back to their first meeting. "He pretended to be my equal, so I had no idea of his true status, and even though I had several suitors, I selected him."

"When did he tell you his status?"

"That evening. Naturally, my parents and I were surprised."

"What about his parents?"

"They objected as anyone in their position would. Edur insisted on staying with me, and they conceded."

"How long have you been together?"

"We are moving toward our fifth yellow harvest. After our ceremony, he gave me this," she held a necklace chain with a small yellow jewel dangling at its end.

"That's a pretty stone; what does the symbol mean?"

"It is his family crest. It means noble."

The vehicle slowed down to a stop. Julie saw a large crowd farther down the avenue, waiting to enter the arena. Artificial flowers, like the ones at the museum, decorated the entrance. A valet opened the door and helped them out. She saw Zorion approaching in the distance; she could smell spearmint long before he reached her. Tearing her thoughts away from him, she remembered Urki's instructions and concentrated on cloaking her power.

Seeing her, Zorion smiled and quickened his pace to greet her. He stood before her, admiring her beauty.

"You look stunning!"

He faced Tionah, "You have done an excellent job!"

Zorion returned his attention to Julie, held his arm for her to take, and smiled, "Are you ready to meet the other sovereigns?"

"As ready as I'll ever be."

Julie walked, holding onto Zorion's arm, turned back to look at Tionah, and wished she could come with her. Seeing her worried, Tionah smiled and waved to her, nodding confidently. They entered a private room adjoining the main auditorium, and Julie felt every eye on her. One by one, they approached her, anxiously waiting for an introduction to the one who saved their world.

Being mindful of Tionah's instructions, she was sure to greet them with her palm forward. However, she found it increasingly difficult to split her concentration between hiding her power from the Skeans and listening to others talk. As the crowd's noise grew, she realized the celebration would begin soon.

Zorion socialized with his guests for a time and returned to her side, "We will be moving to the dais shortly. You will sit beside me, but as Yetta enters the arena, I must move forward and sit alongside Thea," he paused to look at the stage, "The moment she arrives. I am sorry; it is unavoidable because she is Yetta's parent."

"Don't worry. I'm not upset. I understand you still have obligations to her."

"Thank you. Your consideration means a great deal to me. After the ceremony, I will introduce you and the ambassador. I believe presenting the ambassador second will help focus the media's attention on him since I will announce that we have reached an agreement, and tomorrow, we will begin moving to Earth."

"Oh, Zorion, that's wonderful!" she reached up to embrace him, forgetting that Akilians considered public displays of affection inappropriate; realizing her mistake, she let go of him; it was too late because the others had already noticed.

"I'm deeply sorry. Tionah told me it was improper; I got caught up in the moment."

"Do not worry. They will understand. I will make them if they do not," he answered with a wry grin.

"Zorion, we should be going," Gwah urged.

Zorion extended his arm for her to take, so Julie rested her hand on it, and they walked toward the dais, with everyone else following close behind. As they walked the steps, the crowd murmured, seeing Zorion with Julie; their whispers grew louder seeing the other Akilian sovereigns following close behind. Before sitting, Zorion searched the room for Otsoa, who was absent; he did notice that Thea finally decided to show up. Right behind her, Durnah was running to catch up with the group.

She stood beside him, "Otsoa sends his apologies. He is not feeling well."

"Otsoa is sick? He has never been sick for one Terrestrial Revolution in his life," Zorion explained.

"I left him in bed. He did not look well," Durnah reported.

"I will escort you home after the ceremony and visit him. For now, please have a seat beside Thea."

"Thank you."

Pushing aside his worries about Otsoa's health, Zorion moved toward the podium, and the crowd began to quiet. It was clear that they were curious about the unfamiliar guests and why all the sovereigns were together simultaneously. Moments later, Zorion began the ceremony.

Chapter 49

Earth
The Regime - Washington, D.C. - Fort McNair
May 14, 2452

Before dropping through the portal, Wu Luli requested a weapon; Captain Yates refused. She hated going into a combat situation unarmed, but her dad's life depended upon her being there. On the other side of the event horizon, she landed just a few feet from Nick's position, several yards from the entrance, where she last saw her dad. One soldier from Nick's team approached their location.

"I just finished scanning this building section for heat signatures and motion. Based on my readings, all the guards are dead."

"That's why the readings were off in our original scan. Their bodies have cooled down, making their signatures appear blocked."

The rest of his team reported in; he faced Wu Luli, "Every sentry inside the building is dead. Any ideas?"

"I'm sure it's a trap; I do not know what kind he set for us, so let me go inside."

Nick shook his head, "We have to clear it for possible explosives first," he paused to push the microphone to his lips. "Base, we have a problem, over."

"Roger that," General Green acknowledged.

He faced his communication officer, "I want a private line to Nick's comm."

"What's the problem, Nick?" he questioned.

"All the guards inside are dead. Wu Luli thinks it's a trap; she's uncertain what kind. I agree with her assessment."

"How do you want to proceed?"

"I will have my men pull back to defensive positions. We'll need shield generators and ten bomb-seeking androids."

"They'll be there shortly; after they arrive, we'll close the portals, just in case there's an explosion. We'll communicate via satellite from now on."

"Roger that."

His men pulled back to safer positions, and a large android, carrying a shield generator, exited the portal. The other nine would land at different sites around the building. The android set down the shield generator and handed Nick the controls. The shield was up in less than five minutes, so he sent the android inside to root out any explosives.

Having used them before, Nick was glad for their help because they saved many lives. Even if a bomb exploded during their search, engineers made their skeletal frames out of thick titanium bars, protecting them from almost any blast. Also, unlike other androids, engineers did not give them a human appearance because they did not deal with the public.

Instead, their skeletal systems stayed exposed. If caught in an explosion, the force of the blast would go through them rather than push them. It reached the door, and the skeleton-like android used one of its metal fingers to punch through the steel knob, disabling the locking mechanism. Its mechanical arm pushed the door open and leisurely walked inside. Once out of sight, Nick faced the monitor watching the android's movements.

"That's the room. See if our man is inside," Nick ordered the android.

The android punched through the lock and stepped inside the room. The monitor showed an older man sitting in a recliner, watching television. The android performed a visual and electronic scan to secure the area. Satisfied it was safe, Nick instructed the android to remove him; using its multilingual software, it faced the man and spoke in Mandarin.

"Sir, please come with me now!"

Startled out of a sound sleep, the older man jumped. Again, the android repeated its message until he realized it was a rescue, so he got up and followed the android outside, where Nick and Wu Luli waited. Seeing him, Wu Luli ran to meet him. They held each other until Nick and a team member grabbed their arms and pulled them back behind the protective shield.

Wu Luli had tears in her eyes, "I told you I would get you out of here."

Her dad was also misty-eyed, "Yes, but at what cost?"

"I made a deal with the Regime; we'll be safe."

Nick was happy to rescue a prisoner. Still, the situation remained precarious at best.

"Base, we've acquired the target."

"Roger that. What about the building?"

"I'm still waiting for the androids to finish their scan."

The androids cleared the building an hour later, allowing Nick and his men to rush inside and check each room down the long corridor. Nick returned to Wu Luli several minutes later, sitting beside her dad.

"You must come with me."

His tone gave her chills; she followed him and got a sick feeling in her stomach, which was never a good sign. She entered the first room and discovered that her instincts were right again. She saw a woman riddled with bullets sitting in a chair like her dad. She closely examined the body and counted over twenty bullet holes spanning the woman's face and torso. It was an execution. *Why did he spare my dad?*

She looked at Nick and inquired, "Are they all like this?"

He nodded.

She and Nick's team thoroughly searched the room and came up empty until seeing one of the lenses gave her an idea.

"Let's get to his office."

Before moving ahead, he checked with the team, ensuring everything was clear, and they ran to his office. Wu Luli sat in General Ming-tun Fu's chair. His computer was on, and the pointer rested over a folder. At first, she hesitated, not wanting to see what he had in store for her. She clicked the mouse, and a video played. This had to be the worst of all the things General Ming-Tun Fu could have done.

The video showed someone armed with an automatic weapon entering the room. Wu Luli saw her face and gasped because the assassin looked like Wu Luli. The impersonator ruthlessly shot the prisoner until he was dead. She scanned the video's contents and discovered that the assassin had killed every prisoner in the corridor; General Ming-Tun Fu had framed her for ninety-nine murders.

Sensing Nick's presence behind her, she faced him, "I was right; it's a trap, designed only for me."

"Aren't you the woman in the video?"

"No. That is another agent, wearing prosthetics to look like me. He left it here as a message to me."

"Message?"

"Yes, he has sent a copy to every agent, so I now have ninety-nine specially trained killers looking for me."

"We better get you back home."

Captain Yates escorted them to the hospital for a complete exam. Wu Luli explained to her dad what was happening and that an interpreter would meet him at the hospital. Also, she would return at some point.

Once her dad left, she faced Captain Yates, "I need to speak with Michael now."

"After I debrief you, I will contact him."

"No. It's too important. Please, I need to speak to him now!"

Captain Yates hesitated, but hearing the urgency in her voice, he nodded, "All right, I will contact him in the interrogation room."

Several minutes later, Michael arrived, still unhappy to see her, "What do you want?"

His words were curt. Gently, she pulled him close to whisper; he pulled away. The second time, she pulled harder, forcing him to come close, and whispered sharply into his ear.

"Listen to me! You have a spy somewhere in your organization."

"Yeah, you."

"No. I'm talking about someone else. Someone the Regime doesn't know about."

"Why are you telling me?"

"Because you're the only one I trust. I don't know Captain Yates, so I can't tell if someone has compromised him."

"Why do you think there's a spy?"

"Because I left my employer to reenter the Regime, he had no reason to suspect that I would betray him. At his facility, we made a gruesome discovery. General Ming-Tun Fu has one hundred spies in his employment. I recently learned that he had been holding our parents in that building. They are all dead, except for mine, and to make matters worse, he had the killer fitted with prosthetics to look like me and recorded their assassinations. By now, my colleagues have a copy, which means I have a target on my back."

Michael paused to think, "There are only a few people who know about you and why you're here, including the Supreme Commander, so what you're telling me is impossible. Everyone in contact with this mission has top-level clearance, which means they were born in the Regime. There's no way he or she would betray our country."

"General Ming-tun Fu had no idea I was planning to leave him. The only ones who know are you, Captain Yates, General Saunders, and Supreme Commander Porter."

He shook his head, "I don't think it's true. The leak must be on your end."

"At least stay for the debriefing because I might say something or someone's name that will give you a clue as to who it could be."

"I think it's a waste of time. It's obvious that General Ming-Tun Fu ordered one of your colleagues to spy on you."

"We'll see."

They sat, and Captain Yates turned on a video recorder, "Please state your name for the record."

"My name is Wu Luli."

"Would you please explain your first mission to the Regime?"

"I was ordered to replace Chu Lian during her vacation."

"Is she still alive?"

"No. General Ming-Tun Fu ordered me to kill her."

"Did you have plastic surgery to make yourself look like her?"

"No. General Ming-Tun Fu discovered her by accident. He showed me pictures of her. At first, I thought they were of me, but I later learned she was my doppelganger."

"After you arrived, what did you do?"

"It took a few weeks for me to learn how to fit into her life. Part of that was getting acquainted with her friends, which wasn't difficult because she only had a few."

"And her mother?"

"I would only make short video calls if pressed. Other than that, I communicated through text or emails."

"Why did you target Michael?"

She paused, feeling the weight of her decisions. Initially, Michael would not be here for her debriefing; now that he was present, she wanted him to hear it from her since he would find out eventually.

"He had a high clearance level, so I knew that if I could get close to him, I could get his badge. With his identification, I could access the labs on his floor, copy as many top-secret documents as possible, and send them to General Ming-Tun Fu."

In her peripheral vision, she saw Michael instinctively grab for his identification.

"What information did you obtain?"

"It is still unclear what information I sent."

Captain Yates looked at her quizzically, "How did you know it was top secret?"

"I didn't." She took a deep breath. "Standard protocol dictated that I kill him, take his badge, get the information, and get out before anyone knew what happened."

"What stopped you?"

She smiled at Michael, "I fell in love with him, so I couldn't do it."

He remembered the moment she was referring to, and his eyes widened, "You mean that day you knocked the glass out of my hand?"

"Yes."

"Please elaborate," Captain Yates interrupted.

"I invited Michael to my apartment. We ate dinner and I poured him a toxic drink. Before sipping it, he told me he wanted to be with me forever. I remember thinking that no one has ever said this to me before. I knew he was not lying; he had no reason. I imagined my life in ten years and what I saw frightened me. It didn't take a genius to know that if I continued to spy for General Ming-Tun Fu, I would always be alone, never knowing what it felt like to be in a real relationship. As he brought the drink to his lips, I realized I loved him too. Without thinking, I slapped the glass out of his hands."

"What happened next?" Captain Yates asked.

Wu Luli smiled, "We made love for the first time."

She looked at Michael, hoping he was fond of the memory; her grin faded seeing him frown.

"Are you saying that you never took his badge?" Captain Yates inquired.

"That's right."

"What files did you send to your employer?"

"Because of how I felt, there was no way I could hurt him or the Regime, and since Michael often brought his laptop home, I decided to try a different approach."

"Wait a minute! I secured the laptop with a combination lock, and even if you hack into it, the Regime encrypts the files with a twenty-tier security system protecting them, so how could you possibly get by all that protection?" Michael yelled.

"The combination took a few tries; you used my birthday," pausing; Wu Luli smiled softly at him. "I thought it was sweet."

She faced Captain Yates, "Once the lid was up, I turned it on. With no one around, I inserted software that easily bypassed his passwords breaking through the firewalls. It took a few minutes until they fell. Once I was in, I looked for something harmless. There was quite a bit saved. There were many fantastic ideas that I did not send because I knew my employer would do horrible things with them.

"Michael didn't make it easy because the folders did not have labels with a classification; I found a folder titled 'Parlor Game' after searching for a stretch. There were quite a few files with schematics inside. They looked complicated enough to fool my employer into thinking it was something important, so I changed the name to Project X, making it seem like it was highly classified."

In her peripheral vision, she saw Michael's expression turn to horror. The distraction made her talk slower and slower until she finished her thought.

"I didn't think any harm would come of it since it was only a Parlor Game. I broke the files up into sections. I mixed them up and sent them, one by one, to General Ming-Tun Fu. I dragged the process out, knowing I would not have anything else to send back once I finished. A couple of quiet months later, he called me back home."

As she finished speaking, Michael stood white as a ghost. She thought he was going to pass out.

"What's wrong?" Captain Yates wondered.

Panic set in, and his breathing was fast and deep; he pointed to her, "You've destroyed us!"

He ran out of the room.

Wu Luli frowned, "What is he talking about?"

"I don't know, but whatever you copied from his hard drive, I'm guessing it *was* top secret."

Wu Luli sighed, "I thought I was careful. I didn't want to send anything damaging."

"The road to hell is paved with good intentions. Now, why did you return?"

"General Ming-Tun Fu wanted me to retrieve a disc he believed the Regime stole from one of his clients. As part of the deal, he wanted me to kill Supreme Commander Porter too."

Captain Yates frowned, "And the client's name?"

"President Martinez."

Captain Yates entered the information into his tablet, which caused a flashing red light in response, so he inquired, "Can you decipher the disc?"

"Yes. Nathan Mitchell encrypted it. Before disappearing, he worked for General Ming-Tun Fu, so we assumed the Regime grabbed him."

"It wasn't us."

"He disappeared out of a very secure facility. There were no tunnels, no broken locks, and no sign that he left his room."

"It does sound mysterious. Follow me," Captain Yates walked to the door.

Wu Luli followed him through a series of corridors to a lab where two androids stood at the entry. Captain Yates spoke an entry code, and they allowed him to pass. Inside, she saw hundreds of people working at computer stations, and a young man approached them.

"Can I help you?" queried Danny.

"I think we can help you, Danny. This young woman standing beside me should be able to decipher the disc."

"I could use all the help I can get; we've been working on it for days with no success. How can she possibly decode it?"

"Get me to a terminal with internet access, and I'll show you," she reassured.

He showed her to one, and she sat. Her fingers moved across the keyboard swiftly until finding the site where she downloaded an application.

"What's that?" Danny questioned.

"The software you need to decrypt the disc," she answered as it finished downloading.

"Where's the information on the disc?" she asked.

He disappeared for a moment, returned with a data stick, inserted it into the monitor's side, and Wu Luli started the application. Hundreds of windows opened with schematic images, which Captain Yates recognized with wide eyes.

Seeing his expression, she queried, "What is it?"

"It's the schematics for a portal machine!"

"President Martinez would have paid General Ming-tun Fu a very high price for this technology," Wu Luli noted.

"I must return you to the debriefing room and inform Supreme Commander Porter of our discovery!"

Chapter 50

Standing at the podium, Zorion felt excited, preparing to make his speech in front of the large crowd. Soon, everyone would share in his hope of surviving the Akilian crisis.

"First, I want to thank all of you for attending. Before we begin the festivities, I wanted to let everyone know that the Information League broadcasts this ceremony at every station. Later, I will have a special announcement to make. Now, I can see many familiar faces in the crowd. Most attended Otsoa's celebration just a few Terrestrial Revolutions ago. Sadly, I must report that he cannot be here due to an illness."

Hearing soft chatter, he paused until it subsided, "As everyone knows, at the beginning of her eighteenth Yellow Harvest, an heiress receives a coming-of-age ceremony. An assistant told me a hundred eligible suitors are waiting just outside those doors," he paused, allowing a smattering of applause, "Since I have waited for eighteen Yellow Harvests for this event, I see no need to delay the celebration any longer, so let the festivities begin!"

As Zorion returned to his seat, the crowd roared a cheer, and the musicians came into the arena with loud music that echoed throughout the auditorium. The crowd stood and danced as the acrobats entered the stadium. Their performance reminded Julie of the circus acts back home. They performed gymnastic feats, danced, and threw artificial black flowers into the stands.

Half an hour later, they disappeared through the exits the same way they entered. Hundreds of young Akilian females walked onto the center floor, wearing black and red. Their dresses rose in the air as they twirled, reminding Julie of the ballet dancers she used to watch as a young girl. Their precision and timing amazed her; the dance ended, so they formed two parallel lines that led from one of the entrances to a chair. They faced the door, knelt to the ground, spread out their dresses, and bowed forward with their arms extended.

Zorion nudged her, "There she is," he nodded toward the entrance farthest away from their seats.

To Julie's surprise, Yetta wore all black, and if that was not bad enough, she also painted her eyes black. It reminded her of the gothic fashions of so long ago.

"Are you sure she's going to get married? It looks like she's going to a funeral," she whispered.

He looked at her quizzically.

"On Earth, women wear black to funerals," she added.

He gave her a knowing look, "In our tradition, the women wear black because they are Gau's daughters."

Julie bewilderedly nodded.

"I must sit beside Thea now," he lamented.

"I'll be right here, waiting," she smiled.

Julie watched as Yetta passed the women, making the pathway to her seat; each stood and danced behind her. The crowd cheered as she walked to her chair. The noise was so loud that Julie had to cover her ears. The spectator's clamor made it hard for her to focus on her cloak. Urki told her it would be very demanding during her last training session. To make matters worse, the longer she tried to support it, the more difficult it became to control.

Feeling her concentration slip slightly, she refocused her mind to hide her powers. Now was not the time to reveal herself to any Skeans that might be nearby. Yetta took her seat, and Julie saw about a hundred men dressed in formal apparel enter the arena. They marched in a strange and awkward rhythm several times around the auditorium and, in due course, moved toward Yetta in a single file line. They paraded within a few feet from where she sat as they passed by.

They returned to their original formation and stopped moving; the audience was silent as Yetta walked by each admirer. Occasionally, she paused to study a candidate, moved on to another, and repeated the process until returning to her seat.

Taking his cue, Zorion walked to the podium and inquired, "Have you made your decision?"

"I have," she replied.

Since she was wearing a microphone pinned to her collar, her voice echoed throughout the arena.

"Begin the procession," Zorion announced.

Instantly, the suitors moved into a single line; one by one, they approached Yetta, pausing briefly to wait for the signal that she had selected him. If she did not respond, he moved on, and another suitor replaced him. As she turned away each one, Julie became more anxious, wondering whom she would choose. Julie did not know Yetta yet felt nervous for her because she had to make a crucial life decision. A thousand heartbeats later, only a few remained; Yetta raised her staff. Julie saw the confused look on the winner's face.

At the same time, Julie felt a wave of anger wash over her. At first, she thought it was her emotion until realizing it came from someone nearby. The distraction caused her to lose focus, and her cloak briefly vanished, exposing her. She closed her eyes, concentrated on raising the invisible cover around her again, and looked around to see if someone had noticed.

Although no one directly looked at her, she did notice Thea glaring at Ambassador Reynolds, who sat nearby. Seeing her gaze, Ambassador Reynolds smiled and gave her a friendly nod. Without a response, Thea turned her attention back to the celebration. The circumstances were suspicious, and Julie was unsure if it was a coincidence. Her gut was telling her that Thea might be a Skean. Since Thea looked at the Ambassador, she might have thought the power emitted from him. *If that's true, his life could be in danger.*

Having made her choice, the rest of the suitors disbanded and left the arena, signaling the musicians to return and play another song. The newlyweds danced as the music played. The crowd stood, applauded, and threw the artificial black flowers onto the arena floor. The thought of having black flowers thrown at her wedding made Julie cringe. The song ended, so the couple bowed and turned to face everyone in the audience.

As they started to exit, Zorion rushed to the podium, "Yetta, please, do not leave yet. I would ask that everyone stay seated for just a moment. I have news you will want to hear."

His announcement stirred the crowd, so after quieting them, he motioned for Julie and Ambassador Reynolds to come forward.

"I am sure you recognize everyone on the dais, except for these two unfamiliar faces. It has been no secret that we have searched the stars for another planet we could call home. I am pleased to announce that we have indeed found one."

There was loud chatter among the crowd.

"Please, quiet down. There is more I need to say."

The room became silent.

"I have never been a strong believer in miracles, but the circumstances that led to finding this new world have changed my thinking. We discovered a suitable planet through a series of events that I would normally call accidents. We also learned that another civilization inhabits it, so we sent a scout to gather information about their societies. Upon his return, another accident occurred. This young female named Julie followed him here to Akil. With her help, we sent a quick message to their Supreme Commander."

Briefly, he faced her, "Without you, none of this would be possible."

He returned his attention to the assembly, "Within a brief time, they sent Ambassador Reynolds, who brought with him a contract for us to review. This contract is an agreement between our two worlds," he paused to savor the moment. "The agreement, which all of the sovereigns have signed, will allow us to start moving to their world at the beginning of the following Terrestrial Rotation!"

The crowd thunderously cheered. Everyone stood, danced, and threw pieces of their garments in the air or anything they could grab. During their happy response, Zorion looked at Julie and smiled with excitement. It took Zorion a few thousand heartbeats to quiet everyone down again.

"As you know, our numbers are very great. To move such a large group, we must ensure that food, water, and other necessities are available. Therefore, we will send over two thousand Akilians from each city whose abilities lie in construction, engineering, and science. It will ensure that the things we need will be ready when we arrive. I will release more information as time goes on."

He turned to Julie and asked, "Would you like to say something?"

"I don't know what to say. Besides, they won't understand me."

"I have installed a translator in the system, so please, speak a few words from the heart."

Reluctantly, she agreed. Standing at the podium, she could feel every eye upon her. The microphone broadcasted her heavy breathing as she tried to think of something to say.

"Zorion is right. I stumbled onto your world accidentally. I can honestly say that I was frightened because I did not know where I was or who any of you were."

There was some soft laughter as she paused to think of something else to say.

"I have only been here a couple of days, and I have seen enough of your city to know that you are intelligent, kind, and resourceful people. I want to be the first person from Earth to welcome you to our planet, and I look forward to learning more about your history and culture. I hope to meet as many of you as possible. Thank you."

Again, the crowd roared in response. It took Zorion another few thousand heartbeats to quiet them, which allowed him to introduce Ambassador Reynolds and turn the podium over to him. Zorion returned to his seat as the Ambassador gave an over-rehearsed speech. Julie hoped everyone would concentrate on him now; Thea sat beside her.

"You must be the one everybody has been talking about," she whispered.

"I thought my presence here was secret," Julie responded.

"I do not know what it is like on Earth, my dear, but secrets are hard to keep here," Thea grinned.

"How much do you know about me?"

"I know that Zorion created an account in your name."

"I didn't ask for it, and I'm giving whatever's left back to him when I return to Earth."

"Why?"

"Because I can take care of myself."

"It is your loss."

"Yetta looks beautiful today," Julie offered, trying to change the subject.

Thea ignored her comment and questioned, "Tell me about Ambassador Reynolds."

"I can't tell you anything about him. I don't know him."

"That is a shame. I was hoping you would know if he was single."

"Really? Ambassador Reynolds?"

"Why, do you not find him attractive?"

"Uh, actually, no, I don't."

"Perhaps you can introduce me to him later."

"Sure, if you would like."

"Good, I will call upon you if I have a need," she remarked and abruptly left.

Ok, that was weird. Alone again, Julie sat back in her chair, waiting for Ambassador Reynolds to finish his speech. She knew that he was every bit a politician because his oration continued for a long time, and it was about nothing. He finally finished, and the crowd responded again with thunderous applause and shouting. This time, Zorion did not wait for them to settle down; instead, he dismissed everyone and escorted Julie and Ambassador Reynolds off the stage into the private room from where they came. As they left, everyone on the dais walked into the room together. Zorion stayed by Julie's side.

"They seem happy about the news," she yelled over the noise.

"Yes. Still, we have many challenges ahead of us. I only hope their enthusiasm remains strong."

Everyone from the dais was in the private room when Yetta and her new partner walked in. Clearly, Thea was not happy with her; Julie did not understand why.

She faced Zorion, "Did Yetta's ceremony go the way you hoped?"

"Yes. I believe it did."

Nodding toward the one Yetta selected, she quizzed, "What's his name?"

"His name is Taen. I vaguely remember her mentioning him at dinner once, so I am not surprised at her choice."

"Do you approve of him?"

"Many consider moss farmers low in our society. My only concern is Yetta's happiness; Thea does not share my sentiment," he responded, watching them argue.

Julie looked at him quizzically, "Isn't moss essential to your survival here?"

"Yes, I deeply respect our farmers, but Thea is very status-oriented. Even though she has come from a low position in our society, she thinks everyone else is beneath her. It is one of the many reasons we are no longer together."

"I'm glad you're not like that."

"You can thank my sovereign. As I grew up, part of my education included moss farming, among other menial jobs, so I learned respect for those who had to do them daily."

"That's good to know."

Chapter 51

Earth
Spain - Madrid
May 15, 2452

After their meal, Sofia and Isabella stayed in the kitchen to clean up while Vincent, Diego, and Sabina moved into the living room. Sabina had already taken her first steps, so she felt confident walking. She staggered toward Vincent, falling along the way. He reached out to support her. Sabina grabbed onto his index fingers, pulled herself up, and with renewed confidence, put one foot in front of the other, forcing Vincent to stand and walk with her.

Returning from the kitchen, Isabella smiled, seeing him holding her up. Sabina made her way over to Sofia, who spoke in odd-sounding, Spanish baby talk. Vincent thought it was strange; Sabina liked it. A brief time later, Isabella put her down for a nap, and the adults talked for a little longer.

Sofia stood, "I really must thank you for a wonderful evening, but it's time for me to leave because I must go to work in the morning."

"Already?" Isabella asked, disappointed by her early departure.

"I barely avoided a disaster today, so I need to go in early tomorrow to check on a few things."

"Vincent, why don't you walk Sofia home," Isabella grinned.

Reflexively, Vincent gave Diego a look that meant "stop her from interfering," not realizing Sofia saw him.

"Isabella, why don't you come with me into the kitchen, dear," Diego urged.

"Why? What's wrong?"

Gently, Diego took her hand and urged her to move out of the living room, leaving Vincent and Sofia alone. Sofia started for the door before Vincent could say goodbye.

"Sofia, wait," he ran to catch up with her.

Before he could reach her, she slammed the door in his face. Holding onto the knob, he paused before opening it. *She's gone; the dinner is over; just let her go.* Over the years, he learned to trust his instincts, and they were screaming at him to stop, yet for unknown reasons, he ignored the warning, chased her, and caught up as she was unlocking her door.

"Sofia, please wait!"

She removed the keys and turned to look at him with flushed cheeks as anger boiled inside her.

"Why are you so mad?" he wondered.

"I saw the look you gave Diego. It's obvious you are not interested in me."

"Hold on! That's not true. You're jumping to conclusions."

Ignoring him, she spun around and opened her door. She paused before going inside.

"I don't need your pity! If I choose, I could find someone before the night is over. I only came over because Isabella spoke so highly of you. Now I can see you're nothing like she described!"

Gently, he reached to stop her, "Look, you're getting upset for no reason."

"Explain it to me," she demanded, folding her arms in anticipation of a lame excuse.

"Uh, all right. Yes, Diego told me Isabella was setting up a dinner date tonight, and I didn't want to come. It's because I'm always traveling, and it makes it hard on relationships. My last girlfriend hated me for it, and I didn't want to go through that again."

"Humph, it seems I didn't jump to any conclusions!"

Again, she abruptly turned and walked into her apartment. Ignoring his better judgment, he followed her inside and closed the door behind him.

"Look, I'm glad we met. You're beautiful and smart."

At hearing his voice, she turned to face him. Her piercing look would have killed him if her eyes were a weapon.

"How dare you enter my apartment! I didn't invite you in!"

Holding his hands in surrender, he said, "Don't be upset. Just let me explain before I leave."

"You've already explained. I understand. You're not interested because you're afraid. You think I'll hurt you. Now go!"

Adamant to reason with her, he held his ground, "Look, why don't you give me your contact information, and we can start over? I only have a few more cities left on my itinerary, so I'll call you, and we can go out, just you and me. We'll talk about my business and how often I'm away, and if you're still interested, we can try seeing each other."

With a laugh that held daggers, she scoffed at him, "I wouldn't go out with you if you were the last man on Earth! Now leave!"

He did not move, so she used her body weight to push him into the door. Angered, he started to leave but stopped and, without thinking, turned and kissed her. His advance surprised her, yet she did not resist; he pulled away, and she unexpectedly slapped him hard on his cheek.

"Ouch! Why did you do that?"

Without responding, she pushed him against the door again and kissed him. At some point, she ripped his shirt open. Buttons shot in every direction, bouncing off the furniture and the floor.

"That was a new shirt!" Vincent protested, tearing the shirt from her body, partly in retaliation.

They continued to shred each other's clothing as if in a contest. Hours later, Vincent lay face down in her bed, sleeping. Sofia got up, and her sudden movement woke him. He gazed at her naked silhouette as she walked into the kitchen to pour something to drink. On her way back, she carried two glasses.

"I thought you might be thirsty."

"Yeah, I am. Thanks."

He drank the filtered water, set the glass on the dresser, and noticed her staring at him.

"What's wrong?"

"I'm never going to see you again, am I?"

"Of course, you will. I'll finish my itinerary and take some time off. You must understand that what I do for a living takes up much of my time. I'm always going from one city to another, which is why my last relationship failed. That's why I hesitated."

Smiling, she sat beside him and kissed him, "I would like to see you again. Let's try it. At the very least, I could see you on weekends. Portal travel means you'll only be a few minutes away."

"I have plenty of frequent portal miles you can use," Vincent offered.

"You are sweet. Are you hungry? I'll make us something to eat."

"Yeah, I could eat something. You gave me quite a workout."

"I'll be right back."

As she got out of bed, he felt something sharp scrape his arm. Looking down, he saw a two-inch scratch that started to bleed.

"I think your bracelet nicked me," he held up his arm to show her.

"Oh, I'm sorry. I'll get a Band-Aid."

As she retrieved it, he scanned the room to get a sense of her character. From experience, he learned that pictures told a lot about a person; his search came up empty. The absence of any photo made him feel uneasy. To make matters worse, he could see marks on the wall, showing that, at one time, there were pictures in the room. His gut was screaming a warning.

"Hey, Sofia, I'd like to see a picture of your parents."

"I don't have any. I was an infant when they died," she yelled from the kitchen.

"What about friends?"

"My job keeps me too busy. I never had time for friends. Why do you think Isabella set us up?"

Her answers did not put him at ease. He contemplated the situation and decided to dress, but his arms and legs would not move, prompting him to perform a quick body check. He discovered that his head could move, his breathing was not impaired, yet he could not move anything from the neck down.

"Sofia, something's wrong. I can't move. I think you should call the paramedics!" She did not answer, so he yelled again, "Sofia! Where are you?"

Moments later, he heard her walking toward him. Her boots hitting the hardwood floors gave him an eerie chill.

"Why are you dressed?"

She sighed, "Because I'm afraid our time together is over."

"Nicely played."

"Thank you. I must admit, you gave Diego that look, and I thought for sure it was going to take me longer to get to you."

"I almost didn't follow you. Walking out in a huff was a good move. I should have listened to my instincts."

"It would have only delayed the inevitable. You know as well as I that you would have pursued me. I have not lost a man yet."

“How very humble of you. Who hired you?”

He was sure of the answer. Still, he wanted to hear it from her. Without responding, she stood beside him, moved his legs, so they were straight, and pointed his toes upward.

“Dragon sends his regards.”

“Whatever he’s paying you, my employer will double it if you don’t kill me.”

He tried to move his fingers; they did not respond. Meanwhile, Sofia continued her ritual by gently grabbing his hands and crossing them over his chest.

“That’s a generous offer, yet I cannot accept it because I have a reputation to uphold. If people hear that I double-crossed my contractor, I will never work again and could end up dead, most likely by Dragon himself.”

“I can protect you. I *will* protect you.”

She chuckled softly, fluffed his pillow, placed it under his head, and walked to the end of the bed. She had left his head tilted forward enough so that he could look her in the eyes.

“How can a business owner, who travels the world, protect me?”

“Come on. You must know that I’m not *really* a business owner, so think, why would Dragon want to kill me?”

She froze; now he knew she had no idea the kind of trouble that found her.

“You don’t know who I am, do you?”

“I don’t need to know. I accepted a contract, and I must fulfill it. I wish we had met under different circumstances because I enjoyed our brief encounter.”

She opened one of the dresser drawers and retrieved a six-shooter with a suppressor.

As she brought the weapon to bear, he exclaimed, “I’m an agent for the Regime!”

She smiled knowingly, “You’re lying. Dragon gave me your dossier, and I verified its authenticity. You’re a tool salesman for Ultimate Construction.”

“That’s my cover. Dragon killed a Regime comptroller, and I’ve been chasing him all over Europe. He sent you here to stop me because I’m getting close.”

"Now I know you're lying. No one has ever gained illegal entry into the Regime."

"Somehow, he got access to a Portable Vortex Transmitter, and you know how diligently the Regime guards its technology. We're just as diligent in finding those who kill our citizens; if you kill me, they *will* send someone to find you."

"You almost had me, except you have a flaw in your story. In my line of work, I would have heard if someone had obtained the Regime's portal technology. The fact is, you're making this up."

"We just recently discovered the theft, so whoever has it is likely keeping it for personal use."

"All right, if you are a Regime agent, prove it."

"Do you have a computer?"

"I do."

He gave her a website address and password to use. After typing the information, she saw his picture and a complete dossier showing his real identity. Feeling all the blood drain from her face, she threw the computer aside, slammed the gun down on the dresser, and paced, cursing Dragon for getting her into this situation.

"You *should* be mad at him. He set you up. If you kill me, the Regime will stop at nothing to find you. Plan on spending the rest of your life on the moon."

Hearing his words fueled her anger more; a few seconds later, she calmed down, retrieved her gun, and tapped her head with the barrel, thinking of what to do.

"Let me go, and I promise to help you."

"If I don't kill you, Dragon *will* kill me. It's not personal; I don't want to hurt you. At least if the Regime catches me, I will still be alive."

"If you think spending the rest of your life on the moon is living, you're sorely mistaken."

"Damn it!" she paced again.

"There is one more thing you should know."

"What's that?"

"I'm not just an ordinary Regime agent. I have an implant. Come here and look at my hands."

She hesitated and then remembered that he could not move for another two hours; it gave her the confidence to examine his hands.

"I don't see anything."

"Look closer. You'll see tiny metal tips on each finger."

"Interesting, they must be subcutaneous because I didn't feel them when you touched me. What do they do?"

"They add strength to my hands. Now that I can't move, they're useless," he lied.

Curious, she exposed the palms of his hands and touched them to feel the metal running through his fingers. She made contact, and he released a pulse of electricity. The current ran through her body, causing the muscles in her hand to contract, squeezing him tightly. As the current moved through her body, she shook violently, and strands of her hair stood in the air. Moments later, he disengaged his implant, and she fell unconscious.

As he waited for the toxin to wear off, the minutes seemed to pass like hours. During that time, he hoped she would not regain consciousness. Little by little, he recovered control over his body until regaining complete command over his extremities; he retrieved his gun, dressed, dragged her unconscious body onto the bed, removed her boots, and tied her hands and feet to the bedposts. Just in case she woke, he put tape over her mouth, preventing her from screaming, and contacted Diego, who brought Vincent's suitcase.

"I came over as fast as I could. What happened?"

"I'm afraid Sofia is a contract killer hired to eliminate me."

"Aye yigh, yigh! I can't believe it! I had her checked out!"

"Don't feel bad. She's a professional, and Dragon helped her. It was good that she wavered because it gave me a chance to get the upper hand."

"What are we going to do with her?"

They heard her in the bedroom trying to speak through the tape; Vincent grabbed the end and stopped.

"If you start yelling, it'll go right back on," Vincent warned.

She nodded, so he gave a quick pull.

"Ouch!"

"Remember, no yelling."

"That hurt!"

“We need to talk.”

“About what?”

“I’m going to make you an offer. If you help me catch Dragon, I’ll make sure you do your time on Earth. If you don’t, I’ll make sure you spend the rest of your life on the moon. It’s up to you.”

“Those are my only choices?”

“I’m afraid so.”

“What if I make you an offer?”

“What is it?”

“What if we disappear together? I know we would have a great deal of fun.”

“I think we know that I can never trust you.”

“That’s not fair,” she pouted. “Once I discovered your identity, I wasn’t *really* going to kill you. I just needed time to figure a way out.”

“If I were just a salesman, I’d be dead now. Wouldn’t I?”

“Maybe. As I said, I wasn’t happy about it.”

“That isn’t comforting.”

“Fine, I’ll help you.”

“Tell me how you’re supposed to get paid.”

“It is a cash contract, so I must call Dragon to confirm my kill. Later we are supposed to meet me at the Plaza Norte Shopping Center.”

“How will he know you’re successful?”

“I’ll need a photo of you lying in this bed, dead, and your index finger.”

Vincent thought a moment, “Ok, what else?”

“That’s it. I’ll call him to set a time, and we’ll meet at the mall’s center.”

“All right. Diego, you watch her; I’ll contact the Regime. Also, I’ll need a few things for tomorrow. You don’t mind if I invite a small team over, do you?”

“Not at all. Bring all the help you need.”

Chapter 52

Akil

Argi City

The 22,279[th] Terrestrial Rotation of the Second Summer

In the room adjoining the arena, Taen held Yetta's hand and talked with her. Unbeknownst to him, Thea was still impersonating her daughter, Yetta, and her daughter continued impersonating her mother, Thea. Having chosen the wrong Akilian during the ceremony, Thea put Yetta's life in danger. Once Gecheana learned of her disobedience, Yetta would fall from her good graces. Thea suspected that Gecheana was already planning Yetta's demise.

She would not have put Yetta in this position had she not betrayed her; the little wretch deserved Gecheana's wrath. There was a slight chance that Gecheana would order Thea to kill her, which she would gladly accept; even if Gecheana did not give her permission to rid herself of Yetta, Gecheana must restore control of Argi to her because of Yetta's blatant disobedience. Enjoying her victory over Yetta, Thea gently played with Taen's hand as they stared lovingly into each other's eyes.

Having spent some time with him, Thea now understood Yetta's attraction. As with most young Argian males, he was handsome and strong, and the pleasant smell of purple moss filled the air around him. It reminded her of Olan. The difference was that Olan's social status was much higher than Taen's, which meant everything to her. She gazed into Taen's eyes and saw her daughter walking toward them in her peripheral vision. If a glare had power, hers would have burned a mark into her forehead. *So that is what I look like when I am angry*, Thea mused.

"I must speak with you now!" Yetta growled.

After kissing Taen right in front of Yetta, Thea walked with her to the nearest corner, keeping them out of the guests' hearing range.

"Have you gone mad? Gecheana is going to kill me!" Yetta spat with an angry whisper.

"Is something wrong, dear? I thought you said to choose Taen."

"Do not pretend to be stupid! I know what you did! You broke our agreement! You were supposed to choose Noka!"

"I am sure Gecheana will understand. Just blame me for it. Tell her your whole plan and that I disobeyed you; I am sure she will forgive you."

"I *will* tell her what you have done, and I swear, if I get in trouble for this, you *will* suffer!"

"Do me a favor, record that conversation. I cannot wait to hear Gecheana's sword cutting through your neck," Thea laughed.

Yetta stomped away, so Thea returned to Taen's side and smiled, thinking of the pleasures she would have with him later at Yetta's expense.

Chapter 53

Crouched behind a vehicle in the hospital parking lot, Kenny Barnes waited for an opportunity to get inside unnoticed. Hearing a noise from behind, he turned and winced at the pain from the wound in his shoulder. Relieved that no one was there, he turned back and peeked through a hovercar window, hoping to keep himself hidden from unsuspecting eyes. The bullet wound bled steadily enough to soil his shirt, which prevented him from entering public places because someone would notice the blood.

Before leaving his apartment, he hurriedly put together a bag of necessities: a clean set of clothes, Regime Talons, his ID, transport card, computer, and the gun with which the detective shot him. His stomach growled; he realized food should also have been on the list. From his vantage point, he could see the employee entrance. The door opened, and he saw a nurse carrying a medical kit, so he changed his plan as she walked to her vehicle. Instead of coercing her to help him access the hospital, he would convince her to help him.

He kept himself low, scanned the area for pedestrians, and followed her. At the vehicle, she opened the trunk and tossed her bag inside. He took one last look to ensure it was clear and moved up behind her. Before she could close the trunk, he put his hand over her mouth and the nose of the gun into her back.

"Don't move or scream, and you'll live to see another day," he whispered into her ear, as menacing as possible.

Terrified, she froze. Within moments, he felt tears rolling over his hand, covering her mouth.

"Do as I say, and you'll be home for supper, understand?"

Shaking, she nodded.

"I need an injectable sedative. Do you have anything in the bag?" Kenny demanded.

Again, she nodded and reached inside to retrieve a vial with a couple of syringes. Kenny read the drug name on the bottle.

"Phenobarbital? I've never heard of it. Now don't scream, or I'll shoot," he threatened, removing his hand so she could respond.

"Please, just take it and leave me alone!" she begged frantically.

"Put your right hand behind your back and hold the vial with your left."

Whimpering, she did as he commanded, and with his other hand, he grabbed one of the syringes she set out, jabbed the needle into the vial, and drew the serum into it.

"Tell me how much to keep you out for a couple of hours, and be sure you won't wake early."

At hearing his plan to sedate her, she sobbed.

"You better tell me when to stop," he warned as the syringe filled.

She was terrified yet forced herself to focus on the vial, "Stop. That'll keep me out for a couple of hours."

"Ok, now set the vial down."

"Please don't do this," she begged.

Knowing there was little time left, she searched the parking lot, looking for anyone who could help her. She felt the needle enter her neck and knew her chance of escaping had just dwindled. The drug moved through her veins and gave her a warm, soothing sensation. Since her heart was beating fast, it quickly moved throughout her body, making her eyes heavy with sleep, and she knew it was only a matter of seconds. It did not take long for her to feel the drug's full effects. Her fear faded within moments because the medication made her relax and fall quietly into an artificial sleep. Unconscious, she collapsed forward.

Kenny caught her, guided her safely into the trunk, took her purse, set it down on the ground, and tried to make her comfortable. He checked her left hand and did not find a wedding band. After securing her, Kenny locked her inside, jumped into the front seat, opened her wallet to get her address, and rifled through her purse to look for pictures, hoping to avoid surprises.

Inside, he found a family photo of her, a man who might be her ex-husband, and two children. If her children were in a Regime school, they would not be home, and since she was not wearing a wedding ring, there was a good chance they had separated. Kenny considered all the information at his disposal and decided to go. There was a good chance that no one would be there to greet them at her home. If someone were waiting, Kenny had to get the jump on him; confrontations made him nervous.

He carefully drove the hovercar over the grass streets to her cabin in the woods, scanned the landscape, and only saw the forest. If she had neighbors, they would be too far away to see her home with the naked eye. Upon arriving, he parked the vehicle in front of her porch and ran to her door. He decided against using her key to gain access. Instead, he rang the doorbell and waited with his hand on the gun, but no one answered. He continued to knock on the door until satisfied that no one was home and used her key to enter.

With his gun drawn, he checked every room to ensure it was clear and returned to the car to retrieve his hostage. Since a bullet had gone into his left shoulder, he could not carry her in a typical fashion, with one arm under her knees and the other behind her upper back, so he pulled her feet out first and then her upper body over his right shoulder. She was light enough for him to carry without too much effort.

Having searched the house, he knew the location of her bedroom and took her there. He set her on the bed, searched the kitchen, found some plastic ties, hogtied her hands and feet, and checked the bedroom clock. She would wake in about forty-five minutes, and once she felt well enough to help him, he would have her fix his wound and get the hell out.

In the nearest bathroom, he rummaged through her medicine cabinet, found bandages, removed his shirt, and put some gauze over the hole in front of his shoulder. Looking at his back in the mirror confirmed what he knew already. The bullet had gone through. Unable to reach it due to its location, he did his best to tape a large white bandage over the area.

By the time he finished, the bleeding had started to show on the front bandage. Seeing his effort was getting him nowhere and feeling hunger pains, he decided to eat. Later, blood had soaked through the dressings covering his wounds; he knew leaving was out of the question until it stopped bleeding. He returned to the bedroom to wait for his reluctant host to wake and, using her remote control, turned on the television to occupy his time. About half an hour later, she woke.

"Uh, where am I?" she asked groggily.

"Home, lying on your bed," Kenny remarked.

His voice made her jump; the restraints prevented her from moving. She saw his face, panicked, and struggled against the plastic ties.

"Don't; you'll hurt yourself," Kenny warned worriedly.

"I've seen your face! You're going to kill me!"

Kenny looked surprised at her accusation, "Why would you say that?"

"I'm a nurse. I talk to police officers all the time. They told me anytime a kidnapper lets his captive see his face, he or she ends up dead."

"I promise I'm not going to hurt you. Besides, you're not the only one who knows what I look like," he reassured, nodding toward the television.

She craned to look at the current news report and recognized the face on the screen. Underneath his photo, a scroll listed why he was a wanted man. Before it ended, it read that the police considered him armed and dangerous.

"You killed a police detective!"

"It was an accident."

"Ha, right. People who *accidentally* kill police officers fill prisons," she scoffed.

"I'll explain everything later; right now, I need your help with my shoulder. It won't stop bleeding."

She laughed, "You want me to help you; after what you've done?"

"Please, Wendy. I need your help. The sooner I can get this to stop bleeding, the sooner I'll be out of your life."

"How do you know my name?"

"It's on your driver's license."

"You bastard! I can't believe you went through my things!"

"I'm sorry, I'm desperate."

"You could have turned yourself in."

"That's not a choice. Are you going to help me or not?"

"Fine, take off the bandage and let me see the wound."

Gently, he removed the tape; the bandage came off, and blood trickled down his chest. He turned around to show Wendy the other wound.

"That's a through and through. From here, it looks like the bullet just missed your Clavicle bone. If that's the case, all you need to do is clean it and stitch it."

"Fine, show me how."

She laughed, "How do you plan on stitching the hole in your back?"

"I don't know. It's not like I planned on getting shot."

"Untie me; I'll do it."

Kenny chuckled, "Sure, the moment you're free, you'll try to subdue me."

"It sounds tempting, especially since you tied my feet and hands behind me, but you don't have to worry; I took an oath."

"You're a doctor?" he inquired, genuinely surprised.

"I'm a shock trauma physician."

"You told me you were a nurse."

"I was hoping you were looking for a doctor, so I lied. Sue me."

Even in his dire situation, Kenny smiled in admiration for her quick thinking, "I guess you can't trust anybody these days."

"What are you going to do, smart guy? If you don't let me help, you will end up at a hospital anyway, and I can guarantee they'll report it. The police will arrest you before the last stitch is in place."

Feeling helpless, he hung his head down and thought. She saw his distress, felt sorry for him, and hated herself for being sympathetic.

"Why don't you tell me what happened?"

He raised his head to look at her, "Honestly, I'm still trying to figure it out myself. A couple of weeks ago, my boss laid me off from work. They refused my unemployment application, saying he fired me, making it difficult to find work, and he won't return my calls. Last night, I fell asleep on my couch until I heard someone knock at the door at about 10:30 PM. I looked through the peephole and saw an older man holding a badge near his face.

"Before opening the door, I asked him what he wanted. He was investigating home invasions in my apartment complex, so I let him in. We talked in my foyer with the door open for several minutes while he asked me a few questions. I hadn't seen anyone suspicious in the building or heard anything about robberies in our area at all. Before leaving, he asked for a glass of water. As I left to get it, he shut the door behind him, and I watched him lock it; he reached down and pulled a gun from his ankle holster."

"You mean the same gun you used to abduct me?" she interrupted.

He removed the weapon from his belt, held it up, and popped out the roller, "It's empty. I didn't want to take a chance on hurting anyone, including myself."

"Son of a bitch! You mean, you snuck up on me with an empty weapon! You've got some nerve, Barnes!"

"I didn't want to abduct you; I had no other choice."

"Just finish the story."

"I saw the gun in his hand, and it scared the crap out of me. I set the glass down on the coffee table and raised my hands in surrender. I asked him what I did wrong; he said, 'Sorry, kid, I have my orders.' I pleaded for my life, but it made no difference because he told me to sit on the couch. Some kids ran down the hall knocking on everyone's door; it was a prank.

"The knock was enough to distract him. I frantically looked for something to use as a weapon. I saw the vase on the coffee table, and without thinking, I threw it at him. He turned, and it hit him square on the forehead. I instinctively ran toward him, knowing I had to fight for my life, but before reaching him, he brought the gun to bear and shot me in the shoulder. He tried to shoot again, but I grabbed onto the weapon with all my might.

"We struggled for some time. He was much older than me and had a head injury, yet he put up one hell of a fight, and as we wrestled for control of the gun, it went off, hitting him. I'll never forget the look on his face. It was like turning off a machine. His arms fell to his side, and he collapsed to the floor."

"Why didn't you call the police?"

"He *was* the police and claimed he was following orders. I don't know who wants me dead or why, so I got some things together and ran until I saw you in the parking lot."

"What's your plan?"

"I haven't thought that far ahead. I was hungry and bleeding. I needed food and medical attention; I saw you and took a chance."

"Gee, thanks."

"I know I scared you, and I'm sorry about it; as I said before, I'm desperate, and I don't know what I'm doing. Before turning myself in, I need to find out who hired him and why they sent him to kill me. Until then, I can't trust anyone."

"If you don't get that wound cleaned and stitched, it'll get infected, and you'll die a slow, painful death without proving your innocence, so untie me, and I'll stitch it up for you."

Kenny stared at his captive for a long, silent moment, contemplating her offer. Some time passed without a response.

"Look, you have three choices. First, you can clean the wound, stitch the front, and let the back injury continue to bleed. You might have a week before the infection sets in; it might not be enough time to find out what's happening.

"Second, you can go straight to the police and turn yourself in. You'll get the medical attention you need, and you can ask for an MR to prove your innocence. Assuming whoever is trying to kill you doesn't get to you first. Third, you can untie me. I'll clean and stitch your wound," she paused before speaking again. "Then, I'll help you find out who is trying to kill you."

"Why would you help me?"

"I don't know. Maybe I believe you."

He thought about it and knew she was right. On his own, he would last a day or two. Before long, he would spend all his Regime Talons, leaving him broke. Even if he did make it out of state, it would not be long until someone recognized him. The news media was showing his face every few minutes. The police would be on him, with guns drawn, if someone saw him. Since they believed he shot one of their own, it did not take a genius to figure out that they would take him dead rather than alive. Even worse, if the person trying to kill him found him first, he would end up dead, with no one to help him.

He did not know anyone trustworthy, so surrendering terrified him. Since they had paid one detective to kill him, it was not a far stretch to assume there would be at least one more looking for him this very minute. There was no doubt in his mind that he would end up dead no matter what, so he walked behind her, removed a knife from his pocket, and cut her loose.

She rubbed her wrists and ankles, and wobbly stood, "Can I have a drink of water, please?"

"Sure, you should sit until you recover; you don't look a hundred percent yet."

"The sedative is still in my system."

He returned with a bottle of water, and she drank it. A few minutes later, she could stand without feeling dizzy.

"Grab my bag and meet me in the bathroom. I don't want blood on my carpet."

Standing in front of the mirror, he watched her remove a few needles, a bottle of saline, and hydrogen peroxide.

She filled a syringe and grabbed an alcohol swab, "I'll inject a small amount of Novocain around the wound. It will numb it so I can clean and stitch it up."

Having been afraid of needles most of his life, he closed his eyes as she injected the serum; it did not help. Even though she took her time, the Novocain felt like a thousand bees stinging his wound, making him holler out from the pain.

"Ok, lean over the tub so I can clean it."

Although the wound's outer area was numb, he could feel it burning as the peroxide reached deep inside his shoulder. He kept his face down and saw saline, mixed with blood, dripping off his shoulder and into the basin. Wendy cleaned the injuries, stitched his back and front, put fresh dressing and tape over his shoulder, led him to the guest room, and sat him on the bed.

"I'm not tired. Besides, I need to find out who is trying to kill me."

"Have you had a tetanus shot in the past ten years?"

"I can't remember."

Without another word, she removed a filled syringe and stuck him in the arm.

"We'll start looking for your killer tomorrow. Right now, you need rest."

He felt the warmth of a narcotic going through his veins and inquired, "What did you give me?"

"I suggest you lay down before you fall."

“I thought you would help me,” he slurred, drifting off to sleep.

Now that he was unconscious, Wendy had control of her life and called a friend for help.

“Yeah, it’s me. I need a favor.”

Chapter 54

Akil
Argi City
The 22,279[th] Terrestrial Rotation of the Second Summer

Thea and Yetta finally stopped arguing, allowing Zorion to bring Julie over to meet his daughter; unbeknownst to him, Thea was still impersonating their daughter Yetta and vice versa. Behind the mask of Yetta, Thea watched Zorion and Julie walk toward her and Taen. Thea never loved Zorion, yet a twinge of jealousy ran through her seeing Julie's hand on Zorion's arm.

It had been her place for many Yellow Harvests, and now some alien was pawing over *her* property. In the past, she would blame herself for losing control of Zorion. Now she knew better. Yetta was to blame, and Thea would make her pay for that betrayal. As Zorion and Julie came closer, she sensed defiance from Taen, and Zorion noticed it too. Holding back a devious grin, Thea curtsied before Argi's sovereign the way a daughter should.

"Congratulations to both of you," Julie and Zorion said simultaneously.

"Thank you," Yetta and Taen answered in unison.

"I hope you enjoyed the celebration," Yetta addressed Julie.

"Uh, yes, it was different than I expected; very festive."

Seeing that Taen wanted to say something, Zorion excused them from the conversation and took him aside to talk with him privately, and before he could ask what was wrong, Taen verbally attacked him.

"I am giving you fair warning, Zorion. Every Argi moss farmer is united, so if you try to put me in prison or kill me, they will stop all moss shipments, and Argi will starve."

As if slapped on the cheek, Zorion stepped back in shock, "What on Akil are you saying?"

"Yetta told me you tried forcing her to choose someone else. If she refused, you promised there would be consequences."

His accusation angered Zorion. He glanced at his daughter for a moment, wanting to strangle her, but better judgment prevailed, and he reeled in his emotions. Instead of yelling, he spoke in a calm, controlled tone.

"I made no such demand."

"Do not play games with me, Zorion! I am no fool!" Taen snapped, raising his voice.

"I am not playing games! I have never, once, instructed Yetta on who she could or could not be with!" Zorion yelled.

This time, he was unable to keep his anger in check. His loud response echoed throughout the room, attracting everyone's attention. In his rage, he did not care about appearances. All he wanted was an explanation. Adamant about resolving the issue, even with everyone present, he called for Yetta and Thea, still unaware that they were impersonating each other, so when he spoke to Yetta, he did not know it was Thea and vice versa.

Upon their arrival, he glared at who he thought was Yetta with daggers and demanded, "Why would you tell Taen that I forbade you to choose him, knowing I said no such thing?"

Thea, still posing as Yetta, was surprised by the accusation. Not having a prepared response, she did what Skeans always do in these situations: lie, lie, lie.

"I told you some time ago that I cared for him. I clearly remember you telling me you would not allow me to be with a moss farmer."

"That is an out-and-out lie; tell them, Thea!"

"I was there, Zorion. You did tell her she could not be with him."

Even though he knew they were lying, their accusation publicly humiliated him, and his cheeks flushed as rage boiled inside him. Julie had been listening to the conversation. She knew better than to entangle herself with another family's argument but refused to allow their accusations to go unanswered.

"Excuse me," she smiled pleasantly, walking over to where Taen stood. "Forgive me; I couldn't help overhearing that you believe Zorion disapproves of you. I think it is important that you should know that just a few moments ago, he told me how happy he was for you. It may be true that Thea and Yetta believe they heard Zorion say something to the contrary; I would suggest that they must have misunderstood him because he showed no hint of displeasure when I asked about you.”

If looks could kill, Thea and Yetta would have slain Julie at that moment; Taen seemed receptive.

“Is that true?” Taen wondered.

“Absolutely. No one would survive without you, and I do not believe Zorion would have said those things because I just heard him confess how much respect he has for Argi moss farmers. So, there’s no reason for harsh words, especially after such a lovely ceremony,” Julie responded with a pleasant voice.

“Perhaps you are right. Zorion, please accept my apology,” he repentantly answered, with his palm held forward.

Zorion returned the gesture, “I accept your apology, and I swear to you that I have never said anything to the contrary about you. If Yetta is happy, I am happy.”

“Speaking of making me happy, I believe it is time we leave, Taen,” Yetta flirted with a grin.

To Julie’s surprise, Thea could not hide her displeasure with the remark. Julie was unsure if it was because Yetta broke protocol by her innuendo or if it was entirely something else.

“Here,” Zorion handed a set of keys to whom he thought was Yetta. “I purchased a new home for you on level ten. I hope you enjoy it.”

The gift widened Taen’s eyes, “Thank you, Zorion! That is kind of you!”

“You are welcome. I wish you both every happiness.”

As the new couple left, Thea followed them, leaving Zorion and Julie alone.

“Boy, they are a handful,” Julie remarked.

“You have no idea. Thank you for your help because you singlehandedly thwarted a dangerous protest. Had Taen stopped the shipment of moss, I do not know what would have happened.”

“I’m glad I could help.”

*****

As Thea (still posing as Yetta) and Taen walked to their vehicle, Yetta (still posing as Thea) gave her a mental nudge, letting

283

her know she demanded to speak with her privately. Ignoring her, Thea smiled, knowing she had Yetta by the emotional throat. Thea would have the first part of her revenge in just a few hundred heartbeats. Sharing Taen's bed would cause Yetta irreversible emotional pain, which is why she chose this course. Yetta gave Thea a forceful tug at the Avenue, which would have knocked her down except for Taen's help. Realizing that Yetta refused to allow Thea to ignore her, Thea decided to speak with her.

"I will be just a moment, Taen," she released his arm and walked to where her daughter stood.

"I am going to give you one last chance. Come with me now so we can change our identities back to our original," Yetta whispered through gritted teeth.

"No," Thea responded defiantly.

"You openly disobey me?"

"Just as you have done to me so many times before."

Unable to hide her rage, Yetta moved her hands to strangle Thea, who held her hand as a warning.

"Careful; if you kill me, Taen and everyone else will think you are dead. You can no longer show your face again."

"You will pay for this!" Yetta spat, spinning around and stomping off.

As Thea approached Taen, still looking precisely like Yetta, he questioned, "Is everything all right?"

"Yes. Thea wanted to ensure we had everything we needed. Now, we should go. I want to get you home and undressed."

Chapter 55

Earth
Scotland - Edinburgh
May 14, 2452

Dawn left the hotel and headed straight for work in her Mercedes-Benz McLaren SLR, which she bought about a year ago for two million pounds. She sped through traffic and parked inside the garage of Royal Duke Holdings Company, one of the world's top ten conglomerates. The private elevator was only a few steps from her reserved spot and would take her to the hundred fiftieth floor. At the top, the CEO and her best friend, Thomas Mountbatten, lived there for many years. Upon arrival, she saw his secretary, who caught her attention.

"Good morning, Ms. Pierce. Mr. Mountbatten would like to see you right away."

She nodded and headed straight to his office. Seeing he was still in a video conference, she quietly shut the door behind her and waited. It was Thomas' idea to build an office opposite the CEO because he hoped she would use it daily, but her schedule would not allow it. Dawn realized it had been a month since her last visit, so she studied him to find any changes.

True to his upbringing, he kept perfect posture in a tailored suit that fit him flawlessly. He nodded for Dawn to sit, and while patiently waiting, she found herself staring at his wavy, dark-brown hair combed to the side. Soon, her gaze moved to his bright, brown eyes. Unable to resist, she stared at him for a long time. Her feelings for him resurfaced. Keeping him at a distance had been her only way of suppressing those emotions. With a willful effort, she pushed those intimate feelings back down to where they belonged. It was the only way she would get through the meeting without running into his arms. When his conference ended, he turned his attention to her and sighed.

"That was Kathryn Wright, CEO of Sanya Electronix. The TBI raided her company."

"What for?"

"There is a money trail linking the company to the assassination of the Comptroller in the Regime, Washington, D.C."

"I remember reading an article about it. Did the Regime find the person responsible?"

"I'm told the TBI is looking for someone named Kenny Barnes. They recently fired him."

"How bad is it?"

"Oh, it's a terrible mess. I sent our best lawyers to assist them."

"Since Sanya Electronix is a subsidiary of your company, your Public Relations Department must be ready to answer any questions the media will have," Dawn advised.

"I have already notified them."

"Is that why you called me here?"

"No, I," he paused, "I have not seen you in a month. How have you been?"

"Good. In fact," she pulled out a data stick and handed it to him, "our research and development department finally came through."

With a look of surprise, he put the stick into his computer and brought up the information.

"Is this what I think it is?"

"Yes. A vaccine for the common cold."

"Dawn, this is an amazing breakthrough! We're going to make billions with this discovery!"

"I expect my usual payment."

"Certainly, I will have a quarter of a billion in gold bars delivered to your warehouse as usual, but I'm curious; I thought Shire, Inc. was decades ahead of everyone?"

"I had my team working hard all year, and they came through."

"I don't know what to say. This vaccine will help save many lives."

"That's what we're here for," she stood, "Now, if there's nothing else, I'll take care of a few things in my office and be on my way."

"Before you go, we have a shareholder's meeting in three days," he paused, summoning his nerve. "I was hoping you would accompany me."

"You know I have always cared for you, Thomas, which is why I don't think it's a good idea to mix business with pleasure."

"Please, forgive me for questioning you. I didn't mean to upset you by infringing on our agreement. I just have not seen much of you lately. I hope you forgive me for saying that I miss you terribly."

"I'm not upset," she made a point to smile warmly; unable to resist the urge, she walked over and hugged him; it was something she had not allowed herself in a long time.

"You could never upset me. You're the one person I care for and trust the most in this world, so I don't want to do anything to endanger our relationship."

"If you change your mind, the address is in your inbox."

Feeling like a heel, she kissed him on the cheek, "I'll consider it."

"That's all I ask."

Gently, she pushed away from him and walked to her office. On her way out, she could feel his eyes watching and forbade herself from turning to look at him. She did not like to visit him because it was always hard for her to leave. Alone in her office, she stared out over the city through the corner windows. Dawn could not stop trembling from the war raging inside her. The temptation of returning to what they once had was hard to ignore. She had to remain strong because he would distract her from accomplishing certain things on her itinerary.

Using work to regain her focus, she turned on her tablet and reviewed her messages. With so many things going on at one time, it was easy for something to slip by her, so she checked on each project personally. Upon viewing her encrypted emails, her Regime informant delivered two messages containing invaluable information. The first was hard to believe, but she had no reason to doubt her source.

Recently, an alien civilization has contacted the Regime, which will open many doors of possibility for her. Having alien technology at her disposal would push her plans years ahead of schedule. Her informant's other message concerned her, so she contacted one of her contractors using high-end encryption software. His all too familiar face filled the small screen on her tablet.

"Why is the TBI still looking for Kenny Barnes? You need to find him and keep him from an MR scan," Dawn warned.

"I'll take care of it personally."

"Have you tied up the other loose ends yet?"

"Almost. I decided to outsource some help. Sofia came highly recommended, and I'm sure she will get close enough to take Vincent down."

"That's why I'm calling. I've just discovered that Vincent turned her. My source tells me your mark is setting a trap for you."

The other was quiet for a moment, "I will handle the situation."

"You better, Dragon. You know the penalty for being caught."

"I won't get paid," he replied wryly.

"Among other things," she terminated the conversation.

Dawn contemplated Dragon's situation and decided to find a replacement. With a Regime agent on his trail, she could not use him. Nearly an hour later, Dawn reviewed several dossiers of operatives from all over the world. Only one had the qualities that impressed her; he retired years ago. It did not matter because she had a way around that obstacle. The dossier indicated that his last known location was in Panama City, Panama.

She booked passage to Panama City with the International Transportation Station. Hopefully, by tomorrow, she will have a new assistant. Setting that aside, she read a new message from one of her U.S. informants. The information was intriguing and confirmed the rumor of two men having supernatural abilities. It was the break she needed. Now she could prove her dad's theory was correct. All she had to do now was convince one of them to testify on his behalf, and maybe the Regime would release him from the moon prison.

Chapter 56

Akil
Argi City
The 22,279th Terrestrial Rotation of the Second Summer

Once Yetta and Taen left, everyone in the room returned to celebrating the good news that Zorion had delivered earlier. Still, the confrontation with Taen upset Zorion. Seeing his distress, Julie offered him her ear.

"I do not understand why they would accuse me of these things."

"It's obvious to me why Thea sided with her daughter. She wants to make your life miserable."

"I cannot understand why. I have not thrown her out on the avenue. She has a lovely home and plenty of Sovereign Cubes to spend. I fulfill all her needs."

"There was a British playwright and poet named William Congreve who once said, '*Heaven has no rage, like love to hatred turned, nor hell a fury, like a woman scorned.*'"

"What does that mean?"

"It means that even though you are nice to her, you still rejected her. No number of Sovereign Cubes can make that feeling go away. Thea feels like you disregarded her, which means she will try to hurt you somehow, so I suggest you be careful around her."

"That is sound advice. I will do my best, except she always has the advantage."

"Maybe you can try to help her find someone else to focus on."

"I do not understand."

"Find someone to replace you."

"Ah! That is an excellent idea!"

"Make sure she doesn't know that you're involved. It should look like a chance meeting, so if things progress between them, she won't reject him, knowing you had a part to play."

"Tell me; are all the women from your planet as crafty as you?"

"Most, I would think."

"In the meantime, the accusations made me look foolish in front of my friends."

"I'm sure your friends can see what she's doing, and if they are your loyal friends, they will love you just the same."

"Love?"

"Absolutely, don't you see how they look at you? Everyone loves you; your friends love you; the people of Argi love you; I love you."

The moment the words left her mouth, she felt flush. Trying to pretend she did not say anything, she smiled awkwardly. *You should have stopped while you were ahead, Julie!*

"You love me?"

Before she could clarify her meaning, servers came into the room with two carts. The other guests politely applauded the seed's arrival. Using the distraction to get out of the conversation, Julie clapped with the others, turning her gaze away from him. Zorion politely smiled, acknowledging everyone's appreciation of his gift.

Gwah spoke above the noise, "Zorion, I thought this type of seed was extinct."

"They are. It is the last one I have in my private cellar. I saved it for this very occasion."

"What are they?" Julie asked.

"It is the seed of the *Periscote* Tree. This kernel has been in my family for many Yellow Harvests."

"I don't understand. Are we going to eat it?"

"Not at all. It produces liquor if it does not germinate within thirty days after it falls to the ground. I have never tasted it, yet I have read that it is delicious."

"There's only one way to find out."

Everyone in the room watched with enthusiasm as the servers prepared the seed for drinking. First, they set up drinking glasses on a square table in eight short rows; it took four servers to carry the seed to its resting place; the servers set it on top of a round, glossy, black fountain-like table and retrieved a mallet and two steel rods, with a faucet at the end. Julie thought the seed looked like a giant white stone with odd markings.

Using the mallet, he tapped the spout through the hard exterior. Once it was secure, he inserted the other nozzle into the top of the seed. Simultaneously, two servers opened both valves, and a fluorescent, blue liquid poured out the lower tap onto the fountain-like table. Within moments, the liquor shot upwards from the center of the table, about a foot high. The servers waited a few minutes as it circulated and filled the glasses with the fluorescent, blue liquor stream. The angle at which it came from the fountain allowed the servers to fill each glass without spilling a drop.

"Is it supposed to glow like that?" Julie quizzed, gazing at it with a childlike fascination.

"Yes. The brighter it glows, the stronger the liquor will be."

The four servers brought their trays, and each guest took a glass. Julie also took one, swirled the florescent liquor like wine, and sniffed. Her actions caught Zorion's attention, who stared at her quizzically.

"They do this back home tasting wine. It's supposed to bring out the aroma of the drink."

He tried it himself, became happily surprised, and shared the discovery with his guests, who did their best to imitate her. To Julie, the fragrance reminded her of a blend of tropical fruits. Not surprisingly, it still had a strong spearmint smell since Zorion was standing close to her. Everyone sipped their drink. Masked behind a sweet, tropical fruit flavor, Julie could taste the alcohol. It warmed her throat on its way down.

As the evening continued, everyone kept going back for more. As with any party where the host serves alcohol, one drink turns into two and two into three. Before long, everyone was feeling merry, except for Zorion, who stopped after his first glass. The other sovereigns sang old Akilian victory songs, and even though her earpiece did its best to translate, much of the songs stayed a mystery to her.

An hour later, her body had absorbed much of the alcohol she had consumed. Add to the fact that Urki put her through some very rigorous workouts earlier; the combination made her very sleepy. By now, Zorion had left her side to mingle with the other sovereigns, leaving her to sway independently. She carefully walked over and grabbed his arm for support.

"I need to lie down," she whispered into his ear with a slight slur.

"I will call Tionah and have her get your car."

Feeling amorous from the alcohol, she stopped him before he could move.

"I would rather *you* take me home."

Zorion checked his guests before answering. Since everyone was smiling and laughing, he did not think they would miss him in their current state. Besides, when it came to Julie, he did not care much about protocol. Zorion nodded to Broll and led her out onto the avenue. The more they walked, the more support he gave her to keep moving.

Tionah waited for Julie nearby, and one look from Zorion let her know that she would be following them home. He held her hand as she stepped into his vehicle; Julie stumbled, fell onto the seat, and the floor, laughing hysterically.

"Are you drunk?" he queried.

"Yep."

"I am sorry, Julie. I did not intend for this to happen."

"It's all right. Just don't tell Urki; he'll make me do pushups," she whispered and giggled.

"How could Urki make you do pushups? He's dead."

She laughed, "I know…right? It's just weird."

"You are not making any sense," he remarked, helping her back onto the seat.

Zorion sat beside her, and the driver sped off to take her home. She played with the buttons on her door panel along the way, continually causing the side window to go up and down. With genuine fascination, Zorion watched her test all the vehicle's electronic devices. She found the button that brought up a divider between their compartment and the driver and smiled.

"Finally, I have you to myself."

Grabbing his jacket with both hands, she pulled herself to him, trying to straddle her legs to sit on his lap; her dress prevented such a pose, so she sat side-saddle, as it were, and put her arm over his shoulders. Since they were in a small, closed area, Julie noticed the pleasant spearmint aroma surrounding him was more intense.

"Mmmm, you smell good," she slurred.

Speechless, Zorion tried to change the subject, hoping to distract her, "I hear that your parents own a farm. It must be very satisfying to work with animals."

Ignoring him, she took a strand of his hair, brought it to her nose, and breathed deep.

"If I was a cat, I'm sure catnip would smell like spearmint."

"What is catnip?"

Again, she ignored his question, playing with his hair, wrapping it around her finger, and unwinding it.

"You know, I have never liked the look of long hair on a man; somehow, you make it work. It's so thick and wavy."

With both hands, she gently pushed her fingers through his hair, unintentionally messing it up. Zorion enjoyed the attention but had to return to the celebration and did not have time to comb it again.

"Julie, please. I must return to our guests."

"Oh, I'm sorry," she frowned, trying to pat it back into place; all she managed was to make it worse.

"That is not helping," he smiled at her.

Her childlike fascination with his hair amused him until their eyes met, and they stared at each other in silence. There was so little space between them that he could feel her breath on his lips; she leaned in and kissed him. He could not stop himself from giving in to her advance, even though it went against protocol for her to be on his lap, showing affection. Besides, no one could see them.

During their embrace, he instinctively wrapped his arms around her, squeezing their bodies close together. One thing was for sure, Thea never made him feel this way. He felt alive and wanted to tell the driver to keep going; the vehicle came to a stop. Reluctantly, he gently pushed her back.

She fought against him, "What are you doing?"

"You are home."

She sighed, "Walk me to my door."

He helped her onto the avenue and saw Tionah standing by the entrance, waiting for instructions. With a gesture, he instructed her to open it, which she did, and inside, he told Tionah to put her to bed.

"No. I want you to tuck me in," Julie whispered seductively, but she slurred her words.

"I am sorry. I cannot go any farther. As friends, it would be inappropriate for me to be in your private room, even with Tionah present," Zorion paused and faced Tionah, "Make sure she is comfortable. I must return now."

Although Julie protested, he left to return to the celebration as Tionah helped her to bed, where she fell fast asleep.

Chapter 57

Earth
The Regime - Washington, D.C. - Capitol Building
May 14, 2452

Having taken a portal directly to the Capitol Building, Michael briskly walked to Supreme Commander Porter's office to relay important news. It was rare for them to meet, and had it not been for his elevated level of clearance; he would not have made it this far. At the Supreme Commander's office, Michael spoke to his secretary, Mrs. Miller, making a point to let her know it was a matter of national security.

With the Supreme Commander's busy schedule, he could sit here most of the day before seeing him, even with urgent news. Michael's mind raced to figure out how to fix his mistake; nothing came to him. Mrs. Miller told Michael that the Supreme Commander would see him. Michael approached his desk and felt his heart racing, knowing he had to accept responsibility for allowing secret documents to get into enemy hands.

Supreme Commander Porter was still working on something, forcing Michael to wait even longer before telling him. It was as if it were some cosmic joke. Waiting was always worse than dealing with the problem right away. He stopped a few feet from the desk, stood with his arms behind his back, and noticed the Regime's seal hanging on the wall behind Supreme Commander Porter. It had long been a symbol of his country's strength and honor, which was now in jeopardy.

"Have a seat," Supreme Commander Porter turned from his computer.

"Thank you for seeing me, Sir."

Michael sat, but all the adrenaline in his body made him squirm.

"My secretary told me you said there's a threat to our national security?"

"Yes, Sir."

"Why didn't you go to General Saunders?"

"I do not know how high the breach goes."

"Breach? Please explain," he asked with a raised eyebrow.

"During her debriefing, Chu Lian, or Wu Luli, confessed to copying some files from my work laptop and forwarded them to her employer."

"Why are you here? Why isn't Captain Yates in my office?"

"Because he doesn't know what I know, and since I'm not sure who is compromised, I can't trust anyone. I'm not even sure I can trust you."

"If it's as serious as you say, I can see your problem. Still, you must trust someone, so it might as well be me."

"I agree. You first need to know that her employer is General Ming-tun Fu."

"Hmm, that name sounds familiar," he considered, typing into the computer. Moments later, a dossier appeared on the large monitor in his office. "Ah, yes. General Ming-tun Fu. He's a dangerous man. I see he's involved in drug running, espionage, and human trafficking, among other heinous activities."

"He sent Wu Luli here to obtain classified documents."

"Anything specific?"

"No, he told her to send anything she could find."

"What did she get?"

Pausing to gulp before telling him, Michael braced himself for his reaction, "She sent him the schematics to the Mind Reader."

Michael saw his face go pale, clearly showing that the news upset him.

"How did she get to it?"

"As I said, she gained access to my work laptop."

"I assume you had all the security measures in place?"

"I locked it inside a briefcase and had our most advanced security system in place, yet she got through it." Michael paused, shook his head, and continued, "I am deeply sorry, Sir. It's entirely my fault."

"No, Michael. General Ming-tun Fu trained Wu Luli to deceive people and infiltrate. She broke through your laptop securities and the Regime's identification protocols. Also, I understand she's a dead ringer for Chu Lian."

"She is, but there's more. I had the MR schematics on my computer because I was working on a new idea. I wanted to speak to

Chu Lian in her native language. Since I didn't have time to learn it, I figured out a way for the Mind Reader to insert languages into the brain."

Supreme Commander Porter perked up, "That's fascinating, except I don't remember reading about it in my daily briefs."

"That's because we broke up just as I finished, so I hadn't bothered testing it. I created diagrams to embed commands into the subconscious to imprint the brain with a new language. Like the ones we use for our agents."

"If they've put together the machine, they can not only read someone's mind, but they can also command it as well," Supreme Commander Porter surmised.

"Yes."

"Wu Luli should be happy that I keep my word because I want to send her to the moon just on principle."

Michael did not believe Wu Luli targeted the files to hurt the Regime, so he defended her.

"She was trying to find something harmless to send. To hear her explain it, I believe her. I stored the Mind Reader schematics in a file titled *Parlor Game*. She thought it was gaming software."

"Whether she meant to hurt us or not, the result is still the same. The Mind Reader is in the hands of a dangerous man."

"We don't know for sure that he's built the device. Although…"

"What?"

"Before her debriefing, Wu Luli did say she suspected we had a spy in our midst."

"What made her suspicious?"

"Because General Ming-tun Fu knew we were sending an assault team and set a trap for her."

"Were the men able to disarm it?"

"It was not that kind of trap. General Ming-tun Fu killed the parents of every spy in his network, except for Wu Luli's, and left behind a video incriminating her. She believes he already distributed it to her colleagues."

"We must assume he has built the Mind Reader."

"What do you want me to do?"

"This does put us within an interesting conundrum."

"What do you mean, Sir?"

"To be blunt, it is possible you have been compromised and don't know it."

"I agree; it is a possibility."

"Here is what we must do. I will choose an MR tech, and you will choose one; the three of you will clear me first and then each other. Once we can trust ourselves, you will clear the entire MR team. We will move throughout the higher levels of our government to check each person. In the meantime, I'll have Stan Hill put together a list of everyone who had anything to do with the mission. He'll assemble a team of guards to escort each person to your lab. I'll tell them we had reports of a dangerous virus making its way through the population, and we're vaccinating everyone to prevent an epidemic. Instead of a vaccine, you'll inject them with a sedative, and during their slumber, you'll perform the scan."

"Why all the deception?"

"Because General Ming-tun Fu may have given them a suicide directive in case of discovery."

"What if you try to kill yourself after I leave?"

"We'll have to take that chance. I'm sending you a one-time directive to scan my brain. If I refuse, you have the authority to send guards to force me."

"I'll get my lab ready and contact you once I finish."

"I'm canceling everything else I have scheduled for today until I can resolve this issue. The moment I hear from you, I'll be on my way. If I'm not there in fifteen minutes, contact the guards."

"I understand."

Michael left, and a few minutes later, Ms. Miller contacted him on his office com, "Captain Yates is here to see you, Sir. He says it's a matter of National Security."

When it rains, it pours. He didn't want to see anyone until Michael cleared him, but this could not wait.

"Send him in."

Captain Yates briskly walked to Supreme Commander Porter's desk and stood at attention.

"At ease, Captain. Tell me what's wrong."

"Wu Luli deciphered the disc we intercepted. It contains schematics for a portal machine."

"Our technology?"

"It's similar, Sir. Wu Luli said that General Ming-tun Fu hired Nathan Mitchell, a world-renowned engineer, to build one. First, he had to design the schematics, which General Ming-tun Fu sold to President Martinez. The disc we intercepted holds his design. Before building a machine for General Ming-tun Fu, he disappeared, along with all of his work."

"You said disappeared. Do you mean he simply left during the night unobserved?"

"No, Sir. He was under guard and vanished, making them believe we took him."

"This is the first I have heard of it."

"Is there a third party involved who can open portals?"

"Yes. I have already sent an agent to find them. Once we locate the assassin, who killed the comptroller, we'll find this third party, confiscate the schematics and destroy their machine."

"What about General Ming-tun Fu?"

"I will assign an agent to track him down and bring him in too."

"What about Wu Luli? Give her a chance to make up for what she's done."

Supreme Commander Porter was silent for a moment, "If you think she's up for it."

"I do. She wants to find him before he kills her; that's good motivation."

"Very well, you have my approval; just send me a copy of your report."

"Yes, Sir!" Captain Yates saluted and left.

Chapter 58

Akil
Argi City
The 22,279[th] Terrestrial Rotation of the Second Summer

Olan, Dolas, and Molo sat in an adjacent room, waiting for Qual to wake up from his earlier interrogation. It gave Olan immense pleasure questioning him in between punches. To his surprise, Qual lasted longer than most but eventually blacked out from the pain. Olan tagged his ear lobe with a tracer as he sat unconscious and checked his locator to ensure it worked correctly.

Satisfied, he went into the adjoining room, where they waited for him to regain consciousness for most of the work cycle. Qual woke, scanned the room, and found himself alone. He worked to free himself from his restraints and liberated his wrists from the chair; the bonds kept his hands tied together, so he maneuvered them underneath his feet and in front of him.

He stood, looked around the room for something sharp, and decided to use the edge of a countertop. He rubbed the rope back and forth, applying pressure until it unraveled. Within a few hundred heartbeats, he was finally free. The others in the adjacent room watched with some amusement.

Qual approached the door, and Olan signaled that it was time for them to talk. They discussed what to do with their prisoner as Qual carefully opened the door to his room and peeked out. It was clear, so he opened the door wider. In the adjacent room, he heard the voices of his captors. Qual smiled, creeping by the door, believing he outwitted them. At the front door, he turned the knob, and with one quick motion, he pulled it open and ran outside. The trio laughed as they tracked his movements on Olan's locator.

"I cannot believe he is that stupid," Molo remarked.

"It is not so much stupidity as it is exhaustion," Olan added.

"I am still surprised. Qual is supposed to be a trained agent. He should know there would be no way we would ever let him escape," Dolas commented disapprovingly.

"After the beating I gave him and the lack of food and water, I am sure he is not thinking, which is why I put him through it," Olan explained.

"Look, he is on the elevator," Dolas pointed.

"Any bets as to what floor he will get off?" Molo offered.

"I only bet on sure things," Olan remarked.

As the flashing red dot moved, they intently watched until it stopped.

"He is on level four hundred fifty-one, section twenty-nine," Olan noted and faced Dolas.

"It is time for us to go."

"What about me?" Molo inquired.

"You stay here. Once we capture Igon, you can finally go home," Olan promised.

Olan's order disappointed Molo because he wanted to participate in Igon's capture. A few hundred heartbeats later, they arrived at their destination. Olan remembered reading that they had to make them closer together when engineers dug out the lower apartments, so they excavated each level broader, enabling the rock beneath each level to support the homes above.

It meant that the lower the level, the closer the doors were to each other. The government reserved these tiers for low-income Argians. Since homes were cheap near the city's bottom, agents like Olan used them for safe houses. Therefore, it did not surprise him to learn that Igon did the same. Olan and Dolas arrived, kept out of sight, and waited for him to leave.

As Qual stepped onto the Avenue, Dolas whispered, "It looks like he bathed. Do you think he found the tracer?"

Olan checked his locator, "No, I am still tracking him."

"I guess he did not wash behind his ears," Dolas joked.

"It pays to be hygienic," Olan replied.

As Qual moved down the avenue, Olan's locator kept him apprised of his position. Since it was getting late, the crowd was sparse. Olan and Dolas stayed back far enough so that their target could not spot them. By chance, if someone followed him, Qual followed protocol and methodically changed his appearance and attire several times. Olan believed he would have evaded them had it not been for the tracer on his body.

The red light stopped moving, and Olan and Dolas disappeared into the tunnels. As they approached Qual's location, their conversation became louder, so they positioned themselves nearby in the shadows, ready to jump the moment an opportunity presented itself.

"What did you say happened?" puzzled Igon.

"I was about to kill him, but an agent stopped me."

"Did you recognize him?"

"Yes. It was Olan."

"How did you escape?"

"I was alone for a few heartbeats, so I used the opportunity to free myself. Olan and his team talked in the adjacent room, so I slipped out, went to my safe house to refresh myself, and called you."

"You idiot! You have led them right to me!"

"What? No! I ensured no one followed me! I implemented our protocol to the letter."

Forcefully, Igon searched Qual's body for what he knew was on him, touched his earlobe, and hooked the tracer with his fingernail, ripping his flesh along with it.

"Ouch! I thought it was a bump."

Knowing his agent blundered, Igon threw the chip to the ground and crushed it underneath his foot. His gut instincts kicked in, and he scanned the area, searching for his adversary. He backed toward the wall, hoping to hide in the shadows, and grabbed Qual by the collar to pull him along. Little did they know, they put themselves right into the hands of their enemy.

Dolas and Olan jumped out of the tunnel when they were close enough to their position and drove daggers into their backs, just above the fifth rib, preventing them from crying out. They fell unconscious, so Olan and Dolas tied their hands behind their backs; to ensure they would not escape, they tied their hands and feet together and threw them over their shoulders as they disappeared into the hidden tunnel.

Chapter 59

Earth
United States - Texas - Austin - State Capitol Building
May 15, 2452

Jared paced in Sonya's office. It was about 5 PM and only a minute since he last checked. It was getting late. Worried that something had gone wrong, he headed for the door. The sound of voices outside quickened his pace, and after opening it, he saw her approaching with a frown.

"What went wrong?" he asked cautiously.

"Nothing," she realized that her face betrayed her melancholy and smiled to correct her mistake, "Here it is, as promised. Texas is yours."

Excited by the news, he grabbed her by the waist, lifted her, and twirled her around. She laughed with her back arched and her hair flowing out behind her as he spun her. He stopped, allowing her body to slide through his arms back to the floor until they were face to face, and then they kissed.

"What do we do now?" she questioned, anxious to start her new life.

"We must ensure that the Texas military will abide by your decision. If they won't, we could have a long battle ahead of us; if they do, I must contact Supreme Commander Porter to send a team to take possession."

"They've already agreed. I did alert them, so they should be here shortly to report to whomever you plan to put in charge. Now, how about we get married?"

"I must notify Tim of our success before we can leave."

*****

Tim hugged Jared tightly and patted him on the back, "I don't know how you did it but thank you. We finally have a chance at a better life."

"Things should move quickly now that all leaders have agreed. Soon your companies can operate like a normal business."

“We won’t know how to act.”

“I’m sure you will figure it out.”

“Hey, before you go, what *did* you have to do to get her to sign off on it? I mean, she was the Governor of Texas. I can’t imagine she wanted for anything.”

“Money doesn’t buy everything, Tim.”

“That doesn’t mean what I think it means, does it?” he queried with a raised eyebrow.

“Let’s just say the price the Regime paid was nothing compared to what we got in return.”

“Whatever you did, Jared. Thanks.”

Jared shook his hand, “You’re welcome. Now, I must go.”

Chapter 60

Earth
The Regime - Washington, D.C. - Fort McNair
May 15, 2452

General Saunders stood in his office, wearing his best uniform, reading the marriage ceremony script before Jared and Sonya. Just in case Jared got cold feet, he posted a couple of guards at the door because it would not be the first time a groom ran. Jared listened distantly to the General's words, replaying their visit to Market Place, where they bought their rings, his tuxedo, and her gown.

Out of all the things he had to do on assignment, shopping was one of the most daunting; it was something he hated with a passion. On the other hand, Sonya delighted in purchasing her bridal outfit. The salesperson did an excellent job convincing her that the Onyx Wedding Gown would be perfect for her, especially since they had one in stock that would fit her with only a few alterations.

He remembered hearing, *Voluminous layers of ivory tulle veiling wafting over soft bisque silk* until his mind went numb. Jared's attention turned elsewhere as the salesperson continued to talk about the dress. In the background, all he heard was *blah, blah, blah* until Sonya came out of the dressing room spinning. He gave his blushing bride full attention and caught himself smiling.

Realizing it was his wedding day, he decided to enjoy the event. She surprised him by using her Regime Talons to pay for the dress, for which she had plenty. Since she did not hint at him to pitch in, he wanted to do something special for her. He bought a tuxedo and took her to a jewelry store, where they chose the style of rings they would wear.

He insisted on paying for it this time and told her it was a gift from him on their wedding day; her eyes flooded with happiness. It was turning out to be a day to remember, and he was glad to take this journey with her, so even if things did not turn out well for them, they had a memorable day to look back on.

"Do you take this woman to be your lawfully wedded wife?"

The words brought him out of his thoughts, "I do."

General Saunders faced Sonya, "Do you take this man to be your lawfully wedded husband?"

"I do," she smiled at him adoringly.

"I now pronounce you man and wife. You may kiss the bride."

As they embraced, the photographer snapped several pictures. Later, they posed for several more, and after the wedding, they headed to his home on the beach.

Chapter 61

Earth
The Regime - Maryland - Eastern Shore
May 15, 2452

The last portal Jared and Sonya stepped through left them at the nearest Interstate Transportation Station to their house. Since the home was in a secluded area, he had to use a hovercar to take them the rest of the way. The residence Supreme Commander Porter gave them was in a small community near the ocean. Ten houses lining the beach in a remote area made it an ideal place to keep an eye on his new bride. Each property had plenty of wooded land in the back, and the neighbors were only a short walk away from each other and the beach. The sun had set a few hours before, and as they drove over the wet sandy beach, he could see clouds moving in by the moonlight.

As far as she knew, he had lived in this home for a few years. He would pretend to know his neighbors (Regime agents) to keep his cover. During their conversation along the way, he recited a few names from the list Supreme Commander Porter gave him to make it believable. They finally arrived, and he carried her over the threshold at her request. There was no doubt in his mind that she wanted the whole experience of a traditional wedding day. Once inside, he put her down, and they kissed again.

The Regime had already delivered her suitcases and stacked them neatly in the living room. Before leaving the Interstate Transportation Station, they scanned and thoroughly searched them. Had the team found anything suspicious, Military Police would send her back to Texas at once. Just before the ceremony, Jared learned that they did not find anything dubious, which gave him a sense of relief.

"It's awfully chilly for May," she rubbed her arms to get warm.

"It has been cooler than normal, even for Maryland. Plus, I saw a cold front moving this way from the northeast, so I'll turn on the heat to keep you from freezing on your wedding night."

"Thanks," she patiently waited for him to return. "Where's the bedroom?"

"It's the first room on the left, at the top of the stairs."

She pointed at her suitcases and bashfully smiled at him, "Would you mind? They are heavy."

"Sure, not a problem."

He lifted the top case and discovered that she was not lying because they were cumbersome, even for him. Carefully, he climbed the stairs with the extra weight in hand. Inside the room, he set them down on her bed. As she unpacked, his mind fast-forwarded to the next phase of their agreement. Since he still did not know her very well and knew that Regime agents were watching their every move, having an intimate encounter with her this early in their relationship made him nervous.

He had promised himself to take things gradually even though parts of his body preferred to move forward with her expectations; the fact that he was in danger of having feelings for her made him vulnerable. If she hid a secret, the more he cared for her, the more pain he would feel after discovering it.

"You know what, it's late. We should call it a night. I'll crash in the other room," he faked a yawn.

"I'll be finished in just a moment. I was looking for something special to wear."

"I think it's best if we take things slowly."

He could tell it hurt her feelings, even though she tried to hide it.

With a forced smile, she replied, "I understand. Have a good night, Jared."

"It's not that I don't want to - you know - it's just that we don't know each other yet, so I promised myself we would take it slow because I think it would be better if we became friends first."

"You're like a rock, Jared. I don't know too many men who would walk away from an opportunity like this."

"I'm not most men. I'll see you tomorrow."

Before leaving, he stopped. Something had been bothering him, and he needed an answer.

"You're different somehow."

"What do you mean?"

"You're not acting as you did in Texas. You're too agreeable. It's like you're putting on an act for my benefit."

"I'm not acting. It is who I am. What you saw at our first meeting was an act. Remember, I was the Governor of Texas. I had responsibilities that demanded assertiveness and confidence, sort of a mask I had to wear. My stepdad, whom you know as President Martinez, began my training to be a politician early. For politics, I must be one way, and in my personal life, I'm another. During our negotiations, I used all my talents to get what I wanted and needed."

"I'll admit you're very good at it."

"Thank you."

"One thing still bothers me."

"What's that?"

"You risked all those lives to get yourself into the Inner Circle. You could have lived just as well in the Immigration District. Why?"

Sonya blushed, "Do you want the truth?"

"Definitely, you better never lie to me."

"Very well, the truth. I have been a widow for a few years now. My job kept me busy, so it shouldn't surprise you that I haven't dated anyone since I lost him." Her husband's memory caused strong emotions to flood her mind, making her pause to gather her composure, "As you so cleverly guessed during our first meeting, I'm thirty-seven. Also, I'm single, and I don't have any children.

"After losing my husband, I looked hard at my life and didn't like what I saw. The Secession Bill gave me the opportunity I needed. Initially, I planned to ask the Regime to move me to the Immigration District with the rest of the delegates until I read your dossier. The first thing that got my attention was your picture. I think you're very handsome, and I guess that most women do too.

"The second was your accomplishments. Since you're young, I knew it would be a longshot for someone my age to get your attention. Few young men are interested in an old widow, let alone a politician with a questionable past. The truth is that I didn't think I had a chance with you at all. I knew that if I met with you and settled for the Immigration District, you would have agreed, and we would have parted ways, never to see each other again.

"Except I wanted more. I wanted the chance to spend time with you, and I hoped that you would want the same, so I used every advantage I had to persuade you. I promised you love, romance, and excitement, hoping that one or all would pique your interest. I mean to keep that promise if you'll let me."

"What if it didn't work? What if I turned you down?"

"Oh, I would have had a good cry and even laughed at myself for being foolish. Ultimately, I would have accepted your counteroffer and moved to the Immigration District. Life would move on, but at least I tried. At the time, you didn't realize that you held all the cards. Texas needs the Regime's help, and I wanted your help too. I bluffed."

"Remind me never to bet against you in poker."

"You'd be wise not to," she smiled playfully.

"Look, I'm flattered that you did all that to get to know me. I just don't understand why you would want to force a marriage. If you were interested, you could have just let me know."

"I have no intention of forcing you to remain in a loveless marriage. If you remember, I left it up to you how you wanted to pursue the relationship. I completed my goal by getting your attention, you decided to continue, and it still is your choice. All I can do is be myself and hope you like that person. All I'm hoping for, all I want, is a fresh start, and I would like you to be a part of it, if possible."

"What if it doesn't work out between us? What if we can't stand each other?"

"I hope that's not the case. If, for some reason, we don't get along or, if, at any time, you change your mind, bring me the divorce documents, and I'll sign them, freeing you. I'll leave your beautiful home, move to the Immigration District, and be out of your life forever."

"Hmm, so this is the real you?"

"Yep, live and in person, for good or bad."

"You're different; I'll give you that."

"I hope that's a good thing."

"If what you're telling me is true, it is."

"I swear it is."

"Good."

"I'm almost done unpacking this bag. Are you sure there isn't anything I can do or say to convince you to stay? We don't have to do anything. I could even sleep on top of the covers if it would make you feel safe," she inquired, hopefully.

"No. Let's stay in separate rooms until we are better acquainted, but I did enjoy talking with you. If things continue this way, I'm sure we'll get to that part of the relationship soon enough."

"Be careful; I can talk a lot."

"Good. I look forward to hearing more about you."

"Goodnight, Jared," she gave him a gentle kiss on the cheek and returned to her unpacking.

"Goodnight, Sonya."

He felt more at ease with her because the talk helped his nerves. At first chance, he planned to ask the analysts to verify all her statements and claims. He would confront her if they discovered she was lying on any issue, but for now, he needed rest. With his bedroom door closed, he threw on a pair of shorts and a tee-shirt and turned off the light.

Staring at the ceiling, he tried unsuccessfully to get her off his mind; having a beautiful woman sleeping in an adjacent bedroom and knowing she wanted him made it impossible to think of anything else. He rolled to his side a few minutes later and watched the clock; time seemed to drag. Fifteen minutes later, he still had not fallen asleep, and to make matters worse, he heard thunder in the distance.

Crap, I'm gonna be up all night now. The minutes seemed to pass like hours, and the storm soon reached the house. Two flashes of lightning assaulted his eyes, which had finally adjusted to the dark. As expected, a loud clap of thunder followed, shaking the house. As the rumble faded, he heard a knock at the door.

"Jared, are you asleep?"

"No."

"May I come in?"

"I don't think it's a good idea, Sonya."

"Please, just until the storm passes. I'll stand in the corner," she begged.

He sighed, "All right, just until it passes."

As she opened the door, lightning lit up the room, revealing the tight-fitting pink teddy clinging to her figure. She shut the door behind her and stood in the corner as promised.

"Thanks; I'll leave once it's over."

"I would never have imagined that you of all people would be afraid of a little thunder."

"It's more the lightning than the thunder. I saw a bolt strike a friend, and it killed her. I've been afraid of it ever since."

"Why are you wearing that outfit?"

"Oh, sorry. I'm not trying to tease you. I wore it just in case you changed your mind and didn't have time to change before coming to your room."

Again, light flashes lit up the room, and a loud clap of thunder shook the house. She nearly jumped from her spot, squeaked out a quick, girlish scream, yet stayed near the corner. Wondering how long the storm would last, he glanced at the clock and discovered the electricity had gone out.

"We just lost electricity."

"I should have grabbed my robe before leaving since the house hasn't warmed up yet," she shivered.

"Go back and get it."

Another loud clap of thunder rumbled.

"Nah, I'll tough it out until the storm is over."

In the dark, he rolled his eyes, knowing her plan. What bothered him most was that it was working. Being alone in the room with her was just too tempting.

"If you want, you can get under the covers. Just keep some space between us," he put a pillow between them.

"Thanks," she responded, jumped into bed, and pulled up the covers to her chin.

Jared could feel her shivering as the storm raged on. In the dark of night, he could smell her perfume lingering in the air, making her even more appealing. Trying to avoid contact with her, Jared turned away and faced the window. As the storm continued, he somehow drifted into a light sleep and dreamed they were in the throes of passion.

He visualized all the things she whispered in his ear until a loud clap of thunder woke him. The rumble made him sit up, and as he became alert, he realized his encounter with her was just a dream making him relieved and disappointed.

"Are you still awake," he whispered.

"Yes, how could anyone sleep with that noise?"

"Are you still cold?"

"A little; why?"

He moved the pillow and shook his head, thinking, *this is a terrible idea, Jared.*

"Come over here and get warm."

"Are you sure?"

"Yeah. I don't want you to get sick on our wedding night."

She moved over and snuggled close to him with a smile hidden by darkness.

"I could stay like this forever," she grinned, nestling her cheek onto his chest.

They cuddled until the storm passed, and moonlight shined into the room as the clouds dissipated; seeing the light reflecting off her hair, he stroked the delicate strands.

"Jared?"

"Yeah?"

"What are you doing?"

"I'm just running my fingers through your hair."

Sitting up, she looked down at him, "Should I leave? I don't want to go, but I sense that you're about to break your promise to yourself."

"I'm finding it difficult to lie beside you."

"I'll leave."

"No. I don't want you to go."

"What are you saying?"

"I guess I'm not a rock."

Chapter 62

Akil
Argi City
The 22,279[th] Terrestrial Rotation of the Second Summer

Zorion returned to the reception room and listened to the ambassador tell stories for another thousand heartbeats. The ambassador's stamina and experience amazed Zorion, so with the end of the conversation nowhere in sight, he politely excused himself from the festivities. He found Durnah, Otsoa's mate, and ordered her to follow him to his vehicle. Zorion told the driver where to go and faced Durnah.

"How long has he been ill?"

"Four Terrestrial Revolutions. Now I am worried."

"You should have told me he had the sickness."

"It is not the sickness. It is something else. He eats five servings at each meal and eats several times during a Terrestrial Rotation; afterward, all he does is sleep."

"That does not sound good at all."

"There is one other thing."

"What is that?"

"He is growing."

"Growing?"

"Yes. He has grown at least two hand widths taller and is twice his original size."

"Is he fat?"

"No. He is all muscle. His arms and legs are enormous, at least four times their original size. His chest and stomach are like boulders."

"You mean like Tuso?"

"Yes. Exactly like him."

Light from a passing vehicle showed a bruise on her neck.

"What happened to you?"

"Nothing. I bumped into a cabinet this morning."

"A bruise from a mild injury such as that should only take seventy heartbeats to recover. You have been with me most of the Terrestrial Revolution. Let me see the injury."

Hesitating, she turned away from him.

"I can order female assistants to inspect you; they will remove all your clothing. I am only asking to see the injury on your neck."

She unlatched her dress, revealing a dark blue and purple bruise covering her entire right shoulder.

"You should have told me he did this to you."

"It happened this morning. I did not bring his food fast enough, and his temper flared; it was my fault."

"You will stay on level one as my guest until I can determine if it is safe for you to return home."

"But we have not…" she stopped before revealing the secret.

"You have not what?" he demanded.

"We have not completed the ceremony."

Her eyes defiantly flooded with sorrow.

"That does not change the fact that he is hurting you. You cannot return to him until I have determined he is well again."

"Yes, Sir," she spoke softly.

The vehicle stopped, and Broll was already on the avenue, waiting for him.

"Durnah just told me that something odd is happening to Otsoa. He has grown."

"Grown?"

"Yes. He is as big as Tuso, so consider him dangerous. I want him arrested at once; take no less than five guards."

Choosing to err with caution, Broll called twenty of his best guards. Moments later, they broke down the front door and rushed inside. Zorion watched with Broll from the avenue, standing only a few paces away, just in case. They returned without a prisoner.

"The place is empty, Sir."

"Damn him!" Zorion growled. He faced Broll, "I want every sentry, screener, and agent you can spare looking for him. Tell them that if he does not come willingly, take him by force. Run him through if you have to; just get him off the avenue and into a prison cell!"

Zorion returned to the vehicle, forcefully sat beside Durnah, slammed the door shut, and faced her, "He has left, but you will remain under guard on my level until security captures him. He could kill you, and I do not want that to happen."

"Please, do not hurt him."

"That will be up to him."

*****

Igon woke with a sharp pain in his back, took a deep breath, opened his eyes, and saw Olan glaring at him from across the room. Now, all the events over the past few Terrestrial Rotations made sense.

"You must be the one who has been chasing me," Igon remarked.

"You may take comfort that you did not make it easy for me."

"I thought you were in prison."

"It is a long story; the abridged version is that I escaped and have been working as a rogue agent."

"Should I credit you for saving Zorion's life?"

"Yes."

"I do not understand. I have seen a video of you trying to kill him."

"I was coerced by someone powerful."

"He must be strong to have convinced you to betray Zorion."

"I will deal with that individual later. Right now, we have some business to discuss."

"Is Shafe still alive?"

"Yes."

"What about Qual?"

"Dolas has him and the rest of your spy network."

"You have done well, Olan. I would have managed things differently if I knew you were still active."

"Like leaving after your first attempt failed."

"Precisely."

"No sense in dwelling on past decisions. We need to focus on your future."

Igon smiled and turned his head to grab the corner of his shirt collar with his teeth. What he expected to be there was not.

"I cannot allow you to kill yourself."

"Let me go, and I will tell you everything."

"You know how this works. Tell me your name so I can have it on record, and if you give me the information I want, I will let you go."

Igon was silent.

"Very well, we will do this the hard way."

Olan recorded the session and exacted several torture methods on his prisoner; each one was more painful than the previous. It took a few

316

thousand heartbeats until Igon broke. First, Igon confessed to being the Chief Administrator of Vlor's Intelligence Department, just as Olan suspected, and in time, he repeated Elzer's order to assassinate Zorion and revealed several crucial passwords that Olan would use later.

Olan asked his last question about a female's participation in Zorion's assassination attempt. Although Olan was sure Nayrah worked for Elzer, Igon vehemently denied the accusation under extreme duress. It convinced him that she was working independently and with a separate agenda.

Olan faced him, "Elzer is a fool. He should have never tried to kill Zorion."

"I agree."

"Why did you pursue it?"

"Put yourself in my position. What if Zorion told you to kill Elzer?"

"You would not have stopped me."

"Do not be so sure of yourself. I was working with limited resources."

"So was I, and yet, I caught you."

"What will you do with me now?"

"I cannot leave you tied up. I know you will escape before I return," Olan unsheathed his sword.

"What if I promise not to escape?"

"You will forgive me if I do not trust you."

Before Igon could respond, Olan plunged his sword into his chest. It cut a chamber within his heart, preventing him from recovering. Igon would remain immobilized until Olan returned to remove the blade. For a couple of hundred heartbeats, Olan stared at Igon's inert body until he abruptly spun, leaving to continue his work.

Chapter 63

Earth
The Regime - Washington, D.C. - Mercy Hospital
May 16, 2452

Having only a couple of hours of sleep, Michael released another suspected spy and yawned. At least Supreme Commander Porter, Michael, and all the MR tech staff passed the testing, authorizing them for duty. All parties agreed it would be easier to keep up their charade about the epidemic in a hospital rather than the military base. Michael used his emergency authority to obtain a small, quarantined section at Mercy Hospital. It had been a long night, and so far, everyone on the list Stan gave him did not show any signs of MR coercion.

"Who's next, Lisa?" Michael asked as he yawned again.

"General Saunders."

"Get him prepped and contact me after you sedate him."

"Will do."

Michael ran a full diagnostic on the machine following each scan to ensure it was running correctly. Also, he set up the MR machine in an adjoining room to prevent anyone from seeing it. He heard General Saunders' voice in the adjacent room.

"What's all this about, Lisa? I have documents to sign and things to do."

"Sorry, General; there is an outbreak, and the Center for Disease Control has us vaccinating everyone to ensure they won't get the newly discovered Rete virus," she lied.

"Sounds dangerous."

"It could be *if* we don't get it under control," she patted the reclining medical chair with her hand. "Have a seat so that I can give you the injection."

He hesitated.

"What's wrong?" Lisa wondered.

"I don't know. I can't seem to move."

"Some people are afraid of needles. Why don't you sit here instead?" she comforted, pointing at another chair. "It should help you relax."

He moved to the other chair and sat. Lisa noticed his anxiety but did not find anything in his medical records to show that he had issues with needles, so she continued with caution.

"If you look away, it'll all be over in a flash."

She gave him the injection; he pulled away and stood, feeling the burn of the serum.

"What did you give me?" he demanded.

"The vaccine, like I told you. Why are you so upset?"

Feeling the sedative working, he struggled to retrieve something from his trouser pocket. Seeing a pill in his hand, Lisa grabbed his wrist and called for Michael. General Saunders struggled with her to bring his hand to his mouth; Michael ran to help, and before he could achieve his goal, General Saunders fell unconscious.

"What happened?" Michael questioned.

"I gave him the injection, and he tried to take this pill."

"Take it to the lab and ask them to analyze it."

Michael put General Saunders on a gurney with the help of two assistants, and they wheeled him into the adjacent room. He put the headpiece on him and turned on the machine. Thirty minutes into the process, the machine beeped a warning signal. Michael reviewed the data and performed a detailed scan of General Saunders' brain, where the machine found an issue. The machine delivered the results a few minutes later, and Lisa returned.

"What's wrong?"

"I can't believe it; General Saunders is the spy."

Chapter 64

Akil

Argi City

The 22,280[th] Terrestrial Rotation of the Second Summer

Julie agreed to stay, and Zorion's work started piling up, mainly because her presence was a constant distraction, so he arrived a couple of thousand heartbeats early to catch up. Just as he finally completed the earlier work cycle's duties, Shilda called him through the intercom.

"Sir, Dolas is here to see you."

"Send him in."

Dolas reached the door, and after Zorion waved him in, Dolas handed him his report. As Zorion finished reading it, he thought about the earlier work cycle events. First, Olan helped him uncover a significant spy network within Argi. Also, with Shafe's recorded confession, he proved that the order to kill Zorion came from Igon, Chief Administrator of Vlor's Intelligence Department.

Shafe's confession cast suspicion on Elzer; it would not be enough to remove him. Elzer would blame everything on Igon, who would take the fall. Dolas was sure Elzer did not count on Olan capturing Igon, and with his confession, the other sovereigns would strip Elzer of his authority, and his family could not inherit his seat. That piece of the puzzle would be up to Olan to obtain.

"You have done excellent work, Dolas, yet without Igon's confession, I cannot bring charges against Elzer."

"Yes, Sir. I know, but do not worry. We are searching the city for him now. I am sure he is still here. Once we find him, I will personally bring his recorded confession to you."

"How is your search for Olan progressing?"

"Not good, Sir. He is very elusive."

"Yes. I know he will be hard to find because he is still the best agent I have ever known."

"I agree; I will keep looking."

"Very well, dismissed."

As Dolas left, Shilda was on the communicator again.

"Sir, Yanamai is here, as you requested."

“Send her in.”

Seeing her at the door, he could tell by her expression that she still felt uncomfortable since her encounter with Kraeth. *Do not worry. I will avenge you soon enough.*

“Come in, Yanamai.” After she sat, he said, “As you already know, the five sovereigns have agreed to the Regime’s contract. Ambassador Reynolds communicated with Supreme Commander Porter, and we will evacuate Akil at once. Each city is sending their best and brightest to the planet first, along with our historical data and computer technology.”

“Then, it is finally happening,” Yanamai smiled for the first time in a few Terrestrial Revolutions.

“Yes. All your arduous work has saved us, at least some of us, because we can only send a limited number of Akilians each month. They were not ready for three hundred billion mouths to feed, so we will send machinery to dig in the ground and carve out homes while others build tents and community centers.”

“How long will it take to get everyone there?”

“The earliest date is this time next yellow harvest.”

Her smile faded, “Our sun may not last that long.”

“We do not have any other choice. If we send everyone all at once, they will die of starvation or dehydration.”

“What do you want us to do?”

“I am sending you and your sister with the first group. I will ensure your parents are at the top of the list when we allow citizens to go.”

“Why are you sending us?”

“You both qualify as our best and brightest.”

“I cannot leave; I must run the Interstellar Transport Bay,” Yanamai insisted.

“Tadra volunteered to do it.”

“This cannot be happening. I expected to be the last to leave, not the first.”

“Why? You have already given up so much.”

“I cannot leave you or my parents behind.”

“I always knew I would send you first.”

“I cannot….”

"This is not up for discussion. I have made my decision. Say your goodbyes and go. You may leave now."

Although his words seemed callous, even to him, Zorion had to ensure she survived. He knew she could do more with the Regime's support than staying on Akil. It was not how he wanted to say goodbye, but he refused to argue with her about it. She stood and, to his surprise, walked around his desk to face him. He thought she planned to argue with him again until seeing tears in her eyes, so he stood with a gentle smile.

"I know."

What went unspoken between them was the likelihood that they would never see each other again. Knowing Zorion the way she did, he would not leave until the last Akilian was on Earth, and with their sun in its current state, it was unlikely that Akil would still be here by the following yellow harvest. Unable to control her emotions, she hugged him tightly. He put one hand behind her head and the other around her shoulders, pulling her close.

They stood in a silent embrace for a long time until she finally let go, "Thank you for being my friend."

"Thank you for being the daughter I have always wanted."

"Will you be there to see me off?" she asked, sniffling.

"I promise."

He kissed her forehead as a final farewell; she left to get ready and say her goodbyes.

"Hurry, I want you off this planet as soon as possible," Zorion urged.

As she left, Broll stood in the doorway. Grateful for the distraction, Zorion waved him in.

He stood at attention until Zorion questioned, "What can I do for you, Broll?"

"I have heard the news of another attack on your life."

He sighed, "I do not understand why I am so unpopular."

"This attack is of the highest betrayal. Dahmar tells me that Otsoa has been building support in the barracks."

"You think he is planning a coup?"

"My sources confirm Dahmar's report. He intends to kill you and take your place as Argi's sovereign."

"This is happening at the worst possible moment in our history. Argi is the doorway to Earth. No one can come or go without his approval if he gains control of the Interstellar Transport Bay."

"Dahmar plans to interrogate every soldier on level eight hundred. We will know the names of his supporters soon."

"No. Tell Dahmar to stop."

"Why?"

"We must let Otsoa follow through with his plan."

"He will kill you!"

"If so, he cannot claim my seat in the Argi House."

"That is easy enough to fix. Otsoa can order one of his soldiers to kill you for him."

"What if we enact your plan?" Zorion inquired.

"It *could* save your life."

"At the same time, it would reveal his loyal followers without having to waste time interrogating them."

"What happens if he gets around the extra sentries I posted?"

"We will tell the ambassador of our plan, and he can tell Supreme Commander Porter. That way, our allies will know what we intend to do. I do not want anything to stop the evacuation of Akil."

Chapter 65

Early in the morning, guards escorted Wu Luli back to the interrogation room, where Captain Yates waited. She saw a grim look on his face, which made her feel uneasy, causing her to imagine all sorts of tragic scenarios.

"What's wrong?" she asked.

"Am I that obvious?"

"You don't hide your feelings very well."

"Which is why I'm not a spy anymore," he paused to sigh, "please, follow me."

At the end of the hall, he showed her a room with a one-way-looking glass. On the other side, her dad sat drinking a soda.

"What's going on?" she questioned.

"Your dad said he and his wife, Wu Meili, attempted to flee China to the Regime seventeen years ago. He was unsuccessful and had hoped that Wu Meili made it, so we checked our records, and she did."

The door to the other room opened, and an older woman walked inside. Staring in disbelief, they gazed at each other in silence until they simultaneously ran into each other's arms and wept fiercely for several minutes.

"Is she my mother?" she puzzled, also weeping.

"Yes."

"She looks familiar. Have I met her?"

"Based on your debriefing, you have not, but you have seen her picture and communicated by email."

On a small tablet, he opened an image allowing Wu Luli to see the name underneath her mother's photo, and she went pale.

"This can't be right."

"I'm sorry. There is no painless way to say this. After your mother arrived and changed her name to Chu Juan to hide her identity, her daughter's name was Chu Lian, your twin sister."

Feeling like someone had just punched her in the stomach, she collapsed. Captain Yates caught her, set her down gently, left to get a glass of water, and returned to her side.

"I killed my sister," she repeatedly mumbled in a whisper.

"You can't blame yourself. General Ming-tun Fu used you."

"How did he do this?" she managed to ask in between ragged gasps.

"I'll tell you later after you've calmed down."

Anger overshadowed her sorrow long enough for her to squeeze his hand tightly.

"Tell me now!" her voice trembled with anger and pain.

"You were only five at the time. Your dad told us that Ming-tun Fu was a Colonel and had his eyes set on becoming a General. To gain recognition from his superiors, he started an experiment and recruited a hundred children to make them spies under his command. Your dad was in the military and heard of his plans to enlist you and your sister. He did not want that kind of life for either of you and planned to escape.

"To ensure that one of you survived, he sent your sister with your mother to the Regime in a boat. After they left, he put you in his truck and headed for Mumbai, India, where he intended to take a different boat to the Regime; Colonel Ming-tun Fu caught him before crossing the border, where he arrested him, put him in prison, and sent you to his training camp."

Wu Luli thought General Ming-tun Fu had always been one step ahead of her until now; it was clear he planned her sister's death before bringing her into his training camp. Drawing on her years of experience, she analyzed everything from her dad's statement. Since she and her sister were identical twins, General Ming-tun Fu waited years for her to have enough experience to take her sister's place in the Regime. Rather than abduct her, he had her killed. That enraged her.

The problem with executing such a long-term scheme was the variables. Still, it explained General Ming-tun Fu's contingency idea of setting her up to murder her colleagues' parents. To put his emergency plan into effect, he needed another spy inside the Regime. Since Michael was hunting that person now, it left her to pursue General Ming-tun Fu. The next time they met, she would make him pay dearly. Having a new goal, she gathered strength and forced herself to stand.

"I swear on my life; I will kill that bastard and avenge my family!"

"I know you want revenge. If I were in your position, I would too, so if you promise to bring him back alive, I'll give you the mission."

"Are you serious?"

"Yes. I already have Supreme Commander Porter's approval to send you if you bring him back alive. We can't scan his memories if he's dead. If we can get inside his head, we can destroy everything he's built and send him to the Penal Facility on the moon."

Although her rage demanded General Fu's death, she conceded that Captain Yates was right. Death *was* too good for him.

"You're right. It would be satisfying to know he'll spend the rest of his life on the moon."

"Where will you begin?"

"I'll need to return home and search for my contacts."

"Make a list of anything you'll need, and I'll schedule your departure for 0600 hours tomorrow; you should spend some time with your parents and get reacquainted."

"How can I face them knowing what I have done."

"It's not your fault. General Ming-tun Fu abused his power and manipulated all of you. They will understand. Don't deprive them of both their daughters."

"I'll go in a few minutes. I need time to think."

"I'll see you tomorrow at 0600."

She stared at her parents as they sat at the table, talking. Even with everything wrong, she could not get Michael off her mind. Most of her life had been a series of tragedies, and the only time she felt at peace was with him. In time, she hoped that Michael would forgive her; no, she needed Michael to forgive her because she wanted what her parents seemed to have, a lifelong connection.

Even though General Fu had separated them for seventeen years, she could see how much they still cared for each other. Hopefully, Michael would look at her that way again soon. For now, she had to face her parents and tell them what had happened. Summing up the courage to meet with them, she walked into the adjoining room and told them everything.

Chapter 66
Akil
Argi City
The 22,280[th] Terrestrial Rotation of the Second Summer

Standing in the Interstellar Transport Bay, Yanamai and Garbi had teary goodbyes with their parents and friends. Two thousand handpicked Akilians stood in a line that reached out onto the avenue, each saying goodbye to their loved ones. One camera crew from the Information League recorded the event on Zorion's order in the Transport Bay. Yanamai did not see Zorion anywhere; it saddened her because she had hoped to see him one more time before leaving.

After they finished with all their kisses and hugs, Tadra, now in charge of the Interstellar Transport Bay, prepared the machine to open. Out of respect, she asked Yanamai to engage the computer one last time. The camera operator zoomed in on her standing in front of the control panel. Having no desire to make a speech, she pressed the icon, and the portal opened inside the adjoining room.

Spanning the area, the camera operator focused his lens on the event horizon. On the other side, armed soldiers stood scattered about, awaiting the arrival of their guests. Still sniffling, Yanamai moved toward the portal with Garbi close behind. She knew Tadra would keep the door vortex open until the last select Akilians stepped through.

Yanamai kept looking back along the way, hoping that Zorion would show up at the last moment, and at the event horizon, she turned one last time; he was not there. She took a deep breath, threw her bag of clothes over her shoulder, and stepped to the other side, with Garbi by her side.

*****

Using her alter ego of a beautiful debutante, Gecheana exited the intercity train. She arrived with a small entourage that followed her and carried her luggage. Due to Nayrah's incompetence and Jadell's disobedience, her visit to Argi was now necessary to regain control and put her plan to dominate Akil back on track. She sent her soldiers earlier and in different cars to stay inconspicuous. With their help, Nayrah and Jadell would fall.

By now, her soldiers were at Nayrah's old apartment, waiting for further instructions. Gecheana hoped that Nayrah and Jadell would try to reclaim the home during her time here. It would save her from hunting them down. Until then, she had other plans to enact. Having retrieved Gau's sword from the surface, she removed it from her luggage and sent her attendants to the apartment. Gazing at the handle, she smiled, knowing it would be the key to gaining complete control of Argi.

The only thing she needed now was a willing accomplice. Concentrating, she closed her eyes and searched for Otsoa's whereabouts in the city. Having considered all her options, using him was the best choice. She planned to seduce him with an offer that would be hard to refuse. Otsoa was not a Skean, making him easier to manipulate. She also heard reports that he had been gathering support in the barracks.

Having an instant army under her command would help with the coup. The circumstances of this scheme were in her favor. Now all she had to do was find him. She saw an image of him, and a barrack number appeared to her, so she verified its location and left to find it. She exited the elevator and heard a roaring crowd nearby, so she followed the noise to the nearest garrison.

Once inside, the noise level increased dramatically; she quickly adapted. Still using the beautiful debutante disguise, she was too short to see past the soldiers in front of her. Used to having her way, she pushed through the horde with the Night Lord's power until reaching the center, where it surprised her to see how big Otsoa grew. His size and muscle mass increased about four times since his fight with Tuso.

Nayrah must have given him a strength potion. Idiot, if you cannot control him, you do not make him stronger. Currently, he was in the heat of battle. His face was bloody, but his opponent looked much worse. As they fought, Otsoa's challenger tried to keep his broken left arm behind him. Using his right side to defend and attack, he fought bravely yet did not match Otsoa's newfound strength.

The challenger received two solid hits to his face (the second hit knocked out a couple of teeth) and tried to retaliate; Otsoa grabbed his fist with an open hand and squeezed it. The pain made him fall to his knees. Otsoa did not yield and twisted his hand, breaking his competitor's wrist, so the challenger motioned with his broken arm to surrender; the gesture enraged Otsoa, who pummeled the contender unconscious. The beating left them covered in blood.

As his opponent's head hit the ground, the crowd cheered for Otsoa, who raised his fists in victory. The fight was over, so the group dispersed, and Gecheana heard Sovereign Cubes exchanging hands. Still standing near the makeshift ring, Otsoa wiped the blood off his body and put on his shirt, unaffected by the recent combat. It was clear to her that the drug Nayrah gave him also increased his endurance.

Everyone left, except two of his friends, so she expected him to acknowledge her, being the only spectator. Instead, he completely ignored her, and the trio walked by as if she were not there. Before he could leave, she spoke to him with a soft, flirtatious voice, backed by just enough of her Skean power to grab his attention; he faced her.

"I saw you fight. You are good. Perhaps you could give me private lessons," she smiled sweetly at him.

His companions laughed at her comment and gave him a jovial slap on his back.

"Looks like you have an admirer," an associate joked.

"I do not have time for private lessons," Otsoa snapped rudely.

"You will want to make time for me," Gecheana again embellished her words with her seductive Skean power.

He motioned for his friends to go on without him and faced her, "What is it you want from me?"

"You cannot even begin to imagine what I have in store for you."

He surveyed the room and saw they were alone, so he allowed his primitive emotions to take over and responded to her advances with a primal kiss. The touch of his sweaty lips surprised her and made her nauseous. She tried to push him off, but he was too strong, so she called upon the Night Lord's powers and knocked him back a few paces.

"Nayrah!" he snarled.

"No. I am Gecheana, her superior."

"Go crawl underneath the mossy rock you slithered from, you slimy Skean. I do not want anything to do with your kind!"

"You know what I am?"

"Yes. I have done some research, and it is not hard to figure out what you and Nayrah are."

"Relax. I am not here to hurt you. I am here to make you an offer."

"Whatever it is, my answer is no! Nayrah always made me do things that only benefited her, and I always got the blame."

"What if I make an Akilian oath? I swear on my life that I will not intentionally harm you."

"How do I know you will keep your word? I have dealt with your kind before. I cannot trust you."

"I have given you an Akilian oath; you *can* trust me."

"What do you want from me?"

"I want you to be my partner. I know we can accomplish remarkable things together."

"If we are going to be partners, I expect payment before I do anything for you."

"Ask for whatever you want, and I will give it to you."

"There are three things that I want."

"Tell me."

"I want to rule, Argi."

"Consider it yours. What else do you want?"

"I want to join houses with Yanamai."

"What about Durnah?"

"I do not love her. I have never loved her."

"This request will be difficult to grant."

"Then, our deal is off."

"Do not be too hasty. I said it would be difficult. I did not say it would be impossible. Yanamai is no longer on Akil."

"What?"

"She left for Earth earlier this work cycle."

"I know Zorion sent her away to keep her from me. He will pay for this!"

"Once you become Argi's sovereign, you can summon her back."

"She will not return knowing I am in charge."

“What if her parents were in trouble?”

“Yes, she would return to help them.”

“And the last thing you want?”

“I want Nayrah’s head.”

Gecheana smiled, “I will deliver it to you, personally. Now, do we have a deal?”

“Yes. We have a deal. When do we start?”

“Immediately.”

“What do we do first?”

“We will finally kill Zorion. Once he is dead, you can take his place as Argi’s sovereign.”

“I have already made plans to kill him.”

“Tell me, what are they?”

“I have one hundred loyal soldiers. We will storm the Argi House, where my General will kill Zorion, and I will take his seat.”

She refrained from berating him for his stupidity.

“That plan will not work.”

“Why not? I will not kill him; someone else will do it.”

“The law states that if you are part of a plot to kill the sovereign, the other sovereigns will have you executed for treason.”

“I was not aware of that law.”

“That is why you need me.”

“How can we get rid of him?”

“At the appointed time, you will go to a public place, where there will be plenty of witnesses, and I will go with your soldiers to kill him. That way, the Sovereigns cannot link you to his assassination.”

“They are *my* soldiers, loyal to me.”

“Going forward, they will be *my* soldiers, not yours. I will lead them into battle. They will be loyal to me. All I need you to do is gather them together and tell them to follow my orders.”

“They will not follow a female.”

“I will use my powers to persuade them, and with your support, they will obey me.”

“I do not like the idea of giving you control over my army.”

“Again, you can trust me. We are partners in this. I will keep my word.”

“What do you get out of all this?”

"Our goals are similar. I want Nayrah dead and you to rule Argi so we can rule Akil together."

"I never imagined I would rule all of Akil."

"You can, with my help."

"How is that even possible?"

She removed the special sword with her right hand and presented it to him.

"What is that?"

"It is Gau's sword."

"Where did *you* get it?"

"That is none of your concern. All you need to do is show it to the Information League during your inauguration. It will do two things. First, it will prove that you had nothing to do with Zorion's death. Also, Gau's High Priest will confirm you can ignite the sword, so the other four sovereigns must submit to your authority."

"I am not Gau reborn, nor do I have a Skean's power, which means I will fail."

"You do not need to ignite it."

"They will demand to see me do it in front of everyone!"

"If so, you will tell them that the sword is holy and will not ignite it in front of non-believers. Instead, you will do it in front of Gau's High Priest in the privacy of the temple."

"Except *he* will know I cannot ignite it. What happens if he tells the Information League?"

"He will help you because he is working for me."

"He will know I am a fraud, and there will always be a chance that he will tell someone. What if he decides to extort me or us?"

"You do not need to worry about him. I have tested his loyalty many times."

Taking the sword from her, he raised it in the air and yelled, "Let this Terrestrial Revolution be Zorion's last! Gau has returned!"

She smiled, "Gather your soldiers together. He has scheduled another media conference within a few hundred heartbeats. I will attack him there. It will be public and will help with your alibi."

Chapter 67

Jared woke to the sound of clanging dishes from the kitchen. Groggily, he rolled over and, within moments, found one of the hidden cameras embedded in the fire alarm, mounted directly over his bed. Images of his encounter with Sonya last night flashed in his mind. Knowing the Regime recorded all of it made him blush. Aware that unnamed analysts were reviewing his love life, he dreaded facing Supreme Commander Porter and anyone else in the Regime.

Pushing aside his fear, he jumped out of bed, dressed, and headed toward the kitchen; he smelled eggs, toast, and bacon. With a tray of food in her hand, Sonya turned.

"Oh, you ruined the surprise. I planned to bring you breakfast in bed."

"I appreciate it, but I need to get to work."

"I should have negotiated a week off for you; I guess even the best of us slip up from time to time."

"I'll be home by five, so we'll have plenty of time this evening to be together."

"I'll have dinner ready. You will need your energy."

Grabbing a couple of slices of toast, he spooned some egg and bacon in between, making a sandwich, and headed for the door. Before leaving, she caught him and gave him a long kiss.

"Thank you for last night. It was wonderful," she smiled affectionately.

"I enjoyed it too, but...."

"You feel guilty for breaking the promise you made to yourself."

"A little."

"I think you will forgive yourself in time. You're only human, Jared. Besides, I'm glad you reconsidered."

"You didn't make it easy for me."

Sonya smiled, "No. I didn't."

"So, you did plan to come to my room last night and seduce me."

"The storm gave me a good excuse to be there, don't you think?" she smiled.

"You just can't take no for an answer."

"Not if I can change it to a yes."

He chuckled, "You're something else."

"I'm *your* something else," she kissed him. "Now have fun chasing villains. I'll see you tonight."

As he drove off, her smile faded because the thought of performing even one more task for President Martinez wore on her conscience, but the fear of becoming a widow again drove her to keep their agreement. Having discovered several lenses scattered about the house during her morning chores, she returned to the kitchen to clean, keeping the pretense of being unaware of their existence.

She spent an hour cleaning every room in the house and mentally noted each camera location and their blind spots, and with her back facing one of the lenses, she used a small Philips screwdriver to remove the green computer board from her hairdryer plug and slipped it into her pocket. The Regime scanners missed this tiny electronic device, which President Martinez assured her could record and playback video. Since her hairdryer would run without it, no one would be the wiser.

Casually, she threw some clothes in a hamper, carried them down to the basement, and started the washing machine. As it filled, she inconspicuously moved into the lens's blind spot. Using a small stepladder, she peeked above the drop ceiling. With her flashlight, she traced the camera cable to the electric box. Staying out of the camera's view, she walked to it and exposed the camera relay center.

Since there were many wires, she had to trace each one before connecting her computer board to it, which she hid behind some cables. She retrieved a bottle of wine from the rack, climbed the stairs, grabbed her purse, headed for her neighbor's home, and rang the bell twice. Seconds later, a woman opened the door.

"Hi. How do you do? I'm your new neighbor, Sonya; Sonya Stewart," she smiled and extended her hand to greet her.

"Welcome to the neighborhood, Sonya. My name is Sharon."

"Good to meet you, Sharon. I brought you a gift," she handed the bottle to her.

"Wow, a 2443 Chateau Montelena. That's very generous. Please, come in."

Sharon escorted her to the living room.

"You have a lovely home," Sonya observed.

"Thank you. Please, have a seat. Did you say that your last name is Stewart?"

"Yes. Jared and I got married yesterday," Sonya extended her left hand.

"Oh, those are beautiful rings."

"The engagement ring belonged to my grandmother; he picked out the wedding band himself. He has good taste."

"Yes. I can tell. Now, we have a reason to celebrate, so I'll get some glasses, and we can have a drink."

"That would be nice. Thank you."

Sharon was busy in the kitchen, so Sonya walked to the doorway leading to the adjoining room, searched for a computer, spotted one, and returned to her seat; her bottom hit the cushion as Sharon turned the corner. Sharon set two glasses on the table, used a corkscrew to pop the cork, poured the wine into the glasses, and raised hers for a toast.

"May your wedding night never end."

"I'll drink to that."

Gently, they tapped their glasses and sipped the wine.

"Mmmm, that's delicious."

"I should have brought some cheese. I must remember it next time," Sonya remarked.

"Wait. I may have something. Let me check."

Sharon left to retrieve the snack; Sonya slipped her hand into her purse and removed a small plastic bottle used for eye drops. The liquid inside was something Alonso gave her. She removed the little plastic container, put two drops into Sharon's drink, and placed it back into her purse, just moments before Sharon returned.

"Here we go; I found some Pecorino in the refrigerator."

"Oh, that'll go well."

She set down the wooden board, which held the cheese and knife, cut some slices, put them on a small plate, and handed them to

Sonya. For several minutes, Sharon talked without touching her wine, and as time passed, Sonya began to wonder if she would ever drink. Sharon took her glass and sipped it with a morsel of cheese and, within a few short minutes, finished all the wine in her glass.

Soon, her head fell back onto the chair cushion. Sonya walked to her computer and turned it on. As it started, it requested a password. She opened and slammed drawers, looking for a clue, until finding one. It was a picture of Sharon's husband's boat. Sonya typed its name, the computer acknowledged her as the administrator, and she accessed the site Alonso gave her. Once linked to the server, it automatically found Sharon's machine and sent the coordinates to him. Moments later, a location and time scrolled onto the screen.

Sonya entered the coordinate into her wristwatch and memorized the time of their meeting. She covered her tracks by removing any evidence of her search from the browser history; she shut down the computer and returned to clean Sharon's glass, removing the drug's residue. The two drops kept her asleep for about an hour, so Sonya filled their glasses halfway and poured the rest into the sink, hoping to convince her that they had drunk the whole bottle. Sonya kept her eyes closed, pretending to have also fallen asleep, hoping Sharon would think their late morning nap was due to their wine consumption.

"Sonya, are you all right?" Sharon questioned, wiping her eyes. Sonya did not respond, so she groggily stood, walked over to her side, and spoke a little louder, "Sonya, can you hear me?"

Using her best acting skills, Sonya pretended to wake and, seeing Sharon, queried, "What happened?"

"I don't think we can handle our wine," she held the empty bottle. "We fell asleep."

Looking at her watch, Sonya pretended surprise, "Oh dear, I need to get home and start dinner. Jared will be arriving in a couple of hours. I have something special planned for tonight."

"I hope we can get together again soon, but I think we should stick to water."

"I look forward to it. Please give me your number. I'll contact you tomorrow, and we can set up a time."

They exchanged information, and Sonya returned home to prepare for Jared's return.

Chapter 68

It was early, and Yetta stood in the shadows, waiting for Thea to leave the apartment Zorion gave her and Taen. Bad judgment caused her to make the mistake of trusting Thea to follow orders during her Coming-of-Age Ceremony. Out of jealousy, Thea betrayed her by taking Taen to bed. Now, she would make Thea pay for that treachery. The door opened, and Thea stepped onto the avenue, still disguised in her identity.

Yetta saw Thea's smug smile, and it made her angrier than before. With her sword already unsheathed, Yetta ignited it, and as Thea came near, Yetta swung at her neck; Thea blocked it with her sword because she sensed her daughter outside and was ready for the attack.

"I am going to kill you for betraying me!" Yetta spat.

The intense hatred they felt for each other fueled their fight. They moved fast, swung hard, and without mercy. At one point, their swords met, and Thea moved her lips to Yetta's ear to whisper, "I suggest you rethink your plan. You will need my help."

"I do not need the help of a backstabber!"

"Fine, you will fight Gecheana on your own."

"I am not afraid of her. If she were here right now, I would kill her too!"

"You will soon have your chance. My informants tell me she is staying at my old apartment on the lowest level."

"She is in Argi?"

"How can you expect to run a city not knowing who comes and goes? Yes. She is in Argi and plans to take it from us."

"Us? She gave the city to me!"

"Fine. Gecheana is taking it from you, just like she did from me. I suggest we work together, and after we kill her, we can decide who will rule Argi."

"I can beat her by myself. I do not need your help."

"Really? How can you beat her not knowing her location?"

"You just said she is staying at your old apartment."

"That does not mean she is there right now. I feel disappointed, Yetta. I thought you knew better."

"I have not had time to build an information network yet."

"That is another reason you need my help."

She hated to admit that Thea was right. There was no way Yetta could defeat Gecheana independently. She was still beginning to put together her network, and not having current information made her weak. She had no choice, so Yetta pushed Thea back and disengaged her sword.

"Very well, you have a truce until Gecheana is dead, then I *will* kill you."

"Just be ready to act the moment I call."

"You stay away from Taen!"

Thea smiled smugly again and turned to leave, "Do not worry. I had my fill of him during the sleep cycle. You should be more worried about what Gecheana will do to him."

Thea left, and Yetta entered her new apartment. Thea's words haunted her. By selecting Taen during her ceremony, Thea made it clear to all Akil that Yetta cared for him. It was only a matter of time until Gecheana would try to kill him for her disobedience. She would not let that happen. Hearing the Dryer-Booth running, she knew Taen was getting ready for work. As he left the bathroom, she met him.

"Where did you go?" he asked.

"I needed to walk."

"I am surprised you have the energy considering the last sleep cycle," he grinned.

Yetta understood that he did not know it was Thea with him; it still hurt. Seeing his smile was like a punch in the gut, which is what Thea wanted. *I swear, Thea. I will have my revenge!* Yetta loved Taen and used that feeling to push aside her anger.

Smiling, she moved close to him, "Do not leave. We should continue where we left off."

"You are tenacious, my love. I am sorry, I must go to work."

"You must not go to the farm this work cycle or for several."

"I have a responsibility to the citizens of Argi. My farm supplies five percent of the moss eaten in this city."

"I do not care about them. I care about you. I have just learned that your life is in danger."

"What do you mean?"

"I have many enemies and angered one who will kill you to punish me."

"I do not have to run. Moss farmers stick together. I will ask them to set a watch."

"You are only condemning them to an early death."

"You should ask Zorion for some guards."

"They will not be enough."

"Who is this Akilian?"

"She is powerful and dangerous. It was one of the reasons why I did not want to join our houses publicly. Now you have become a target."

"What about my farm?"

"I will hire someone to watch over it for you. Now please, my love, let me take you to the Intercity Transport Station."

"Where will I go?"

"Go to Vlor and wait for me there. Before you leave, I will give you enough Sovereign Cubes to live on for thirty Terrestrial Revolutions."

"How will you find me?"

"Do not worry. I will. Now we must go before she strikes."

"I need to pack some clothes."

"No. You do not have time. You can buy new ones once you are safe."

"Zorion just announced that the evacuation of Akil is underway. What if he calls my name?"

"Do not worry, my love. At the right time, I will ensure you get off Akil safely."

"All right. I trust you, Yetta. Lead the way."

At the Intercity Transport Station, Yetta withdrew enough Sovereign Cubes for Taen to live on during his time in Vlor. She kissed him goodbye and watched him get on the train. It disappeared into the tunnel, and she turned to prepare for the fight ahead.

A loud banging on the front door woke Julie from her sleep. She started to get up and fell back down on the pillow. The alcohol was still in her system, and she had all the hangover symptoms. The only thing she wanted to do was sleep, yet the banging persisted, so she mumbled a few swear words, forced herself out of bed, and answered the door.

"Go away, Tionah," she growled.

"Good morning to you too, Julie. I anticipated your illness and brought a special moss drink for you," she entered the apartment.

The thought of drinking green moss made Julie gag in her current physical state.

"Oh, it is not that bad. Try it. It will make you feel much better," Tionah urged.

She took a hesitant sip of the green concoction and gagged, "That's disgusting."

"Hmm, I do not understand," Tionah took a sip of her own. "It tastes fine to me."

"Moss is difficult to eat when I'm feeling good. With a queasy stomach, it's impossible."

"I will leave it on the table for you, just in case. I recommend that you eat something. It will help to absorb the alcohol in your system."

"What happened last night? I don't remember anything after my first drink."

"Are you sure you want me to tell you?"

"Uh, oh. What did I do?"

"I took the liberty of looking up the correct Earthian phrase. If I am correct, you *threw yourself* at Zorion."

Julie's head fell into her hands.

"Oh, no. I owe him a huge apology."

"It will not be necessary. You are his friend."

"He's going to get one anyway. I haven't had a drink in years. The liquor they served last night reminded me of the gelatin shots I used to swallow in college. It tasted great going down; three or four drinks later, I couldn't remember my name."

"Right now, Zorion is holding a media conference to address Akil's evacuation protocol. If you hurry, I think you can catch him before he leaves the dais."

"All right, I will go freshen up. I don't want him to see me like this."

Before reaching the bedroom, Julie spun around and questioned, "You said the only plants that survived were the different mosses, right?"

"Yes, why?"

"I keep smelling spearmint in Zorion's presence. On Earth, it's an herb we use to flavor candy and gum. I was just wondering how it got here."

"Is spearmint a pleasant smelling and tasting herb?"

"For me, it is. It's my favorite flavor."

"Interesting, and you only smell it around Zorion?"

"Yeah."

"The herb does not grow here, but what you are experiencing sounds familiar."

"What do you mean?"

"I have told you how we select our companions. It sounds like you are becoming Akilian."

"Are you saying I smell spearmint because I like him?"

"I think your feelings for him are deeper than that."

"It is true that I do care for him."

"Since we are on the subject, you must understand what he is risking by meeting with you."

"Risking?"

"Yes. As Argi's Sovereign, our society holds him to a high standard. If the Information League finds out about your *dates*, the elites will remove him from his position for breaking our social laws."

"I had no idea. Why would he risk so much to rendezvous with me?"

"It should be obvious."

"His feelings for me are no reason to risk his position."

"I have been told that he has explained his dreams of you."

"Wow! Akilians gossip just as much as we do."

"It is my job to know the things important to my employer. Based on what I have heard, he does not just like you; he is very much in love with you."

"Impossible, we just met!"

"He has had those dreams for nearly one of your Earthian years, so from his perspective, he has known of you for that long."

"What do you expect me to do, marry him?"

"Yes. If you care for him."

"I will repeat it; we just met!"

"I have read that some people from your world marry within a short time. You call it love at first sight."

"Those marriages don't last."

"You are different, Julie. You are an Akilian woman now, which means you know you and Zorion are compatible. That is why you smell spearmint in his company."

"How can you be so sure?"

"You must trust your new instincts. The longer you wait to unite your houses, the more likely an Information Gatherer will see you and Zorion together. If that happens…."

"He'll be removed."

"Exactly."

"At least there's no pressure," Julie quipped.

"I do not mean to upset you. I only wish to make you aware of what society expects of you. If you do not wish to join houses, you must clarify so Zorion does not continue to put himself at risk. He is too important to the city."

"Thanks for telling me. I had no idea. I'll need to think about this before I make my decision. I imagined getting married one day; I didn't dream it would happen this fast," Julie explained and started to leave.

"Before you go, would you like me to open this package?"

Julie glanced at it and guessed it was the suit Urki ordered for her, "No. I will open it in private."

She took it from her, retreated to her bedroom, opened the box, and removed the thin, white bodysuit. Based on Urki's description, it should cover her from top to bottom. The headpiece was separate from the rest of the garment, and there was a belt to carry her sword. She bathed, put on the uniform, slid on the headpiece, and looked in the mirror; all she could see was a bright, reflective light. *It may hide my identity, but it will make me a target. I need to speak to Urki about this.*

She spoke a few words wearing the mask to test the translator. She did not know a word of the Akilian language, yet it interpreted the English words. It also distorted them so that the Akilian words spoken did not sound female. She removed the headpiece and the light faded. Quietly, she peeked out of her bedroom and saw Tionah watching television, so she sneaked out the side door and ran to the cave.

"Urki! Urki!"

"Yes, Julie. I am here."

"This uniform you ordered is too bright. It'll attract too much attention."

"It is the best I can do for you. It will hide your identity and prevent anyone from being able to copy your image."

"Excuse me?"

"Unlike the people of your world, Akilians have a unique ability. They can change their appearance to that of anyone they meet."

"Are you saying they're shapeshifters?"

"Yes. I guess you could describe them that way."

"How can they do that?"

"They have done little research on it because most of our focus has been on trying to find a new planet. Nevertheless, our scientists know that an Akilian body has something like sonar. Depending upon the individual, most only have a range of five to ten paces. The brain sends several consecutive sonar waves to a bone in the nose that receives the signal and transmits an exact, three-dimensional image of the targeted humanoid back to the brain, which signals the body to release a chemical that allows them to change shape. Once he or she achieves the desired appearance, the brain signals the body to release another chemical to neutralize the first, and the form becomes semi-permanent."

"Are you saying that Tionah could make herself look like me?"

"She is taller and broader than you, so she could only change into a larger version of you."

"That's creepy."

"It was something their bodies developed over time after our sun changed into a red giant."

"Just to be sure, are you saying that while I'm wearing this uniform, no one can scan me?"

"Correct."

"I plan on wearing it all the time."

"I suggest you wear the uniform underneath your outer garment. If you have time before a fight, look for a secluded area, remove your outer garment, and put the headpiece on. It will activate the uniform's reflective properties, so no one will know who you are."

"This planet is getting stranger by the minute."

"Believe me. Yours is just as strange to us. Now, we must continue with your training."

"I have to see Zorion first. I need to apologize for my actions last night."

"Your apology can wait; we must return to your training."

"Sorry, I *must* leave. Tionah is in my living room, waiting for me to get ready. She's probably already looking for me."

"This does not help our situation."

"The moment I return from speaking with Zorion, I'll come back and practice. I promise."

"Before you go, there is one more thing you need to know."

She sighed loudly, "What is it now?"

"If you are in a fight, the only way you can kill an Akilian is to remove his or her head. It would apply to the Skeans as well."

"Oh, come on. You're joking with me now!"

"I do not joke."

"What happens if I stab someone in the heart?"

"The injury will only disable him or her because the heart will mend, and the body will rejuvenate in time."

For a long silent moment, she stared at him in disbelief. He did not flinch or comment further, so she rolled her eyes in frustration and stomped off.

"Fine; I'll cut their freakin' heads off!"

Chapter 69

Earth
The Regime - Washington, D.C. - Mercy Hospital
May 16, 2452

Waking from a drug-induced sleep, General Saunders opened his eyes to find Michael and Lisa staring at him.

"What happened?"

"You've been out for a couple of hours," Lisa said.

"Asleep?"

"Yes. I'm sorry to be the one to tell you this, General. Someone implanted a command into your subconscious. As a result, you've been sending classified information to an unknown source," Michael explained.

"What? That's a lie! I would never betray the Regime!" he exclaimed, sitting.

He immediately regretted it and collapsed back onto the pillow.

"You haven't betrayed us, Sir. Someone got to you. If you don't believe me, look at the monitor," Michael pointed to the screen. "Do you see the red area?"

"Yeah."

"That's where they put it. I just spent the past two hours removing it. After that, I sent my findings to Supreme Commander Porter and cleared you for command."

"Are you sure you got it all?"

"Yes, Sir. Every bit of it. I completed a thorough search and repair."

"Did you have to download any of my memories?"

"No. It wasn't necessary. A quick scan showed that they erased the hours before they made contact. You don't have that memory anymore, which means you don't know who did this to you."

"How long have I been spying?"

"I think at least a few months."

"Months!"

"It must have started when you went to Great Britain for a meeting. Do you remember going?"

"Yes, I remember!" General Saunders snapped. "Whoever did this to me, I want the son of a bitch's head on a platter!" he yelled, struggling to get off the gurney.

"Please, General. Give yourself some time for the drugs to wear off," Michael warned.

"Damn the drugs!" he shouted, ripping the tubes out his arm.

"General, wait, let me help you!"

Lisa rushed to remove the I.V. needle from his hand, put a bandage on his arm, and helped him stand. At first, he swayed a little until getting his bearings.

"Here's a list of the men I've cleared; until we catch whoever did this to you, we'll never know who or how many are still compromised."

"I'm going to make it my number one job to find him; he'll wish to have never been born!"

*****

Michael cleared the rest of the suspects on the list, returned to his lab, and mass-produced the Martian bacteria. Having received a large order from Supreme Commander Porter (enough to inject thousands of people), he needed to get a head start. Michael inserted the bacteria into the Petri Dishes and put them into the incubator, wondering whom Supreme Commander Porter planned to use all the serum on. Usually, Supreme Commander Porter told him how he would use his discoveries, except this time. Michael shut the door on the last one and headed toward his office. Lisa stopped him, calling him over to her workstation.

"What did you find?" he asked.

"I've been trying to identify the unknown element we found in the moss. I completed a full battery of tests but found nothing, so since our theory has been that the suspect was eating it, I decided to mince the moss and insert it into the daily food of one of our mice."

"Your results?"

"In only a few short days, the mouse showed noticeable increases in energy levels, and the blood work showed that he was healthier than before the experiment. Also, it had better muscle tone, increased strength, and stamina."

"Had?"

"Yes. It died this morning in the best health of its life."

"That's strange. If the suspect was eating it, how is he still alive?"

"Maybe it reacts differently to humans than mice. We could ask for a volunteer from the Penal Colony on the Moon."

"I agree. We never get conclusive findings using animals, so send the request saying it's an alternate food source. Don't mention moss. I don't want to raise any eyebrows. We'll grind some up and mix it with the food, so the volunteer won't know what he's eating."

"Ok, I'll start on it right away; before I go, there's some more bad news."

"What's that?"

"Do you remember I told you that the black moss somehow sprang up overnight?"

"Yeah."

"I tested it on another mouse; it died right away."

"How could that be? It grew from within the others."

"The unknown element within the black moss is poisonous. As to how it sprang up, I can only guess that there were some spores mixed in with the other species, and they grew in the moist atmosphere of the terrarium."

"All right, move forward with the volunteer testing, and don't use the black moss in their food. I'll visit it later. Since it's poisonous, I'll keep it separate from the others because I don't want it tainting them. I hope we can figure out another application for it later. If the other moss proves to be an alternative food source, we may have discovered the key to good health."

Michael gave Lisa instructions and walked to the back room, where they hid the specimens. Even in the low light, he could tell it was growing at an alarming rate, faster than any other plant growth; learning that the black moss rose about three times faster than the others was upsetting. They completed a thorough search, yet neither he nor Lisa could match the moss to any species on Earth.

The results only brought more questions. *Since the moss can proliferate, it should be easy to find on Earth, so why has no one seen it?* The only answer that made sense was that the moss was not from this world. This conclusion also meant that the man they captured, who died jumping through the unstable portal, was also an alien. Voices in the adjoining room brought him out of his thoughts. Before leaving, he sprayed the moss with a water mist, closed the lid to the terrarium, and returned to find Alex and Lisa talking.

"What's going on?" Michael inquired.

"General Saunders called an emergency meeting at Fort McNair," Alex replied.

"He did?"

"Didn't you get the email?"

Shaking his head, he looked to Lisa for confirmation; she shrugged her shoulders.

"We didn't have time to check them yet," she walked to her computer, reviewed her inbox, and nodded, "Yep, there it is."

Michael confirmed his invitation, and they briskly walked to the elevators. They stopped at the assembly hall, where they had to wait in line for about fifteen minutes at the checkpoint because each person had to surrender their identification for the sentries to scan.

"General Saunders is getting paranoid," Alex mused.

Knowing what happened to him, Michael bit back a retort because it was top secret. He could not leak the information to Alex, even though he trusted him with his life.

"It can only mean that whatever he has to say must be highly classified," Michael offered instead.

"Since he's holding the meeting in the auditorium, he must be summoning the whole base," Lisa added.

Thousands of people entered simultaneously, making the noise level almost unbearable. They found a seat, and a minute later, the meeting started as the lights dimmed and the stage lit up. There was an immediate hush as General Saunders appeared from the right side of the stage. Michael watched him closely; the General did not seem to be showing any signs of stress from the ordeal. Since his job offered daily tension, he could hide it.

"I'll start by reminding everyone here that you have all signed a confidentiality agreement with the Regime. Make no mistake; the Regime considers the information revealed in this meeting top secret. Speaking about what you hear today with anyone outside this room will bring swift punishment. The Regime will prosecute those individuals to the full extent of the law."

"That means you will receive a life sentence in the penal colony on the moon," Alex whispered to Michael.

"Two days ago, the Regime received a distress call. What makes this situation unique is where it came from," he paused before continuing. "The request was sent by a stranded civilization on a frozen planet called Akil, on the other side of the Milky Way."

The attendees began murmuring, so he paused briefly, "I think you can understand the gravity of the situation. If this news were to go public, the United Nations would try to stop or sabotage our effort to rescue them. Even if they agreed to help, politics and red tape would delay it. The aliens said their planet is orbiting a red giant in their message, and a nearby star rapidly depletes its plasma.

"They are running out of time, so we must act quickly. In return for our help and hospitality, they've offered to share all their technology with us. Since they made contact from the opposite side of the galaxy, it is obvious that their portal technology is hundreds of years ahead of ours. Incorporating their knowledge into our space program will allow us to do things we only dreamed possible."

Alex grabbed Michael's arm and smiled, "We're going off-world, buddy!"

"Not me. I have no desire to leave Earth."

"In return, Supreme Commander Porter will allow them to live in the Sahara Desert," again he paused as the murmuring became loud. "Now, I don't want anyone here to panic. I have not seen anyone from this civilization, but I've read that they are humanoid and look very much like us."

Pausing, he looked at his watch and continued, "A portal between our worlds will open within the hour. It will stay that way until the last of the voyagers arrive. We expect two thousand aliens in the first wave, which will begin in an hour. These are our new allies and friends. They will be strangers in a strange world, so I expect everyone to make them feel welcome.

"They will bring earpieces that translate our language to theirs and vice versa. You'll need to wear one at the Sahara base. A few select scientists will work here to update our portal machine. Anyone working with them should keep their earpieces on your person in case you need to communicate.

"They will go through the standard process. We will search them for weapons, give them Regime identifications, add their name and I.D. to our database, and test them for diseases. If they pass, we will offer them food and shelter, so we have a lot of work to do."

Again, he paused because the murmuring became loud, so he motioned for everyone to quiet down, "I know you have a million questions, but we don't have time for Q&A right now. Everyone here has a job to do. You'll find your orders at your workstations, so I suggest you return to your offices, read your assignments, and start working. You're dismissed."

In unison, everyone stood and headed for the exits. At their lab, Michael and Lisa brought up their assignments on their computers.

"Looks like you will assist me, Lisa. General Saunders has already selected a team to evaluate their blood for diseases. He wants us to oversee it until we're satisfied that everything is running smoothly. Then, we're to return here," Michael remarked.

"I recognize most of the names on the team, so it shouldn't take us long to get everything set up," Lisa noted.

"Good, I have things here I need to finish."

"I don't like that we don't know anything about these aliens, yet Supreme Commander Porter invited them to live on our planet. What if they invade?" Lisa speculated.

"I'm sure he's considered all the possibilities. I can't believe he would knowingly put us in danger."

"It's what you don't know that ends up killing you."

"I hope you're wrong. Anyway, let's get going before we wait in another long line to get to the Sahara base."

On their way, they ran into Alex, who was going in the same direction.

"What do they have you doing?" Michael questioned as they headed for the elevators.

"They want me to monitor the event horizon from our end and gather information. After your team clears the scientists, the General assigned them to collaborate with me. We are supposed to convert the Mars Outreach Facility into our own S.P.M.," Alex explained.

"S.P.M?"

"Yeah, Super Portal Machine. Do you like it? I thought of it on my way over."

"I like Interstellar Transportation Station better," Michael stated.

"I do, too," Lisa chimed in.

"Whatever. Anyway, how many are on your team?"

"We have twenty-five technicians. Michael and I will oversee the setup and return once things are up and running," Lisa offered.

"Supreme Commander Porter is spending plenty of Regime Talons on this program," Michael commented.

"Think of what we're getting in return! Imagine being able to go to a distant planet in an instant. We could colonize some and use others for their natural resources. The possibilities are endless!" Alex exclaimed.

"You're right. We could end up landing on a world where the parasites get inside the human body and eat the insides until they jump out of the chest," Lisa quipped.

"You've been watching too many horror movies. We would take precautions," Alex insisted.

"I hope we find a cure for some of the more serious diseases our society still has to deal with," Michael commented.

"You see, Lisa, Michael has a better outlook than you. I think it is an exciting time to be alive!" Alex delighted.

Chapter 70

Akil
Argi City
The 22,280[th] Terrestrial Rotation of the Second Summer

Tionah paced in Julie's living room and rechecked her timekeeper. It had been more than a thousand heartbeats since Julie left to change, and she was beginning to worry. Concerned for her safety, she walked to her bedroom door and knocked. After waiting for a proper amount of time, Tionah called for her again. There was no answer, so she opened the door, searched the room, and did not see Julie anywhere; she found the side door ajar and started to walk toward it but stopped because a bright white light approached her. In a panic, she ran for the guards. Upon their return, they found Julie sitting in the kitchen.

"Where did you go?" Tionah asked.

"I was sitting near the fountain. Why?"

"Did you see the bright light?"

"Nope, sorry," Julie shook her head to reinforce her lie. "Are you ready to go?"

Confused, Tionah frowned for a moment, put on a rehearsed smile, and escorted Julie to her hover vehicle to speak with Zorion.

*****

Disguised as Reenah, Nayrah passed through the screener as usual with a finger wave. The screener blinked a few times and let her pass. As she approached the courtyard in front of the Argi House, Nayrah saw about a thousand spectators waiting for Zorion to return from the conference. With the news of Gecheana entering Argi, she cloaked her powers to stay hidden, took a position in the shadows, and watched anxiously, waiting for the events to unfold. The crowd pressed close to one another, making it difficult to spot any familiar faces. As her gaze moved across the mass, she saw a debutant standing on the stairs leading to the City Capitol.

Usually, there would be no need for concern, except Nayrah saw her giving signals similar to how Gecheana taught her. *What is*

352

she plotting? It is not like her coming out of the shadows and getting her hands dirty. She saw a prominent business owner respond to her command, and a closer look revealed that he was carrying a sword underneath his suit. *That is no business owner. That is a soldier!*

She realized what was about to happen and scanned the pressing horde, only to find more soldiers disguised as civilians. *She plans to assassinate Zorion!* Although Nayrah had no love for him, Argi was her city. If anyone were going to kill Zorion, it would be her, but only when *she* was ready for him to die. One thing that troubled her was how quickly Gecheana found so many soldiers to fight for her cause until she remembered reading an informant's report saying Otsoa had been recruiting.

It all made sense to her. *Gecheana has control of Otsoa! Once Zorion is out of the way, she will be free to rule Argi through Otsoa!* The fundamental part of Gecheana's original plan was the same; only the players had changed. Now, instead of Nayrah controlling Argi through him, Gecheana planned to do it herself. *Not while I am still breathing!* Gecheana might find her, so she meditated with her eyes closed, using her powers to decide when and where to intervene and stop her.

"There he is!" a civilian yelled.

His voice ripped Nayrah from her concentration. She saw Zorion stepping out of his hover vehicle near the dais. He walked toward the Capitol steps, and the crowd cheered his name as he greeted them with his palm facing forward. It surprised her that he only had twenty of his elite guards protecting him. *Broll must be slipping.* As he moved closer to Gecheana's position, Nayrah walked toward him with her hand on her sword's hilt.

Sensing everything around her, she knew Broll was searching the crowd for any would-be assassins. Even though she used the Night Lord's power to push her way through the crowd, their sheer volume slowed her progress. She saw Zorion reach Gecheana's position in her mind's eye, so it was only a matter of moments now. Someone screamed. Looking through the multitude, she saw Gecheana had stabbed him in the belly, bringing him to his knees.

The violent attack scared everyone, causing them to rush for an exit. Had it not been for the invisible wall protecting Nayrah, they would have trampled or carried her away. Most of the crowd left, allowing Nayrah to see Gecheana holding her Skean sword high, ready to strike. Before she could bring it down through Zorion's neck, Nayrah thought to reach out with the Night Lord's power but sensed an alien presence nearby that stopped her. Gecheana felt it because the distraction caused her to lose focus. As a result, the energy flow ceased, and her sword dimmed, weakening it. As she brought it down to kill him, Broll's blade stopped it.

Having failed at her first attempt, Gecheana signaled her soldiers to attack. Within moments, the remaining spectators removed their outer garments, exposing swords fastened to their belts, and attacked Zorion's elite guards. As the battle for Zorion's life raged on, Nayrah watched with delight, if for no other reason than to see Gecheana fail.

Still distracted by the stranger's presence, Gecheana had to divide her concentration between fighting Broll and searching for the intruder. Broll kept Gecheana distracted, allowing two elite guards to drag Zorion off to the side, set him down against the wall, and take a position in front of him with their swords drawn. To even the odds, Broll whistled loudly, calling for more elite guards to join the fight. Returning to the shadows, Nayrah watched and waited for the stranger to make his appearance.

Chapter 71

Earth
The Regime - Africa - Sahara Desert - Fort Levan
May 16, 2452

Michael, Lisa, and Alex stepped through the event horizon and landed at Fort Levan in the Sahara Desert. The trio took the glass tube walkway to the warehouse, where the Regime set up an Interstellar Transportation Station. Outside the tunnel, they saw green grass and trees surrounding the base of several tall buildings. In the distance, a large portal fed the human-made Sahara Lake, and at the east end, a herd of camels gathered to drink; just as they were about to enter the warehouse, Michael noticed something on the horizon.

"Look! A sandstorm is approaching!"

Standing in the shadow of the building, they watched as an intimidating, dark cloud rushed toward their location and hit the small town's shield. The wind and sand climbed over the invisible dome, blocking the sun.

"I have seen enough," Lisa commented nervously. "Let's go."

Inside, they stopped at an Information Station. Michael was first to type in his name to get directions. Based on the diagram, the building had four floors and was the size of a large warehouse. The Information Station's directions showed that they were standing on the second floor at its west end, so they had to go eastward to reach their destination.

Along the way, Michael sent instructions to his team to prepare the rooms for their visitors. They gazed through a thick, bulletproof glass barrier at the end of the corridor where sentries stood in a semicircle formation and faced the wall at which he expected the portal to open. They also saw a thick, yellow line on the floor for the aliens to follow. For a few minutes, they all watched, knowing they were taking part in a historical event. No one outside their level of clearance would ever hear about this day.

Michael spoke up, breaking the silence, "Lisa, you and I will be working in room twenty-three on the second floor. Alex, where will you be working?"

"After putting on my hazmat suit, I need to set up my instruments near the event horizon to take some readings, and once security clears the scientists, they'll let me know. After that, I'll escort them home to begin work on our *Interstellar Transportation Station*," he made a mocking sound for the last three words.

"Be careful, Alex; you don't know what kind of radiation that vortex might produce," Lisa warned.

"I'll be fine. I won't get close until my gauges tell me it's safe."

They heard an alarm echoing throughout the complex. Simultaneously, a yellow siren, fastened to the wall in the landing bay, flashed. Moments later, a vortex opened against the north wall.

"Wow! There wasn't even the smallest vibration," Alex noted with amazement.

They watched with great fascination as two women stepped through the event horizon. Once they were inside, others accompanied them. A recorded announcement played, telling them to follow the yellow line. One of the women put a translator in her ear.

"Even though General Saunders said they would look like us, they're still not what I expected," Michael remarked.

"I thought they would have tentacles or large green skulls; man, was I wrong! Those girls are hot!" Alex enthusiastically noted.

"Those poor women traveled from the other side of the Milky Way to be safe, and all you can think about is how you're going to bed them," Lisa responded, aggravated.

"Hey, don't hate the player; hate the game," Alex bantered with a wry grin.

"It's not a game, Alex. One day you will realize it, but it'll be too late," Lisa snapped.

"What's wrong, Lisa? Why are you so angry at Alex?" Michael asked.

"I don't like the way he treats women."

"I think we should get going. I'll see you at Fort McNair, Alex," Michael interrupted, attempting to prevent an argument between them.

Michael and Lisa went to their room, where several other scientists on his team waited for him. They were all anxious to see alien blood under a microscope. Everyone put on their protective gear and inserted the translators that the aliens delivered to them, and Lisa let in their first guest. Michael recognized her as one of the twins first through the portal.

Michael tried unsuccessfully not to stare. Alex was right; she was beautiful. Lisa took her temporary identification card and entered her information into the main computer. Her picture and personal information appeared on his monitor, so Michael typed his data as the technician on duty and approached her.

"Welcome, Yanamai. My name is Michael, and this is Lisa."

He extended a gloved hand to greet her. Staring at the alien's extended hand, Yanamai hesitated to return the Earthian's greeting; she did a few uncomfortable moments later.

"I don't see your last name," Michael noted.

"We do not have last names in our world," she replied dryly.

Sensing she was not in a pleasant mood, he smiled politely, "It doesn't matter. Your identification card will have your picture and number on it. Just make sure you don't lose it."

"I'm not a child; I know how important the card is," she retorted, with a hint of annoyance in her voice.

"All right," Lisa interrupted. "I'm going to take a small sample of your blood. You're going to feel a little prick on your finger."

"Ouch!" Yanamai exclaimed, rubbing her finger.

"Sorry, there's just no painless way to get a blood sample," Lisa remarked, putting the blood onto a test strip, and giving it to one of the accompanying scientists to examine before placing another sample into their diagnostic machine.

"Wow! Everything looks normal. Your blood shows no signs of disease, and your DNA closely matches ours, with only a few minor differences! It's going to change everything we believe about evolution!" Michael explained.

"Am I free to go?" I have work to do," Yanamai queried, completely uninterested.

"Uh, sure. You're cleared to…" before he could finish, Yanamai stood, snatched her badge out of his hand, and left without saying another word.

"What a bitch," scowled Lisa.

"I'm sure she's just having a bad day," Michael reasoned.

"You always try to see the good in people, except you tend to project what you wish he or she would be like instead of how they are."

"This is different. She's just left her home planet and landed in a strange world, so I can understand why she would be irritated."

"I think she ought to show a little more gratitude because we're saving her life."

"Perhaps she'll come around."

"She better, or I'll send her back home myself!" Lisa yelled, hoping Yanamai would hear her.

Chapter 72

Earth
The Regime - Washington, D.C. - Fort McNair
May 16, 2452

Michael had screened thirty aliens and sent his findings to a few anthropologists who would appreciate the data collected. Since his team had things under control, he and Lisa returned home to Fort McNair. They were tired and hungry, so they stopped by the cafeteria for a bite to eat. Coincidentally, they met Alex at the back of the line.

"How was your day?" Alex asked.

"Other than changing the way we think humans evolved, the day was uneventful," Michael quipped.

"Are they human, inside and out?"

"Every scan and diagnostic show they're as human as we are with a few minor differences in the DNA."

"What does that mean?"

"I'm uncertain. We still need to figure out what those dissimilarities are. What about you? What have you learned about long-distance portals?"

"Quite a bit. I'm currently collaborating with a team of one hundred new arrivals to upgrade our machine."

"How long will that take?"

"Not long. They brought most of the equipment with them. Our biggest task will be creating enough energy to run it."

"How do they do it?"

"Solar panels, or as they call them, energy consoles."

"Really? I didn't think that would generate enough power, especially if their sun changed into a red giant."

"They've figured out a way to increase the panels' power output. Yanamai thinks that our sun will allow them to recharge the capacitors in one fourth the time, which means we can have a permanent doorway open in a few days."

"Are you working with Yanamai?"

"Yeah, she's the head of the portal team, and I asked her to meet me here for dinner."

"You do work fast. I'll give you that," Michael shook his head.

"Where is she? I need to warn her about you," Lisa scanned the crowd in the cafeteria, hoping to find her.

"You must be excited about operating a permanent event horizon," Michael interrupted, changing the subject to distract Lisa.

"Yeah, I am. I reviewed some of the Akilian schematics and realized it would have taken us hundreds or even thousands of years before we figured it out. Their understanding is far advanced. I feel like a child compared to their scientists," Alex answered.

"I understand how you must feel," Michael offered.

"Our last meeting had heated discussions about running power lines through the vortex between our two worlds," Alex noted.

"Isn't that dangerous?" Michael frowned.

"They don't seem as concerned as I am," Alex explained.

They talked and loaded their plates with food. Michael found a bowl of hot soup, set it on his tray, headed straight for the cashier, handed her his money card, and saw Alex waving to someone in his peripheral vision. The cashier handed him back his card, so Michael spun around to leave, crashing into Yanamai, spilling his hot soup all over her shirt and jacket.

He could not understand what she was saying with his translator in his pocket. By her tone, it was not pleasantries. To be helpful, he grabbed a handful of napkins and dabbed her clothes until she snatched his wrist, stopping him. The look on her face told him everything he needed to know. *Back off!*

"Yanamai, I am deeply sorry; please, forgive me," Michael hoped she had turned on her translator.

She blotted her soaked clothes and continued to speak in her native tongue. Michael's hand moved to his pocket to retrieve his translator, but she stomped off before putting it in his ear.

"Boy, you know how to make a good first impression," Alex joked.

Michael sighed, "Yeah. Now you know why I didn't sign up to be an ambassador. The Regime wouldn't have any allies."

"Here," Lisa handed Michael her tray. "Get us a table, and I'll go back and get you something to eat."

"You don't have to," he replied; she left before he could stop her.

"Come on, Alex. I need you by my side to ensure I don't drench someone else on my way to a table."

A few minutes later, Lisa joined them. She sat across from Michael, still fidgeting with his shirt, trying to sop up remnants of the spilled soup on his clothes.

"May I sit here?"

The voice was familiar to everyone at the table. They turned to look at the new arrival. Her presence surprised them.

"Yanamai?" wondered Alex.

"Are you sure you want to sit here?" Michael added.

"Yanamai is my sister. I am Garbi."

"Oh, I remember Yanamai mentioning you. Sure, have a seat," Alex smiled flirtatiously.

Garbi sat beside Lisa, across from Alex.

"I remember seeing you two at the landing site. You look like identical twins," Michael noted.

"We are not twins. I am her *younger* sister."

"I'm amazed at how much you look alike," Lisa observed.

"It's not that unusual. Siblings share much of the same DNA. If their parents are the same, each child will have half of its DNA from each parent, which means siblings will share at least half of their DNA," Michael explained as if quoting one of his elementary school theses.

Alex faked a yawn, "Thanks for that boring explanation, Mike."

"I did not think it was boring. I am interested in biology," Garbi smiled cutely at Michael.

"You'll be happy to know I've studied the female anatomy very closely," Alex added. "Ouch! Why does everyone keep kicking me?"

Like Julie did at the mall, Lisa glared at him, yet her warning did not stop him. Instead, Alex recited his family's genealogy, making sure Garbi knew that he was a descendant of James Shaw, the man who opened the first portal on Earth. As Alex continued his verbal montage, Michael watched in amazement how easy it was for him to talk to women. During the entire meal, he kept Garbi's focus solely on him; Lisa could not take it anymore and asked Garbi to tell them about her home.

The rituals and lifestyle of her society fascinated Michael, mainly how they chose partners. To him, it seemed like it relieved the men from most of the burden, and as always, Alex could not keep himself out of the conversation for long. Within a few minutes, he turned the discussion into a debate about which was better, sight or smell, flirting or being direct. Michael watched and listened as Garbi, Alex and Lisa argued over the pros and cons, keeping himself out of the exchange due to his limited experience on the subject.

An hour later, Michael decided it was time to leave, "I'm going back to the lab. Lisa, I'll see you tomorrow. Alex, you too. Garbi, it was a pleasure to meet you," Michael extended his hand.

Garbi did not return his farewell.

"Would you mind walking me home? I have some questions I would like to ask you."

Everyone at the table looked surprised, including Michael.

"Uh, are you sure you don't want Alex to walk you home?"

"No. I asked *you*."

"Yeah, Michael, she wants *you* to walk her home," Lisa added, giving Alex a triumphant smile.

Michael did not share in Lisa's enthusiasm because if experience had taught him anything, it was that women preferred most anyone other than him, so against his better judgment, he inquired, "What's your apartment number?"

"183."

"It's in the east wing. Follow me."

It was quiet for most of the walk to her apartment; she broke the silence in the last hallway, "I suppose you are wondering why I chose *you* to walk me home."

"I can guess, but go ahead and tell me."

"I considered how Earthians pursued one another and found it tedious and unnecessary. However, Alex made it seem exciting."

"Before you go any further, I can tell you that Alex is not interested in a committed relationship."

"Why should that matter to me?"

"I have no idea."

"What I want is your help."

He sighed, "What do you want me to do?"

"I want you to teach me how to flirt."

"That's something you should ask Lisa. It's not a question a woman would ask a guy."

"I disagree. A guy (as you say) can tell me what is most effective."

"Fine, let me think. Usually, if a woman wants Alex's attention, her first step is to lock eyes with him and give him a coy smile."

"I see, so the first step is to capture the other's attention and hold it."

"Exactly. If Alex is interested, he'll stare back and wait for a signal. There are too many to mention; I've seen some women twirl their hair and others lick their lips or caress a body part with their finger. Alex would perceive that as an invitation to approach."

"Interesting. Is all this done without speaking?"

"It's called body language. Once Alex meets whoever is flirting with him, he'll talk to her. Don't ask me what he says because I'm usually on the other side of the room, drinking a beer alone, so I can never hear him. They will gaze into each other's eyes, kiss, and leave together, leaving me stuck with the bar tab again."

"Where do they go?"

"Somewhere private so they can be alone, usually his apartment."

At first, she looked at him quizzically, not understanding until her eyes widened, "Oh, they go somewhere to copulate."

"That's one way of putting it."

"I think this is my apartment."

"Yep, 183. I hope my advice was of some help to you. I'm sure you and Alex will have a wonderful time together. See you next time."

As he turned to leave, she gently grabbed his arm, "Please, wait; I have not had a chance to practice."

"I don't want to be part of your experiment."

"Oh, stop your whining and look at me."

Reluctantly, he did; her lips curved into a soft smile and her come-hither-eyes made him feel very uneasy.

"Yeah, you got it. Now it's time for me to go," he said.

Again, he turned to leave; before he could take a step, Garbi removed a pin, releasing a swirl of thick, yellow hair that fell down her shoulder to about her mid-thigh and shook her head to toss it around. *Great, now I need a cold shower. Thanks for teasing me, Garbi.* He wanted to leave, yet something kept him from going. Probably because he could not take his eyes off her, she was a natural flirt. As if he had not suffered enough, she began twirling a strand of her hair while slowly and seductively approaching him. Inches away from his face, she licked her lips and stopped before they touched him. The smell of honeysuckle was on her breath.

"Do you know what I would like?" she whispered.

He gulped, "I have no idea."

"I would like for us to go on a date."

"All right, that's enough practice. I can't be your Guinea Pig anymore."

This time, he intended to leave, no matter what she did, because he could not stand knowing that she meant her flirtations for Alex and not him. She gently took his hands as he turned to leave and lightly rubbed the tops with her thumbs.

"You are trembling," she whispered.

"Am I?"

"Do you want to go on a date with me or not?"

"Enough, Garbi! I can't take your teasing anymore!"

Without another word, she leaned in to kiss him. Reflexively, Michael backed up until her front door stopped him from going farther. With nowhere to go, they finally met, and she pressed her lips firmly against his. During the kiss, two lines of thought crossed his mind, the first was that she was interested in him, but his logical side overruled his foolish hope, convincing him of the second line of thought; this was practice for Alex.

Although she hurt his feelings by teasing him, he decided to enjoy the moment. Even if she was doing this for Alex, at least he had a chance to kiss one of the most beautiful women in the galaxy. It was an opportunity he did not believe would happen again. The door he was leaning on opened, and they stumbled into Garbi's apartment until Michael ran backward into her sofa. With Garbi still in his arms, the two bumped their foreheads and landed on the cushions.

"Ouch!" they said in unison.

For a moment, they looked at each other until realizing someone had opened the door, and they burst into laughter, rubbing their foreheads.

"What are you doing?" Yanamai demanded.

"What does it look like we're doing?" Garbi sarcastically answered.

Yanamai recognized Michael from their earlier confrontation in the cafeteria.

"What are you doing with this clumsy alien?"

Ignoring her sister, Garbi took Michael's hand and led him back into the hall for some privacy.

Again, she kissed him; he pulled away, "Look, I can't take this anymore. I need to know if you're doing this because you like me, or are you practicing for Alex?"

"What makes you think I am doing this for Alex?"

"During lunch, you only spoke with him, and you seemed to be having a fun time, so I thought you were interested in him."

"I picked *you* to walk me home."

"In my experience, it doesn't necessarily mean anything. Besides, you asked me for advice on flirting, so it seemed logical that you wanted to know for Alex."

"No, Michael. I used the excuse as a ruse to flirt with you."

"Are you sure?"

"Yes," she nodded.

"Garbi, please send him away. I could use your help with these calculations," Yanamai yelled from the apartment.

"Can you manage them alone?"

"No! Now please get in here!"

"Give me a moment," she snapped and faced Michael, "I am sorry, I must go. How about we meet for breakfast tomorrow morning?"

"Sure, I'd like that. It is the most important meal of the day." *Why did you say that?*

"Meet me here tomorrow at 7 AM."

"All right, I'll see you then."

She gave him another kiss and stepped inside her apartment, leaving Michael alone with his thoughts. *Did that really happen?* He entered his lab, sat, and replayed the events in his mind, imagining what his life would be like with Garbi.

Chapter 73

Akil
Argi City
The 22,280[th] Terrestrial Rotation of the Second Summer

As Julie's hover vehicle approached the city's Capitol, she saw hundreds of people running away from the stage where Zorion planned to make his speech. At the same time, she felt a sense of urgency and faced Tionah, "Call for help, now!" Even before the vehicle stopped, Julie jumped out and hit the avenue running. Remembering Urki's suggestion, she looked for a place to change.

Through the dispersing crowd, she saw a public restroom nearby. Hoping it was empty, she ran into it, checked to ensure no one was there, removed her outer layer of clothing, slid the headpiece on, and attached her sword to the belt; it took her less than fifteen seconds to get ready. She exited the bathroom and discovered that the crowd had left. She sprinted to the courtyard and saw Broll defending Zorion from two soldiers on the dais. To her dismay, Zorion rested on the floor, severely injured and unable to move.

She ran, unsheathed her sword, and mentally pushed air into the handle, extending the blade like an antenna. As she moved toward Zorion's position, energy flowed through her body into the power transfer gem within the sword's hilt, igniting the blade. Soldiers on both sides stopped fighting. Gecheana, brawling in their midst, also paused to gaze at the newcomer. Since the bodysuit reflected all the light in the room, making her appear as a brilliant white illumination, they had no idea who or what they saw.

Julie reached the dais, drawing all eyes to her. The soldiers attacking Broll stepped back a few paces, not knowing what to expect; even Broll stood ready to defend himself against the unknown intruder. Moving toward the two attackers, Julie cut through their swords, and with a fast-spinning motion, she removed their heads. Seeing how easy the unknown entity brought down their colleagues, Gecheana's soldiers fled.

Julie looked at Broll through her mask and hoped he considered her an ally, even though he could not see her. Knowing that the new combatant just helped kill two traitors, Broll cautiously nodded his acceptance while holding his hand up to block out the harsh reflection of her suit. Broll kept an eye on his new ally and ordered the rest of his elite guards to chase the fleeing soldiers, who left Gecheana alone.

Still posing as a beautiful debutante, Gecheana studied the new arrival. Since only a few Akilians remained, the only sound was Julie's sword humming with the High Lord's power running through it. Gecheana knew it was the Saiph. Using the Night Lord's power, Gecheana darkened her eyes to look past the blinding light to discover the Saiph's identity using her mind, but something prevented her from detecting the form behind the illumination.

Even though facing the Saiph was her worst nightmare come true, she was not going to let her fears prevent her from moving forward with her plan to kill Zorion. If the Saiph intended to protect him, she would confront the Saiph head-on. Gecheana cautiously stepped over the fallen and approached the dais, using the right-side steps. On the stage, her crimson and white blade extended from the hilt in her hand. Broll raised his weapon, ready to fight; Julie moved in front of him and motioned with her hand for him to stay behind. Reluctantly, Broll obeyed, for now. Julie held her sword up and was ready to defend, waiting for the Skean to get closer.

Gecheana stopped several paces away, "We were winning until you arrived. In a few hundred more heartbeats, I would have killed enough elite guards for my soldiers to overtake them."

Not knowing how to respond, Julie shrugged her shoulders. Her response angered Gecheana. Feeling the attack before it happened, Julie moved her sword in the exact spot to block the Skean's blade as it came rushing at her. Before she knew her next move, Julie felt her arms, legs, and body moving to attack. The two blades arched in semicircles, humming as they cut through the air. Every time their swords touched, positive and negative energy rushing between them echoed throughout the courtyard.

During practice with Urki, Julie felt something take hold of her and move her in unexpected directions. Fighting a Skean heightened that sensation. For the first time in her life and since her training, Julie felt the High Lord's power take complete control of her body. She moved unimaginably as invisible hands guided her through the fight faster than even her eyes could see. At one point, Julie swung horizontally, and the Skean jumped high in the air, landing behind her.

Feeling the attack before it came, Julie put her sword over her shoulder, protecting her back, and spun around to face her opponent. Having placed herself between the Saiph and Broll, Gecheana was one step closer to carrying out her goal. Seeing that the Skean got by his new ally, Broll moved forward to join the fight. He brought his sword down, thinking it would meet flesh and blood until the Skean moved her sword through it as if it had no substance, severing his blade in the middle. Having gotten the Skean's attention, Broll stepped back, trying to avoid the unusual sword she wielded.

*****

From the shadows, Nayrah watched with amusement as Gecheana approached the dais. At least for her, it was easy to see that Gecheana was frightened. Slow and cautious was never Gecheana's fighting style; that changed with the Saiph. Nayrah listened to Gecheana's taunts as they faced each other, except the Saiph did not respond. Details like that did not escape Nayrah's attention. She was unsure why the Saiph did not speak but had an idea. *I hope the Saiph removes your head, Gecheana.* Nayrah watched the competitors closely as their swords met.

Gecheana's moves almost made her laugh, yet the Saiph did not fight much better. It seemed as if the Saiph allowed its power source to make all the moves, which was a novice mistake. Still, Nayrah felt privileged to watch a battle between light and dark. It was something that had not happened during her lifetime. Even better was that Gecheana was the one who had to fight instead of her.

Gecheana put on a disappointing display. Never had Nayrah seen such sloppy footwork with awkward defensive blocks and offensive strikes. As a Skean, it was embarrassing to watch. Her technique was messy; she was off balance and often unnecessarily backed up. Now that Nayrah knew Gecheana's weakness, it allowed her an opportunity to kill her. Assuming the Saiph did not do it first.

Gecheana jumped over the Saiph, getting herself closer to Zorion. Nayrah admired Broll's skill as a fighter, but he was not fast enough or strong enough to defeat Gecheana because by wielding a

Skean sword, she could cut him down in one or two heartbeats. Gecheana sent an invisible wall of energy toward the Saiph, pushing him or her to the right side of the dais, giving her space to focus on Broll.

As Nayrah watched the drama unfold, she saw Broll fly off the dais. She thought Gecheana did it until realizing the Saiph rescued him before Gecheana could thrust him through. Landing headfirst onto the stone seat that circled the fountain and walled in the water, Broll fell unconscious. It was another novice move from the Saiph. An experienced fighter would have pushed Broll out of the way without harm.

With no one between them, Gecheana moved toward Zorion for the kill. As she approached, Nayrah reached out with her mind and tripped her. Gecheana tumbled forward and landed at Zorion's feet. *The only thing missing is a moss-woven bow and gift bag.* Nayrah saw the Saiph running to catch up and tried to strike at Gecheana, who lay prostrate. Gecheana moved out of the way and was on her feet again to defend herself. Nayrah spat a curse, refusing to help the Saiph anymore, just on principle.

Once again, their swords arched in the air as they moved about the dais. To Nayrah's disappointment, the Saiph almost beat Gecheana a few times, yet Gecheana found a way to escape and recovered each time. Finally, Gecheana pushed the Saiph off the dais, stunning him or her long enough to reach her goal. Nayrah watched as Gecheana stood over Zorion with her sword raised. The Saiph cried out with a distorted voice, "No!"

*****

With all her might, Julie pulled the Skean toward her; it was too late because she had swung her blade through Zorion's neck. As the Skean soared through the air toward her, Julie stood, ready to attack; they clashed awkwardly, and Gecheana hit the ground, rolling away from Julie. Gecheana stood and walked toward her opponent with a slight limp on her left leg.

Knowing her injury could cost her life, Gecheana smiled, "We will meet again soon."

369

She spun around and limped away, disappearing into the shadows of the avenue.

*****

Nayrah tried to watch the Saiph as he or she ran to Zorion's side, but the glare made it impossible to figure out what it looked like behind the blinding light. Nevertheless, she could sense a deep sadness coming from within. Nayrah heard the approaching emergency vehicles and watched the Saiph run out of the courtyard toward the public restroom. Before the Saiph could reach the door, Nayrah blocked the path.

Startled, Julie ignited her sword and stood ready to fight another Skean, except this Skean raised her arms in surrender, "Relax. I am not here to fight you; instead, I want to welcome you to Akil."

Julie stood silent and on guard.

The Skean continued, "I suggest we work together, at least briefly."

"I do not work alongside Skeans," a distorted voice informed.

"Do you know how many of my kind are here?" Nayrah asked, looking down at her fingernails as if holding a casual conversation with a friend.

"No," Julie replied, her voice still muffled.

"Well, let me educate you. I have four Skean sisters, and although we call each other sisters, we are not biologically related. You just fought our mother, Gecheana. Also, my sisters and I have given birth to one Skean each. Therefore, we outnumber you considerably."

"What you say may or may not be true; since you are a Skean, how can I possibly trust you?" Julie questioned, her voice still distorted through her suit.

"I agree; you should never trust a Skean," Nayrah chuckled. "However, considering your circumstance, you must take a chance because it will allow you to put the odds in your favor. Would you rather fight one Skean or eleven?"

Julie did not reply.

"I know you think it might be a trap, and you are wise to be cautious because I *will* betray you after we have killed the other

Skeans, so I will give you an Akilian oath that I will not attack you before that time."

"I will have to think about it," Julie responded warily.

"I understand that it is not an easy decision to make. Here is my contact information. If you decide to work with me, let me know soon. Now that Gecheana fought you, she knows you are a novice."

"Why do you think I'm a novice?"

Nayrah chuckled a little longer this time, "I have been doing this all my life. I can spot a beginner from far away, and you, my dear," she pointed her finger at the Saiph, "are a student."

"I just might surprise you."

"Perhaps. Remember, the longer you wait, the more time you give Gecheana to gain complete control of Argi. Once you become too much of a nuisance, she will call for my sisters to help get rid of you; then, it will be too late for either of us."

Keeping her sword at the ready, Julie cautiously took the small data stick from the Skean.

"Do not forget, we do not have time to waste," Nayrah warned, spun around, and leisurely walked away.

Julie returned to the restroom to change and discovered that the bag with her clothes had disappeared. She frantically searched for it until hearing the bathroom door squeak as it opened. Still wearing her camouflage outfit, Julie peeked out of one of the stalls and saw Tionah holding it in her hand.

"Looking for this, Julie."

Knowing that Tionah knew her secret, Julie removed the headpiece and saw her smiling.

"I knew it!" she exclaimed. "The moment I saw the bright light earlier, I knew there was a Saiph among us!"

"Who are you going to tell?"

"No one, unless you permit me to tell my priest."

"Why would you tell him?"

"There are many on Akil dedicated to Lehoi, just like those who follow Gau."

"Where have I heard that name before?"

"I will tell you more about her later; for now, it would be nice if you put your outer garments on. Your suit's reflection is very bright and hard to look at."

As Julie dressed, Tionah saw tears, "What is wrong?"

"Zorion is dead. I couldn't save him."

"Oh, dear. We cannot take you back to your home."

"Why not?"

"Because his heir, Otsoa, will rule in his place."

"Is he that bad?"

"I heard that he is troubled. There have been rumors that he recently changed physically and has become aggressive."

"Do you think he had anything to do with Zorion's death?"

"If the rumors are true, the soldiers who attacked Zorion were loyal to him."

"Was he with them?"

"No, I did not see him. If he did play a part, it would be best for you to hide. Since I am your domestic, Edur and I will also go into hiding with you."

"Why? I haven't done anything to him."

"Zorion cared for you. That is all the reason he needs. He will not hesitate to imprison or even kill you."

"The Regime will find out and cut off all relations with Akil."

"Which is why we cannot give him the opportunity. Too many lives are in jeopardy."

"I need to get back to my apartment somehow."

"I can send for your things."

"I do not care about my things. I need to get back to my teacher, Urki."

"Urki died a long time ago."

"It's a computer-generated hologram. He's been teaching me how to fight and about the Skeans."

"How wonderful! Do not worry. I will help you get back after we find a safe place to hide. Your vehicle is just outside. We should go now."

Nodding, Julie followed her to the vehicle. As it took off, she saw Zorion's lifeless body lying on the dais, surrounded by emergency personnel, and as he disappeared from her sight, she burst into tears.

Chapter 74

Earth
Spain - Madrid
May 16, 2452

While waiting for General Saunders' reply to his requisite for supplies and personnel, Vincent reviewed the dossiers of qualified agents his team needed to capture Dragon and discovered that the Regime recently gained a Chinese spy. Vincent reviewed her file and hoped General Saunders could convince her to help. Since there was only a tiny window of time to catch Dragon, he contacted the General directly, whose image appeared on his computer display.

"How can I help you, Vincent?"

"The Supreme Commander has tasked me with finding and capturing the Comptroller's assassin. So far, he's evaded me, but you have someone on the base that should be able to help. Her name is Wu Luli."

"Why do you think she can help?"

"I reviewed her dossier and memory photos from the MR and found this," he paused to send him a copy of the image.

"You are saying this is Dragon?"

"Yes. Wu Luli knows him."

"Captain Yates is still interrogating her."

"I understand you want to get as much information from her as possible, but this mission is time-sensitive, and I don't want to lose him again. He's always one step ahead of me. It's as if he has access to the Regime server or has someone on the inside feeding him information."

Vincent's theory brought a chill down the General's neck. Since Michael told him the disturbing news (that he was the traitor), the only way to know how much sensitive information he gave away was to assign a technician to check his computer. The Regime also hired an investigator to retrace his steps for at least two months. Knowing someone forced him to betray his country made him angry. To make matters worse, he could have been the one who kept Dragon informed of Vincent's movements, putting his life in danger as well. Armed with this latest information, the General contacted the technician to find any transmissions he may have sent to Dragon; if he found out who was behind this, that person would pay dearly.

"I'll get back to you," he abruptly disconnected.

Vincent thought it was odd for the General to disconnect yet did not let it distract him from the mission to prepare Dragon's trap.

Chapter 75

Earth
The Regime - Washington, D.C. - Fort McNair
May 16, 2452

With Lieutenant Colonel Jones by his side, General Saunders marched into the interrogation room; Captain Yates stood at attention.

"Where's Wu Luli?" General Saunders demanded.

"She's in the adjoining room with her parents."

"I'm sorry to break up the family reunion, but I need her help," he said unapologetically.

Captain Yates nodded and retrieved Wu Luli, understanding the General's mood; to the General's surprise, she seemed calm, considering her recent experiences. Agents who could hold themselves together during such a crisis were well-disciplined and good at their job. Knowing this made it easier for him to give her the order.

"There is an urgent matter I can use your help with."

"What is it?"

With his right hand, General Saunders motioned for Lieutenant Colonel Jones to hand her the photo.

"You recognize this man?"

"Yes, but it's been years since I've seen him. He was one of General Ming-tun Fu's agents and disappeared a few years after General Fu forced me into the program. His name is Chen Heng."

"I have an agent in Spain who has been tracking him all over Europe."

"What does the Regime want with him?"

"He killed Comptroller James Bradley using portal technology."

"The disc the Regime retrieved destined for President Martinez had the schematics for a portal machine. Do you think Dragon is working for the U.S.?"

"It's possible. We'll know for sure once we apprehend him. Now, are you going to help us catch him?"

"Certainly, anything you need. Just tell me what to do."

"Come with me."

Chapter 76

While doing his best to stay sad and respectful, Otsoa mournfully climbed the Argi House's steps, where a staff member greeted and escorted him to the dais set up inside Argi's capitol building. Outwardly Akilians saw a grieving heir, but on the inside, he celebrated Zorion's defeat. Now he was free to rule Argi his way, and anyone who defied him would suffer his wrath.

Inside the Argi House, a few Information Gatherers huddled near recording devices as they prepared for the inauguration. Sitting in the front row, waiting for Otsoa to arrive, Broll, Dolas, Dahmar, and several other Argi's Chief Administrators stood as he approached the stage. Before the celebration, the media broadcasted a special report informing everyone that during a rebellion, someone killed Zorion. However, Broll, Dolas, and Dahmar could not find any evidence linking Otsoa to Zorion's murder.

Since more than fifty witnesses testified that he was with them at the time, Dolas had to dig deeper to find proof and do it secretly once Otsoa took Zorion's seat. Many of his sources suspected Otsoa had something to do with Zorion's death. Still, none of the Chief Administrators could stop him from claiming his inherited position without witnesses.

Having no choice, Broll, Dolas, Dahmar, and the others pledged their loyalty to him. If they refused, Otsoa would dismiss them or worse; the cameras were ready and Gau's High Priest, Elazar, began the ceremony by blessing Otsoa in an old Akilian dialect long forgotten by all except Gau's ministers. Elazar finished the blessing, allowing Otsoa to recite the Akilian Oath of Office. Afterward, the Chief Administrators moved, single file, onto the dais. They bowed, took his hand, and kissed it, symbolizing their Akilian oath, promising their loyalty, and recognizing his sovereignty.

Broll bowed before him and took his hand, giving Otsoa a deep sense of satisfaction. Not too long ago, he told Broll he would serve under his authority one Terrestrial Revolution. Otsoa also cautioned

Broll to treat him respectfully; Broll ignored his warning. As the new sovereign, Otsoa would find a way to make him pay for his insolence. All the Chief Administrators pledged their loyalty to him and returned to the front row. Otsoa stepped up to the podium to speak.

"My fellow Akilians, this is a sad Terrestrial Rotation for all of us. Zorion was a beloved parent to me, yet all Argians loved him. Although we will miss him, we cannot dwell on former administrations because our lives are at risk. Even though it will be difficult, we must push forward to the future and forget the past. I assure you that I will not rest until every Akilian lives safely on Earth.

"My first order of business will be to set up a good working relationship with Supreme Commander Porter and ensure him that we will keep our end of the contract. I do not doubt that Zorion is smiling up at us from Gau's dark, divine abode, knowing that we will be successful in our endeavor. I know that change is difficult, and I promise to do my best to make this transition as seamless as possible."

"Were you involved in the plot to kill Zorion?" an Information Gatherer yelled from the audience.

The crowd mumbled, hearing the question.

"I have heard of these rumors, too; even though the circumstances of my inheritance may seem questionable, I have brought proof that I have not broken Gau's law."

He reached down, unsheathed the sword from his belt, and held it horizontally for all to see. Since he did not have a Skean's power, Gecheana extended the blade before giving it to him, forcing air into the hilt and locking it in place. Even she could not ignite the sword because the power transfer gem was unique and only recognized Gau or his descendants. As the camera zoomed in, he rolled the hilt so they could see all its markings and spoke the words Gecheana made him rehearse.

"I could not have broken Gau's law because his spirit ascended from his holy dwelling place and took its abode in me. It guided me to the secret location where it rested for so many Yellow Harvests. Now I humbly ask High Priest Elazar to verify its authenticity."

Elazar stood beside Otsoa and accepted the sword to examine it. Secretly, Elazar had already authenticated it because Gecheana had met with him earlier; the room was silent as he studied the hilt and the blade. Elazar pretended to study it for a few hundred heartbeats until he decided it was long enough.

"This *is* Gau's sword!"

Everyone in the assembly gasped, and the Chief Administrators mumbled to each other about the consequences of Elazar's proclamation.

"Thank you, Elazar," Otsoa replied.

"Ignite the blade, Otsoa!" some yelled from the audience.

"This sword is holy, and I will not ignite it in front of unbelievers," he paused to look at Elazar and continued, "But I will ignite it privately before the High Priest in his temple."

The gathering began to mumble again until Elazar faced the audience, "I swear that I will give you an honest report."

Some still whispered, saying they would not believe him, while devout Gau followers professed that they would accept the High Priest's word.

"Let us go to the temple," Otsoa remarked.

Everyone dispersed to get as close to the temple as possible. Even though the crowd would not see the event, most wanted to say they were there when it happened. By the time Otsoa and Elazar arrived, word had spread, and a large crowd gathered in front of the temple. As Otsoa's guards pushed through the crowd, many spectators tried to look at the sword as the High Priest carried it above his head for all to see.

Before entering, Elazar turned to face the observers. Everyone bowed their heads except for some of the Chief Administrators and a handful of spectators who doubted. Elazar made a mental note of those who did not bow, spun, and closed the door behind him. At Gau's larger-than-life stone image in the holiest of all places within the temple, Elazar handed the sword back to Otsoa.

"Gecheana said I could trust you," Otsoa commented.

"Yes, I have spoken to her, and I know you cannot ignite the sword, so do not fret, Otsoa; I will tell everyone you did."

"Good, with your help, my transition to becoming Argi's Sovereign will go smoothly."

"You have my word, Otsoa. Everyone will believe that Gau visited you."

"What did Gecheana offer in return for your support?" Otsoa asked.

"She did not offer me anything. Gecheana is a Skean, and I am her humble servant; she did say that this announcement would bring more into our congregation."

"Ah, I see. The more Akilians worship Gau, the fuller your coffers become."

"The scrolls teach us that Sovereign Cubes solve all problems," Elazar articulated.

"Indeed, they do, Elazar, and now, we should return to our beloved citizens and give them the good news."

Chapter 77

Earth
Regime - Georgia - Fulton County
May 16, 2452

Wearing her police uniform, Officer Ashley Hale stepped out of the Fulton County Interstate Transportation Station and into a rented hovercar. She started the engine, and the car rose off the ground, so she moved the lever to the right, spun the vehicle around one hundred eighty degrees, and hit the thrusters. The journey from New York City was a long one. It took at least fifteen minutes to get through customs and land in Fulton County, Georgia; Ashley visited Wendy often and had become accustomed to the hassle.

During their last conversation on the video com, Wendy requested her help as soon as possible. On any other occasion, Ashley would have waited until the weekend, but the tremors in her voice reeked of desperation. Knowing Wendy was afraid of something, Ashley took a personal day off from policing the streets of New York and hurried over. Ashley smiled on the way to Wendy's house, thinking of their days together in High School. They grew up in New York City in the same apartment complex and did everything together, even though Wendy was a few years older.

Wendy had left New York City to practice medicine in Georgia. Still, they continued to stay connected and met throughout the year. The last time Ashley saw her was a month ago. She approached Wendy's home, throttled down the engine, and the hovercar coasted to the parking spot in front of the porch, so she shut the car off and knocked on the door.

"I'm so glad you're here. Please, come in."

Wendy's voice was a mixture of panic and relief.

"What happened, Wendy?"

"Follow me."

Ashley's hand moved toward her gun as Wendy led her upstairs because the unknown made her feel uneasy. Ashley stepped into the guest room and recognized the man sleeping on the bed. Instinctively, she removed her handcuffs from her belt and moved toward the suspect to apprehend him; Wendy stopped her.

"That's not why I asked you here."

"Don't tell me you're helping him."

"Well, sort of."

"Are you crazy? Every Regime state is looking for him! You can go to jail for aiding and abetting!"

"I know; just hear me out first."

Ashley listened to Wendy's explanation of how she and Kenny came to meet and the circumstances he claimed led him to her.

"How can you believe him?"

"I have my doubts; that's why I called you. I want to be sure. I was hoping you could help me get him to an MR machine."

"I don't know how to work one of those things."

"The police have technicians run them all the time. Don't you know anyone who can? I was hoping someone owes you a favor."

Ashley thought momentarily, "I know someone in New York, but it's too risky to take him there. I'll ask if she can refer me to someone here in Georgia. Where's your video com?"

"Over there."

Ashley made a few calls and returned, "I have an address in Sandy Springs. It's in the Immigration District. We'll have to take the hovercar; if he's spotted on any of the transportation stations' cameras, they'll be on us in seconds."

"Fine, I'll drive."

Chapter 78

Akil

Vlor City

The 22,280[th] Terrestrial Rotation of the Second Summer

Disguised as a business owner, Olan stepped off the Intercity Train onto the Vlor platform. As he headed for the avenue, video displays along the way caught his attention. Olan read the scroll on the right side of the screen and learned that someone had killed Zorion. The news made him sick, so he sat and watched the current broadcast to get the details. It did not take long for him to discover that Otsoa's inauguration was underway. He spat on the ground in disgust.

The ceremony ended, so he contacted Dolas to find out more details; he could only confirm that Otsoa had nothing to do with the attack. Even so, he would continue to investigate the matter. Fury raged within him as he heard Dolas detail his suspicions, yet he could do nothing to stop him without evidence.

"Do you think Otsoa helped plan Zorion's death?" Olan wondered.

"I do unless you think Igon had a backup plan."

"Anything is possible, but one thing is for sure, Igon will take credit for the attack, whether he is responsible or not."

"What will you do?"

"I will move forward with my original plan," he disconnected before Dolas asked any more questions.

The less he knew, the better. Waving his right arm, he got the attention of a '*pay to ride*' vehicle and jumped inside.

"To the Capitol Building."

He disappeared into the tunnels surrounding the city, changed his identity to match Igon's, and used the tunnel's secret entrance to get to Igon's office, bypassing all the screeners that would have searched him. Olan accessed Vlor's database using Igon's credentials and sent a copy to Argi's server, where Dolas could access it anytime.

Later, if Olan survived the mission, he could access the database and copy it for a detailed analysis. Dolas would have to do it alone if he did not return. Olan almost smiled at how easy it was to access Igon's private office. If he had not tried to kill Zorion, none of this would have been possible, yet he would trade all the information to have Zorion back. At least this way, his death would have meaning.

Olan originally planned to kill Elzer, disguised as Igon; this scheme assumed Zorion would still be alive, and Elzer's order to kill Zorion would die with him. Now that Zorion is dead, his goal is the same, except his reason for killing Elzer changed from protecting Zorion to revenge. He copied the last file within the database, returned to the tunnels, and headed to Vlor's Capitol Building. Satisfied that no one saw him, he appeared from the shadows looking exactly like Igon, walked to Elzer's outer office, and gave the assistant Igon's name.

"Is he in?" Olan requested, precisely looking like Igon did before interrogating him.

"Let me see if he is available."

It only took a few heartbeats before Elzer happily allowed Olan's entrance to see him. Olan stood at the door and waited for Elzer's approval, which would come once his conversation ended with the other in the room. He felt anxious standing at the door but kept his emotions in check. It was no time to make a mistake. *Patience, you will have him soon.* Once their conversation ended, the other left.

"Ah! There you are! Come in, come in. I did not think I would see you for a few more Terrestrial Revolutions," Elzer said joyfully.

Obeying Igon's master, Olan stepped inside and shut the door behind him.

Elzer moved close to him, just a few hand widths from his ear, and whispered, "Tell me, was that you the Information Gatherers were talking about earlier?"

"Clearly, who else could get to Zorion except for me?"

"Ha! I knew it!" Elzer exclaimed; soon, he frowned, "What about the guard they caught?"

"Dead, I made sure of it."

"Ah! You are the best, Igon!" He paused again, rubbed his chin, and inquired, "How did you do it? My information says that a female killed him and had a small army helping her."

"I used my imagination on this one. The female was Lirain, one of our agents in Argi. I disguised her as a Skean to play on their

383

superstitions. The small army consisted of a bunch of degenerates who needed a cause, so I gave them one."

Elzer heard the word Skean and felt chills because of his encounters with the one who helped him build the time machine. Still, he did not let it dampen his good mood.

"You have outdone yourself, Igon! Tell me what you want, and I will grant it!"

"There is one thing I would like you to do for me," Olan whispered, bringing Elzer closer to hear him better.

"Tell me, my friend. Anything you want, it is yours."

"I want you to die!"

Simultaneously, Olan spoke his last word and plunged a dagger into Elzer's throat. The knife passed through his voice box, preventing him from calling or whispering for help. Elzer fell to his knees and looked at Igon, bewildered at his betrayal. With his free hand, Olan dragged Elzer to the nearest wall and glanced back at the door. *It will do.*

The area was out of the secretary's sight, so she would not see Elzer's body lying on the floor after he left. Olan wanted to gloat by revealing himself but did not want to waste the opportunity, so without saying another word, Olan unsheathed his sword and decapitated him.

"That is how you kill a sovereign, you *putok*!" Olan whispered a spat.

Olan aimed the torso at the wall until his heart stopped, keeping the blood spatter to a minimum. He removed his coat, turned it inside-out to hide the bloodstains, used a clean cloth to wipe away any blood left on his hands and face, stepped outside, and told Elzer's assistant not to allow any disruptions for at least a thousand heartbeats. Olan would be on an Intercity train heading home before she found Elzer.

Chapter 79

Earth
Panama - Panama City
May 16, 2452

Wearing a short blonde wig and brown-colored contacts to match her fake passport, Dawn stepped through the event horizon onto Panama's International Transportation Station. Using her private portal machine would risk having the Regime tracing its signature back to her home, so she used public transportation. Besides, the trip only took a few seconds, except for the screening process, which cost her twenty minutes due to a minor discrepancy with her passport. Not having time to spare, she headed straight for the elevator.

She allowed herself the luxury of looking out the large glass windows along the way. Panama City's International Transportation Station sat atop the highest skyscraper in Panama. At one hundred fifty floors, it loomed over the whole municipality. In the distance, she saw Punta Paitilla's white, sandy beaches. Like any other vacation spot, the locals and visitors were lying on the beach and swimming in the ocean. The turquoise-colored water made her long for a short respite, but there was no time for such pleasures.

In the parking garage below, she found the medical van complete with a gurney and emergency equipment her assistant had requested hours before. Although she preferred to drive sports cars, it was necessary on this trip to have a vehicle that could accommodate a disabled passenger, assuming she could convince him to leave with her. Dawn punched in a security code, the van unlocked, and she drove toward her destination.

Thirty minutes later, she arrived at a single-family, beachfront home, stepped out of the van, and saw a dilapidated property. *I hope I'm not too late.* Upon arriving at the door, she knocked several times before hearing movement inside.

"Who is it?" a gruff voice asked from behind the door.

"My name is Dawn Pierce. I'm here to speak with Ethan Brun, please."

"What do you want with him?"

"I'm here to make him an offer."

"I'm not interested in what you're selling. Now leave me alone!"

"I'm not selling anything. I'm here to offer you something you dearly need."

"What's that?"

"Time."

"What kind of nonsense is this?

"If you open the door, I'll explain everything."

There was a long pause until Ethan disengaged the locks and partially opened the door. She saw a large, older man sitting in a wheelchair gazing up at her through the crack in the door. He paused briefly before opening it enough for her to walk through. She closed it behind her and followed him into the adjoining room, which he left cluttered with clothes and empty food containers, giving the home a distinct, rotten odor. Before she could say a word, he spun his wheelchair around and pointed a gun at her. She raised her hands to show she was not a threat.

"Did Heinrich send you?"

"Who?"

"Don't play games with me, missy; I'll shoot you between those pretty brown eyes."

"I'm not here to hurt you, Ethan. Besides, if I wanted you dead, all I'd have to do is wait a few more weeks."

"I live under an alias. How did you find me?"

"I searched until tracing your steps here. Once I discovered the name you're using, I pulled your medical records; everything is digital nowadays, meaning nothing is private."

"If you're not here to kill me, what do you want?"

"I'm here to offer you a job."

"Sorry, honey. I've killed enough for one lifetime. Besides, do I look like I'm in any condition to work?"

"What if you were young again?"

Ethan raised his weapon to take better aim; his hand shook even more with his arm extended.

"You better start making sense, or I'm gonna pull the trigger."

"Have you heard of Clone Replacements?"

"Vaguely, I think they make clones of pets that have died or something."

“That is their main source of business; they can also make human clones.”

“That’s illegal.”

“Someone who works there owes me a favor.”

“What good does a clone do either of us? I’ll die in a few weeks, and the clone will not have my memories or thoughts. I won’t live long enough to train him.”

“There’s been a technological breakthrough in the field of memory transfer.”

“Are you saying what I think you’re saying?”

“I propose we create a clone of your body and stop the aging process at twenty-one. Then, we transfer your memories and your conscience to an exact copy of your younger self. By tomorrow morning, you could be in a new body with perfect health in the prime of your life. Also, as a signing bonus, I’ll ensure they remove any genetic flaws, like tremors,” she nodded at his hand, holding the gun.

“What would I have to do for such a prize?”

“I’ve read your dossier and can tell that you are very good at following orders.”

“A lot of good it did me.”

“You took the blame for the Logan massacre.”

“That’s why they call me the Butcher of Logan County, even though it wasn’t my fault. The intel was bad.”

“You took the blame anyway. Anyone else would have told what really happened; you covered up for your superiors.”

“I got a dishonorable discharge and lost everything except my freedom.”

“Is that how you ended up working for German Intelligence?”

“I had no choice. No one would hire me.”

“Is Heinrich your old boss?”

“Yeah. After collaborating with him for ten years, he shot me in the back. I lost the use of my left leg. My pension defaulted, so I took what he owed me. Last I heard, he put a price on my head, dead or alive.”

“If you choose to come with me, you will walk again. I’ll even help you kill Heinrich so that you can get rid of the bounty on you.”

“Why go through all the trouble? There must be others who are younger and stronger that could do the same job.”

“Believe me. I’ve looked around; no one has your experience and character.”

“I don’t know. It sounds too good to be true. Let me think about it for a couple of days.”

“You could be dead in two days, Ethan. I need to know now. Are you coming with me, or do I look for someone else? I don’t have much time to spare.”

Ethan rubbed his chin in thought because he did not know what to make of this blonde-haired beauty. Her offer was very tempting, but he knew there would be a catch because there was always one; his only alternative would be dying here in pain as cancer ate through his body.

“Where is this facility?”

“Scotland.”

“I don’t have a passport anymore. I didn’t think I’d be going anywhere.”

“Don’t worry. I took the liberty of getting you one. Now, what do you think?”

“All right, I’ll do it.”

“Excellent! You won’t regret it! Outside, there’s a medical van waiting for you. It’ll take us to Panama’s International Transportation Station, where we’ll go to Scotland so that you can start your new life!”

Chapter 80

Dawn returned to Scotland with Ethan and drove him to the Clone Replacements facility under the cloak of darkness. She took him inside the building, where her friend Blair waited for her.

"Hurry, this way," Blair urged Dawn to follow her.

It was a short walk to the room Blair set aside for Ethan's overnight stay. Once they were safely inside, Blair took a sample of Ethan's blood and inserted an IV into his arm. Dawn ensured Ethan was comfortable and left with Blair to the lab, where Blair put a drop of his blood into a machine for analysis. The monitor lit up, with hundreds of green and red numbers representing sections of Ethan's DNA. The red numbers represented areas of defects, which she would correct before creating the clone.

"How long until I have the finished product?" Dawn asked.

"His new body will be ready by tomorrow morning, but as you can see, he has some genetic anomalies that need repair before I can start the growth process."

"Make sure you fix them all. I don't want him to have any problems, and don't forget the failsafe."

"I won't."

"Good, I want to ensure he obeys like the others."

Chapter 81

Akil
Argi City
The 22,280[th] Terrestrial Rotation of the Second Summer

Reaching the halfway mark to Argi, Olan sent Elzer's assistant a copy of Igon's video confession. The one where he said that Elzer sent him to kill Zorion. The Information League announced the news of Elzer's death within a few hundred heartbeats of his departure, and hearing them say he died from the sickness was not a surprise. Elzer's heir would not pursue his killer, knowing that whoever killed him would release Igon's confession to the news media.

Having completed his mission, he sat back and enjoyed the pomp of the reporting. Afterward, they gave an update on Zorion's death. The description of the female killer surprised Olan because he did not know her yet believed Nayrah would do anything, including changing her image, to kill Zorion. It seemed like a desperate move. *She must have run out of patsies.*

There was something odd about the situation, but one thing was sure: he would avenge Zorion's death. An intense guilty feeling washed over him for not protecting his friend from the attack. At first, it overwhelmed him to tears until he thought of killing Nayrah, which gave him focus. Now he had a new mission to complete. He stepped onto Argi's Intercity Platform and checked his messages. Having received one from Dolas, he ran to meet with him. In the room, within the secret tunnels, he found Dolas pacing.

"Where have you been?" he asked anxiously.

"Vlor."

"It *was* you who killed Elzer!"

"Do not worry. They will not pursue it. I sent them a copy of Igon's confession, detailing Elzer's involvement in Zorion's assassination."

"That is one issue resolved. Still, there are many more. Have you heard anything new about Zorion?"

"No, but the female they described must be Nayrah."

"Are you sure?"

"My gut tells me it was her, and it looks like she decided to get her own hands dirty this time."

"Zorion's death set off a chain reaction. Otsoa has already taken the oath of Sovereign and is considering invading Vlor before Elzer's heir takes his oath."

"That would be foolish. Vlor would attack us!"

"Otsoa is not listening to his Chief Administrators or advisors."

"How did he come up with the idea?"

"I took the liberty of installing some surveillance cameras in his office before he took the oath. He is taking advice from this female," he played it for Olan to see.

"I do not recognize her."

"He calls her Gecheana."

"It is odd that he would take advice from a female, especially now that he is the Argi's Sovereign."

"Do you still think it is Nayrah?"

"Again, it is possible. She would not use the same likeness as the one who killed Zorion. It might be another alias; no matter who it is, we must get rid of her if she gives him such foolish advice."

"It is easier said than done because from what I can tell, once she leaves his office, she disappears from the surveillance view."

"That does make it more difficult, but not impossible."

"There is more. Otsoa ordered all his Chief Administrators to monitor Argi's elites and anyone with a claim to the Argi House."

"For what purpose?"

"He wants to know who is against him and kill them. He has become paranoid."

"We must get Va'ron safe before moving against Gecheana and Otsoa."

"It will be difficult getting to Va'ron because Otsoa assigned thirty sentries to protect him."

"With some surveillance, we should find a weakness, even though his advisor is good at putting up a defensive perimeter."

"There is something else you should know. Julie has disappeared."

"Did he kill her?"

"No, I have spotted her domestic on level five hundred twenty-three."

"Did you erase the surveillance video?"

"Yes. I told my video technicians to send all future records to my Information Terminal; if I can find her…."

"We cannot let him kill her. It would destroy our relationship with Earth; they will shut the portal and leave us to our fate."

"I will try to help her."

"No. If Otsoa catches you, he will kill you both. I need you on the inside. Give me the address, and I will help them find a more secluded place to hide."

"There is yet one more thing you should know before leaving."

Olan sighed, "Tell me."

"I have assigned agents to watch all the other Chief Administrators. They spotted Broll in the northern section of level three hundred fifteen. They have seen him buying moss and taking it to this address," Dolas handed him a data chip with all the requested information.

"Who does he know on that level?"

"No one. The apartment is in his name only; he is obviously hiding someone."

"Who?"

"I could investigate if you want; he might have participated in Zorion's assassination."

"Unlikely. Do not probe into it. I will take care of it. Meanwhile, keep your eyes open for anything out of the ordinary and keep me informed," he paused to put his hand on Dolas's shoulder, "We are at a pivotal time in Akil's history. We will all perish if we do not rid Argi of Otsoa, Gecheana, and Nayrah."

"You know I will do whatever it takes."

"As will I. Thank you, Dolas, for believing me," Olan spun around and left before Dolas could respond.

Knowing the levels between five and six hundred were home to the middle class, Olan dressed to blend in, strolled past the marketplace like their group usually moved, and saw Julie's domestic with a basket full of moss. He shook his head. *Sloppy, very sloppy.* From the shadows, he waited until she opened the door. Before she could close it, he rushed toward her and pushed her down. Inside, he shut the door and unsheathed his sword. Having heard the commotion, Edur ran in from the adjacent room. Seeing a stranger holding a blade to Tionah's neck, Edur froze.

"Do not hurt her, please!" Edur begged.

"Where is Julie?" Olan demanded.

"She is not here," Edur insisted.

Knowing he was lying, Olan pressed his blade harder on Tionah's neck, drawing some blood. Tionah did not scream even though Olan terrified her.

"Leave her alone," Julie stepped out from behind Edur.

"You are all pathetic. Do you not know Otsoa is looking for…."

Before he could finish his sentence, Julie sent a wave of invisible energy that slammed into him, knocking the sword out of his hand and landing him on the floor, stunned. Before he could get back on his feet, Julie stood over him, holding a glowing, white blade to his throat.

"Kill him! He is a traitor!" Tionah yelled.

"She wants me to kill you. What do you think I should do with you?" Julie quizzed.

"I am here to help you," Olan insisted.

"He tried to kill Zorion!" Tionah yelled.

"Is that true?"

"I was merely a tool in the hands of someone with powers like yours, and even though she used her abilities to force me to attack him, I resisted enough to spare his life. Moreover, I saved him from Elzer, who sent a spy to kill him."

"Lies," Tionah spat.

"You can ask Dolas to confirm my story. He took my position as Chief Administrator of Argi's Intelligence Department. His contact information is in my pocket."

With his life on the line, his calm manner impressed Julie, yet she would only trust her newly discovered instincts. Those feelings told her that he was not a threat. Still, it did not hurt to have more information.

"Why did you come here?" she demanded.

"I came here to relocate you because Dolas's agents have already found you. He has put them on other assignments for now; if you do not leave, Otsoa will learn of your hiding place."

"So, he does want to kill me," Julie wondered.

"Of course, you were a friend of Zorion's."

"He must be insane. If he hurts me, Supreme Commander Porter will close the portal to Earth."

"Someone named Gecheana is advising him. It is someone I know as Nayrah in disguise."

"No, Gecheana is Nayrah's mother. She is the one I fought, trying to protect Zorion."

"How do you know?"

"Because Nayrah confronted me earlier. She told me Gecheana is her Skean mother."

"Did she tell you anything else?"

"Yes. She said that there are eleven Skeans on Akil."

"There are real Skeans on Akil?" Tionah queried, frightened.

"I used to think they were fables, but knowing what she did to me and seeing your powers, I believe they are real," Olan admitted.

"I still do not trust him," Tionah warned.

"I think we should," Julie countered, retracted her blade, latched the hilt to her belt, and extended her hand to help him.

"Are there any more of you on Akil?" Olan inquired hopefully.

"No."

"Can you defeat them?"

"Not on my own; Nayrah wants us to work together to eliminate the others, and once her family is dead, we fight to the death."

"You cannot trust her," Olan warned.

"Yeah. I figured that out already, except I don't have many options. I'm still a novice, and I'm alone. Even worse, Nayrah knows I just started learning."

"You are not alone. You have us," Olan pointed to Edur, Tionah, and himself.

"It may not be enough. Nayrah gave me this in case I decided to contact her and join forces," she handed the data stick to Olan, who inserted it into his communicator.

"It is Nayrah's number; I have called many times before."

“What do we do now?” Tionah questioned.

“The first thing we must do is get out of this apartment. The government knows you are here, so it will not be long until Otsoa finds you. After that, we must go down to the lower levels. I am thinking twenty-four,” Olan suggested.

“No one lives down there. It is dark and cold!” Tionah protested.

“Exactly the reason we must go there. Guards and spies do not bother going to that level, and more importantly, there are no cameras,” Olan explained.

“Julie is our guest here. We cannot have her live in such filth,” Tionah insisted.

“It is up to you,” Olan faced Julie.

“If it’s safe, we should go; I need to get back to my apartment first and speak with someone,” Julie explained.

“I recommend against that. If anyone sees you, they could capture you, even with your special abilities,” Olan warned.

“I must speak with my instructor about the Skean’s offer,” Julie insisted.

“Very well, I will take you there after we relocate all of you; for now, we must go before someone discovers us,” Olan remarked.

Chapter 82

Earth
Spain - Madrid
May 16, 2452

Vincent reviewed a final checklist detailing the mission with his team gathered in Sofia's apartment. To ensure Sofia would not make a run for it at the mall, he injected her with a newly developed tracking serum General Saunders recommended. Moments later, Vincent received an alert that a portal was about to open, so he and his team cleared the room. Moments later, Wu Luli stepped through the event horizon to join him. Without delay, he put her to work, analyzing the mall's blueprints to find the best places for his agents to hide. Places, she thought Dragon would not look.

"How will I prove to Dragon that I killed you?" Sofia asked.

Vincent handed her a data stick, put it into her phone, and viewed the pictures.

"These are photos of me in a death pose. We used pig's blood to make it look authentic," Vincent replied.

Sofia nodded, "The bullet hole in your head looks real enough, but he's also expecting your finger."

Vincent removed a small plastic bag from his pocket and handed it to her, "This is a synthetic flesh duplicate of my finger that our lab techs grew overnight. It has my fingerprint and DNA, so he won't have any reason to doubt you."

"It should be enough to fool him, except I have a bad feeling about this," worried Sofia.

"You'll have the full support of my team. We'll be there to help you if anything goes wrong," assured Vincent.

Wu Luli reviewed the photos and the finger, confirming the evidence was convincing.

"It would fool me."

"Excellent!" He faced Sofia, "Give him the photo and the finger, collect your payment, and walk away."

"He'll be expecting me to be armed. I'll need a gun," Sofia advised.

Having removed the ammunition from the chamber and clip, Vincent handed her gun back.

She sighed, "What good is a gun without bullets?"

"She's right, Vincent. It would help if you gave us loaded weapons," Wu Luli added.

"I'm sorry, ladies. General's orders. Neither of you will be armed."

"Dragon will have a backup plan. If he thinks it's a trap or your agents approach him, innocent people will get hurt."

"Most of the exits have foyers with double doors, so we'll activate the automatic locks, which will trap him, and before he can even try to escape, I'll have thirty men surrounding him inside the foyer and in the hallways with protective shields."

"It sounds like a good plan. I hope Dragon cooperates," Wu Luli commented.

"He'll have no choice this time," Vincent assured.

*****

Standing on the second floor at the mall crosswalk, about fifty yards from Sofia's position, Vincent searched the area, using specially designed glasses made to act like binoculars. He used a remote in his pocket to zoom in and out inconspicuously. Dragon scheduled their meeting at 10 AM, which was only a few minutes away. Not willing to take any chances, Vincent had several backup procedures.

First, he had his agents positioned where Wu Luli suggested. Second, he stationed agents at all the exits, which would lock on his command. Third, his technical team would activate a disruptive field encompassing the mall to prevent another portal escape upon Dragon's arrival. Finally, just in case he did make it past his team and outside the mall, his friend Diego had more than one hundred plainclothes police officers waiting in the parking lot covering each exit.

Once inside, there was no way Dragon could escape, at least in Vincent's view. As he scanned the mall for some sign of Dragon, his gaze caught Sofia waiting for him. Wearing the latest Madrid fashion, she blended in with the crowd, apart from the red scarf around her neck, so Dragon would know it was her. Vincent protested the tight-fitting garment; Sofia insisted it resembled her usual outfits.

The last few minutes passed by like hours. Occasionally, some men would stop to speak with Sofia, hoping to make a connection. Vincent placed a small transmitter on her collar without her knowledge, which allowed him to listen in on the conversation. He tried to ignore it, yet part of him felt jealous, as her admirers wanted to convince her to join them for lunch or dinner. With a polite smile, she sent them on their way and continued to wait for Dragon. At about ten-fifteen, an older man approached her from the building's west side. At first, Vincent thought nothing of him until noticing his walk was too spry for someone his age.

"Ok, everyone, he's here. Stay sharp!" Vincent whispered into a small communicator.

Vincent watched intently, expecting Sofia to show him the photos and finger, but without saying a word, the older man retrieved a small revolver from his pocket and shot Sofia directly between the eyes. Staring in disbelief, Vincent watched Sofia fall, motionless. Hearing the gunfire, nearby mall patrons screamed and ran for the exits. The older man spun around and headed for a stairwell to the first floor. Vincent turned to Wu Luli, hoping for an answer as to why Dragon went off-script.

Seeing she had no idea, he brought his communicator up and yelled, "Lock this place down and find him!"

Vincent ran to Sofia, knelt beside her, motioned for Wu Luli to follow him, and contacted his tech team to disengage the field disrupter long enough to notify the Regime's medical emergency team, who would open an emergency portal inside the mall.

"I need help now! GSW to the head! Hurry!"

Knowing he could do nothing more for Sofia, Vincent scanned the mall for Dragon and saw him running toward a stairwell. Instinctively, he reached for his weapon, aimed, and fired several times. Patrons, running for the doors, screamed as they dove for the ground. Vincent heard the high-pitched sound of miniature remote-controlled cars as they zigzagged through the chaotic rush of the fleeing crowd. Abruptly they stopped near a group of potted trees and exploded. Dirt, debris, and smoke filled the air, and as it finally cleared, two agents were down, and Vincent did not see Dragon anywhere.

"Where did he go?" he shouted over the noise of the fleeing mob.

Wu Luli pointed to the stairwell, "He went in there."

The medics arrived and hooked Sofia up to a machine that kept her heart pumping and pushed air into her lungs.

"I have two more men down there!" Vincent yelled.

The paramedics nodded, and another team appeared from the vortex to help the other injured men. Sofia's paramedics put her on a gurney and returned to the hospital in the Regime. Using his communicator, Vincent directed two nearby agents to stay on the second floor and search the first floor from above; he ran to the stairwell with Wu Luli close behind him. Vincent stepped out the first-floor door and scanned the crowd to find Dragon waiting for him. He barely heard the gunshot over the noise; Vincent felt the bullet hit his shoulder.

"Damn it!" Vincent yelled.

"What's wrong?" Wu Luli wondered.

"He shot me in the same shoulder as last time we met. Son of a bitch!"

"Give me your gun. I'll follow him."

Vincent hesitated.

"Come on. You're bleeding too much. If you start running, you will bleed out before you catch him," she urged.

He swore under his breath, "Here. Take the magazines too. I'll contact Diego and tell him to keep watch. Dragon shouldn't get out. I only dropped the portal disrupter long enough to get Sofia to the Regime. The paramedics will have an emergency DNA rejuvenation powder that will accelerate my arm's recovery enough to stop the bleeding. I'll catch up to you after it's healed."

She stuffed the ammo clips into her belt, grabbed the gun from his hand, and chased Dragon. She stepped out into the hallway with the weapon raised, ready to fire, and half expected Dragon to shoot at her; he was nowhere in sight. Instead, she saw a nearby exit door closing, ran through it, and saw Dragon amid others, running down a long corridor that led to the outside. His journey ended because Vincent sent orders to lock all the doors.

Turning to find an alternative way out, Dragon saw Wu Luli, who knew Dragon would feel trapped and become more deadly, so she prepared herself for the inevitable. As expected, he fired several shots in her direction. He missed her and hit several bystanders who did not duck in time. She wanted to help the wounded, but her training forbade it, so she returned fire as he ran through the crouching spectators to the doors.

He stuck a clay-like ball to the door's deadbolt area and lay prone on the ground. There was an explosion, and the doors flew open. They stood at the same time and fired their weapons at each other. One of his shots grazed her right shoulder as she put one into his thigh. Having injured him, she hoped he would be easier to catch; he was not. With his right hand, he threw a similar ball of clay-like material in her direction.

Knowing what was coming, she dove the other way moments before the explosion. She recovered and heard gunfire outside. Upon reaching the door, she saw several of Diego's officers lying on the ground. The explosion caught them off guard, injuring them. Only one was conscious, and he was still shooting at Dragon from the blacktop where he lay wounded. Screeching tires caught her attention, and she saw Dragon racing off in a small car.

The car sped away as she tried to catch him on foot. On the street, she stopped a motorcyclist by pointing her gun at him; the motorcyclist almost wrecked and ran away, leaving it behind. With the bike still running, she hopped on and sped off in pursuit. By weaving in and out of traffic, Wu Luli gained on Dragon.

It was not hard for her to follow him because he left a trail of wrecked vehicles in his wake. To lose her, he drove through side streets, parking lots, and even a tennis court before stopping his car in front of a residential area. Wu Luli finally caught up as he disappeared inside one of the homes. She dismounted, raced to the nearest door, and found it locked. Having no chance of surprising him, she shot the doorknob and kicked in the door.

Before rushing in, she stepped out of the doorway in case he was lying in wait; nothing happened, so she ran inside the house, ready to fire at anything that moved. Carefully and methodically, she checked each room on the first floor; there was no sign of him until she stood in the dining room and heard a noise on the second level.

She crept up the steps, and at the top, she saw Dragon standing in the farthest bedroom doorway with a young woman in his grasp. He kept the barrel of his gun set firmly against her temple. She had not been a Regime agent long enough to study their hostage negotiation technics; one thing she was sure of, the Regime would not want this person harmed.

General Ming-Tun Fu only trained her to take hostages, not save them, so this situation stumped her. Trying to get a closer vantage point, she moved from the stairs to the first room. Her gun stayed pointed at him on the way to her new position. Hidden behind a wall, she tried to think of what to say. She chose to take the direct approach.

"Drop your weapon, Chen Heng," she spoke, in a manner, so calm that she could have been ordering a glass of wine in a restaurant.

Recognizing her voice, Dragon peeked from behind the head of his hostage.

"Wu Luli? Is that you?"

"Yes."

"Why are you chasing me?"

"I work for the Regime now."

"You've gone rogue too?" he queried behind the crying woman, keeping his head hidden.

"Yes."

"I've heard there's a price on your head and that it's up to one billion Yuan."

"I'll have it up to a trillion before I finish with him."

"Perhaps we could make a deal."

"General Min-Tung Fu's agents don't make deals; you know that."

"What if I told you I know where he is?"

His offer was tempting, except she had no way of verifying his information.

"Sorry, no deal," she answered indifferently though the rejection was hard to say.

"I heard you killed the parents of all the other agents."

"News travels fast."

"Why would you do that?"

"You know me. What do you think happened?"

"I think General Ming-tun Fu set you up as he did me before I quit his employment."

"Is that why you left?"

"I had no choice. I demanded to see my mother. He refused, so I snuck in to find her; the bastard killed her before I could get her out."

"Why didn't you kill him for betraying you?"

"I was alone and labeled a traitor. I had to run. I think you can understand my position."

Even though his story was interesting, she knew he was telling her these things to stall.

"Drop your weapon, Chen Heng. Let me take you in, and I'm sure the Regime will work out a deal with you."

"I thought you don't make deals?"

"I don't, but the Regime might if you surrender now."

Training kept her voice calm. Inside, she was concerned for the hostage's safety; it was a strange new feeling. She used a technique General Ming-Tun Fu taught her; she exhaled and relaxed her body to clarify her aim.

"Sorry, surrender is not an…."

Before Chen Heng could finish his sentence, Wu Luli fired her weapon. The first bullet hit his gun, which flew out of his hand. Instinctively, his hostage dropped to the floor. Now that she was out of the line of fire, the second bullet struck Chen Heng in the stomach. Having lost a large amount of blood from his leg wound, he was already in a weakened state, so the second shot put him down. He landed on the floor, and his back came to rest on the bed behind him. Using his left hand, he put pressure on his stomach to slow the bleeding but did not have much time before his blood supply ran out. Now that she had ended the threat, Wu Luli instructed the former hostage to go downstairs and call the police.

"I'm taking you back with me so they can fix you. Later, you'll tell me where General Ming-tun Fu is hiding."

The idea of someone capturing him made Dragon laugh, which caused blood to trickle out of his mouth.

"My employer will not allow anyone to catch me."

"I don't think he has a choice."

"You are naïve, and you won't survive for long on your own in this business; I give you a week."

She tried to make him comfortable with a pillow until Regime medics arrived.

"You hear those sirens? That's the Regime coming to arrest you," Wu Luli warned.

A small portal opened above his head, and something dropped through the event horizon, which quickly closed. The device landed on the bed, just behind Chen Heng's head; the strange-looking sphere had a digital timer counting down from ten. Knowing it was a bomb, she spun around as the counter changed to nine and ran down the stairs, skipping several steps.

Without explaining, she grabbed the former hostage by the arm and pulled her out of the house. As they cleared the doorway, the device exploded with enough force to send them airborne onto the street. Their landing was hard, giving them only scrapes and bruises. Wu Luli looked back at the house and saw that the explosion had destroyed the top floor, leaving the lower half intact and burning. Within moments, the police arrived.

"What the hell happened?" Vincent demanded.

"He killed Dragon," Wu Luli clarified.

"Who did?"

"His employer."

Chapter 83

Akil
Argi City
The 22,280[th] Terrestrial Rotation of the Second Summer

With Julie behind him, Olan guided her through the secret tunnels to her apartment. Like a child at an amusement park, Julie saw the passages with wonder.

Most of their journey was quiet until Olan asked, "How did you get your powers?"

"I was lured into eating black and white moss by their smell. Urki told me I died and revived. He also said that the High Lord chose me to fight these Skeans on Akil."

"It is as I suspected. The myths of Skeans and Saiphs are true."

"It's the first I have ever heard about it."

"How long have you had your abilities?"

"Only a few days."

"Yet you have the power to shove me aside like a toy. You seem strong for a novice."

"Not strong enough to save Zorion."

"He would have been honored at your attempt to help him."

"It doesn't help knowing I failed him."

At the top level, Julie tried to make him stay behind; he refused, insisting on staying by her side. Reluctantly, she showed him the cave where Urki existed as they walked toward the first room.

"Interesting. I thought I knew every secret place in this city."

"It holds more mysteries than any of us realize," Julie remarked.

She called for her instructor in the circular, domed room, "Urki, where are you?"

Urki materialized nearby. Seeing Olan, a sword materialized in his hand, and he swung at Olan to kill him; before the edge came close to his neck, Julie's sword was in her hand, blocking his strike.

"What the hell are you doing?" Julie challenged.

"I am programmed to train and protect you; this Akilian is Olan, the betrayer. You must not trust him," Urki warned.

"Do not believe everything you read in the city's database," chided Olan.

"He's on our side, Urki. Now put away your weapon!" Julie demanded.

Reluctantly, Urki did as Julie commanded, "Every report indicates that this Akilian betrayed Zorion."

"I was manipulated by a Skean, you one-dimensional simulation!" Olan chided.

"How do we know you are not under its influence right now?" Urki suspected.

"He's not. I would know, wouldn't I?" Julie wondered, still unsure of her abilities.

"Perhaps. Trust him at your peril," Urki answered, glaring at Olan.

"This planet is full of peril," Julie remarked.

"I am aware of your fight earlier today. You did well," Urki noted.

"Not well enough to save Zorion," Julie lamented.

"At least you survived, but with more practice, you can beat the Skean next time," Urki insisted.

"I think today will likely be my last practice, at least for a while. After the fight, another Skean named Nayrah approached me to talk."

"This is highly irregular. Saiphs and Skeans have nothing to say to one another. What did you discuss?"

"She told me that the one I fought was her Skean mother, and she has four sisters."

"There are six Skeans on Akil?" Urki asked.

"No, eleven, including their children."

"Why would she tell you this?"

"She wants my help to kill them."

"Speaking strictly as an Intelligence Officer, if I were in her position, I would have no problem lying to you. I would tell you there are eleven when there are only two; if I successfully convinced you to join me, I would plan to kill you the moment you struck down the other Skean, taking away any chance of having you fight back, and there would be no one to oppose me," Olan explained.

"He has a point," Urki added.

"She knows I am here, and if I refuse to help her, what's to stop her from finding and killing me tomorrow?"

"Nothing. I know firsthand that Nayrah will sacrifice anyone to attain her goal," Olan warned.

"If you stay here in this cave and cloak your powers, she cannot find you. Olan can deliver your food until you are ready to fight them," Urki added.

"What good does that do any of us? They're out there now! Plotting, who knows what. If I don't try to stop them, they could take over Akil. This way, if Nayrah is telling the truth, the odds will even," Julie commented.

"What if she is not telling the truth?" Urki asked.

"I agree with Julie; she does not have a choice. Nayrah *will* try to kill her if she does not help, and time is running out for Akil. If they gain control, we will all die. Besides, I will fight alongside her," Olan offered.

"You will only be fodder for the Skeans," Urki imparted dismissively.

"Then, I will be fodder, but I will defend her with my life," Olan insisted.

Urki paused as his software analyzed the situation and calculated all the variables.

"Based on the information you have given me, I agree with your assessment. The odds of this Skean looking for you if you do not help her are high. I warn you never to trust a Skean. They are known for lulling their enemies into a false sense of security and striking unexpectedly."

"Don't worry. I always have an uneasy feeling around her."

"That is the High Lord urging you to fight," Urki instructed.

"Yeah. Well, that urge will get me killed if I don't learn to fight better."

"I agree, so we should begin the next phase of your training."

Chapter 84

Earth
The Regime - Washington, D.C. - Mercy Hospital
May 16, 2452

Sarah woke and tried to sit up, but Larkin's arms prevented her from moving; last night, they shared a small mattress beside their daughter. Gently, she elbowed Larkin to wake him, and they walked to Sable's bed as she watched television.

"How are you feeling, sweetheart?"

"Ok, mommy."

"Are you hungry?"

She nodded eagerly.

"All right, I'll go fetch you something."

Sarah started to leave until Sable hollered for her.

"Mama, mama, look!"

Sarah turned back and saw Sable pointing to the television. Curious about her daughter's fascination with the TV show, she walked over and watched with Larkin. Instead of cartoons, Sable selected a documentary on the history channel, and the topic of discussion was the Butcher of Logan County, who massacred women and children during the Oklahoma conflict of 2395. A picture of Sergeant Ethan Brun appeared on the screen during the commentary, and Sable became excited.

"That's him, mama. That's him!"

"Who, sweetheart? Who is he?"

"The bad man who wants to hurt us."

"That can't be him, Darlin'; that happened more than fifty years ago," Larkin explained.

"But papa, I saw him clear as day. He hurt us."

Sarah looked at Larkin, bewildered, "He must be in his eighties by now."

"If he's even still alive," Sarah added.

They watched in horror as the commentator gave gory details of the brutal attack that killed more than two thousand women and children seeking refuge in a hospital. The correspondent went on to say that he escaped from prison before his trial, fleeing the U.S., and to this day, no one has ever seen him again.

"She must have seen this at home, and the images have been giving her nightmares," Sarah concluded, turning to face Sable, who hid under the covers.

"She's acting scared," Larkin noted.

"We'll call Dr. Grant again and tell him what we discovered; maybe he can tell us what to do to help her through it," Sarah remarked.

"I'll contact him after breakfast," Larkin answered.

Chapter 85

Earth
Regime - Maryland - Eastern Shore
May 16, 2452

Sonya prepared one of her best dishes, ran upstairs, and set candles everywhere in the bedroom. Jared returned home, so she fed him and took him upstairs for a candlelit encounter. Later, they lay intertwined on the bed, both panting from their vigorous activity.

"Would you like some water?" Sonya asked.

"Yeah, I'm thirsty."

She reached for a pitcher on her nightstand and filled a glass for him. He drank all of it and rested his head on the pillow with her in his arms. Jared stared at the tiny camera lens above him and longed to regain his privacy.

"I met our neighbor, Sharon, today. Would you mind if I invited her and her husband over for dinner this Saturday?"

"Sure."

"I like her. Maybe one day we can be good friends."

"All we can do is try."

"What do you think about going on a boat this Sunday?"

He did not respond, so she questioned, "Jared?"

She gently shook him; he did not even stir. She looked at the empty glass on the nightstand, and her smile faded. Even though she hated the thought of drugging him, President Martinez gave her no choice. If he were to wake up at night, everything she risked would be for nothing. She poured the rest of the water down the drain to ensure he did not take more of the drug.

Before leaving the second floor, she returned to the bedroom, blew out the candles, and slipped back into bed. Several minutes later, she used her remote to send a signal. The small, green board she inserted into the camera relay center started recording. Per Alonso's instructions, she waited five minutes, allowing the chip to store enough video to play in a loop.

Since it recorded them sleeping, she had to stay completely still, so, during playback, the analyst watching could not detect the same clip repeating. She believed the Regime observers would not even pay attention unless she got up but had to take every precaution. At last, the timer on the remote beeped, so she sent another signal to start the loop. The green light on her clicker lit, allowing her to move freely.

Before getting up, she made a mental note of her current position, ensuring the same pose upon returning and avoiding tipping off the analyst. Since the drug put Jared in such a deep sleep, it should prevent him from moving during her errand, just in case she took a quick photo with her cell phone. Now ready to leave, she went downstairs and retrieved a hidden bag of clothes.

She changed and headed out to the beach. She walked for a spell and glanced at her watch. It was 10:32 PM, and the compass found in the outer ring of the watch face pointed in the direction she needed to go. As she walked along the beach, searching for the drop-off point, the cold ocean spray landing on her cheeks helped to keep her sharp. The closer she came to her destination, the faster her watch beeped.

She found a small immersible resting on the shore; her high rubber boots kept the water from contacting her skin. Still, the ocean spray felt cold for May. The waves moved the immersible around, making it tricky to grasp the package. She retrieved a medium-size steel case and pressed a button on the immersible. Its engines sprang to life, disappearing back into the ocean from where it came.

The return trip was uneventful, but she would not enter the house until completing her task. She walked to the hovercar, opened the trunk, and placed the case inside. She opened the lid, retrieved a small tablet nestled at the top in a foam package, and saw a metal panel with a lock. Without the key, she tried to jimmy the lid; it would not budge.

It was clear that President Martinez took measures to ensure that only the recipient, who had the key, could get the money; she sighed in frustration, closed the lid, and took the tablet with her inside the car. She connected it to the vehicle's onboard computer and reprogrammed it to send the car's current location to the satellite, no matter its actual position.

She scanned the area to ensure no one was watching, started the engine, causing the car to rise, and using the tablet, she started its GPS guidance system to lead the way. It showed that her destination was a hundred miles inland. Knowing that security would catch her using an Interstate Transportation Station, she had to drive the distance.

She knew the Regime was watching her, which meant they did not trust her. Anyone who saw a video of her carrying a suitcase late at night would confirm their suspicions. She traversed small trails and open fields for two hours until reaching her destination, where she removed the suitcase full of Regime Talons from the trunk and tossed it into the large dumpster stationed at the Market Place's northeast corner, as instructed.

Having completed the last task for President Martinez, she returned to the vehicle with haste, started the engine, and sped away. She returned home and used the tablet to put the vehicle's application back to its original settings. Then, she ran into the woods with the tablet, buried it in a shallow grave, silently closed the front door behind her, changed back into her nightgown, hid the clothes she wore during her mission, and quietly climbed the stairs.

She looked at the photo before slipping back into bed. Jared had not moved an inch in the past six hours. Relieved that she did not have to reposition him, she slid into bed. She ensured her position was the same as before, turned off the playback feature, reinstated the video to a live feed, and drifted off to sleep.

Chapter 86

Earth
Regime - Maryland - Sandy Springs - Immigration District
May 16, 2452

Ashley stepped out of the hovercar at her friend's address, casually walked to the door, and knocked. Moments later, a young man answered, wearing an old food-stained shirt with torn jeans.

"Sorry, I must have the wrong place," Ashely hoped it was a mistake.

"Are you Beverly's friend?"

"Yeah."

"I'm Kaleb," he extended his hand.

She shook it and inconspicuously wiped it on her pant leg, making a mental note to take a cleansing shower and throw away the pants. Before entering, she scanned the room behind him to ensure it was safe and motioned for Wendy and Kenny to follow. Until she was sure Kenny was innocent, Ashley insisted he wear the handcuffs, so they kept his hands hidden underneath one of Wendy's old jackets.

Once inside, Kaleb led them to his basement; along the way, Ashley saw all kinds of equipment scattered about in every room and the hallway, leading her to believe he lived alone. The conditions some people were content living in always amazed her. The basement was in worse shape than the upstairs; Kaleb pointed to an old, shredded chair, so Ashley walked Kenny over and motioned for him to sit. Even though it was more clutter than dirt, she found it hard to tell the difference. Kaleb dug through a pile of junk in front of him, retrieved a syringe, and began filling it with a serum.

Kenny panicked, "Is it necessary?"

"You need the serum, or else the MR won't work," Kaleb explained.

"How many times have you used that needle?" Kenny asked.

"Just a few," Kaleb remarked.

Kenny turned to Wendy for help, who noticed his distress and had mercy, "Here, I have a new one in my bag."

Tossing the other syringe back onto the pile of debris on the table, Kaleb took the clean needle from Wendy, filled it, and stuck

Kenny in the arm. As the drug moved through his veins, Kaleb started the machine. It stalled a few times, so he kicked it and hammered it until it whined as the motor sped up. Once the headpiece was on, images flashed on a few monitors; some had cracks on their surface.

"You only have to go back a couple of days," Wendy offered.

Watching Kenny's life unfold, they searched for the detective who had visited him two nights before. It did not take long for the machine to find it.

"There he is," Wendy remarked.

With the press of a button, Kaleb slowed the machine, and they watched the episode as seen by Kenny's eyes. It ended, and Ashley removed his handcuffs.

"I'll need a copy of that memory on a data stick," Ashley requested.

Kaleb finished downloading the images and handed them to her, so they left, with Kenny in the back seat, alone this time. Kenny had been through hell but was glad to have someone believe in him again.

"What do we do now?" Kenny inquired.

"We go back to Wendy's and get some rest. Tomorrow, I'll take this flash drive to the local police station, send the information to the TBI, and wait for a response. Hopefully, if things go right, by this time tomorrow, you should be a free man."

"I like the sound of that."

www.ingramcontent.com/pod-product-compliance
Lightning Source LLC
Chambersburg PA
CBHW070234200726
48293CB00005B/1615